A Million Dreams

A Million Dreams

DANI ATKINS

HEAD of ZEUS

9 7 5 3 1 2 4 6 8

A catalogue record for this book is available from
the British Library.

ISBN (HB): 9781789546163
ISBN (XTPB): 9781789546170
ISBN (E): 9781789546156

Typeset by Divaddict Publishing Solutions Ltd

Printed and bound in Great Britain by
CPI Group (UK) Ltd, Croydon CR0 4YY

Head of Zeus Ltd
First Floor East
5–8 Hardwick Street
London EC1R 4RG

WWW.HEADOFZEUS.COM

A Million Dreams

To my mum
I wish you could have read this one

PROLOGUE

10 Years Ago

Beth

'The sooner we begin your treatment, the better the chances for a successful outcome.'

The words that reshaped our future – reshaped everything – were softly spoken. I looked across the desk, beyond the files and X-ray envelopes, at the doctor who was patiently waiting for our world to stop spinning as we absorbed the news.

I was gripping Tim's hand so tightly I was probably crushing bone against cartilage, but my gaze was fixed on the oncologist, whose eyes revealed far more than I think he knew. Behind the rimless glasses, I saw the glimmer of a truth he was not prepared to share with us on that first black day. The chances of success were small. My ability to read faces, to pick up on tiny nuances others failed to see, had always been an asset in my work. On that day, it felt more like a curse.

'I see from your file that you and your wife don't have children, Mr Brandon.'

Tim shook his head, and I felt the tremors racking his body begin to spread to mine. I was shaking in both body and voice as I answered for him.

'We've only been married for two years. We were planning on waiting a little longer before starting a family.' I looked at the doctor, whose face was beginning to swim behind my tears.

'I know this is a lot for you to take in, but without wishing to add to the decisions you are now facing, I have to urge you to think about safeguarding and preserving your fertility.' Perhaps Tim understood instantly what the oncologist was talking about, but I was several pages behind him. 'There is a strong possibility that your treatment will affect your ability to father a child in the future, so at this point we would recommend you to consider freezing your sperm.'

For one crazy moment I imagined he was talking about doing so at home, where it would sit on the shelf beside the packets of pork chops and Birds Eye peas. It took a few moments for the image to disappear.

'There are several fertility clinics that we can refer you to. They will be able to explain the various options open to you. These can range from freezing sperm to even freezing embryos, if you should choose.'

'Embryos?' Tim asked, his voice ringing with confusion.

'It's one option to consider. There are excellent statistics for successful pregnancies resulting from cryogenically stored embryos. For couples your age and in your situation, it is definitely something worth thinking about.'

***

We had visited a clinic just two days later. Scarcely enough time to consider what we were doing, or why. The possibility of Tim facing a life-threatening disease was still so overwhelming to us that everything else seemed like white noise. We'd left the fertility clinic with armloads of pamphlets and advice ringing in our ears. In the end, we had made the decision not because of the success rates, graphs, or testimonials we'd read until late into the night, as though cramming for an exam. We'd made the decision with our hearts.

'We'll be making a baby,' I said, snuggling up against the man I loved and trying not to notice how much thinner he seemed than only a month or so earlier.

'And then freezing it. We'd quite literally be putting our child – or children – on ice.'

'Actually, I think they store them in liquid nitrogen,' I corrected, a new expert in a field I'd known next to nothing about only a few days earlier.

'We'd also be putting you through all kinds of invasive procedures unnecessarily. Because there's nothing wrong with *you*,' Tim had said, and it was impossible not to hear the pain and regret in his voice. He was angry. No, more than that, he was *furious* with his body for failing him so cataclysmically for the first time in all of its thirty years.

'We don't know how long it's going to take you to beat this thing,' I reasoned, hoping the positivity in my voice was powerful enough to fool him. 'And it could be *years* before we're ready for children. This way we won't have to worry about whether my fertility has dropped off by the time we're ready. We'd already have a freeze-dried baby all ready to go.' .

'Just add water,' he had joked, pulling me even closer against his bony ribcage.

'Exactly,' I said, my mouth against his skin, where hopefully he couldn't feel the trembling of my lips or the dampness on my cheeks from the tears that were falling silently in the darkness of our bedroom.

'Let's go for it then,' he whispered into my hair. 'Let's make some babies.'

1

Beth

I have a good nose. I don't mean its shape, which is fairly ordinary and fits in perfectly well with my other features. (My husband, Tim, once claimed that I'm beautiful, which was charmingly biased and also inaccurate.) What I mean about my nose is that my sense of smell is uncommonly acute. Admittedly, I didn't fare quite so well with some of the other senses; for a start I'm completely tone deaf, which is kind of funny as I ended up falling in love with a musician. But a good sense of smell is a definite advantage if all you've ever wanted to do is work with flowers, or better still own your own florist shop. Happily, I did both.

'Is there anything else you'd like me to do before I leave for the day, Mrs Brandon – er, I mean Beth?'

I looked up from the bouquet of peonies I was tying and smiled at Natalie, my assistant, who even after six months of working for me occasionally forgot to call me by my first name. My fingers were working at speed, securing and knotting the rustic string around the stems with the dexterity of a practised fisherman.

'Have you any plans for this afternoon?' Natalie asked as I followed her to the door and flipped the swinging sign from 'Open' to 'Closed'.

'Nothing particular,' I replied with a smile as I ushered her onto the pavement and slid the bolt in place. She didn't know me well enough to spot the lie. It was a smooth eviction, and hopefully she hadn't noticed my haste.

Standing in the empty shop, I let the familiar odours and sounds settle around me, like a security blanket. The buzz of the overhead lights and the hum of the large refrigerators where the most delicate blooms were stored combined to drown out the sound of traffic from the high street. The shop was in a great position, and its reputation had grown steadily in the six years since we'd opened it. I ran my hand over the polished wooden counter, waiting for the usual grounding sensation to calm me. But today the shop failed to work its magic.

Early closing day was typically when I met with clients or caught up on paperwork, but there was something else on my agenda for this afternoon. I only managed to eat half of the meal-deal sandwich I'd bought that morning before throwing the rest into the bin beneath my desk. Perhaps I should have done the same with the strong Americano coffee, because the last thing I needed was an extra injection of caffeine, not when I was already so wired.

'This is ridiculous,' I muttered to myself as I went through the familiar ritual of locking up the shop and setting the alarm. 'I'm only speaking to my husband. Why am I so uptight?'

Because you know he won't be happy about this, an annoyingly accurate inner voice replied. I drowned it out by turning up the car radio to a volume usually favoured by teenage boys, and wove through the early afternoon traffic.

The car park was gratifyingly empty and I didn't pass a soul as my feet travelled on cruise control down the familiar twisting pathways. Even the scurrying squirrels who called this place home remained in their trees, as though respecting our need for privacy. My stomach was churning and gurgling with a mixture of eagerness and trepidation, forcing occasional splashes of acid to burn their way up my throat.

The thick cardigan I'd pulled on before leaving the shop was redundant, and I shrugged it off in the sunshine as I walked. Even so, beneath the weight of my shoulder-length hair, tiny pinpricks of perspiration erupted like measles spots on the back of my neck.

As I walked to meet him, it occurred to me that almost *every* important moment Tim and I had shared had taken place outdoors. We'd never engineered it, but looking back over the history of us, from our very first kiss (on a rain-drenched street corner) to the day two years later when we'd stood by the edge of a lake in front of our family and friends and promised to love each other for ever, we'd been outside. All our significant moments had been beneath a ceiling of clouds or stars. Even Tim's proposal had been al fresco, stunning me halfway through a countryside picnic. I could still remember how his dark brown eyes had softened as he reached across the plaid blanket for my hand, carelessly knocking aside the remains of our lunch. 'Marry me, Beth,' he'd whispered, looking almost as surprised as I'd been by his words. Then his mouth had covered mine, almost smothering the excited 'yes' I'd given in reply.

It was only right, therefore, that this next life-changing conversation – the one I'd been rehearsing all morning – should be held beneath a blue, cloud-wisped sky, with only the chirruping birds as witnesses.

He was waiting for me beneath the shade of a tall oak tree, and I hurried to him as my stomach tied itself into an unimaginable tangle of knots. I felt like an actor who'd suddenly forgotten their lines moments before their cue. My carefully constructed argument covering the points I wanted to make – and the objections I knew he'd scatter like landmines in my path – had suddenly deserted me.

It was still a struggle not speaking to him every day. Perhaps that's why my voice shook in a way it hadn't done when I'd run this conversation past the buckets of gerberas and carnations in the sanctuary of the shop we'd set up together. I cleared my throat.

'Timothy,' I began, which must surely have put him on high alert, as I hardly ever used his full name. I swallowed down a lump of anxiety that was lodged in my throat like a boiled sweet and tried again.

'Tim, I've got something I want to say, and I don't want you to interrupt or chip in until I've finished, okay?' I gave him no chance to interject and dived right in. 'I've given this a lot of thought over the last few weeks – well, months actually – and I think we should try again. I think we owe it to ourselves to give it one last go.'

I hadn't realised I was pacing as I spoke, until I saw I was no longer beside him. I retraced my steps. 'I know what you're going to say: that we tried before, *twice* before,' I added ruefully, as if he might somehow have forgotten our previous failures. 'But this time, I've got a feeling...' My voice drifted away, and I instantly corrected myself. 'No, it's more than that. I'm *certain*. This time everything is going to work out just the way we wanted.'

I lifted my head and pushed back a thick lock of copper-shot hair that had fallen across my face. 'Okay,' I corrected, sounding suddenly sad, 'maybe not *exactly* the way we wanted. But something good can still come out of all of this. Something wonderful.'

I dropped my gaze to my feet, but I could still imagine his eyes lasering through me. 'The shop's doing really well now; financially, we're in a good place. And Natalie is ready to take on more responsibility.' I could feel the acid prick of tears, but I didn't want to stop, not now I'd finally found my stride. 'I don't want to wait any longer. I'll be thirty-six next year,' I reminded him, because he'd always been shockingly forgetful about birthdays and anniversaries. 'I'm already what they'd call elderly – *geriatric*, probably.'

I looked around, making sure we were quite alone and not overheard before continuing. 'I've contacted the clinic.' I imagined, rather than heard, his gasp of disapproval. 'They said it could be different this time. I could try it without the drugs, so there'd be less chance of me feeling so sick.' I gave a small laugh, which almost – but not quite – managed to hide the fledgling sob beneath it. 'Unless of course I get *morning* sick,' I joked. No one laughed. But then I hadn't really expected that either of us would.

I looked back towards him, feeling the first escapee tears beginning to course down my cheeks. I grappled in my pockets for a tissue packet, furious with myself for not having had the foresight to bring one. There'd always been zero possibility of me getting through this without crying.

'We've got one last chance, my love. There's just one embryo left, and I want to try for it.' My words rode the sob like a surfer on a wave. 'I want to have your baby.'

My words hung on the air, like the strains of an instrument long after the song has ended. I scrabbled in my handbag on another fruitless tissue hunt. Who comes to a place like this without one? I sniffed inelegantly as I crossed the space between us. 'Aren't you ready after all this time to be a daddy?' My fingertips reached out to him. The stone felt cold as I traced the outline of his name in the white-flecked marble. *Timothy Brandon.* And beneath his name was the date, which was etched in my heart even more deeply than it was into the stone marker. September 10th 2014. The day I lost my husband.

Mascara was probably running down my cheeks, and I was sniffing like a runny-nosed toddler in the absence of a handkerchief. 'For Christ's sake, where's a bloody tissue when you need one?'

'Here,' said a voice from somewhere behind me.

I don't think either me or the stranger who was holding out the unopened packet of tissues expected me to shriek quite as loudly as I did.

'Sorry,' said the man, taking a quick step backwards, his much-needed packet of Kleenex going with him. 'I didn't mean to startle you.'

'Well, you did,' I retorted, embarrassment making me sound angrier than I should have been. 'I thought I was alone here.'

I looked around at the rows of orderly headstones. It was my preferred time of day to visit Tim's grave. Midweek, mid-afternoon; you were practically guaranteed to have the place to yourself.

'Me too,' said the man smoothly. His eyes held a challenge and I quickly reached out and took the packet from his still-outstretched hand before he changed his mind. He politely pretended not to hear while I made good and noisy use of the tissues. It was a sound I'm sure Tim's immediate neighbours were all too familiar with. I plucked a second square from the packet – just in case – and passed them back to him.

'Please, keep them,' he said, his eyes kind and knowing. 'It sounds like your need for them might be greater than mine.'

His words made me uncomfortable, but that didn't excuse my knee-jerk reaction: 'Were you *eavesdropping* on my private conversation?'

The man's eyes, which were an unusual shade of grey, like slate after the rain, widened a little at my confrontational tone. 'Quite unintentionally, I assure you.' His voice was measured, but I caught the smallest flare of his nostrils, like a dragon waiting to exhale flames. 'Although I'm not sure it can legitimately be called "private" when you're broadcasting it loudly to anyone in the vicinity.'

He had me there, but embarrassment made it impossible to hear the sensible voice of reason in my head, the one that was telling me to thank him politely and walk away. 'There *was* no one around. I checked. And it was a very personal conversation.'

The man sighed, and I wondered how many times he was

going to end up regretting his good deed for the day. From the expression on his face, quite a few, I imagined. 'I've been here for the last forty minutes.'

I rammed the tissues he'd given me into my pocket, and heard a teenage-worthy petulance in my voice, which I should have outgrown several decades ago. 'Well, you must have been hiding, or something.'

There was something in his eyes that told me I'd crossed a line, and all at once I remembered where we were.

'I was kneeling down,' he said quietly. 'Tidying my wife's grave.'

My eyes dropped and I saw two damp circles darkening the denim of his jeans, verifying his words. 'I... I'm so sorry,' I said awkwardly, trying to squeeze the apology past my foot, which was firmly lodged in my mouth.

The man shook his head, and as he did I noticed the small scattering of grey threads at his temples. He was older than I had first thought, perhaps in his early forties. Although his lean frame and casual clothing gave the impression of someone younger.

'Don't worry about it,' he said, but I got the impression he was still annoyed with me. That made two of us, because *I* was annoyed with me. 'Anyway,' he continued, 'I was about to go, so I'll leave you in peace to finish your... conversation.'

'No, please, don't go because of me. I feel like I've chased you away.'

'Not at all.' His mouth betrayed the polite lie. 'I can always come back later.'

He turned to go and I felt a rush of shame. In my job, I was used to dealing with the bereaved. And never, in all my years as a florist, had I spoken to a grieving relative in such an unthinking way.

'I really *am* sorry,' I said to his fast-retreating back. For a moment, I thought he was going to carry on walking, but he slowed and then turned around.

'Forget it,' he said, and then his face softened as he added, 'It sounded as if you and your... partner—'

'Husband,' I corrected softly.

There was empathy in his eyes as he nodded gently. 'It sounds as if you have a lot to discuss.'

He strode away, surprisingly silently for such a big man. No wonder I hadn't heard his approach. I dug my hands into my pockets, my fingers curling around the stranger's gift, as I crossed back to Tim's headstone. The grass was slightly damp, but I dropped down onto it, sitting crossed-legged as I leant forward with my forehead resting against the cool marble. 'Don't say a word,' I warned my ever-silent husband. 'Not one single word.'

The random encounter with the stranger in the cemetery kept popping into my head over the next few days, and I cringed *every single time* I remembered how I'd behaved. Of course I would apologise if our paths ever crossed again, but I really hoped they didn't. It felt weird knowing that a total stranger was the sole keeper of a secret I hadn't yet shared with either my family or friends.

My hands stilled their work sorting out the early morning delivery of blooms from the nursery. The baby Tim and I had hoped for felt so close, all I had to do was reach out and pull it towards me. We had one last chance to make our dream a reality. Deciding to go ahead with the IVF by myself was both terrifying and exhilarating. A baby. A tiny human who would be half Tim, and half me. It was a tangible way for him to live on in my life, in more than just my heart and memories. I pulled up the tall stool at my workbench and sank shakily onto it. It was a huge decision, a life-changing decision, and making it alone had never been my intention.

I closed my eyes, knowing when I did the cool storeroom of the florist shop would disappear and I would once again be transported back to the oncologist's office, hearing the news that would devastate our life and shatter the future we'd dreamt of. The ringing of the shop's doorbell was a welcome intrusion as it jerked me out of the old memory I visited far too frequently.

'Crazy Daisy' had always been so much more than a business to me. It was something Tim and I had dreamt up and created together; at times from his hospital bed, or during the long days between treatments, when he'd not been well or strong enough to return to his teaching job. The shop felt like our child, our firstborn, and I was fiercely protective of it.

When Tim lost his fight to stay with me, when all I'd wanted to do was curl up in a ball of misery and join him, it was the shop that dragged me from my bed each morning. To abandon it felt like I'd be abandoning him. And that was something I would never do. Without Crazy Daisy, I doubt I'd have got through those first dark months of grief and despair. But now, five years on, I was ready to create one last piece of magic with the man I loved. It wouldn't be easy. I knew that. I was going to worry that I was doing it all wrong every single minute of the day. Without Tim's calming influence around to dial me down, I was probably going to be an absolute nightmare of a parent. And I could hardly wait to find out.

2

Beth

After Tim died, I'd visited the cemetery every day. It hadn't been healthy – I could see that now – although at the time I'd refused to listen to my worried parents or my sister, who'd voiced her concern all the way from Australia, where she now lived. Eventually my visits had decreased to just once or twice a week. Anything less than that still felt wrong.

There were always more people in the cemetery at the end of the day, and I recognised the faces of several 'regulars' as I passed them. Some looked up from tending their loved ones' graves, and nodded like commuters who travel the same route for years but never say a word to each other.

Graveyards have their own etiquette. It's okay to nod. Even a watery smile of recognition is permissible. But what you're *not* meant to do is intrude on any conversation being held with a lost loved one. The man who'd offered me his tissues the other day had clearly never learnt that. I wondered if he was recently bereaved.

'Hey. It's me again,' I said to the white plinth that had withstood so many of my tears in those early days, I'm surprised the stone hadn't eroded away. I'd been a mess; totally unprepared for life without the man I loved beside me. You'd have thought my early premonition at that first oncology appointment would have prepared me better, but when Tim finally slipped away, after the bravest and hardest-fought battle, I was left reeling.

I lifted the bunch of flowers in my hand. 'Don't get excited,' I told his headstone, 'these aren't for you. They're an apology for a man whose wife lives over there somewhere,' I explained, nodding my head in the direction the man had come from the other day. 'Give me a minute to find her, then we can carry on with our chat. We still have a lot to discuss.'

In any other location, I'd probably be certified as crazy for talking to Tim in the way I did here. But in this place it was so normal, it was practically obligatory. Beneath our feet were our loved ones. The people we'd shared our lives, our hearts and our souls with. To *not* speak to them in exactly the same way as we'd always done, well, *that* would be the madness.

An uncanny instinct led me to the right plot. In a row of lichen-covered, weed-strewn markers, her memorial was scrubbed clean, and the surrounding ground was neatly tended and planted with small flowering shrubs. The epitaph carved into the light grey marble was simple rather than flowery, but no less poignant. It said that the woman at my feet was Anna Thomas, wife of Liam, and a quick sad sum confirmed she'd been young – exactly the same age as I was now – when her life had been cut short eight years earlier. What a waste.

I crouched beside the headstone and carefully set down the small bunch of yellow roses. Not many people understand the language of flowers anymore, but as a florist I was fluent. These said 'sorry', and drew a concluding line beneath my unfortunate meeting with Anna Thomas's husband. Tucked among the tightly furled blooms were two things: a small card, on which I'd written *Thank you*, and an unopened packet of tissues. I figured he'd be able to work out who they were from.

'So what's new? What have you been up to recently?'

'Nothing much,' I replied. *Except preparing to get pregnant.* For a horrified moment I thought I'd said the words out loud, but my sister's face on my laptop screen looked neither stunned nor shocked, so I don't suppose I could have.

It was morning in Australia and Karen was sitting in her preferred spot for our Skype chats, on the deck of her Sydney home against a backdrop of tropical blooms. I'd long since seen through her not-so-subtle attempt to lure me subliminally to the other side of the world with exotic foliage.

Our calls were the highlight of my week. She was half a world away, but she was still my best friend, and the ache of missing her had never gone away, not even after all these years. I still longed for the smell of her shampoo when she hugged me, the graze of her lips against my cheek when she said hello, or her hand squeezing mine for those moments when words just weren't enough. We'd always been close, even as children, and although I'm sure we must have squabbled the way siblings do, the memory of it was buried so deeply beneath missing her, I truly couldn't recall it.

We knew each other's secrets: first crush; first kiss; first sneaked cigarette; first time with a boy: *'Honestly Bethie, I don't know what all the fuss is about; it was all over in seconds.'* That one still made me smile, although one devoted husband and two small children later, I doubt she still felt the same way. But now I was keeping the biggest, boldest secret in my entire life from her, and every time I opened my mouth I was scared it was going to come tumbling out.

'How are Mum and Dad?' Karen asked, momentarily disappearing from my screen as she reached for her glass of orange juice.

'The usual,' I replied in sister shorthand. I knew she'd be able to translate that one: Mum was busy with her book club, volunteering and amateur dramatics, while Dad was trying to pretend that retirement wasn't boring him to death, or that his arthritis hadn't deteriorated from slightly troublesome to seriously debilitating.

Karen pulled a face that I recognised only too well. The guilt that was never far away scored a sneaky bullseye. It was no secret that my parents had always intended to spend their retirement years in Australia. The pull was perfectly understandable: the weather was better for a man with Dad's condition; plus, fifty percent of their offspring lived there, with one hundred percent of their grandchildren. It was really all about the maths.

I'd always suspected that Karen had a secret master plan to move our entire family 'down under'. It had been a clever long game. She'd fed our parents titbits of information about beachside retirement properties beside golf courses, and had even sent links to Tim about teaching jobs with funny notes attached: *Didgeridoo skills not needed for this one!*

Although we'd never pursued it, I could see Tim's curiosity had been piqued. Karen knew I wanted to live by the coast again – and there was plenty of that in Australia. So mission (semi) accomplished. Or at least it might have been, until there was a persistent stomach spasm that wouldn't go away, and a perpetual sickness that caused the weight to drop from Tim almost overnight... and suddenly all talk of living elsewhere disappeared. We were much more focused on just living *at all*.

I hadn't expected that Tim's illness and battle to survive would alter my parents' plans. It had never been said – in fact, it had been actively denied many times – but everyone knew the real reason my parents had never emigrated. *I* was the reason. And the guilt of that weighed down heavily on me. Karen had two adorable children whose growing-up was being watched at a distance by their grandparents, and nothing anyone could do or say was ever going to make me feel better about robbing them of that. Except, perhaps, by giving them a third grandchild – one that no one was expecting.

A chorus of kookaburras chirruped noisily from a tree behind Karen as seven-year-old Aaron edged his face before the camera.

'Are you coming to see us soon, Auntie Beth?' Aaron asked, his question a serpent's lisp owing to the absence of his front teeth.

'Nice one,' I said to his mother over the top of my nephew's tousled blond curls. 'Clever change of tactic.' She knew better than anyone how much I loved her two little boys.

Karen answered with a grin that even I could see was identical to my own. 'I figured he'd be harder to disappoint,' she said, dropping a reward kiss onto her son's head.

'We've been through this a thousand times before. You know I can't just shut up the shop and take off.'

'I thought that's why you hired your wonder woman assistant.'

My smile felt suddenly strained. For a moment, I came perilously close to letting Karen in on my secret. Very little shocked my big sister, but I bet if I said: *Actually, I hired Natalie so she'd be able to look after the shop while I have a baby*, I could wipe that knowing look clean off her face. But I wasn't about to say that. Not yet. Call it superstitious, but it felt too much like counting your chickens before they've hatched, or the IVF equivalent: counting your embryos before they've thawed.

Luckily, a noise somewhere off-screen distracted Karen, and she glanced towards it with a small frown. 'Uh-oh. Sounds like Josh has just woken up. I thought we'd be safe for another twenty minutes. Sorry, hon. I'm gonna have to cut this one short.'

'Give him a big kiss from me,' I said, waggling my fingers at the screen. 'We'll chat again next week.'

Karen's eyebrows drew together to form a single blonde line. She was much fairer than me, and seven years in the New South Wales sunshine made her look like a native Aussie.

'You sure everything's okay, Bethie? You sound kind of... preoccupied.'

How did she do that, even from the other side of the world? How did she see through the distortion of pixels and look straight into my heart? Out of sight of my laptop screen I crossed my fingers like a child, to cancel out the lie.

'I'm absolutely fine. Stop worrying.'

Sleep took a long time coming that night. I hated lying to my family, but after the pain of the first two failed IVF attempts in Tim's final year, I didn't want anyone to know what I intended to do, until I knew it had been successful. *Or so they can't talk you out of it?* asked a voice in the darkness, which I recognised as mine. I turned over and thumped my pillow with an angry fist, as if the words had emerged from its memory foam filling. 'No,' I replied, reaching for the pillow on what I still referred to as Tim's side of the bed. I curled my arms around it, but it was a poor substitute for the man who should be lying there. 'I just don't want to get anyone's hopes up, that's all.'

3

Izzy

Here it was again. The worst moment of the whole week. Those dreadful five minutes when I stood in front of the man I still loved and tried to pretend I was okay with this; that I couldn't remember when 'goodnight' was murmured from the safety of his arms in the bed we shared, and not awkwardly on the doorstep of a house he no longer lived in.

'His homework's in there. It's all done,' Pete said, passing me the superhero-emblazoned backpack. Our fingers grazed in the transfer, and I felt his instinctive reaction of withdrawal even before I saw the flicker in his hazel eyes. Fortunately, our eight-year-old son, Noah, was happily oblivious to that reaction. He hopped impatiently on the doorstep beside his father.

'Can I go in now, Dad? I don't want to miss my TV programme.'

Pete's hand came out and ruffled our son's thick dark hair. 'Of course you can, kiddo.' Noah threw his spindly arms around Pete's waist, holding on a little longer, squeezing a little tighter, than he would have done before the separation. 'I'll see you in two weeks,' Pete said, his words disappearing into the shock of ebony hair, as he bent down to plant a kiss somewhere in the region of Noah's slightly crooked parting.

'You'll see him before that,' I reminded him. 'You *are* coming to the school show next week, aren't you?' We both heard the censure in my voice, even though he didn't deserve it. Pete wasn't the kind of dad who opted out of those sorts of events. I couldn't remember him missing a single nativity play, sports day, or sharing assembly. He was the crazy parent leaping up and down on the playing field sidelines as though it was an Olympic event, or holding his phone up high (annoying everyone behind us) to record every performance. We used to watch those videos together, curled up on the settee, our hearts beating in perfect synchronicity with love for our child. Did he watch them alone now, or was there someone new in his life who he shared them with? It was a question I didn't feel brave enough to ask.

'I could never forget that,' Pete assured. 'Not when it's your *big starring role*, Mr Zuko.' Pete grinned as he took a step backwards. I knew what was coming next. You don't spend fourteen years with someone without knowing all their party pieces. He pantomimed slicking an invisible comb through a hairline that wasn't quite as lush as it had once been. *'Will you still love me when I'm old and I've lost all my hair?' 'I do, hon, I do.'* The memory caught me unawares. That had been us, only a year ago.

Pete was in full swing now, his hips grinding in a way no eight-year-old wants to see, but Noah was convulsed with laughter as his father extended one arm and swept it slowly from left to right. His moves might be pure John Travolta, but his voice certainly wasn't.

Noah and I winced. It's safe to say that the musical talents that had secured Noah the lead role in the school production hadn't been inherited from either of us. Dogs started howling whenever I sang, and Pete (who loved karaoke far more than a man of his age and lack of talent really ought to) was almost as bad.

I watched Noah race down the length of the hall towards the lounge, seeking the TV's remote control with the accuracy of an Exocet missile. I waited for a moment, until I heard the familiar theme tune playing – as usual – a little too loudly, knowing the volume would provide an effective mask for our conversation. I turned to the man who inhabited a curious no man's land: no longer my current husband, and not quite yet my ex.

'These came,' I said, reaching for the small bundle of mail I'd been collecting. I no longer wondered if the reason so much of his post was still delivered here was that subconsciously Pete intended to come back. In reality it was probably because he was slow to realise that things like re-routing your mail don't magically happen, courtesy of internet elves. Paperwork and organisation had always been my thing, not his. *'Classic control freak'*, he used to tease, softening the criticism with a kiss or a hug. Pete's domain had always been the practical, hands-on tasks. These days I stopped my own dripping taps and eliminated my own spiders. Pete was just taking a little longer learning to pick up the reins.

He took the letters from my outstretched hand. No touching this time, he made sure of that. One by one he flicked through the pile. 'Bill. Bill. Bill. Rubbish. Rubbish. Rub—' His fingers stilled on the envelope I had deliberately placed at the bottom of the stack. He plucked it from the others, his eyes fixed on the white oblong, which bore the name of not one addressee, but two: Mr Peter Vaughan and Ms Eliza Bland. Every year I wondered why we never bothered telling them we were now married – and had been for the last eight years. It was ironic, we'd left it so long to ask them to update their records that their mistake was now about to become the truth again. Would I take back my maiden name? It was one of a thousand questions about my future I couldn't face answering.

There was only one place that still addressed us in this way. Pete didn't need to slip his finger beneath the seal to know who the letter was from or what it was about.

'Oh,' he said, his voice – the one I'd always been able to read so accurately – suddenly a mystery to me. 'Is it that time already?'

I nodded, not quite sure if my voice was steady enough for use.

'What do you want to do?' he asked, his voice low, and before I had the chance to say shouldn't we be making that decision together, he felled me with his next words. 'How much is it?' It was the first time in ten years he'd ever asked that question, and it cut like a knife that he did so now.

I gave a sad shrug. 'I don't know. I didn't want to open it without you.'

His eyes asked *Why?*, but thankfully his voice remained silent. He tore at the seal and extracted the folded letter, tilting it slightly so we could both read it.

The wording from the clinic was the same every year. For them, it was just one more piece of business; a formality. But this year our automatic *'Yes, of course'* and *'We'll find the money from somewhere'* was no longer a foregone conclusion.

'Three hundred pounds,' Pete said quietly, his focus on the bottom line of the letter, while my own lingered on the question they asked us at this time every year: do we wish to continue with another year's storage for our frozen embryos?

My eyes lifted to Pete's. I had no idea what he was thinking, but for me the feelings were still the same. There were two potential people stored in a tank of liquid nitrogen, just waiting for us to release them. They were Noah's brothers or sisters, or could be. And yes, I knew we'd run out of money to continue with further rounds of IVF, having only just clawed our way out of the debt our previous efforts had got us in. But somehow, from somewhere, each year we'd found a way – however tough things were– to keep ticking the box that said 'Retain the embryos'.

'Who knows, we might just win the lottery,' Pete used to say. And even though he'd never been a gambling man, I had loved the way he believed there was still a chance we might one day have the house full of children we'd both always dreamt of.

Pete scratched absently at the space just below his left ear; it was something he always did when faced with a problem. I hated the fact that what had once been a source of hope for both of us was now an issue that had to be resolved. A problem. The contract we'd signed with the clinic ten years earlier had made it clear that we both had to be in agreement about the outcome of any frozen embryos. Who would arbitrate now if I said yes, and he said no?

Pete carefully refolded the letter and slipped it back into its envelope. 'I'll find it from somewhere. Send them a cheque.'

Words were beyond me, and there were now two Petes standing on my doorstep instead of one. I addressed them both in a voice that was little more than a whisper. 'Thank you.'

All the Petes shrugged, because by now he'd quadrupled. 'You never know what's going to happen,' he said, turning away and stepping back down onto the front path. 'We might just win the lottery.'

I closed the door behind him and leant weakly back against it, feeling in some strange way that we already had.

By the age of thirty-four, I thought my life was figured out. Pete and I had weathered all kinds of storms over the last fourteen years. We'd survived the years of bad jobs and no money, and could look back on them with nostalgia – even the early days in that shoebox of a flat above the takeaway shop. Pete had been on an apprentice's wage at the garage back then, and my monthly take-home pay as a receptionist hadn't been much better. But when I look back on those days I remember only the love and the laughter... so much laughter.

We faced every challenge life threw at us together, including infertility. I've heard that it can sometimes break couples; that relationships can crumble under the strain.

Not ours. 'We're titanium strong,' I used to say, tempting the Fates, which I now realise were just biding their time to bring us down. After a struggle that brought us even closer together, Noah had finally arrived eight years ago, and turned us from a couple into a family.

And that joyous time, when everything should have been wonderful, was when – if I'd been listening closely enough – the first distant rumblings of thunder might have been heard. Those early days of parenthood hadn't been smooth sailing. And a lot of that was probably my fault. I'd been an anxious mum and Noah had been a fractious baby, suffering badly with eczema and allergies throughout his toddler years. We'd practically had our own parking spot in the doctor's surgery in those early years, but then every mum worries about their newborn, don't they?

It's unusual for a building to be toppled by a single blow. The same can be said for a marriage. There were two wrecking balls that brought ours down: money issues and my out-of-control protectiveness of Noah. Two years ago, the first cracks had started to appear, growing a little deeper with every red-inked bank statement. The debts were what started to drag us under. They were a mobster, encasing our feet in concrete shoes. The descent from having everything we wanted to realising we might be broken beyond repair had been shockingly fast.

'Did you have a good time this weekend?' I asked Noah, tucking the duvet securely around him; a small boy-shaped Egyptian mummy, encased in a Spiderman quilt. I bent to kiss the soft peach of his cheek, secretly sneaking in a quick hit of cleanly washed little boy.

'Yeah. We went to the cinema, and then to the park to

play football, and we ate lots of pizza and ice cream and doughnuts.'

I did my best to keep my face neutral and not register my disappointment that Pete persisted in following the Homer Simpson eating plan on his weekends with Noah. All that did was make my healthy-eating food regime seem dull in comparison. That was the way of it though. Noah's weekends with Pete were full of fun things, father-and-son bonding things. It wasn't the first time that the realisation panicked me. What if one day Noah asked if he could live with his dad instead of me? It seemed unthinkable, but after witnessing the disintegration of a marriage I'd thought was indestructible, nothing was impossible.

We'd waited so long to have him in our lives that losing Noah became my greatest nightmare. And there it was; the missile that had helped shoot down a marriage we'd thought was rock solid. My overprotectiveness, which at times had bordered on an obsession, and my failure to realise I was pushing away the one person who was trying to help me. *I* became the problem.

It was inevitable that the dream would return that night. It had a tendency to find the cracks in the walls I'd constructed around me and drive straight through them whenever it got the chance. It always started in exactly the same way...

The sun was hot on the back of my neck as I walked across the gravelled car park. I leant forward and adjusted the canopy on the pushchair, making sure that Noah was completely shaded. Not that he was in any danger of burning, for I'd practically dunked him in a vat of factor fifty sunscreen before we'd left the house. Still, it pays to be careful.

'Shall we pick Daddy some lovely fruit?' I asked my two-year-old, who was singing happily away to himself as we crossed to the entrance of the farm shop. Noah smiled broadly up at me and nodded, with absolutely no idea what I was talking about. To be honest, I wasn't exactly sure of the set-up here myself as this was the first time I'd visited the 'Pick Your Own' nursery. It was also to be the last.

'Basket or punnet?' asked the pretty young assistant in her vivid green apron, holding both options aloft for me to choose from.

'Basket,' I said decisively, smiling down at Noah. 'That way we can pick even more.'

'We close in an hour,' the young girl reminded me. 'So make sure you're back here by then so we can weigh the fruit you've picked and work out the bill.'

I felt deliciously rustic with the basket swinging from my hand as we left the shop and headed towards the rows of fruit trees and bushes in the adjacent field. The lateness of the hour meant that the only other pickers we saw were all heading back towards the shop and car park. I glanced at my watch, realising we were going to be late getting back home, so delved into my pocket to send Pete a message. My searching fingers found only a neatly folded tissue and some wisps of fluff, but no phone.

'Damn,' I muttered, hesitating for a minute and looking back towards the car park. I'd left my phone on the passenger seat while I was strapping Noah into his buggy, and had forgotten to pick it up. I debated going back for it, but it was a long hot walk over uneven ground, and the

rows of strawberry bushes were right there in front of us. I chose not to return to the car.

Ignoring the nearest bushes, I decided to walk to the furthest row of shrubs before starting to pick the fruit, imagining they'd be the least depleted by other pickers. The light was dappled beneath an overhead lattice of grape vines, although the late afternoon sun was still surprisingly hot. Despite my constant stream of chatter, I wasn't surprised when I peered beneath the pushchair's canopy to see that Noah had drifted off to sleep.

I lost track of time as I began plucking fruit from the bushes, picking far more than we could probably use, unless I decided to go into serious jam production. Eventually the basket became too heavy for the crook of my arm, so I moved Noah's legs to one side and wedged it on the footrest of the pushchair. Noah didn't even stir, and I remember staring down at him, marvelling as I always did at the incredible length of his long dark lashes, fluttering against the soft skin of his cheeks as he slept.

The basket was almost full when I noticed a large cluster of ripe strawberries at ground level. I put the brake on the pushchair, even though the ground was perfectly flat, and moved a few steps away to pick the last pieces of fruit to complete the basket.

I thought at first he was giggling. What kind of mother does that make me? How could I possibly have mistaken my child gasping for breath for laughter? I was kneeling on the grass and turned to look over my shoulder when I heard him. The smile poised and ready on my lips froze into an expression of terror. Something was wrong; terribly, terribly wrong.

Noah's face was blotchy. Only a minute ago it had been a soft pink colour, now it was red with fiery raised splotches, most of which had erupted around his mouth. Even as I looked at them, his eyes were starting to swell shut. In each pudgy hand, Noah held the lush red strawberries he'd taken from the basket, their fateful juice still dribbling down his chin and onto the white of his T-shirt. It looked horribly like blood. But far worse than his appearance were the long wheezing gasps he was making as he struggled to breathe.

The handful of strawberries I'd gathered flew in every direction, exploding like bright red shrapnel all around us as I ran back to Noah. I threw the basket of fruit off the footrest, but the damage its contents had caused was already done. Neither Pete nor I had a history of allergies and I'd never seen anyone in anaphylactic shock before, but I had absolutely no doubt that was what I was witnessing right now. Noah, who'd never eaten a strawberry in his life before today, was paying the price – the very worst price imaginable – for my negligence.

My fingers struggled on the harness of the pushchair as I tried to release him. Every second counted, and I was losing precious ones as I fumbled ineptly on a clasp I did up more than twenty times a day without even thinking about it.

'It's okay, sweetie, it's okay. Mummy's got you,' I said through terrified sobs as I finally succeeded in freeing Noah from the buggy. I pulled a bottle of water from beneath the pram and poured it quickly over Noah's lips, which were already swollen to twice their usual size. But it was only when I opened his mouth, to swill out the remains of the juice that was like poison to him, that I realised how much trouble we were in. His tongue was so enlarged it filled his *tiny mouth, practically obscuring his airway.*

'Help!' I screamed into the deserted rows of plants and shrubs. 'Somebody please help me. My baby's choking!'

I prayed for the sound of another voice, or the pounding of feet running our way, but all I could hear was the gentle song of bird call and the lazy buzz of honey bees.

Abandoning the pram and my handbag, I held Noah tightly against my chest and began to run.

Sometimes the dream ended there, with me sprinting along the endless rows of fruit bushes, the farm shop always tantalisingly just out of reach in the distance.

Sometimes I made it to the shop, only to find the 'Closed' sign swinging on the door and the lights turned off. In that version of the nightmare I would race towards the only vehicle left in the car park – mine – with Noah gasping for breath in my arms, only to discover the doors were locked, and my car keys out of reach in the depths of my abandoned handbag. Through the windscreen I could see my phone light up with an incoming call from Pete as Noah began to grow floppy in my arms.

In the way dreams have a habit of doing, the ringing phone morphed seamlessly into the trilling of my alarm clock. It was probably my imagination, but it sounded almost irritated that I hit the 'snooze' button three times before finally hauling myself out of bed. I hadn't always been like this, but sleep and I appeared to have fallen out of love with each other lately. I no longer leapt from my bed with a spring to my step or a glowing brightness in my green eyes. The reflection I glimpsed in my bedroom mirror looked more like a bloodhound who'd indulged in yet another night on the tiles. It would improve after a reviving shower, but that particular remedy would have to wait a little longer.

'Muuuuuuum!' wailed Noah, as I stumbled blearily into the bathroom. I backed out, with a quick apology, surprised to find him even awake at this hour, much less already in the shower. Confused, I pulled the bathroom door shut with a click. Eight was an awkward age for boys, and these days my presence in the bathroom was no longer welcome. It was a brief glimpse through a door of a place no sensible parent wants to visit. Puberty. My mouth twisted into a small wry smile. All too soon we would need to be having the kind of talk that was probably going to embarrass the hell out of both of us. Maybe that was something Pete should tackle on his own, I mused, as I walked to the top of the stairs and saw the laundry basket, with its lid bulging open. Having spent most of the previous day catching up on the washing, I had no idea how it could be full to overflowing so soon. Spiderman's face stared up at me from the wicker depths.

A small alarm bell sounded in the back of my head – one I had no intention of pushing the snooze button on. As kids go, Noah was pretty fantastic. He kept his bedroom tidy, and could navigate a route for dirty plates to the dishwasher with only one request from me. He even remembered to put the toilet seat back down again (better than his father ever did). But still, changing his bed sheets was a new and unexpected development. I pushed open the door to his bedroom and sure enough saw that Robert Downey Jr was now on Noah's bed – not literally, of course, just his Iron

Man persona. I think I already knew the answer as I returned to the laundry basket and gathered up the bedding in my arms. He'd buried the damp sheet in the very middle of the bundle, and my heart broke to think of him carefully trying to conceal it from me. I glanced back over my shoulder at the closed bathroom door, because the last thing Noah would want or need was to come out now and find the evidence he was trying so hard to hide right there in my arms.

By the time he joined me in the kitchen I was sitting at the scrubbed pine table, a cup of coffee and a slice of toast I had no appetite for on the table before me. A tiny piece of my heart splintered off when I saw his quick nervous glance at the washing machine. Flashes of red and blue patterned duvet cover were just visible beneath an ocean of white suds. He didn't say anything and I would sooner have lived through a dozen root canals than utter a single word to make him feel uncomfortable.

I pinned my jolliest smile on my face, and reached for the cereal box. He watched me carefully as the golden clusters hit the bowl. He looked like a nervous gerbil biting his lower lip anxiously, the way he does if anyone should happen to ask him 'what's nine times seven?'. That one I could help him with, but with this... I was suddenly helpless. Noah hadn't wet the bed in over five years. While Pete and I had been busy congratulating ourselves on our civilised and polite separation, assuring ourselves that we were still committed members of Team Vaughan, how had we failed to see that one member of the team was struggling? I needed time to think about what I should do now, and suddenly the leisurely morning I had planned was about to be replaced with one spent on my laptop googling for a solution.

Noah was halfway through his breakfast before I spotted the thin leather bracelet fixed around one small bony wrist. It appeared as he stretched across the table for a second slice of toast and I knew he'd seen my expression of surprise by the way he quickly tugged the white cuff of his school shirt back down to cover it. Twice in the space of less than half an hour, my son, who I'd always believed told me everything, had revealed a secret.

'What's that?' My voice was just the right amount of curious.

'It's a bracelet,' he mumbled, and I could have left it there, *should* have left it there, except his cheeks had suddenly gone bright red, the way they used to do when he was teething. As he now had a full complement of teeth, the heightened colour had to come from embarrassment.

'Where did you get that?' I asked, laying my hand down on the table, palm-side up, in invitation. Noah fidgeted on his wooden kitchen chair for a moment before laying his wrist on my hand. It was an unremarkable piece of jewellery, but something I couldn't imagine his dad buying. Like a lot of mechanics, Pete didn't even wear a wristwatch, and the only piece of jewellery he'd ever owned or worn was his wedding ring. It still sat on his finger, as did mine. I dreaded the hurt I knew would come the first time I saw his left hand without it.

So it was hard to imagine Pete buying this ethnic-looking bracelet for our son. A mother's instincts are sharp; so too are a wife's.

'Maya bought it for me on Saturday. There was a stall selling them in the park.'

'Uh huh,' I said, very pleased with the way I sounded

just the right amount of pleasantly interested. Maya was the receptionist at the garage where Pete worked. She was a few years younger than me, wore way too much mascara, and tops cut so low that hardly anyone bothered looking at her eyes anyway. She was pretty, and divorced, and fancied my husband; had done from the first moment she'd joined the staff of the garage three years earlier. Pete hadn't seen it, not even when I'd jokingly pointed it out to him. Only now it didn't seem so funny. *'Does she?'* he'd asked, truly not sounding even the least bit interested. *'Well, that's a shame for her, because the only woman I happen to fancy is...'* There'd been a long pause as he'd come up behind me at the sink and wound his arms around my waist. *'...you,'* he had whispered in my ear, and then kissed my neck in the way he did that always made my knees forget how to hold me up.

'Yuck. That's so gross,' Noah had declared, watching us with undisguised disgust from across the kitchen. Parental canoodling was possibly the very worst thing he could imagine back then. How could he possibly know how much worse it got when the canoodling stopped altogether?

'So Maya came to the park with you, did she?' I was pleased at how I'd managed to make my words sound like idle curiosity and less like bullets being fired from a gun.

'No. We bumped into her after we'd played football,' Noah exclaimed, opening his mouth and biting off a huge chunk of toast. It felt like an eternity before he was ready to speak again. 'But then Dad invited her to join us and we all went for ice creams and then she bought me this cool bracelet with my name on it and everything. Do you like it, Mummy?'

Once, a very long time ago, I'd promised myself never

to lie to my child. And yet it was surprisingly easy to do so now. 'I love it. But I'm afraid you can't wear it to school, honey, it's not allowed.' I reached for the press-stud fastening and removed the thin strap from his suntanned wrist. As I looked into his huge brown eyes I felt a familiar tug of love, laced with a feeling of panic I hadn't been expecting. Would I have to share his love with another woman one day? Would Pete eventually find a new partner who'd become my son's stepmum? Would another woman tuck him up in a bed I'd never see; read him stories I'd never hear; and kiss him goodnight on the weekends he spent with his dad?

I palmed the bracelet, squeezing it so tightly I could feel the sharp edges of the leather digging into the skin of my hand. 'You can wear it when you get home this afternoon. Hurry up now, or you're going to be late for school.'

There were a few lingering mums chatting in the morning sunshine when I pulled up outside the green wrought iron primary school gates, but most had already dispersed. The traffic had been particularly bad that morning.

'Shall I come in and explain why you're late?'

'No!' Noah exclaimed, with the kind of horror only an eight-year-old can effectively pull off. 'That would be soooo uncool.'

I reached over and smoothed back a thick strand of dark hair that had fallen across his forehead. It gleamed like sealskin in the rays of sunlight filtering through the windscreen. He was several shades darker than Pete and a whole colour chart away from my own tawny locks.

'Would Danny Zuko's mum come into school and speak

to his teacher?' Noah challenged, his small pointed chin nodding emphatically as though he'd scored an irrefutable winning argument.

'You feel okay, don't you?' I asked, my fingers itching to rest against his forehead to perform a quick temperature check. There was a time when I did that almost automatically, but I was better now. Mostly I kept the urge under control.

'I feel fine,' Noah assured.

'Got your EpiPen?' One day I would let him go without asking. But not today.

He held his book bag up and waggled it by way of an answer.

'Okay then, my little T-Bird. Scoot. Get the heck out of my car.'

Noah grinned, leapt out, but before running into the building he turned and glanced back over his shoulder. There it was, the grin I loved, all teeth, crinkled eyes, and freckles. '*That* was cool,' he said approvingly, and then was gone.

The car park of the veterinary practice was already full, and I had to circle it twice before finally finding a space. I followed a woman cradling a sick-looking dog in her arms up the path to the surgery. Her red-rimmed eyes were as sad as a basset hound's as she lifted them to mine in thanks when I held open the door. I'd worked at the practice for three years and still found it hard not to get caught up in the heartbreak of the job. It was a hard equation to balance: the joy of loving a pet versus the pain of losing them. The same could possibly be said of a husband.

It was nine months, two weeks and four days since Pete had walked away in tears from our family home, carrying a motley collection of mismatched suitcases in his arms and the memory of that last dreadful argument in his heart – the one when I'd told him to leave. And I still couldn't decide whether the joy of loving him for fourteen years outweighed the pain of living without him for almost a year.

I made my way to my desk, evicting the practice's moggy, Buzz, from my chair, as I did each morning. 'Really, Buzz? Every single day?' I asked, gently nudging the reluctant feline until he sauntered lazily away with a vengeful look in his baleful green eyes. A low rumble of laughter came from the direction of the reception desk, where a tall, well-dressed man waiting to be served had witnessed my confrontation with the cat. He smiled briefly before his attention was claimed by whoever was pulling sharply on the lead curled around his hand.

My job didn't require me to help out at Reception, but the man was clearly dressed for somewhere other than a visit to the vet's; he stood out like a thoroughbred in a string of ponies. More than that, he had a nice air about him. I hadn't reached the point of 'noticing' other men yet, but if I ever *did* get there, he was the kind of man I'd like to meet.

'Can I help you?' I asked, approaching the reception desk with a smile. Whatever animal the man had on the end of the lead was clearly growing increasingly agitated. I could hear a plaintive whining and the scratch of claws on linoleum as it tried to make for the exit. I peered over the desk and his small Jack Russell terrier barked vociferously up at me. Its owner was considerably more courteous.

'Thank you,' he said, sliding a printed bill across the counter towards me. 'I'd like to settle this now, if that's possible.'

'Of course,' I said politely, swivelling the invoice around and trying to keep my features neutral. The amount would have secured storage for our frozen embryos for the next two years.

'Could I have the name, please?'

'Sally,' he said, flipping open his wallet.

'Erm, yours, not hers.'

His laughter set the excitable little dog off again. 'I'm sorry. You'd think with the amount of time I spend here, I'd know the drill by now.' His face sobered, and the fine traces of lines, which the amusement had smoothed away, settled back into place.

'Thomas,' he said, reciting his address to help me find his account on the computer system. An impressive list of invoices popped up on the screen, many of them equal in size to the one he was paying today.

'Sally's quite a regular patient, isn't she?' I observed, wondering too late if my comment bordered on being rude. I was about to apologise, but Mr Thomas just shrugged good-naturedly and slid a credit cards towards me. 'If I stop to think how much this little dog has cost my wife and me over the years...'

I processed the transaction and handed him the card reader. 'I'm sure she's worth it,' I said, suddenly thankful that despite Noah's persistent requests, we owned nothing more expensive to keep alive than a lowly goldfish.

'Well, have a nice day,' I said.

'You too,' Mr Thomas replied politely, already heading back to his life and out of mine. 'I'm sure I'll be back here and seeing you again before too long.'

But the next time I saw Mr Thomas it was in an entirely different location.

4

Izzy

The message came through on my phone. I stared at it for ages and delayed replying for so long Pete probably thought I hadn't received it. When the screen went black, I kept pressing the home button to summon up his words again.

> Was wondering if you'd like to grab a bite of lunch before Noah's show? There's something I'd like to ask you. We could meet at the pub near the garage? TB.

Only I didn't want to text back until I'd forensically dissected his invitation. It was unprecedented. We didn't do this kind of thing anymore, not since Pete and I had stopped sharing a bed, an address, or anything at all, except for Noah – obviously, *he* was something we'd always share. Since our separation, all contact was always in the presence of our son, who we passed between us like a relay baton.

The last full conversation Pete and I had held in private had been the one where we'd discussed how to break the news to our little boy that Mummy and Daddy weren't

44

going to be living together any more. We'd agreed that I should be the one to say the actual words, but when the moment came they'd burnt like bile in my throat, searing it closed. Pete had to take over, reaching for Noah's small hand and gripping it tightly as our words tore his world apart. Pete's other hand had held mine. I took comfort in that for all kinds of reasons. It made me think that perhaps this separation might only be temporary, a blip we'd be able to get past. But somehow we never did.

And now he was inviting me to lunch, away from the familiar surroundings of the home we still owned; away from our child. I ping-ponged backwards and forwards all afternoon, unable to decide if this request for a meeting was a good sign or an extremely bad one.

'There's no way of knowing unless you go,' said Maggie, my work colleague and friend, looking up from a clipboard where she was busy ticking items off a delivery note. 'You *are* going to go, Izzy, aren't you?'

I sighed as I lifted a sack of dog kibble from the floor, my face half hidden behind it. 'What if he wants to talk about going ahead with a divorce?'

'What if he wants to talk about coming home?' she countered straight back.

'Maybe he wants to tell me he's met someone else?' Maya's face, followed swiftly by her memorable cleavage, popped into my head and refused to leave it.

'Or maybe he wants to tell you that he still loves you.'

I had to hand it to Maggie, she was playing her cards well, and I liked her hand much better than my own.

'You have to go,' Maggie said, ending the conversation on a decisive note, almost as if she didn't know I would be spending the entire night tossing and turning, debating on whether or not I'd made the right decision.

'I know I do.'

My reply was so breezy I could practically feel it gusting through the air from my phone to his.

Sure. I can do lunch before the show. One o'clock? See you then.

Never in the history of texts has anyone spent so long debating whether or not to end their message with an 'x'. It went in and came out no less than five times before I finally lost patience with myself and pressed 'Send' without it.

The weather was hot, too warm for jeans, my preferred choice of outfit, or at least that's what I told myself as I delved deep into my wardrobe and pulled out a floaty calf-length skirt and a short-sleeved top with a flattering V-neck. I stared at the woman in the mirror, who'd let her hair hang down in soft waves rather than clip it back in its usual sensible ponytail. I'd never been one for wearing much make-up, except for special occasions, but even I had to admit that a couple of strokes with a mascara wand and a smear of lip gloss made a big difference. Even Noah noticed when I wafted into the kitchen on a cloud of the perfume Pete had bought me two Christmases ago.

'You look pretty,' he declared, which earned him a quick kiss dropped onto his thick dark hair. 'But you smell kind of funny.' There's nothing like an eight-year-old for taking you down a peg or two.

Fortunately, excitement about his show that afternoon meant Noah was too lost in his own thoughts to spare any for what might be happening in *my* day. I tried to bury the idea that Pete was going to ask if he could come back home, but it kept clawing its way back to the surface.

The pub was busy; Pete had always called it a popular 'watering hole' for the nearby offices and building sites, and the phrase certainly rang true as I squeezed and excuse-me'd through the crowds. Laughter as shrill as hyenas' from a cluster of smartly dressed women was answered by deeper, antelope-like snorts of amusement from their male colleagues. At the bar, a trio of dust-covered construction workers grunted like warthogs as I walked past. It felt a bit like being in a David Attenborough documentary.

Miraculously, I managed to score a suddenly vacant table and quickly slid onto a chair, in a manner Buzz the cat would clearly have applauded. The thought made me smile, and my lips were still gently curved when the chair opposite me was pulled out and Pete sat down.

'Hey you,' he said, and the use of his old greeting almost undid me. He moved in for a hug before stopping to question if he should, and ended up hovering so close I could smell the oil from the cars he'd been working on that morning and a lingering whiff of his shower gel. It was all achingly familiar.

'It feels odd being out without Noah,' Pete said, as we browsed the pub menu.

'I did ask the school if he could join us for a swift pint, but they said he had double maths and then needed to get ready for the show.'

It felt good to hear Pete laugh – properly laugh – again. It was even better seeing the flicker of surprise in his hazel eyes, almost as if he'd forgotten that I could be funny. I couldn't blame him for that, because I had too.

'I'll have the ploughman's, please,' I said, wondering how awkward it would be if I offered to pay for my own lunch. Luckily, Pete got to his feet to head to the bar before I had the chance to find out.

'Won't be a minute,' he promised, and then muscle memory or a long-remembered habit reached out from the past to sabotage him. As he turned to go, his hand fell lightly onto my shoulder, giving it a gentle squeeze. Two sets of suddenly indrawn breath and the hand was whisked away. We both pretended that it hadn't happened; it seemed safer that way.

By the time Pete returned with a pint for himself and a glass of wine for me, I'd given myself a stern talking-to, and was trying to pretend that none of this felt weird or uncomfortable. Except that it did. And it wasn't helped by the couple of glances I'd intercepted from him, which had suddenly made the smooth Chardonnay much harder to swallow.

Pete was scratching that spot beneath his ear again, a sure sign that he too was nervous, and suddenly the need to know what we were doing here made me bold.

'You said there was something you wanted to ask me?' I prompted, my hands fiddling with the stem of my wine glass as my entire future hung on a pivot.

Pete's smile looked nervous. 'Yes, there is.'

The pub faded away, and suddenly it was just the two of us staring at each other across a small table roughly the width of the Grand Canyon.

'It's about Noah.'

Keep smiling, I told myself, despite the fact I could already feel the grin sliding from my face like a melting waxwork. *Don't let him see that you were hoping this lunch was about us.*

'I'd like to take him away.'

You'd have thought that after so many years together, he'd have found a better way of phrasing it. Pete looked mystified as the colour drained from my face, before realising that I'd misinterpreted his words.

'On *holiday*,' he clarified rapidly. 'I'd like to take Noah away on holiday. It's been a really tough year for him, but he's coped with it all so brilliantly. He's such an amazing kid and he deserves a break.'

Part of me wanted to know if Pete meant a break from me. I was several glasses of Chardonnay shy of being brave enough to ask *that* one.

'He *has* coped well,' I agreed, although it was hard to dismiss the memory of Noah's concerned expression as he watched the washing machine remove the evidence of how he might *not* be doing quite as well as we thought. I hadn't told Pete about it, because it felt as though I was betraying Noah. 'But a holiday...' I continued hesitantly, as though the word was vaguely familiar, but I couldn't quite recall what one was. 'Do you mean abroad?'

Pete nodded. 'It would only be for a week, Iz. You'd be able to phone him every day and Skype too if you wanted.

I'm pretty sure the villa has Wi-Fi.'

I reached for my glass of wine, buying myself time to collect my thoughts, which were galloping through my head like escaped ponies.

'Someone at work has offered me the use of their family's place in Cyprus for a week, rent free. It sounds great. It's right by the beach and it even has its own swimming pool.'

Had the last nine months erased all memory of me from Pete's mind, I wondered? Didn't he know I was already cataloguing everything that could possibly go wrong: planes plummeting into the sea; sunstroke; food allergies, fish hooks embedded into tender fingers; or drowning in your very own swimming pool? I already knew I wouldn't sleep for the entire week.

'All I'd need to buy are the flights and I've seen a good deal on those.' I hated that there'd already been so much behind-the-scenes planning before he'd even thought of mentioning it to me.

'Noah doesn't have a passport.' It was the only objection I could think of that didn't make me sound like the world's worst overprotective mother.

'We've still got time to get one. I've checked it out online.'

What I really wanted to ask was how he could afford this type of holiday, given how tight things had been financially over the last few years. But that was a wife's question and no longer mine to ask. I sighed and looked out through the pub window. Outside, the warm weather had brought out an unexpected number of shorts wearers, and practically everyone was sporting sunglasses. Everyone looked like they were on holiday.

'I won't let anything bad happen to him, Izzy. You can

trust me, you know that.' Pete's hand stretched across the table and took hold of mine. I was so shocked I forgot to snatch it away. How long had it been since I'd felt his warm, oil-stained fingers wrapped around mine? But as comforting as his touch was, it couldn't tether me to the present, and I was travelling back to an uncomfortable time when my concerns about Noah had crossed a dangerous line. A time when every little illness had me racing to the doctor. And Pete had never once criticised me. He'd been on my side, even when I was wrong. That kind of support, loyalty and patience is hard to forget, even when you're firmly headed on the pathway to divorce.

'What if he gets sick while you're away? What if he has an allergic reaction to something?'

Pete did a pretty good job of swallowing his sigh, but I heard it anyway.

'I'll take all his medications. But you have to admit he's been pretty healthy for a while now. He's finally growing out of it, just like they told us could happen.'

My eyes were busily inspecting the grain pattern of the wooden tabletop, so I missed the reproach on his face, but I heard the trace of censure in his voice. 'I know what to do if he isn't well, Izzy. I might live away, but I'm *not* an absent parent. I never have been. You know that.'

I *did* know that, but it didn't make the letting go any easier. 'What if you can't get his special milk over there?'

'Then we'll take it with us,' Pete countered reasonably. 'Or I'll just pour beer on his cornflakes instead.'

How could he still do that? How was he able to conjure up a smile I would have sworn was impossible to find?

'Relax. I've got this, Izzy.'

'Yeah, well, that's what I thought… but we both know exactly—'

'That was *years* ago,' Pete interrupted. 'And it wasn't your fault. The only person who's ever held you responsible for what happened that day at the farm shop is *you*. It was never me.'

Pete was ploughing on with his carefully prepared argument, not yet realising he'd already won. I sighed, knowing – as I'd done all along – that there was only one answer to give him. I was going to have to say yes.

'Just one last question,' I said. The lines on my soon-to-be ex-husband's face deepened into grooved fantails at the edges of his eyes as he beamed back at me. They faded faster than a shot of Botox when I asked: 'Who owns the villa in Cyprus?'

He could have lied, I'd have been none the wiser if he had, but Pete had always been unfailingly honest, and I simply don't think it occurred to him not to tell me the truth.

'It's Maya's family, actually.'

I didn't think my day could get any worse, but it just did.

5

Beth

'There's a strange man in the shop asking for you.'

I was in the back room, working on an arrangement of jewel-coloured gerberas, leaving Natalie to handle the shop. I'd heard the low rumble of voices as she dealt with a customer, but then she'd startled me by bursting through the bead curtain that separated the two areas. I paused before inserting a crimson red stem into the display, and looked up curiously.

'What man? And how is he strange?'

Natalie glanced over her shoulder, as though the mysterious customer might have followed her into the back room. 'He said he was looking for someone who might have bought a bunch of yellow roses from us, and then he described you perfectly, right down to the colour of your eyes.'

I knew in that moment *exactly* who was waiting for me on the other side of the bead curtain; what I didn't know was *why* he was there. I set the secateurs down on the workbench and wiped my damp hands on the apron I'd tied loosely around my hips. 'Would you mind finishing this up for me, Nat?' I asked. Her disappointed expression revealed she'd much rather have followed me back into the shop.

He had his back to me and appeared totally absorbed with the contents of a bucket of pink carnations. It's not a big shop, and it certainly seemed much smaller with one of its tallest ever customers on the other side of the counter. I hadn't realised when we'd been out in the open, but in here, with his head practically grazing the dark beams of the low ceiling, I realised he must easily be three or four inches over six foot.

He heard my footsteps and spun around. The expressions on his face kaleidoscoped from shocked to surprised, before finally settling on confused.

'It's you,' he declared, smiling, although clearly bewildered. Deep fan lines radiated out from the edges of his grey eyes. He either grinned a lot or spent a great deal of time squinting into the sun, for the lines seemed fairly well established.

He was dressed more formally than the first time we'd met, in black trousers and a pale shirt unbuttoned at the neck. 'Do you *work* here?' he hazarded. It wasn't exactly an inspired deduction, as I'd just emerged from the back room.

'I *own* here,' I corrected, and even I could hear the pride in my voice.

He paused, and I could practically see the wheels spinning in his head. 'So... is your name Daisy?'

For a moment I couldn't follow his logic, and then realised why he'd jumped to that conclusion. I wasn't sure whether to laugh or be offended. '"Crazy Daisy" is the name of the shop,' I said, my lips only just managing to suppress a smile. I thrust my hand out, as though we were in a business meeting. 'Beth,' I supplied. 'Beth Brandon.'

If he was surprised by the formality of my gesture, he hid it well. His own hand was almost twice the size of mine, but the handshake was everything it should be: brief, firm, and not at all damp.

'I'm Liam,' he said. 'Liam Thomas.'

'I know,' I said, my tongue running away with itself before I could stop it. The man's eyebrows drew a little closer together. 'I saw the name on your wife's headstone,' I admitted awkwardly, which made me sound like some weird kind of cemetery stalker.

Thankfully, he let that pass. 'It *was* you who left the roses on Anna's grave?' Again, it wasn't an Hercule-Poirot-worthy deduction. I'd always expected he'd work out who they'd come from.

'I felt I should apologise again,' I explained. Liam Thomas made a small hand gesture, which I took to mean that it really hadn't been necessary. His grey storm-cloud eyes widened slightly when I continued without preamble: 'Why were you looking for me? Come to that, how did you track me down? There's at least a dozen other florists in town.'

I was unusually awkward around this man, and somehow everything that came out of my mouth sounded like an accusation.

'It wasn't exactly difficult,' said Liam, extracting from his pocket the card I'd left with the flowers. Printed on the back was the name of the shop. It was almost as if I'd *wanted* him to seek me out.

I felt a flush start at my collar bones and begin to creep steadily up towards my hairline. This was the second time I'd questioned this man's motives, when really the only one acting weirdly here was *me*. 'Well, it was very nice of you to thank me,' I said, in my best 'let's wind things up now' tone, 'but it really wasn't necessary.'

'I didn't come here to thank you,' Liam replied. 'I came to see if this belongs to you. I found it near the flowers.' He delved into his back pocket and extracted something delicate and sparkly. He held it in his hand, although really it belonged on mine. I gasped as I looked down at my naked wrist, unable to believe I'd mislaid something so precious and not even noticed it was gone. I lifted the bracelet from his palm, my fingers curling convulsively around it like a Venus flytrap.

'I was right then. It's yours?'

I nodded fiercely, my throat too tight to actually speak. Enfolded within my palm was Tim's last gift to me. A gift that, if not for the kindness of this stranger, I'd probably never have seen again. My emotions were like wires, shredded of their protective outer sheath. That's the only explanation I can give for embarrassingly dissolving into tears of relief.

Liam Thomas looked aghast and glanced towards the back room, obviously hoping for help in the shape of Natalie to emerge. When none came, he ran his hands over his pockets as though performing a self-service pat-down.

'I'd offer you a tissue, except you already took my last packet,' he said.

There was a box I kept beneath the counter for emotional customers, and I reached for it now, dabbing furiously at my eyes to stop the flow. There was probably very little left of my make-up by the time I was done, judging by the mascara stains on the wad I dropped into the bin.

Liam had spent the last few minutes carefully inspecting the grout on the tiled floor, and probably couldn't wait to get out of there fast enough, and I could hardly blame him. But once again, I'd misjudged him.

'Look, if this isn't too strange, do you feel like grabbing a coffee or something? I think I spotted a café on the other side of the street.'

I nodded. Rosemary's Kitchen was a popular spot with many of the shop owners. It was somewhere I felt safe and comfortable. Perhaps that's why instead of politely declining the invitation, I looked up into Liam Thomas's concerned face, and found myself saying: 'Okay.'

6

Beth

The rain that had started to fall made Rosemary's appear even cosier than usual. The windows were steamed up, turning the interior into a secret coffee-scented oasis; a refuge for weary shoppers and tearful florists.

I left the shop without giving Natalie a chance to ask why I was disappearing off for coffee with a stranger. 'Won't be long,' I promised, hoping to avoid her curious gaze, and probing questions about my red-rimmed eyes.

I've always walked quickly, '*like you're about to miss a train*', Tim used to joke, but even my usual pace was slow beside the long-legged stride of Liam Thomas. We paused at the kerb for the lights to change, and when they did I felt the barest graze of his hand touching my back as we stepped onto the zebra crossing. It was gone long before we reached the other side of the road.

Politely, he held open the café door, and then stood back to allow me to walk through it. Like Crazy Daisy, Rosemary's Kitchen was housed in a sixteenth-century building with low ceilings and narrow doorways. I passed close enough to Liam for my sensitive nose to pick out the base notes of his shower gel or body spray. The cocktail of bergamot and vanilla was pleasing, but the proximity and undeniable manliness of the aroma disturbed me. It awoke dangerous memories that I'd thought were safely locked up in my past. They had no business making their presence felt here with a total stranger.

Except this stranger was a man who actually knew more about me than even those closest to me, I acknowledged, as I allowed him to steer a path towards one of the secluded booths at the back of the café.

'Is here okay?' I'm sure what he really meant was: *Are you comfortable sitting this far away from the other customers with someone you don't know?* The fact that he'd thought to ask answered that question for me. Even in the middle of a deserted cemetery he'd posed no threat or given me a single moment of disquiet. I had no qualms at all as I slid into the booth.

Liam folded his tall body onto the seat opposite me. The sheer length of his legs meant that our knees were touching, so I swivelled to one side to avoid the contact.

'Hello, Beth. We don't normally see you here at this time of the day. What can I get you? Your usual?'

I nodded, smiling as I looked into the kindly face of Rosemary, the café's namesake and owner. 'And how about you, sweetheart?' she asked, turning her attention to Liam. I saw her eyes twinkle appreciatively as she took in my companion, despite the fact he was a good ten years her junior. Her wide red-lipstick smile and impressively endowed chest usually vied for the attention of most male customers, but Liam was looking only at me. I think that scored him big points with Rosemary, and maybe with me too, if I was honest enough to admit it.

'I'll have whatever Beth is drinking,' he said, passing his menu back unread. It was the first time he'd said my name, and it felt both strangely odd and familiar at the same time.

When Rosemary bustled away to get our coffee, there was a small awkward moment between us. I was trying very hard not to fill it by apologising again, but the urge to do so was strong. I truly don't think I'd ever said 'sorry' so many times to someone I scarcely knew.

I rearranged the bowl of sugar sachets, and then moved the glass vase holding a carnation several times before forcing my hands to be still. When I glanced up, I saw Liam watching me with a thoughtful expression on his face. There was a quiet and peace about him, as he patiently waited for me to settle. I had a sudden insight that he used those qualities to good effect however he earned his living. He could be a detective biding his time to uncover the truth; or a priest, listening without judgement to a confession. He cleared his throat lightly as though about to speak, and my eyes flew upwards. *Don't be a priest.* The thought popped into my head so unexpectedly that for a moment I thought I might actually have said the words out loud. He was still looking at me as though I was relatively sane, so I don't think I had.

'It's nice here. Cosy. Do you—'

'—come here often?' I completed cheesily. It was exactly the right thing to say, and the sound of the ice cracking was a very welcome interruption.

'That did sound incredibly corny,' he admitted, with a self-deprecating laugh.

I felt an unexpected sense of peace wash over me. It came on so suddenly that the revelation was almost a shock. This man was going to be my friend. Maybe not right now... but definitely at some point in our future. I hadn't felt so certain about anything in a very long time, but oddly about this, I had no doubts. It immediately relaxed me.

Rosemary arrived with two caramel lattes with extra whipped cream, and even though I suspected Liam was more of a strong espresso kind of a man, he accepted my choice of drink with good grace.

I waited until we were alone again before lifting my wrist, around which Tim's bracelet was once more securely fastened. 'I can't thank you enough for returning this to me. It... it was...' Embarrassingly, I could hear a tearful catch in my throat. I washed it down with a large mouthful of latte. 'It was a gift from my husband.'

Liam nodded knowingly, and it wasn't just the polite and well-intentioned lip service that people pay to the bereaved. He understood; he really did. Because he'd been walking down this particular road even longer than I had.

'It's the small things that can set you off, isn't it?' he said, startling me by practically reading my thoughts, as though they were floating in great big cartoon bubbles above my head. 'Some stuff you can let go. Some of it you pack up in a box and give to the charity shop, but other things... weird stupid things... well, they'd be what you'd reach for if your house was on fire.'

I looked up, and the depth of understanding in his

slate-grey eyes almost took my breath away. For the first time, I realised how good it felt to talk to someone who actually *understood*. I'd never wanted to visit a bereavement group or see a counsellor. My misery was so deep it had wanted no company. But now, sitting here with a man I didn't really know, I wondered if I'd been wrong. Perhaps being in a boat with other shipwreck survivors actually *did* help after all.

'Tim's dressing gown is still on the back of my bathroom door,' I said, shocking myself as the words popped out of their own volition. Perhaps Liam really *was* a priest! That certainly wasn't anything I'd admitted to anyone before.

'Anna's toothbrush is still in the bathroom cabinet,' Liam countered, seeing my confession and raising it.

We nodded in total understanding, and I saw the same recognition of a future friendship glint in his eyes. I could tell it surprised him, but then he gave a small private nod to himself as the idea, once sown, quietly began to take root.

'People don't understand, do they?' he asked gently, as though testing my own grief for rawness. It was still an open wound, but one I was hoping to finally close with the baby. 'They say "give it time", as though the pain of losing the person you love most in the world has an expiry date.' Liam took another mouthful of coffee, not quite managing to hide a wince at its sweetness. It made me smile. We were both quiet for several moments, and I honestly hadn't known I was going to ask the question, until the words came tumbling out.

'What happened to your wife? To Anna? Was she sick?' To me, illness, or more specifically cancer, was the personal grim reaper who'd stalked Tim in the shadows for years before finally snatching him away from me.

'Car accident,' Liam said, his voice devoid of all emotion. To some, his terse explanation might have sounded brutal, even uncaring, but not to me. I knew from experience that would be the only way he'd ever be able to get the words out. 'Some idiot driving a truck and texting at the same time, ploughed through a junction at speed. Anna's car was in his path.'

'Oh God, Liam. How awful,' I said, and before I knew what I was doing my hand reached across the table and briefly squeezed his. For a moment his fingers froze under mine, before relaxing and returning the squeeze with one of his own.

'I should have been with her. We always drove in together. But that morning I was waiting for an important call, so she left without me.' He shook his head, and I thought I saw the diamond glint of tears in his eyes. 'She died surrounded by strangers. I think that was one of the hardest things to accept.'

I swallowed a lump the size of a golf ball back down my throat. Tim had died in my arms, in the quiet hours of the middle of the night, when so many brave fighters finally lose their battle. The last thing he saw was my face; the last words he heard were me telling him I loved him and that it was okay to go. It was an odd thing to be grateful for, but I really was.

And of course there was something else I was grateful

for. Because even though Tim was gone, a part of him still remained and soon – through the miracle of science – he would hopefully live on.

'Do you have children?' I blurted out, shocking myself yet again that my internal filter appeared to be totally AWOL today. That was quite a personal question to have asked. Fortunately, Liam didn't appear offended by my blatant curiosity. 'Not unless you count Sally.'

'Sally?'

In reply, he pulled out his phone, his long fingers sliding over the screen until he found an image, and then inverted the mobile to show me. The screen was filled with a photograph of a rather scruffy-looking terrier. I've always liked dogs, and was fairly sure I recognised the breed.

'Jack Russell?'

'Through and through,' he said with a smile. 'Funny thing is, I've never really been into dogs. But she was Anna's pet before we were married. It really was a case of "love me, love my dog".'

'She looks cute,' I said, passing him back his phone.

Liam smiled and it elevated his face from merely good-looking to something that would make most women's breath catch in their throat. Most women's; not mine.

'She's actually a pain in the arse. She costs me a fortune each month at the vet, and she's old and cranky. The postman's terrified of her, and if I don't let her out into the garden by six in the morning, she pees all over the kitchen floor.'

I laughed, and it felt more natural and comfortable than it had done for a very long time. I hadn't realised this whole baby plan thing was making me so uptight.

Liam gave a small, embarrassed laugh. 'Actually, I don't know how I'd have got through these last eight years without her,' he admitted, fiddling with the spoon sitting in the oversized saucer of his drink. 'Sally knew what had happened to Anna. That day, when I finally got back from the hospital, the neighbours told me she'd been howling for hours. She'd started at about the time of the accident. She'd never done that before, or since.'

The weirdest things can bring you to tears, and the thought of Anna's dog crying in an empty house and somehow knowing that her owner had died was enough to do it for me. Liam looked up and silently slid a paper serviette across the tabletop towards me. It took two further serviettes plucked from a nearby table before I was done.

'I'm not usually like this,' I protested. From across the café I could see Rosemary eyeing me with concern. Just one nod of my head and she'd come over, I knew she would. I gave her a watery smile and shook my head, holding her at bay.

'It's just this... It's just this baby business,' I said, feeling embarrassed but knowing I owed him some sort of explanation. 'It's making me even more emotional than usual.'

'You don't have to say anything,' Liam interrupted, holding up a hand as though stopping traffic. 'You were quite right in what you said at the cemetery. That's very personal stuff, that I had no right overhearing.'

This time we were arguing on opposite sides of the fence, which felt a little odd. 'You did nothing wrong. I was hardly being discreet about it.'

I looked up and saw he was once more watching me

carefully, waiting for whatever it was I wanted to say, and also for the things that I did not.

'I think, maybe, a part of me wanted someone else to know. Sometimes this whole decision feels too huge to keep to myself.'

'So why are doing that? Do you have family? Friends?'

I nodded, affirming I was well represented in both areas. Although even as I did so, I acknowledged that since Tim's death I was guilty of keeping my friends at a distance, especially the couples. It hurt less that way.

'But you've not said anything about this to any of them?' There was a definite policeman's probing in his intuitive observation.

'No. Not a word. They think we used up all our chances when Tim was still alive. Nobody knows about the one last embryo.'

'Because...?'

I shook my head. 'Because it's so big, so important, that to share it might make it not happen. That I'll somehow bring bad luck on myself.'

His eyes warmed and this time *he* reached for *my* hand. I had almost forgotten the comfort of fingers entwined around mine in support. 'I'm sure that's not true. Perhaps what you really need to do is convince *yourself* you deserve some good luck now.'

'We both do.' And even though I hardly knew him at all, I really felt that to be the truth.

'Then here's to finding it,' he said, lifting up his half-empty coffee cup and proposing a toast. I raised my own cup and we clinked the thick earthenware mugs so loudly that for a moment I thought we'd cracked them.

'Thank you for this,' I said, and I knew I didn't need to explain exactly what I was thanking him for. He already knew it was for the coffee, the understanding and the unshakeable belief that somewhere out there we were both owed a better future. 'I promise that the next time we meet I won't burst into tears.'

His eyes lightened interestingly whenever he was amused. 'Good, because frankly I've been a little concerned about your reaction to me.'

He paid the bill, even though I insisted I should pay half. When we got to our feet, I was surprised to discover I'd been away from the shop for over an hour. Liam Thomas was very easy and comfortable company.

It was only as we said goodbye on the pavement outside the café that I realised I'd said *the next time we meet*, as though it was a foregone conclusion. Despite the pleasant hour we'd spent in each other's company, neither of us had mentioned repeating the experience. He had his life, and I had mine. And mine was hopefully soon about to become even more busy. Perhaps he realised that.

Still, my words had been a little presumptuous and I was still wearing the pink blush they had brought to my cheeks when I crossed the road and entered Crazy Daisy once more.

'There you are,' exclaimed Natalie as the door clicked to a close behind me. 'I was beginning to think you'd been kidnapped by your mystery man.'

I skirted around the edge of the counter, shrugging off my jacket as I went. 'Nothing that dramatic, I'm afraid. I just lost track of time. And he's *not* my mystery man – he's just

67

someone I bumped into recently. Were you busy?' I asked, hoping to steer her interest away from my visitor.

'I wasn't, but your phone certainly was.'

I looked at her blankly for a moment before patting the pocket of my jeans where my mobile should be. All I could feel was my hip bone. Natalie didn't appear to notice that my face had grown pale. There was a weird taste in my mouth, which I couldn't swallow away. Strange, I'd never realised that anxiety had its own peculiar flavour before.

As though from a distance, I could hear Natalie's voice. 'You left your phone on the workbench and it's been ringing almost constantly for the last hour or so. I guess someone wants to get hold of you really badly.'

I squeezed past her, forcing myself to neither run nor pounce on the phone as though it was about to get away. It's hard to appear nonchalant when your hand is trembling so much you can scarcely read the numbers on the screen. She was right; the same caller had tried to reach me six times *and* had left two voicemail messages. It was a number I recognised.

'Anything urgent?'

'No,' I replied, lying instinctively.

This was the call I'd been waiting two weeks for. It was the reason I showered with my phone resting on the bathroom shelf; why I cooked with it propped against the hob; and why I slept with it nestled on Tim's pillow – for luck. Two weeks ago, I'd been for a preliminary scan at the fertility clinic. It was the first step on my long journey to becoming pregnant, and the results would inform the doctors whether they were able to go ahead with the IVF.

This was the news I'd been waiting for and I didn't want

to hear it with anyone else around. It took a huge effort to lay my phone back down, as though it wasn't a ticking bomb with the potential to explode my dreams into smithereens.

'Why don't you head off early today as we're quiet?' I suggested. Trying to sound casual and breezy made my voice taut, like the string of an instrument right before it snaps.

'But we've still got—' Natalie began in protest.

'I'll do it,' I interrupted, cursing myself for hiring someone so diligent. I picked up her handbag and rugby-ball-passed it into her arms, while steering her firmly towards the door. She was still looking suspiciously at me through the glass panel as I pulled it shut behind her. My smile was false, but I held it firmly in place until she gave a small shrug and finally turned to walk away. As soon as she'd disappeared from sight, I slid the bolt on the door and flipped over the 'Closed' sign.

Unease followed me like a ghost as I walked on shaky legs back to the workroom. My worries hadn't been unfounded because something must have shown up on the scans. Why else would the clinic be trying so hard to get hold of me? I could feel the dream of Tim's baby disappearing like a mirage in the desert.

The back room was full of lilies and jasmine, but all I could smell was the sickly waft of my own perspiration. I listened to the voicemail messages, but they told me nothing I hadn't already worked out for myself. The clinic wanted to talk to me urgently and asked me to phone them as soon as I got the message. I glanced at the clock. It was almost five, and I had no idea if they'd still be there.

The switchboard operator sounded like an android

whose dial had been set to 'maximum cheery'. 'I think they've already left for the day,' she said in a sing-song tone, when I asked to be connected to the doctor's office.

'Could you try anyway,' I pleaded, anxiety making my voice as sharp as a knife slicing through her jolly veneer.

'Of course. Please hold the line.'

I leant back against the workbench as I heard the extension ringing plaintively in what I presumed was an empty office. Any moment now I would hear the irritating operator, inviting me to try again in the morning. But I was wrong, for after about the fifteenth ring, a slightly breathless voice came on the line.

'Doctor Alistair's office.' The woman sounded like she'd been running.

'Hello. My name's Beth Brandon. I believe you've been trying to get hold of me.'

The doctor's secretary gave a small sound, difficult to decipher over the phone. 'Oh, yes, Mrs Brandon. Hello. Thanks for getting back to us.'

'Is something wrong? Has something shown up on my scans?' I asked, unable to stifle the question.

The woman paused for not just one beat, but two, before replying. 'Erm, you'd need to speak to Doctor Alistair about that. He was wondering if you'd be able to come in to the clinic for a meeting.'

'Right now? Today?'

My suggestion left her wrong-footed. 'Er, no. Everyone's already left for the day.' She sounded worried that I might ignore her words and turn up on their doorstep anyway. 'In the morning,' she said, wresting back control of the conversation. 'Can you get here for ten o'clock?' She sounded nervous, and with perfect clarity I realised this woman already knew why the doctor wanted to see me.

We hung up, and I sensed her relief that our call was over. My own relief didn't have any hope of kicking in until the same could be said for my meeting with the doctor. And maybe not even then.

7

Izzy

We weren't late. There was plenty of time before the show started, but Pete had insisted we leave the pub with an hour to spare. We were well ahead of the other parents, which allowed us to claim two front-row seats in the school hall. Pete settled himself happily on one of the slightly-too-small-for-adults chairs, and began checking the camera settings on his phone.

The relief that our lunch had gone exactly the way he'd hoped it would was coming off him in palpable waves, while I was doing my best to conceal my own disappointment.

'I don't know about you,' Pete confided in a whisper, as he eyed the stage where Noah would soon perform, 'but I'm feeling kind of jittery for him. Was he okay this morning?'

'He wasn't nervous at all.' I smiled as my eyes found Noah's name on the cast list that had been left on every chair. 'It's as if performing is second nature to him.'

'Well, he definitely doesn't get that from me,' declared Pete. I bit my lip to stop the smile as the image of my husband singing lustily along to various karaoke machines filled my head.

An hour later my cheeks were aching from smiling widely, and my palms felt sore from clapping. All the children had put on an incredible performance, but in my own – obviously unbiased – opinion, Noah had stolen the show. Although admittedly the seven-year-old Pink Lady who'd spent most of the performance dealing with a troublesome wedgie had come a close second.

I was pretty sure I'd seen the sheen of proud tears in Pete's eyes when the curtains had finally drawn to a close. Around us the applause was fading, but Pete was still clapping heartily. Any minute now he's going to start whooping and calling for an encore, I thought, and Noah's going to start wishing he had far less embarrassing parents.

'When did he get to be that good?' Pete asked, as though I'd somehow been keeping our son's musical talents from him.

'I have absolutely no idea,' I answered honestly. 'I knew he could sing well, but not *that* well.'

'You should think about sending him to stage school,' declared Samantha Coleman's mother, whose own eight-year-old was enrolled in so many extracurricular activities, I'm surprised she had any energy left for school. Pete's eyes met mine and we both subtly shook our heads. It was good to know that married or separated, we were still on the same page about that one. Noah had been through enough changes recently. Pulling him out of a school he loved just because he had musical ability wasn't even a consideration.

***

The pizza restaurant was still fairly quiet when we arrived for Noah's celebratory meal. It wasn't yet six o'clock and apart from a handful of elderly diners enjoying the early-bird special, we had the place to ourselves. Several of them looked our way and smiled as we walked three abreast through the swing doors, laughing and talking animatedly about the show.

A young waitress with dramatically pencilled eyebrows showed us to one of the booths usually reserved for larger groups after Pete whispered something in her heavily pierced ear. Whatever he'd said had softened the expression on her face and she'd smiled broadly at Noah and then brought him a free glass of Coke.

'Told her you were famous,' Pete confided with a wink, which made Noah splutter noisily into his drink. I smiled as I watched them, realising just how much I'd missed seeing how good they were together. Pete was a natural at parenthood; he always had been.

We'd ordered our pizzas and were in the middle of toasting Noah's success with fizzy drinks when the cutlery on the table performed a tuneful tinkling percussion as Pete's phone vibrated against it. He went to switch it off and then stopped as he read the caller's identity.

'Sorry,' he said, getting to his feet and stepping out of the booth. 'I need to take this.'

A frisson of irritation ran through me. 'Can't it wait – our pizzas will be here in a minute?'

Pete slipped on his sunglasses, making his eyes deliberately hard to read as he shook his head. 'No. I have to take this now.'

He strode away, already answering the call on his way to

the exit, but he didn't venture far from the doorway; I could still see him through the huge plate-glass window. He had his back to us, but there was something about the way he was standing and the set of his shoulders that bothered me.

Noah was talking, but my attention was split. Who was the caller Pete felt he couldn't put off? Maya's name kept bobbing to the surface, like an unsinkable float. Of course, I had no reason to think it was her, but whoever it was, and whatever they were saying, was clearly affecting my husband. His arms were gesticulating with an emotion it was impossible to name: anger; passion, or something else entirely?

The pizzas arrived, delivered with a flourish on huge pieces of slate. The waitress even performed a tiny bow as she placed Noah's before him. 'Here you go, superstar.'

Noah was delighted, but I was still too distracted by whatever was happening on the pavement outside the restaurant.

'Go ahead,' I urged Noah, who was salivating as he looked at the fully loaded Margarita in front of him. 'Don't wait for Daddy, I don't know how long he's going to be.'

Determined not to ruin the meal for Noah, I pulled off a triangle of my own pizza and sank my teeth into it, wincing as I instantly burnt the roof of my mouth. Somehow that too became Pete's fault, which meant by the time he slipped the phone back into his pocket and re-entered the restaurant, I was already mad at him. But my anger evaporated away almost immediately when I saw the expression on his face as he headed towards our table. He looked dreadful. Beneath the tan he'd acquired over the last few weeks, his skin appeared ashen. He looked as if he'd aged ten years from the man who'd left us less than ten minutes earlier. When he took off his sunglasses, there were shadows living behind his hazel eyes that hadn't been there before.

'What's wrong?' I asked, all hostility now forgotten. Pete had the look of someone who'd just been told of a death, and I was already mentally cataloguing our elderly relatives, wondering which one it was.

'Nothing,' he lied. His eyes flashed meaningfully towards Noah. I was burning with curiosity, but Pete was right, this was Noah's party, and whatever it was that Pete had heard on the phone, it would clearly ruin it.

Pete did his best to carry on as though nothing had happened. I don't know if he managed to fool Noah, but he certainly didn't fool me. He laughed too loudly, and his smile was a rictus, grisly and unnatural. He chomped determinedly through the food in front of him, as though completing a challenge. I doubt he tasted a single mouthful.

We'd agreed that Pete would mention the Cyprus holiday to Noah during the meal, but as we moved from pizzas to small mountains of ice cream – which Noah had no trouble demolishing – Pete said nothing. Was that what the angry phone call had been about? Had he and Maya had a falling out – I refused to call it a break-up, for that implied they were joined in a way I simply couldn't cope with right then. If they *had* argued, perhaps she'd withdrawn the offer of the villa, and *that* was the reason Pete now looked so crushed. It was a theory, but I think even then I knew it wasn't the right one. Every straw I grasped for slipped frustratingly through my fingers.

Pete settled the bill without even checking the amount and got to his feet. We'd driven to the restaurant in separate cars, so this should now have been the natural conclusion to the evening, but as we stood on the pavement, Pete looped one arm around Noah's bony shoulders.

'Why don't I follow you guys back home?' Noah's eyes lit up, as if he'd just won a prize, while mine clouded in confusion.

'I should probably have a look at the problem you said you were having with the back door,' Pete added. Fortunately, Noah was still too delighted to hear his father was coming back home with us to notice my mystified expression. Either I'd been struck with a sudden case of amnesia, or my husband had just invented a convenient ruse in order to speak to me in private.

'The door? Oh, yes. That would be... erm, really useful.' Fortunately, you don't have to be very good at acting to fool an eight-year-old, and Noah didn't seem to realise something was very wrong here. And whatever it was, it had all started with that phone call.

8

Beth

I was there before the clinic opened. I parked in a far corner of the car park, beneath a row of eucalyptus trees, watching through the windscreen as the spaces around me gradually began to fill. My eyes followed the clinic staff as they made their way towards the main building. Some of them had an 'It's Friday' spring to their step; others walked with more reluctance. I recognised no one. But it had been quite a long time since I'd been a patient here; the staff had probably changed many times over in the last ten years.

My attention was continually drawn to the bank of empty spaces reserved for the senior members of staff. The names on the first three bays were unfamiliar to me, but the fourth one bore a small neat plaque reading 'Doctor M J Alistair', and just looking at it made my heart beat faster and my palms grow clammy. The bays were filled within seconds of each other as a cavalcade of dark, expensive vehicles swept in quick succession into their allocated spots. Dr Alistair emerged from his car, carrying a large leather briefcase. He was engaged in conversation over the roof of his car with a colleague in the adjacent parking place, even before he'd closed the driver's door. The vague notion I'd had of hijacking him on his way into the building had been taken from me. Yet my hand remained on the door latch as I watched him disappear from sight into the clinic's modern interior.

I glanced at the clock on my dashboard – I'd been foolish to arrive so early, but going to the shop would have been almost as impossible as staying at home. I hated lying to Natalie, and yet I'd done so surprisingly convincingly at seven o'clock that morning.

'A migraine? Oh, that's horrible. Go straight back to bed and keep the curtains shut.'

I looked at the sunlight streaming in through my kitchen windows, which wasn't bothering my eyes or my head at all. I was showered, dressed, and three coffees into a day that I already suspected would see a caffeine overload.

'I'm sure I'll be in later. Can you handle things until then?'

'Seriously, Mrs B,' said Natalie, 'I can manage just fine. Take the day off.'

More guilt, because she sounded so concerned about a headache that I didn't even have. I was putting a lot on my assistant's shoulders, even though I knew she was more than capable of rising to the challenge.

'And don't worry about the shop,' she added warmly. 'I'll take good care of your baby until you're back.' I did a very poor job of turning my gasp into a cough at Natalie's unfortunate choice of words. I thanked her and hung up before I was forced to tell yet another lie. I didn't want them piling up against me, like black marks on some cosmic scoreboard.

Twenty-five minutes before my appointment time, I gave up all pretence of waiting patiently and left my car. Perhaps the doctor would be able to see me early. Perhaps I'd been worrying needlessly, and there was nothing wrong with my scans. Perhaps the urgency I perceived existed only in my head. Or perhaps not.

The foyer was an elegant calming oasis of glass, marble and thick dove-grey carpet. It looked more like an exclusive hotel than a medical facility, which I imagine had probably been the interior designer's brief. Huge pots of exotic foliage were artfully positioned, but I scarcely glanced at them as I approached the reception desk on legs that felt decidedly shaky.

The young woman behind the highly polished counter looked up from her computer screen with a polite smile of welcome. 'Can I help you?'

'I have an appointment with Dr Alistair. My name is Beth Brandon.' Her fingers flew over a concealed keyboard and a tiny hint of a frown crumpled her brow. 'I... I'm a bit early,' I apologised.

'Please take a seat and I'll let them know you're here,' she said, gesturing towards a low leather couch.

I did as she asked. More waiting. And now a different clock face to study on the ivory-painted walls, as the minutes ticked by with an infuriating lack of urgency. There was a fan of morning newspapers laid out on a low table, but even the headlines couldn't hold my attention. That wasn't the type of news I was interested in today.

'Mrs Brandon?' For someone who'd been waiting for this moment for the last seventeen hours, I had a surprising urge to pick up my handbag and head straight out the door without ever looking back. It took more courage than I was expecting to quash that instinct and get to my feet.

The doctor's secretary led me down a maze of carpeted corridors towards a suite of offices. She kept up a stream of polite conversation, which I suppose I must have responded to appropriately, although I have absolutely no recollection what either of us said. All sounds were muffled beneath the resounding timpani beat of my heart. The musician in Tim would have liked that analogy, and just thinking about him calmed me, as if he was striding beside me. It was only when we came to a halt before a door that the enormity of what I was doing hit me. The last time I was here Tim and I had been a team, undertaking this project to protect our future. Now I was facing it alone.

'Here we are,' announced the doctor's secretary, and it was only in those final seconds that I realised she too was nervous. I had no idea why. She knocked lightly on the door panel, standing politely to one side when a voice from within invited us to 'Come in'.

My first surprise was that I hadn't been ushered to Dr Alistair's private office, where I'd imagined we were heading. Instead, I appeared to be in a small meeting room, with a long lozenge-shaped glass boardroom table. The second surprise was that on the opposite side of that table, lined up and waiting for me like a panel interview team, were *four* individuals.

My confusion must have been instantly apparent by the way my steps faltered as I entered the room. All four people rose to their feet, but Dr Alistair was the only one I recognised. There were two other men, both dressed in almost identical dark suits, and a middle-aged woman with the kind of fiercely pinned hairstyle that looked both incredibly uncomfortable and complicated to achieve. Dr Alistair was the first to extend his hand across the glass chasm of the boardroom table.

'Mrs Brandon, good morning. Thank you for coming in to see us today.'

I'm sure my handshake was the type I most detested, weak and floppy, but I was too confused by the veritable crowd of people present at a meeting I'd thought would be for only the two of us. Where were the medical charts, the screens to hold the images of my scans? There was no examination couch, no blood pressure monitor, and not a single neck had a stethoscope swinging from it. It dawned on me slowly that this was not a medical consultation, it was a business meeting.

Dr Alistair introduced me to his colleagues in turn, whose names I immediately forgot almost as soon as they were given to me. But I did retain their job titles: a member of the board; the clinic's practice manager; and lastly, bewilderingly, their legal representative.

'Please sit down, Mrs Brandon,' urged Dr Alistair, as the party on his side of the table took their seats in perfect unison. There was a single upholstered swivel chair on my side of the table, which the secretary held out for me. In her eyes was a brief flash of sympathy, the kind I recognised only too well from the weeks and months after losing Tim. I had to fight a rather embarrassing urge to grab the woman's hand and ask her to sit beside me, to even things up a little. When her boss thanked and then dismissed her, I got the impression she was glad to leave. Her parting glance as she slipped from the room confirmed that whatever news I was about to receive, it wasn't good.

I was offered – and declined – refreshments, although I did take a very necessary long sip from the glass of water that had been poured for me. My mouth and tongue felt like sandpaper, but that was hardly surprising. I looked up and interrupted a silent conversation voiced only in eye movements between the four clinic employees on the other side of the table. Dr Alistair gave a small, almost reluctant nod, and cleared his throat. He sounded like *he* needed the water even more than I had.

'I'm sure you've been wondering why we asked you to come in today, Mrs Brandon... er, Beth.'

Dark-suited man number two, on the doctor's right, the one whose job was involved in the clinic's legal dealings, flinched visibly at the use of my forename. A small silent warning bell went off in my head.

I replaced my drinking glass on the table with deliberate care, affording the simple task much more concentration than it required. 'Well, I assumed I was here to discuss my recent ultrasound scan.' The practice manager dropped her eyes, but not before I'd glimpsed something that closely resembled anguish in their depths.

I sat up a little straighter, determined not to allow my voice to betray the nervousness that was thrumming through me like an electrical pulse. 'I thought we'd be discussing the mechanics and the timing of the procedure and how it would differ from my previous two rounds of IVF.' Dr Alistair met my eyes. Although he was too practised a physician to allow his face to give much away, his features revealed that he'd rather be anywhere else than facing me across this table. 'But now I'm not sure. Was there something wrong with my scans? Is it bad news?' That had been my worst-case scenario fear for the last few months. It was the one thing I had no control over. Would my own body reject the plans that my heart and head so desperately wanted?

I looked in turn at each of the four faces opposite me and knew, even before Dr Alistair began to speak, that the problem was so much bigger and so much worse than anything I'd spent sleepless nights worrying about.

'Your ultrasound scans were absolutely fine. They showed a very healthy uterus. There was nothing on any of the images that would lead us to have concerns about your ability to carry a baby to term.'

There was a long pause. In any other situation it might even be called a *pregnant* one, but I was in no mood for such irony. In the end, I was the one who filled the silence by saying the word I believed everyone in the room was waiting for.

'But…?'

There was a pen in Dr Alistair's hand. It looked expensive, Montblanc, maybe. He'd unclipped it presumably to make notes, but instead was absently gouging the delicate nib into the leaves of a ruled pad in a series of frenzied doodles. I doubted very much if it would ever write properly again.

'We have a problem concerning your frozen embryo.'

The blood drained from my face. I felt it go.

'What kind of a problem?' Whose voice was that? It certainly didn't sound like mine, although as no one else had spoken, I could only assume that it was.

There was sorrow on the doctor's face as he slowly

destroyed my future. 'The embryo you and your late husband stored at our clinic is… is regrettably no longer available.'

'What does that mean?' I asked, aware that my voice had risen significantly in both pitch and volume. 'How can it not be available? Did the storage tank fail? We were assured that couldn't happen. We were told there were alarms, and back-up provisions.'

'There are, there are,' said Dr Alistair, his hands making calming gestures, which at this point in time were totally redundant. How could I possibly remain calm? My chance, my *only* chance of having Tim's baby was slipping through my fingers, and I had no idea what had happened.

'The clinic, as you know, has numerous safeguards in place to ensure the care of the embryos we store for our patients.'

'Then what the hell happened to mine?' I shook my head, as though that would stop the tears that were already stinging my eyes. 'Ours,' I corrected quietly. 'Ours.'

Wordlessly, the practice manager pushed a box of tissues across the glass surface towards me. I focused on that rather than on the face of the doctor who had once again begun to speak.

'Sometimes, even though everything is in place as it should be… systems fail, things go wrong—' I saw the legal man's arm reach over as fast as a cobra and squeeze the doctor's forearm, halting him.

'What happened to my baby?' I demanded. My words were emotive. For the doctors and embryologists it might be just a collection of cells in a Petri dish, but for me it was a child. Mine and Tim's.

'You have to know that this terrible situation is totally without precedent at this clinic. Today, with our electronic double-witnessing system, it certainly couldn't happen. But eight years ago...'

'What do you mean? What happened eight years ago? How long have you people known there was a problem with our embryo?'

It was the practice manager who spoke then. 'The discovery was only made yesterday. It's as much of a shock to us as it is to you.'

I very much doubted that, but I could no longer speak, for uncontrollable tremors were thundering through me.

'The problem with the embryo, *your embryo*, occurred eight years ago,' Dr Alistair confirmed.

Eight years? But Tim was still alive then, still battling with the cancer that would ultimately defeat him. Eight years ago, I hadn't even had my first round of IVF.

'As you know, ten years ago three of your embryos were cryogenically frozen and stored at our clinic,' continued the practice manager, consulting a thick sheaf of papers before her. 'Five years later, two of those embryos were used by you in rounds of IVF, which unfortunately were not successful.' Her eyes went to the doctor. It was clearly his job to pick up the explanation from there.

'That should have left you with one remaining embryo, which we were hoping to implant now.'

There were tears running down my face, which I didn't even bother trying to wipe away.

'What happened to my embryo?'

Whatever I'd been expecting, it certainly wasn't to see the physician's own eyes fill with tears, as he shook his head from side to side in disbelief. 'Eight years ago, one of your frozen embryos was mistakenly removed from its dewar – the container in which it is stored.' I knew the names of the equipment in the lab; that wasn't the explanation I needed now, and I think everyone in the room knew that. 'And that embryo... your embryo...'

'Died?' I asked, my voice lost and broken. It was the most terrible thing I could imagine, but there was so much worse to come.

'No,' said the doctor, looking in actual physical pain as he forced the words out. 'Your embryo was mistakenly implanted in another patient.'

The room was spinning, and for one awful moment I really thought I would be physically sick as the doctor's words infiltrated every cell in my body, like a contamination.

'And when they discovered the mistake, what did they do? Did that woman have a termination?' The thought felt like a scalpel gouging out my own flesh.

'No one discovered the error,' said the board member softly. It was his first contribution to the discussion. 'This tragic mistake was only uncovered yesterday.'

'So what is it that you're saying?' I asked. I was on my feet without any recollection of how I got there. 'That her pregnancy continued?'

They nodded. Every single one of them, but it was Dr Alistair who delivered the final blow. The coup de grâce. 'Yes, Beth, it did. Eight years ago, she gave birth to a child. A child she has no reason to believe is not hers. *Your* child.'

★★★

I shouldn't have driven home. The fact that I can't remember a single moment of the journey proves that. That I did so without wrapping my car around a lamppost is a miracle of sorts. The end of the meeting at the clinic was a blur. I can remember hearing their repeated assurances that a *full and thorough investigation would begin immediately*' and having to restrain myself from screaming out that it was too late. They couldn't undo what had already happened. There was no way to right this wrong.

I could feel my control slipping away, and like an injured animal I was desperate to get out of there. My hip collided clumsily with the table, knocking over the water jug, and in the resulting confusion, as files were snatched from the slowly growing puddle, I made for the door.

'I have to go,' I can remember declaring. 'I can't be here. I can't do this now.'

The room seemed to have suddenly elongated, the way they do in dreams, moving the doorway agonisingly further away. By the time I reached it, the practice manager was beside me, her hand resting lightly on my shoulder. One look at my face made her quickly withdraw it.

'Mrs Brandon, I realise this must be a terrible shock.'

I looked at her dumbly as though she was speaking in a foreign language. Shock didn't even come close to describing how I felt right then. There simply weren't words to convey the emotions coursing through me: despair, grief, and anger, so much anger. I clawed for the door handle. I had to get out of that meeting room, out of the clinic, and far away from these people whose incompetence had destroyed my future.

I was still shaking when I finally let myself into my home. It had taken four attempts before I'd managed to align the

Yale key in the lock. I think that used up the last reserves of my control. I leant back against the closed door and sank slowly down to the floor. With my head on my knees, I sobbed in a way the walls of my home hadn't heard for a very long time. I'd never been pregnant, I'd never held my child in my arms, I'd never looked down and seen my husband's eyes in our baby's face. And now I never would.

The shadows had travelled across the floor to the far reaches of the room by the time I eventually dragged myself to my feet. I went straight to the kitchen and drank three full tumblers of water, one after the other, knowing I was probably still seriously dehydrated. My throat felt raw and I didn't have to look in a mirror to know my eyes would be red and puffy. I took the coward's way out and opted to text Natalie rather than phone, to let her know I wouldn't be coming back that day.

She replied with a message of 'Feel better' and a row of emojis, which bizarrely made me cry all over again. I was a mess, and knowing that did nothing to help. I was probably still in shock, still trying to process how on earth this could have happened. Now, and only now, I finally regretted not confiding in my family about the last embryo. If I had, I would at least be able to turn to them now. But my stupid need for secrecy had led me to share my plans with no one. Except, of course, Liam Thomas. I pulled off the clothes I'd worn for the appointment as though they were tainted, glad I had no way of contacting Liam, because the need to share this burden was so overwhelming I might not have been able to stop myself from trying to drag him into this horrible mess.

That night, for the first time in ages, I pulled Tim's dressing gown from the bathroom door and wrapped it around me before sliding into the bed we had once shared. The smell of him was long since gone from the fabric, yet still I buried my nose into the folds of material, desperate to catch one last hint of him. 'I'm so sorry,' I crooned, in the quiet of my empty room. 'I'm so sorry, baby.' In my head he said it was all right. In my head he told me that it wasn't my fault; that there was nothing either of us could have done to prevent this. In my head he told me to close my eyes and try to rest. 'I miss you so much.' I said the words to the empty room, knowing that somewhere, somehow, he would hear them.

9

Izzy

Out of a habit I thought I'd forgotten, I automatically pulled my car over to the far side of the drive to allow Pete to park beside me. Noah skipped ahead to the front door while Pete and I locked eyes across the roof of his car. Mine were so full of questions I could hardly see straight, but he answered them all with a tiny shake of his head. *Not yet.*

It was weird sliding my key into the lock and feeling Pete standing right behind me once again. We must have crossed this threshold together thousands of times before. Yet all I could remember were the times when after doing so, our lives had changed. Like when he'd carried me over the doorstep when we'd returned from our honeymoon, and had collided into the frame after misjudging the opening. And then eight years ago, with infinitely more care, as we'd carried our precious newborn into the house for the very first time. Or the day of my mother's funeral, when I'd been blinded by tears and Pete's arm around my waist had been my guiding strength and support, in every sense of the word. The way it had always been.

Beginnings and endings. Those were the moments that filled my head now as we walked into our house. It was impossible to shake the feeling that whatever had happened today would be added to those occasions.

Amazingly, given the size of the meal he'd just eaten, Noah raced straight to the biscuit tin as soon as we entered the kitchen. I was distracted, so caught up in the overwhelming feeling of déjà vu at seeing Pete in this room again, when usually he ventured no further than the doorstep, I forgot to voice even a token objection.

Noah was reaching for Pete's phone, scrolling through the collection of videos from the show. Under cover of the tinnily reproduced rendition of 'Summer Nights', I drew Pete to one side. There was a tremor in his forearm as I laid my hand on it.

'What's this all about? It's got something to do with that phone call, hasn't it?'

Pete glanced towards Noah, whose head was beginning to droop as he watched his own performance. 'Let's wait until Noah has gone to bed.'

From the look of our sleepy son, I would get my answer soon enough.

'Is it something bad?' I asked, my voice little more than a whisper.

'No,' he said, which should have calmed me, except I'd known immediately that he was lying. Had he forgotten that his voice always gave him away?

Noah yawned hugely, revealing a mouth dusty with biscuit crumbs. 'You look exhausted, my little rock star,' Pete declared, crossing the kitchen and ruffling Noah's thick dark hair lovingly. His strong fingers lingered among the ebony strands, looking down at them almost in wonder. Inexplicably, I shivered.

'Why don't you take him up, and I'll make us both some coffee,' suggested Pete.

I opened my mouth to protest but he was already reaching for the cups, as if making himself at home like this in the house I'd asked him to leave nine months ago was perfectly normal.

Noah was so tired he stumbled like a drunken party goer as I followed him up the stairs. 'Have you had a good day?' I asked, suddenly overwhelmed with a fierce feeling of love and protectiveness.

'The best,' confirmed Noah sleepily. 'It's great to have Dad here again.'

For once he offered no complaint as I stood in the open bathroom doorway while he used the loo and gave his teeth a dozen half-hearted swipes with the toothbrush. I was so anxious to return to Pete waiting in the kitchen below, I didn't even bother asking him to clean them again.

'I was so proud of you today,' I said, dropping a kiss on the smooth skin of his brow as I tucked him in. 'We both were,' I amended.

Noah mumbled a response, but was already tumbling into sleep. He was snoring gently by the time I reached the bedroom door and let myself out of his room.

Pete was standing beside an open kitchen cabinet, staring blankly at the packets of sugar, flour and other cake-making ingredients.

'Where's the bottle of brandy we used to keep in here?'

I was so stunned I forgot to remind him that I didn't have to run it by him if I wanted to rearrange the kitchen cupboards. I reached into the larder unit and extracted the bottle of amber-coloured alcohol. We only ever used it at Christmas to ignite the pudding, or when Pete had a cold and insisted that a hot toddy trumped a dose of Night Nurse to help him sleep. Except Pete wasn't sneezing right now.

The coffees were already made, and before I could stop him, Pete unscrewed the bottle and poured a generous slug into both cups. That was the moment when my concern turned into fear. Why did we need brandy?

'Sit down, Izzy,' Pete said, and there was a tremor to his voice that I truly don't think I'd ever heard there before.

Blindly, I reached for one of the pine kitchen chairs and sank down onto it. He pushed one of the coffees towards me. I caught a waft of the potent alcohol and my already nervous stomach rolled queasily.

'Pete, what's going on? What is this all about?'

He shook his head and took a large mouthful of the high-proof coffee before replying.

'That phone call I had this evening...' The world stopped turning and balanced on a pivot as I waited. 'It was from a doctor.' He swallowed awkwardly, as though the words were reluctant to leave him.

'A doctor? Why?' My voice was a hushed whisper, as though we were in danger of being overheard. 'Are you sick? Is that what this is about?' A cold finger of dread ran lightly down my spine, and with his next words I thought my worst fears were confirmed.

'I don't know how to say this.'

'Pete, you're scaring the shit out of me. What *is* it?'

He reached across the table and gripped my hands tightly within his, but not before I noticed that his were trembling.

Fear was releasing adrenaline into my veins, and I still had no idea what this was all about.

'They made a mistake, Izzy. A dreadful, awful mistake. And they've only just discovered it.'

'Who made a mistake? You're not making any sense.'

He was in pain, I could see that, actual physical pain. And he was openly crying, and I could think of only two other occasions in all our years together when I'd seen him do that. I blinked away the memory of his face crumpling when nine months ago I'd asked him to move out. That had been bad, but what he was about to tell me now was clearly even worse.

'The Westmore Clinic. They fucked up, big time. Noah isn't our son.'

'Why don't you go to bed?'

I shook my head, which did little to help the pounding headache that had definitely settled in for the night. My throat felt raw and my eyes were dry and scratchy and probably impressively swollen. Pete was a blurry mirage in the dimly lit lounge, a hazy shape shrouded in shadows on the opposite settee. The only light in the room came from a single low-wattage table lamp, and frankly even that felt too bright.

'I wouldn't be able to sleep. And what if Noah woke up and needed me in the night?'

'Then you'd be in the room next to his, the same as always,' reasoned Pete. '*I'm* the anomaly here. I'm the one who he'd be confused to find.'

I was surprised by the wave of panic that suddenly hit

me. 'You're not thinking of leaving, are you?' Where was the capable single parent who'd coped so very well over the last nine months? She seemed to have disintegrated on hearing the news Pete had delivered earlier that evening.

'I'm not going anywhere, not tonight,' Pete confirmed. His words felt like a blanket, and I wrapped it around me, yet still the chill found its way in.

'I don't understand what you're saying.'

That had been my initial reaction to Pete's shattering revelation. It was a phrase I kept repeating, as though my brain refused to allow any other thought process to intrude until I'd got beyond that initial hurdle. Except now, hours later, I was still no further ahead. Everything about this situation was so incomprehensible I could feel myself being swallowed whole by the enormity of it.

'Tell me again,' I urged. 'Tell me *exactly* what Dr Alistair said. Every single word.' Obediently, Pete recounted the brief telephone conversation... for the fourth time, even though I already knew it so well I could have recited it myself without a single prompt.

'He began by saying there was no easy way of putting it, so he was just going to have to give it to me straight. And then he confirmed he was calling about your IVF treatment.'

I nodded impatiently, wanting him to fast-forward to the crux of the story again.

'The crazy thing is,' Pete said with a humourless laugh, 'I thought they were ringing about the cheque we'd sent them. I thought it must have bounced. I had no idea...Never in a million years did I think... Well, you wouldn't, would you?'

'And then?' I urged, as though one more telling of the tale would make the nightmare somehow more believable. But of course it didn't.

'Then he just came straight out and said it: *"The embryo we implanted in Izzy wasn't hers. It belonged to another couple".*'

Bile rose in my mouth and I swallowed it down determinedly. 'Did he say why they phoned you and not me?' I suddenly thought to ask.

'He said they'd been trying to reach you, but the number they had on file wasn't working.'

My eyes met Pete's. 'They still have my *old* number.'

He nodded solemnly. 'Thank God for that,' he added. 'I wouldn't have wanted anyone else to have broken this news to you.'

That reminder of his fierce protectiveness was almost enough to set me off again. 'But he still didn't explain how it had happened?'

Pete shook his head. 'Apparently there's going to be a full investigation.'

'But they checked. On the day they did the transfer, I remember them checking, don't you?' I asked Pete desperately. I saw the memory of that day in his eyes, almost as brightly as it was in mine. The small sterile room, the gowned doctors, and Pete's hand holding mine tightly as the hatch between the treatment room and the lab opened up and the dish containing our embryo was passed from technician to physician. They'd verified my name, my date of birth, and double-checked it all against the wristband I was wearing. Everything had been absolutely correct.

I could still remember that magical moment when we'd

watched the monitor as the catheter delivered its precious cargo inside me. We'd both held our breath as we stared transfixed at the screen as our embryo settled into its home for the next nine months, totally unaware it held the weight of a million hopes and dreams upon its microscopic shoulders.

I still had the ultrasound image one of the clinic staff had handed me. 'For your baby album,' he had said. And Pete and I had both laughed, almost giddy with excitement.

'What happens now?' My voice was hollow and trembling, because every single answer to that question terrified me.

'I don't know, Izzy. I don't think anyone does.'

I must have climbed the stairs half a dozen times that night, drawn up the treads by an overwhelming urge to check on Noah. It had been years since I'd been this anxious, yet the old obsession felt horribly familiar. *Oh, hello. So you're back again, are you?*

Noah had been sound asleep each time.

I crept back down the stairs, hoping that the silence in the darkened lounge meant Pete too was asleep. I should have known better.

'He's fine, Izzy. You don't need to keep checking on him.' The old words fell so easily from his lips. We were back there again, but this time it wasn't just a new mum's paranoia we were dealing with. This time there was a real and tangible threat to our family life.

'What do you think we should tell him?' I asked, curling

up on the vacant settee and drawing the soft fleecy throw back over me.

'Nothing.' Pete's voice was quick and decisive. 'There's no need for him to know anything about this. Not yet. It will only scare him.'

I could hardly argue with that, because it was terrifying the life out of me, and Pete too, despite his best efforts to hide it from me. Had we been right in deciding not to tell Noah anything about our IVF journey until he was much older? He'd recently started to question the story about the stork, so how the hell were we now supposed to explain that the fabled bird had made a terrible mistake?

Dawn was still several hours away when a question punctured the quiet darkness like a rocket, taking with it all possibility of sleep. 'The embryo – the one they *should* have implanted in me, what happened to it?' Pete's breath caught in his throat as the nightmare took on a new and horrible twist. 'If what they're saying is right – if the embryos *did* somehow get muddled up – was ours mistakenly implanted into this other woman?'

There was a rustle of a blanket and a soft sigh of settee springs as Pete got to his feet and crossed the room. He eased himself down beside me, his strong arms forming a protective circle that I willingly fell into. I buried my face into the warmth of his chest, as the fabric of his T-shirt absorbed a new batch of tears.

'What happened to the baby we were meant to have?'

10

Beth

I slept badly, tossing and turning for most of the night. At just before five I gave up all hope of sleep and got out of bed. I reached for my phone and composed a message to Natalie, which I sent quickly, not bothering to check it for typos, knowing that if I gave myself a chance to think, I might reconsider.

The only time I'd closed the shop before had been when Tim had died, but doing so today felt like the right decision. I'd kept my family out of the picture for too long, but now events were too big, too life-changing for me to tackle alone. I needed their advice; I needed their support; I needed... I needed them.

I drove via the shop, stopping briefly to stick a notice on the door apologising for the unexpected closure due to a 'family emergency'. My lips twisted bitterly at those words, but I could think of no others to take their place. That was going to be the issue in the weeks and months ahead; even this early I could see that. This situation was so rare, so horribly unique, I would continually be swimming through uncharted waters. But I would go wherever I had to go, and do whatever I had to do, until the decision I'd reached in the early hours of the morning became a reality. I would find my child, and somehow I would get them back. And the person I needed to consult first on that long and impossible task was my father.

I visited my parents every six weeks or so, if their social calendar (which was far busier than mine) permitted. This unplanned trip, just a fortnight after I'd last seen them, was bound to trigger alarm bells. I stopped twice during the motorway drive: once for a breakfast that I couldn't eat, and just moved from one side of the plate to the other; and the second time for a much-needed reviving coffee. Three hours behind the wheel after a largely sleepless night wasn't exactly a great combination. I leant up against the bonnet of my car, sipping my latte in the watery morning sunlight, and wondered if I should phone ahead and tell them I was on my way. But to do that would raise inevitable questions, questions that would be far easier to answer in person.

My parents still lived in the home on the coast Karen and I had grown up in. It tethered me to the past in a thousand different ways. A lifetime of memories was locked into the mortar of the building, every one of them as substantial as the grooves notched into the doorframe charting our height over the years. I tried to shake off the ache of nostalgia I was feeling. I was hankering for the past, which was no surprise when the future I'd planned on had suddenly been snatched away.

Although I had my own key to their door, I rang the bell,

not wanting to scare either of them into an early heart attack by strolling in unannounced. As I waited, I looked down at the bunch of flowers in my hand, as though noticing them for the first time. I always brought something from the shop whenever I visited, and this morning I'd reached blindly for the first thing my hand fell upon. My lips twisted as I studied the bouquet of black-eyed Susans, feeling it was something more than coincidence that my subconscious had chosen these particular flowers – the flowers of justice.

I heard my mother's footsteps crossing the parquet flooring to the front door, and was surprised to discover I was actually shaking with nerves.

'Beth!' she exclaimed, her hand going to her throat in a very theatrical way. Her recent enthusiastic involvement in the local amateur dramatic society had a habit of spilling over into real life. It was something both Karen and I found hilarious.

'Whatever are you doing here?' And then, before I could decide which of my prepared white lies to go with, she jumped in with a fairly accurate guess. 'Is something wrong? Has something happened?'

I leant forward and kissed her soft cheek, mindful not to ruin her carefully applied powder and blusher.

'Nothing's wrong, Mum.'

'Is Karen okay? What about the boys?'

I shook my head and gently slipped my arm around her shoulders, steering us into the hallway and shutting the front door. 'Everyone is absolutely fine, Mum. Can't a person just decide to drop in on her parents for a surprise visit?'

My mother's periwinkle-blue eyes were magnified behind the lenses of her glasses, but I suspect she didn't need them to see through my flimsy explanation. She kept looking at me curiously as we entered the bright modern kitchen, which smelled pleasantly of the bacon they'd had for breakfast.

'Is Dad not around?' I asked, feigning a nonchalance I was far from feeling. Now that I was here, I had a sudden burning desire to get this over and done with.

'He had an early round of golf at the club. He'll be back soon.'

'Oh,' I said, disappointed that my big reveal was now going to have to wait a little longer.

Mum looked at me, her brows furrowing as though concentration alone would enable her to work out why I'd unexpectedly come home. *Good luck with that, Mum.* She was torn, that was easy to see. Should she attempt to winkle the truth out of me (in a way we both knew she was perfectly capable of doing), or let me explain it in my own time? I shouldn't have been surprised that her maternal radar had picked up on something. She'd known when I'd scraped her car shortly after passing my driving test; she'd known about the secret party that had left wine stains on the carpet; and she'd known, just from my voice, that the news was bad after Tim's first doctor's appointment. But however good her intuitive powers were, there was no way she would ever guess the reason I was there today, because it was – even to me – still totally unbelievable.

Luckily, my interrogation was put on hold by the timely ringing of the telephone. I wandered into the lounge, grateful to the unknown caller who'd distracted her with questions about rehearsals, understudies and script changes. 'Sorry about that,' my mum apologised when she joined me fifteen minutes later. I was staring at the row of family photographs on the mantelpiece as if I'd never seen them before. There were several of Karen and me when we were younger, but most of the newer frames held images of my nephews. I'm not sure what expression my mother saw on my face as I stared at the photograph of Karen in an Australian maternity ward, a newborn Josh cradled in her arms, but it was enough to make her hurry across the room to my side.

'Beth? What *is* it? What's wrong?'

I shook my head and grappled for a lie she might possibly believe. I couldn't find a single one. 'It's nothing, Mum. Honestly.'

Anxious to escape her probing gaze, I carried my small overnight case up to my old bedroom. A mosaic of old photo-booth images, many curled with age, were still held in the frame of my dressing table mirror, but none of them looked anything like the pale, haunted woman staring back at me in the glass. Tim would have been disappointed in me; *I* was disappointed in me. I pinched my cheeks hard enough to make the pallor disappear, but the look of vulnerability wasn't so easily fixed. I would need to work on that.

The sound of the front door closing was followed by a low rumble of conversation that was impossible to decipher. It was time. They were in the kitchen, and my dad got to his feet and enfolded me in a hug, which I held on to for a little longer than normal. Today, thirty-five didn't feel too old for that kind of support.

'What a lovely surprise, darling,' he said, doing a careful scrutiny of my face before gently releasing me.

I sat down at the kitchen table and my parents pulled out chairs opposite me. It felt horribly similar to another table, where twenty-four hours earlier I'd learnt the news I was about to share. Wordlessly, my mother slid a hot drink towards me, and then sat back and folded her arms expectantly.

I took a moment to draw strength from the love and concern on their faces and felt a pang of guilt for the weight I was about to place on their shoulders. I'd already ruined their retirement plans once, and unless a miracle occurred in the next few minutes, I was about to upset them all over again. I took a fortifying gulp of tea and jumped straight in.

'Firstly, I want you to know that I'm not sick. It's nothing like that.' I saw the relief course through my mother like a sound wave. That was *her* greatest concern, and it felt good to dismiss it. 'And I've not broken any laws, so I'm not going to jail.' I wasn't being deliberately flippant. This time it was my father who sighed thankfully. As a retired solicitor, that would have been *his* personal nightmare.

'But there *is* something you want to tell us?' probed my mum, like a Spanish inquisitor.

I nodded, staring into my mug as if the script I needed might miraculously have appeared inside it.

A chair scraped across the tiled floor as my mother suddenly sat up straighter. There was excitement and hope in her voice. 'Have you met someone, Beth? A man?'

My head shot up. For one split second, Liam Thomas's face had flashed ridiculously into my head. I blinked it away, annoyed with my subconscious for having conjured it up. There was only one man I cared about. Tim. And I still felt very much married, rather than widowed. Somehow, I suspected I always would.

'Mum, please stop guessing. You're making this even harder.'

I saw the disappointment on her face. She really *had* hoped that had been my news. My father reached for her hand and gave it a loving squeeze. His solicitor's patience was kicking in. He inclined his head, waiting for me to disclose whatever it was I'd come there to say.

'You remember before Tim died we tried several rounds of IVF with the embryos we'd had frozen?'

They both nodded, and I saw my mother draw her lips tightly together, as though it took all her restraint to prevent them from asking another question.

'As you know, we weren't successful.'

Sadness for my loss shone from their eyes, so poignantly that I had to look away. Just a few more sentences; that was all I needed to find the strength for. Then they'd know it all.

'Well, what we didn't tell you at the time was that there was one last embryo left in storage. Tim and I decided to leave it until... Well... we just decided to let it remain at the clinic.'

I looked up, feeling almost like a teenager with my apology. 'I'm sorry we didn't tell you this at the time.' They nodded, and I think they understood why. Shortly after my last IVF attempt, Tim's health had seriously declined. It had been the beginning of the end.

'Anyway, a few months ago, I made a really important decision. I decided I wanted to go ahead and use that final embryo. I wanted one last chance to have Tim's baby.'

'Oh, Bethie. Why did you never say anything?' I counted

the seconds in my head, waiting for the next, inevitable question. I only got to 'three' before it shot out on a huge gasp. 'Oh my goodness! Are you pregnant? Is that what you're here to tell us?' My mother actually clapped her hands together in glee, something I truly don't think I've ever seen anyone do in real life before. She looked so happy for me, so thrilled that in the aftermath of such tragedy there would be something beautiful waiting for me. But this story wasn't destined to have that type of happy ending.

And that was when I began to cry.

They were out of their chairs in an instant, with surprising speed for a couple in their sixties. They flanked me as I wept, face down against their kitchen table. Tears of empathy were already in my mum's eyes, and she still had no idea why. I had to get this over with.

'Yesterday, I visited the clinic and was told that there'd been the most terrible mistake.' There was no easy way to say these words. They spilled out of me like a sickness. 'Our embryo was given to another patient. Another woman got pregnant with our baby.'

Shock is a funny thing. It affects people differently. My mother's face drained of all colour, whereas my father's went bright red, as though rage was a hue, and its pigment was seeping through his pores.

They were stunned, starting sentences then leaving the words hanging in the air as their thoughts were whipped away. Strangely, telling the story out loud for the first time had given me a strength that I hadn't felt since those first dreadful moments in the clinic.

My father got to his feet, using one hand to steady himself on the chair before moving to a kitchen cabinet and reaching for a bottle of Scotch. My mother was more of a Harveys Bristol Cream kind of person, and I seldom drank spirits, but neither of us said anything as he poured three sizeable measures into glasses and brought them to the table. It was only midday, but I was grateful for the cauterising effect of the fiery liquid as it burnt its way down my throat.

'Obviously, I wanted to tell you this in person,' I said, shaking my head when my father offered to refill my glass. I'd not eaten anything since the day before, and the single shot was already coursing dangerously through me. His hand shook as he replenished his own drink. He'd always been a quiet man; moderate in temperament and slow to anger. But when it came to his girls – and I included my mum in that description – he was a fierce David who any Goliath should fear.

'I need your advice, Dad,' I said, wondering how many years it had been since he'd heard those words from me. 'I need to know what my rights are. Whose side is the law on? Is it the other woman's, or mine?'

It was several years since he'd retired, and I was asking him questions I doubt had ever cropped up when he'd overseen a thousand house sales, or drawn up hundreds of wills. For a moment he looked older than his years, as he ran his hand through a head of hair that was considerably less plentiful than it used to be.

'To be perfectly honest, Beth, I don't have a clue. It's not my area. But don't worry,' he urged, reaching for my hand and sandwiching it between his. 'I'll make some calls. Talk to some people – experts in this field.' It was the answer I'd driven three hours to hear, and tears of relief sprang to my eyes.

'We'll sort this out, I promise.' The adult in me knew better than to believe him, but the child in me gave a sigh of relief and nodded fiercely.

I left on Sunday afternoon, with the kind of pang I hadn't felt since my university days. I named the emotion as I rejoined the motorway and began my journey back. I was homesick and missing a time when no problem was so great that your parents couldn't fix it.

My dad had disappeared into his study shortly after I'd dropped my bombshell, and hadn't emerged for a great many hours. Occasionally, snippets of his telephone conversations filtered through the closed door. Words like 'negligence', 'paternity' and 'compensation' made me flinch, as if they were bullets travelling across the hallway to find me. Eventually, my mother had reached for the TV remote, turning up the volume and drowning them out with the banality of Saturday night entertainment.

I'd slept surprisingly well, but I think that had more to do with emotional exhaustion than the comfort of my old bed. I was just finishing my breakfast when my dad entered the kitchen and handed me a single sheet of paper with a name and telephone number written on it.

'Everyone I've spoken to agrees this is the guy you need to talk to. He's a medical negligence lawyer, and he's expecting your call.' I gave a huge gulp, and reached shakily for my coffee. It was suddenly sounding very, very real and incredibly scary. And there was an important question, that I could no longer avoid asking.

'This kind of thing... This kind of case... do you happen to know how much it's likely to cost me? I mean, I'm pretty sure I can get a second mortgage against the house or—'

My dad shook his head and looked across the room at my mum, who'd been standing at the sink washing the same plate for the last two minutes. She gave him a small nod and my dad reached into his pocket and drew out a slip of paper, sliding it face down across the table towards me, as though we were playing poker.

'What's this?' I asked, reaching for the slip, which I already recognised as a cheque. Even so, I repeated those words at a considerably higher pitch when I saw the number of zeros and my own name on the payee line. 'I can't take this. This is a huge chunk of your savings. This money is supposed to be for both of you. It's for your retirement.'

'You're going to need it if you decide to pursue a legal claim,' my father said, ever the pragmatist.

'*You're* both going to need it too. This is the money you've set aside to visit Karen to see your new grandchild.'

My mother abandoned the ridiculously clean plate and came to lay one soapy hand on my dad's shoulder, letting me know this decision was unanimous.

'Well, now I'm using it so I can see my *other* grandchild,' my dad said, his voice not entirely steady. There were no words to express my gratitude, and thankfully they didn't seem to expect any.

***

My parents' unswerving support left me more than a little emotional and also totally unprepared for my sister's reaction. Just half an hour into my journey home, her name had lit up my phone screen, and I'd happily switched on the loudspeaker. I'd been intending to call her, and it didn't surprise me that she'd had the same impulse. It happened so many times, we'd finally stopped finding it remarkable. What *did* surprise me was her reaction to the news.

'Mum's just told me what's happened,' Karen began with absolutely no preamble. This was clearly not the kind of conversation that was going to start with *Hello* or *How are you?* 'What an absolute disaster. I can't believe it. How are you holding up?'

'To be honest, Karen, I don't really know. I don't think it's even sunk in properly yet. It's just such a nightmare.'

'Do they know how it happened? I thought that kind of screw-up was meant to be impossible?'

'So did I,' I said despondently. 'I guess I'll find out more when they've done their investigations. Did Mum tell you I've got an appointment with a medical negligence expert?'

'Yeah, she did,' confirmed my sister. From somewhere behind her I could hear a background soundtrack of screeching lorikeets, and my nephews' laughter. The distance between her life and mine suddenly seemed far greater than the miles between us. We were living in different worlds.

'Although compensation isn't what I'm interested in,' I said, carefully switching lanes as I drove, both literally and metaphorically.

'Well, you should be. Those bloody idiots should be held responsible for what they've done to you.' The line went quiet for a few seconds, and when she next spoke Karen's voice was suddenly more cautious and tentative. 'What *is it* you're interested in, Beth?'

She was my sister, the person I'd always believed knew me better than anyone else. The fact that she even had to ask that question surprised me.

'Finding out where our baby is – Tim's and mine. *That's* my priority. That's the only thing I care about.'

More silence, only this time it seemed almost disapproving.

'Beth, I don't want to sound like I don't understand how painful this is for you, but what you're looking for no longer exists. There isn't a baby anymore. It's a child. *Someone else's child.*'

'No, it's—' But she wouldn't let me speak.

'Mum said this all happened eight years ago?'

'Yes,' I confirmed miserably.

'So this child is about a year older than Aaron is now,' she declared. The thought jolted through me. Our children were cousins, close in age. But that wasn't the point Karen was trying to make. 'This child has known no parents other than the ones who've loved them their entire life.' She was quiet for a moment, her voice shaking with emotion. 'Just the *thought* of someone trying to take your child from you is the stuff of every mother's nightmare.'

The fact that this was exactly what had happened to me didn't even seem to have occurred to Karen. Unbelievably, her allegiance appeared to be with this other faceless mother. 'If anyone tried to take Aaron or Josh from me, if they tried to tell me that they weren't mine, I'd do anything, give up everything, to stop them. You have to know going into this what you're going to be up against, Beth. It's a fight I don't think you'll ever win. More than that, it's a fight I don't think you *should* win.'

11

Izzy

It's funny how a sound you'd once have happily committed manslaughter to stop could now be so comforting. The low, rhythmic snort that used to set my teeth on edge was a lullaby in reverse, crooning me awake. That I slept at all was astonishing; that I did so cradled in my soon-to-be ex-husband's arms practically defied belief.

Long probing fingers of early morning light searched for the gaps in the curtains, painting the lounge in the sepia between night and day. In even the worst of situations, there are a few blissful seconds of amnesia on waking, before reality comes crashing back again. My fleeting moment of peace was lost as I struggled to remember why I was lying across Pete's chest, his hand resting comfortably in the curve of my waist.

And then it hit me. I stiffened suddenly, my body no longer rising and falling with the movement of Pete's ribcage.

Noah.

The clinic.

The mistake.

The memories hit me like a series of punches, each

one determined to send me to the mat. Carefully, I eased myself free of Pete's hold. His breath ruffled my hair as I manoeuvred myself across his body. He murmured something in his sleep, which was thankfully too indistinct to make out. I was glad it wasn't a woman's name; I was glad it wasn't *mine*.

Barefoot, I headed for the kitchen, closing the door behind me with a silent click. I leant back against it, waiting for my racing pulse and ragged breathing to return to normal. There are some situations that look better in the light of day. Middle-of-the-night disasters can suddenly seem fixable by dawn. But not this one. Despite the sunlight streaming in through the kitchen window, I shivered violently.

Two mugs of tea later, Noah and Pete were still fast asleep and the warmth of the kitchen was making me feel nauseous. I couldn't remember the last time I'd slept in my clothes, and the thought of a refreshing shower led me tiptoeing like an intruder up the stairs to the bathroom.

It was a relief to step out of the crumpled garments, and as I waited for our temperamental shower to heat up, I stared at my naked reflection in the bathroom mirror. I was much skinnier than I used to be, and even I could see I looked worse for having lost the pounds. My body was like a roadmap, telling the story of where life had taken me. I was okay with my boobs not being as full or perky as they'd once been, because they'd been used the way nature had intended.

An old memory floated down through the years, of nursing Noah in a rocking chair in the middle of the night. A floorboard had creaked and I'd looked up to find Pete standing in the doorway watching us. He'd looked awed, like someone witnessing a miracle. If I lived to a hundred, that would still be one of my most cherished memories.

My hands slid past my ribcage, stopping as they reached the thin spider's web of silvery stretch marks across my stomach, their filigree pattern glinting beneath the bright overhead spotlights. Those scars were mine by right, they were proof of the child I'd carried inside me, and for the first time ever I was actually *pleased* I'd not used the oils that could have prevented them. My cheeks flooded with warmth as the memory of Pete tenderly tracing each line with his lips came into my head and refused to leave.

I spent too long in the shower, finally emerging from the closet in a cloud of steam, like a scene from a film, with salmon-pink skin and fingers wrinkled like prunes. Noah's open bedroom door and carelessly thrown-back duvet got me moving, though. I spent less than two minutes rummaging for clean jeans and a plain white T-shirt, before dragging a comb through my wet hair. Without bothering to check my reflection, I hurried on to the landing, anxious to avoid the questions that would be asked should Noah find his dad asleep in the lounge.

Halfway down the stairs, I realised I was already too late. A delicious smell of frying bacon was coming from the direction of the kitchen and my stomach, which had failed to grasp the gravity of our situation, growled like a traitor. A thousand weekend mornings flashed before my eyes as I walked into the room to see Pete at the hob, with the makings of a mountain of bacon sandwiches on the worktop beside him.

'Ah, there you are,' he announced unnecessarily, as if this was just any other Saturday morning. I felt wrong-footed, as though the last nine months might simply not have happened at all.

'Hey, Mum, guess what? Dad didn't go home last night, he slept here! And he's made us breakfast.' Noah reached hungrily for the topmost sandwich from the pile Pete had carried to the table.

'I see that,' I replied, turning to Pete and trying to rearrange my features to look like someone who *hadn't* woken up in his arms a short while ago.

'You don't mind, do you?' he asked, and for a moment I wasn't sure if he was talking about raiding my fridge or sleeping beside me on the settee.

'No, that's fine,' I replied. My answer covered both options.

'Dad said the three of us could go for a walk this morning.' I looked over the top of our son's head to find Pete staring meaningfully back at me.

'Only if your mum agrees,' he reminded Noah, his eyes on my face. *We still have things to discuss*, they silently reminded me.

My nod was so fleeting a single blink could have missed it.

'Yay!' cried Noah, blissfully unaware that anything was wrong. And that was just how it was going to stay, I vowed. His delight was simple. He was going to spend the morning with the two people he loved most in the world, and he wasn't the only one who needed that, I realised.

When Noah left the room, the air of false normality went right out of the door with him. I panicked for a moment, wanting to call him back, afraid of being alone with my own husband for reasons too complicated to identify.

'Let me help you,' offered Pete, making me jump, for I'd not heard his barefoot approach as he joined me at the sink.

'No. I've got this.' My voice sounded too bright and too brittle, as if the slightest thing might cause it to shatter. 'You can use the bathroom if you like. Some of your old stuff is still at the back of the wardrobe.' I flushed then, hiding behind the fall of my hair as I wondered if he'd ask me why I'd never bothered returning it. I was afraid to look into his face, scared he'd be able to tell just how many times I'd opened up the wardrobe doors, needing to see his things still there. It was a harmless addiction, or so I'd told myself.

'We need to work out what to do next, Iz,' Pete said solemnly, his face naked without the jolly mask it had been wearing for Noah's benefit.

'I know,' I said, focusing all my attention on the brilliant green jet of washing-up liquid arcing into the sink. Pete's hand fell lightly onto my shoulder, and I gave an involuntarily shiver. I turned to look up at him, and perhaps he realised that I needed more time before revisiting the topic we'd soon be unable to avoid.

'Later,' I said, my words falling somewhere between a question and a plea.

His hand squeezed my shoulder gently before falling away. 'Okay,' he agreed.

'Black with two sugars,' said Pete, setting the cardboard drink carrier with the cups of steaming hot coffee down on the picnic table.

I murmured my thanks, my eyes fixed on Noah, who was

standing by the edge of the lake with half a loaf of stale bread in his hands and an extraordinary number of ducks and geese circling with interest around his feet.

More than anything, I wanted to go and join him at the water's edge, and pretend this was just another family outing to Hornfield Forest, which had been a favourite outdoor spot of ours for years. It was a perfect location to have chosen for today, and not just because the sun was shining down, and the gentle breeze rustling through the trees made the five-mile walk more comfortable. The forest held happy memories for us as a family.

By unspoken consent, we'd waited until we reached the lake with its small outdoor café before returning to the topic we'd left very much unresolved in the middle of the night.

'I've been thinking,' I said, automatically dropping my voice down low, even though there was no danger of Noah overhearing us from where he stood. 'How do we even know that they made a mistake all those years ago? I mean, before anything else, shouldn't we insist they produce proof that Noah isn't biologically ours?'

'You mean aside from the fact that he doesn't look like either of us?'

I made a small dismissive sound. 'Lots of kids look totally different from their parents, but it doesn't mean they're someone else's.'

Pete sighed softly. 'But it might explain those characteristics of his that have always puzzled us.' My face clouded with confusion. 'That he's so gifted musically, and also incredibly bright,' he expanded.

'I'm going to try not to get offended that you don't think either of those attributes could have come from our own gene pool.'

Pete's smile was so fleeting I only caught the tail end of it before it disappeared. 'I imagine the first thing they'll want to do is a DNA test to prove things one way or the other.'

I could feel my teeth grinding together and forced my jaw to relax. The irony that the miracle of science that had given Noah to us could also end up being the tool used to take him away wasn't lost on me. The lump in my throat dissolved into tears, and I had to look away for several moments before I had control of my voice again. Pete's expression, when I explained those fears to him, went from incredulous to genuinely horrified.

'No one has said anything about taking Noah away.' There was a brusque quality to his voice, as though every one of his emotions was encased in sandpaper. The threat of his own tears made him angry, and he spilled a small puddle of coffee as he set his plastic cup back down on the table.

'But they haven't said they *won't* try to do it, have they?' Sometimes saying the thing you're most afraid of out loud lessens its impact. And sometimes it doesn't make any difference at all.

Pete shook his head, his eyes going to our son, who was still happily feeding the flock of birds, completely oblivious that his once certain future had now turned into a huge question mark.

'No judge would ever rule that a child should be taken away from his parents.' Pete's voice had become a defiant growl.

'Even if it turns out we're *not* his parents?' Our eyes met and held. 'What if they say we have to swap back? What if the other couple want their embryo back?'

'He's not an embryo. He's my son,' Pete declared, not even bothering to wipe away the tears that were falling silently from his eyes. 'We'll go to the press or the TV if we have to. We'll do whatever it takes to get public support.'

'That might not count for much if the law says he can't stay with us. And do we really want our lives turned into a tabloid sensation?'

'We might not have a choice,' said Pete darkly. I shuddered, despite the warmth of the day. We were both private people and the thought of having our family thrust into the limelight like that filled me with horror. What would it do to Noah? What would it do to us?

'I've spent his entire life worrying that something terrible will happen to him. I've read every childhood illness book I could get my hands on. I could spot a meningitis rash from fifty paces. But *this*? *This*? How was I ever supposed to protect him from this? And yet we have to do something.'

'So what's your plan? What do *you* think we should do?' There was a challenge in Pete's voice, which almost made me hesitate. But the idea that had been circling my head all morning, like a plane waiting to land, had to be given its voice.

'I think we should go away. Leave. Go abroad. Go somewhere they won't be able to find us.' It was a child's solution. A *scared* child's solution. But at least he didn't laugh out loud at my suggestion.

'How on earth could we do that, Izzy?' Pete asked reasonably, reaching for my hand, but I snatched it away. I was in no mood to be sensible or practical. All I could feel was that time was quickly going to run out, and thrumming within me was a mother's primal instinct to protect her young. And I was very much afraid I wasn't going to be able to do that if we stayed here much longer.

'Just think about what you're saying for a moment, Iz. You're talking about kidnapping our own child as though it's a sensible option.' My scowl was dark as he took aim and began shooting holes in my plan. 'Where would we go? What would we do for money? And what about Noah's school and all his friends? Not to mention the house, the mortgage, and both our jobs. Where in the world do you think we could run to, where they wouldn't be able to find us and make us come back?'

'We could get new passports, with different identities. We'd go somewhere without an extradition treaty.'

'You're talking about things that happen in the movies, not real life. I barely knew where I had to go to get a *legitimate* passport, much less a fake one. We're not going on the run. This isn't a *Bourne* film, Izzy, it's real life.'

Nothing had *ever* felt less like reality than the situation we were currently facing. Beneath the table my hands were balled into fists of frustration, even while the sensible part of my brain was admitting that of the two of us, Pete was the only one talking sense.

'We need to fight this, of course we do. And we will. But we can't do it outside of the law. We have to prove that even if the clinic *did* make the world's most colossal mistake, there has to be another solution. No one on God's Earth is going to take our child away from us.'

'So what do you suggest we do?'

'We get legal advice. The very best that money can buy.'

My sigh was resigned, because deep down I knew he was right. But finding that kind of help on two salaries that teetered each month on the brink of being overdrawn sounded almost as unrealistic as going on the lam.

'We'll do this,' assured Pete, with a confidence I wanted so very much to believe. I felt the squeeze of his fingers against mine and looked down in surprise. We were now holding hands across the tabletop, and I had absolutely no idea when or how that had happened.

12

Beth

'Is there anything else you'd like to ask me at this point, Mrs Brandon?'

I looked across the leather-topped antique desk at the man who I'd come there to meet, and shook my head. There were probably a hundred questions I should be asking, but most of them were shouted down by just one: *How on earth did this happen?* But for now, William Sylvester, the lawyer my father had found for me, didn't have the answer to that one.

He got to his feet and extended his hand, indicating that this introductory meeting had come to a close. He was everything you'd expect a young, dynamic and successful lawyer to be. Dressed in a well-cut suit, which occasionally revealed glimpses of the Rolex on his wrist, he wore the trappings of success with a casual nonchalance.

I placed my hand in his, noticing obliquely that his manicure was far neater than mine. His handshake was firm and brief, and bizarrely for a moment it reminded me of Liam Thomas's. That man had a curious habit of hijacking my train of thought at the most inopportune moments. And here, in the plush offices of a legal company I'd never have been able to afford without my parents' help, he was the last person I should be thinking about.

'If you'd like to wait in Reception,' Mr Sylvester suggested, already guiding me gently towards the door, 'I'll have my PA return your documents when she's finished making the necessary copies.'

I gave a small nod, still feeling overwhelmed in a way I hadn't been expecting. Having spent most of the morning online, researching the man I was meeting that day, I'd hoped to feel better prepared for this preliminary appointment. But whatever comfort I'd found in his outstanding reputation had evaporated when I began researching cases similar to mine. That's because it hadn't taken long to discover that there *weren't* any. Admittedly there'd been fertility clinic mistakes before – they'd happened in practically every country of the world. But those mistakes had been uncovered much earlier, directly after implantation, or if not then, at birth. The outcomes were mixed, but almost all seemed to result in protracted legal battles. But there wasn't a single instance I could find where the error hadn't come to light until eight years later.

I'd closed the shop early, and given Natalie the rest of the afternoon off, which at least spared me from having to lie to her again. When the truth came out – and it *would* come out, I knew that – I was going to have a lot of explaining to do. Like a mole struggling in sunlight, I turned away from that glaring thought, filing it under the category of 'Things I'll worry about when I have to'.

The solicitors' offices were located in an area of town I

was unfamiliar with. Flanked by expensive-looking mews homes with impressive river frontage views, the Regency building looked like a town residence in a TV period drama. I'd arrived for my appointment carrying a bulging folder of documents, which William Sylvester's attractive PA had quickly relieved me of. They were needed to run financial checks, and also to confirm my identity. If the clinic had been as diligent as the lawyers were in that respect, we wouldn't be in this mess in the first place, I thought with bitter irony. The thought stung like a barb, burrowing beneath my skin, which already felt as if it was stretched too thin to offer any protection.

Behind a mahogany desk, a pretty blonde receptionist looked up and flashed a dazzling smile in my direction. Did *everyone* who worked here look like a model? Even the man standing in one shadowy corner of the room had an aura about him. His height and the breadth of his shoulders beneath a charcoal grey suit jacket hinted at a gym-frequenter's physique, and his hair was thick and springy, casting its own shadow against the silk-wallpapered wall as he leafed through a magazine. There was something about the way he stood that felt familiar.

And then he turned around, and my mouth went instantly dry. Liam Thomas. Here. Our paths had crossed again, only this time it felt like one coincidence too many. As ludicrous as it sounded, could he actually be *following* me?

His eyes passed politely over me, and then, with an almost comical double-take, flew back to my face. His lips turned up at the corners in a ready smile as he eliminated the distance between us in three long strides.

'Beth. What are you doing here?'

'I was going to ask *you* the same thing.' Did he hear the thread of suspicion in my voice? Perhaps so, because his warm smile suddenly looked a few degrees cooler. 'I had an appointment here this afternoon,' I continued. 'And you…?'

'Work here,' Liam completed equably.

As if on cue, the blonde receptionist reached for a file on her desk. 'I think this is the one you were looking for, Mr Thomas.'

He accepted the manila file without taking his eyes off me. It gave him an excellent opportunity to watch me turn from flamingo pink to puce.

'You said you had an appointment?' His attractive features wore a puzzled veneer. 'It wasn't with me, was it?'

I shook my head, wishing more than anything that the phone would ring or someone would come in with an urgent query to divert the receptionist's open fascination away from our conversation.

'No, it was with William Sylvester.'

Liam's forehead concertinaed into a frown. 'Bill?'

I nodded. It probably wasn't the right moment to say that his colleague hadn't seemed like a 'Bill' kind of a guy.

'But Bill was meeting with Graham Simpson's daughter Elizabeth this afternoon…' Liam's voice trailed away.

Worlds were shifting and colliding, and there was nothing I could do to stop them. They were going to travel on their own trajectories, whether I liked it or not. My voice was low, but I'm pretty sure the receptionist managed to hear me just fine.

'*I'm* Elizabeth. Simpson was my maiden name, and Graham is my father.'

The truth unravelled across Liam's features, one strand at

a time. The names 'Elizabeth' and 'Beth' matched together like playing cards in his eyes. His head shook slowly from side to side as the truth of what I was doing there began to unfold, filling the space between us. But it was his mouth that was the most expressive. From the tightening of his lips, I realised he already knew *exactly* why Graham Simpson's daughter was meeting with the firm's medical negligence lawyer. A sound of sympathy escaped him, because of course Liam Thomas already knew my story, and had done so for far longer than anyone else.

'Are you okay?'

Not even remotely, I thought sadly. If I was honest, I felt more overwhelmed and lost than I'd done since the night Tim had died, and perhaps he saw that on my face.

'Come and sit down for a minute,' he invited, taking my arm and guiding me out of the reception and into the sanctuary of an office that looked practically identical to the one I'd just left, apart from the eye-catching display of abstract art on its walls. Liam led me towards a large green chesterfield, and I folded onto the comfortable leather like a deflated crash dummy.

'Sorry. I'm not usually this much of a wuss,' I said. I was going to have to develop a much tougher carapace if I was serious about going ahead with legal proceedings. William Sylvester had been very clear about that. This case wasn't going to be an easy ride.

Liam shook his head. 'No apologies necessary. Can I get you a coffee?' He glanced at his watch, which looked just as expensive as his colleague's, although considerably less ostentatious. 'My assistant has left for the day, but I'm sure I can rustle us up a couple of cups.'

'That's really kind. Thank you.'

It felt a little weird being alone in his office, and as I waited my attention was drawn to the striking artwork hanging on his walls. Each piece was equally dramatic and compelling and they drew me to my feet, begging to be examined more closely. There was no need to read the signature in the bottom right-hand corner to know they'd all been painted by the same artist. I was leaning in closer, trying to decipher the name, when the office door opened and Liam re-entered carrying two mismatched mugs. One was plain, but the other had a slogan I'd have blushed to say out loud.

He grinned when he saw me looking at the crockery, and instantly ten years were shaved off his age. 'I've no idea where they hide the posh china. I think they must lock it up at night so the partners can't get their hands on it.'

So, he was a partner in this highly successful legal practice. That shouldn't come as a surprise; they didn't give you an office this size if you delivered the mail. Did Liam Thomas also work on the firm's medical negligence cases, I wondered? Would he be involved in mine? I felt momentarily thrown, as though I was standing on a fault line while plates were shifting.

He came to stand beside me, passing me the profanity-free mug. 'It's only instant, not caramel latte, I'm afraid. Although I *was* tempted to drop a random Mars bar I found in the kitchen into it.' His teasing humour came as a surprise and was an unexpected bonus if this man *was* to become my friend.

'This is perfect,' I said, lifting the steaming coffee to my lips and looking up at him over the rim of my mug. 'I was just admiring your artwork. It's very striking. I really like it.' My words were genuine. The bold acrylic colours reminded me of a profusion of wild flowers grouped together in an ad hoc bouquet. Clashing hues jostled against each other, like angry commuters defending their personal space. It shouldn't have worked together, and yet it absolutely did.

Liam's expression grew softer and perhaps that's what made me look more closely at the signature on the painting. The letters reformed into a name I finally deciphered: *Anna*.

'Your wife was the artist?'

He nodded, and there was pride in his smoke-coloured eyes. It was there too in his voice. 'She was very talented.' His words made me feel humble, as though I was peeking through a curtain at their relationship and viewing something very private.

'Was that her profession?'

Liam smiled, turning away from his wife's creations to face me. 'No, it was just a hobby, albeit one she was passionate about. She actually worked as a school teacher.'

I gasped softly, feeling something stronger than mere coincidence at work here. 'So was Tim.'

Liam looked at me for a very long moment, as though half a dozen questions were queued up, just waiting to be asked, and he wasn't sure how to phrase any of them.

'Is there somewhere you need to be right now?'

That certainly *wasn't* a question I'd been expecting. 'No.'

'Do you fancy grabbing a bite to eat somewhere?' It was a casual invitation, without any overtones of being a date. And yet still I hesitated. Should we be doing this? Was it unethical in some way? Did being friends with this man cross some professional boundary?

'Look, you have to eat, and I have to eat, and it might be nice not to be doing it alone for a change.' I could feel the 'yes' coming up from a place deep inside me, where the loneliness lived. 'Okay. I'd like that.'

The building was quiet now, most of the employees having already left for the day. But as we walked along the carpeted hallway I realised one office was still occupied. From beneath a door I'd recently walked through, a sliver of light sliced into the corridor. Behind the panelled oak, I recognised the voice of the man I'd met with earlier, who appeared to be talking animatedly on the telephone. I heard the words 'unprecedented', 'in vitro' and 'media circus' float into the hallway like spilled secrets. I shivered, knowing the case he was discussing was probably mine. As if in confirmation, Liam's hand was suddenly against my back, gently urging me forward and out of earshot.

I followed him through the darkened reception and out onto the street. I blinked in the glare of the early evening sun, which was still strong enough to dazzle, and took extra care as I descended the steep marble steps in my unaccustomed high heels. I'd dressed formally for my meeting that day, hiding behind the armour of a business suit, but it was such a contrast to my everyday wear I felt as if I was wearing a costume in a play.

'There's a restaurant in the square nearby that should have a table this early in the evening. Or we could go further afield if you'd prefer?'

I shook my head, already unsure whether I'd made the right call by agreeing to have dinner with him. But I could see no polite way of backtracking, so the sooner we ate, the sooner the evening would be over. The thought was supposed to leave me comforted, but for some reason it had the opposite effect.

'Are you okay to walk there?' he asked politely, holding out one arm with an almost old-fashioned display of good manners. My cheeks felt warm as I pretended not to see the gesture. There was a tug of war going on inside me: one side was pulling for me to make this man my friend, while the other was tugging just as hard to maintain nothing more than a cool and professional relationship. It would be interesting to see which side won out.

'I'm more of a Converse than a stiletto girl,' I admitted, as I fell into step beside him. 'They're much more practical for work.'

Liam kept up a steady stream of interested questions about Crazy Daisy, which took us all the way to the square he had mentioned. There was an almost continental atmosphere to the lively plaza, home to several restaurants and bars, all of which appeared to be doing a roaring trade. Although it was only just after six o'clock, many outdoor tables were already occupied by people winding down after a week at work. All around us, men were tugging off jackets and unknotting ties and there was a relaxed buzz in the air, interspersed with laughter and the sound of clinking beer bottles and wine glasses.

'Inside or out?' asked Liam, coming to a halt beside an Italian restaurant with white-clothed tables set up on the pavement beneath a brightly coloured awning.

'Would you mind if we went inside,' I replied, feeling

the need to put greater distance between us and the noisy revellers.

The interior of the restaurant was charming and brought an instant smile to my face. It was decorated to make diners feel as if they were in a garden, with indoor trees, enormous planters of flowers and twisting overhead vines. Had Liam chosen this place to appeal to the florist in me, or was I overanalysing his motives? We certainly had our choice of tables and I was particularly pleased when we were shown to one near a small sparkling fountain, which gurgled pleasantly beside us.

'It's lovely here,' I said, thanking the waiter who'd unfurled my napkin with the flourish of a magician. It was almost a disappointment when he draped it across my lap without producing a white dove from its folds.

'We come here quite a lot,' said Liam, and for a moment I thought he was referring to his late wife and had used the wrong tense. It was a habit that had taken me years to get out of after Tim had died. Even now, I still slipped up occasionally. 'Clients really seem to like it,' he added.

I felt as if a pitcher of ice cold water had been tipped over my head. *Clients.* The restaurant was just around the corner from the firm, so naturally this is where they took their clients. This was why Liam had invited me here. He was a senior partner in the firm I'd engaged to take on a high-profile and probably very lucrative case. I wasn't dining with a potential friend; I was being 'entertained'. The realisation made me uncomfortable.

I gave myself a mental shake and rearranged my thoughts back where they belonged. This was a good thing to know, because if this *was* a business dinner there was nothing to stop me from doing some further probing. But before I could decide where to begin, Liam torpedoed my idea clean out of the water.

'Before we go any further, I should let you know that I'm not going to be able to discuss your case with you, or anything Bill has spoken about.'

My face must have taken on the look of a child who's just been told Christmas has been cancelled that year. Liam drew in his lower lip, his teeth leaving a small white bite mark on the pink skin, which was really hard not to stare at. 'Is that what you were hoping for?' he asked softly. 'Was that why you said "yes" when I asked you to come out this evening?'

Maybe. Possibly, I admitted silently. 'Of course not,' I denied on a rush. Liam's eyebrows rose, and his forehead found every one of his frown lines and settled into them comfortably. 'Although it's only natural to have questions about how this kind of case usually progresses. How long it normally takes, and what kind of success rates people in my situation can hope for. That sort of thing.'

Liam's head was shaking regretfully even before I'd begun my list. It told me everything I already knew. I reached for the glass of wine I'd ordered, and took a long sip before answering. My laugh didn't sound natural, but that's probably because it wasn't.

'I guess the reason you can't say anything is that there *aren't* any legal precedents like mine, are there?'

For the first time, Liam looked uncomfortable in my company. I imagine I wasn't the only one who was suddenly thinking this whole dinner suggestion had been a really bad idea. Fortunately, our waiter chose that moment to materialise beside the table as if he'd been magically conjured up. In his arms were two large leather-bound menus. As we browsed through the selection of dishes, the sun began to dip in the sky, its early-evening rays still powerful as they passed through the restaurant window and found our table, irradiating the silverware in a dazzling glow. Rainbow prisms bounced off the drinking glasses, making me feel like a sepia impostor in a world of colour.

'So, how are you feeling now after your meeting with Bill this afternoon?'

'I thought we weren't allowed to talk about that?'

Liam shifted a little uncomfortably on his chair. 'Not in specific terms, perhaps. I was just hoping you feel you've got the right people working with you to get the outcome you want.'

'Does that outcome include getting my child back?'

Liam's eyes widened and he looked genuinely shocked. That's what happens when the unspoken elephant in the room suddenly charges at you, head on. 'Is that what you're hoping for, Beth?' His voice was neutral; there was no hint of whether he approved or disapproved of that plan.

'Absolutely,' I said, which would have been so much more convincing if my hand hadn't suddenly begun to shake so badly my wine glass collided with the bread plate and the water jug before I finally set it back down on the table. 'Will you be working with William on the case?'

There was no imagining the look of relief in Liam's eyes as he answered me. 'No. It's not my area of specialism. I handle the firm's corporate cases. William's our medical negligence expert. He's the best in his field.' Quite unexpectedly, Liam's hand moved across the crisp white tablecloth. For a moment I thought it was reaching for mine, I *still* think that was his intention, but at the last moment he diverted it, and plucked up a breadstick instead.

I waited until a passing waiter was safely out of earshot before asking the man opposite me: 'I suppose you know the full story about what happened with the clinic?'

Liam nodded, and my relief at not having to explain it again was tangible. Liam's face wore an appropriately sober expression. 'It's one hell of mess. A total fuck-up.'

I almost snorted into my drinking glass, surprised that anything about this awful situation had the power to make me laugh. 'Is that a legal assessment, or just your personal one?'

'Both.' Liam's smile was a fleeting ghost as the waiter placed plates of steaming pasta before us. 'Bill discussed your case with all the partners before agreeing to meet with you.' Liam looked down, as though the design circling his dinner plate suddenly warranted closer inspection. 'It's not one any firm would undertake lightly,' he said by way of explanation.

'Because it's so unusual, or because it's unwinnable?'

Liam gave a small start. 'You're not afraid of asking the hard questions, are you?' There was a glimmer of admiration in his eyes, yet still he sighed before answering me. 'Nothing's unwinnable, Beth,' he said quietly. 'You just have to decide at what cost.'

I watched the DVD when I got back home that night, even though it wasn't our anniversary, Tim's birthday, or any other date when I gave myself 'permission' to relive the best day of my life. The need to see his face again burnt like a flame within me. The panic that I could no longer remember his voice or the sound of his laughter faded away, as it always did the second his face filled the screen. He raised his glass of champagne to the camera, and winked broadly at whoever had been recording the footage of his last morning as a single man. 'Welcome to our wedding,' he said, and through the lens and the lost years his eyes found and held mine, and I could breathe again.

13

Izzy

'Okay, so you have to imagine it when I'm ten pounds lighter and wearing industrial strength magic knickers.'

I looked up as the changing cubicle curtain was drawn back and Maggie stood before me in yet another dress.

'Hmm… nice,' I said, with the same tepid enthusiasm I'd given the first three outfits.

'You don't like any of them, do you?' asked Maggie, sounding despondent. 'I'm *never* going to find a dress for Jonathon's wedding.'

'I'm sorry,' I said. 'They all look great, it's just… I've got a bit of a headache, that's all.'

'Oh, sweetie, you should have said,' cried Maggie, her eyes already searching for her handbag. 'I think I've got some pills with me.'

She was so lovely, and I felt like the worst kind of friend by lying to her. 'That's okay, I've already taken some.'

I hadn't wanted to come on this shopping expedition, even though I'd agreed to do so weeks ago. 'I don't want to go,' I'd told Pete, sounding very much like Noah on the first day of a new school term. 'I don't want to be apart from him, not even for a minute.'

Although Pete's eyes had been sympathetic, his voice had been firm. 'We can't do that, Iz. We've got to carry on as if everything is absolutely normal. If we don't, he'll realise something is up. I'm going to take him swimming this afternoon, the way I'd planned, and you're going to go shopping with Maggie.'

So here I was, in a top-end department store, probably ruining what should be a wonderful experience for my friend. 'Try the blue one on again,' I said, forcing myself out of my private world of despair. Maggie plucked the silk dress from the hook, but there was concern in her eyes as she pulled the curtain shut again.

'I really think this might be the one,' she declared a few minutes later, pirouetting like a jewellery-box ballerina in front of the mirrored walls of the changing rooms.

'You look lovely,' I said, a lump forming in my throat at the delight on my older friend's face.

'Hey,' she exclaimed. 'What's up, honey? You're not meant to cry when you see the mother-of-the-groom's dress – unless she looks bloody terrible, of course.' There was a pause, which I realised too late was when I was supposed to laugh. 'You wait, in no time you'll be doing this for Noah. People always talk about how hard it is for dads giving their daughters away, but what about us mums giving away our sons?'

She didn't know – how could she? – that her words pretty much encapsulated the fear coursing through me like a virus. For a moment she thought I was laughing, but her smile faltered then froze as she realised the sounds she could hear were sobs.

'Oh my God, Izzy. What is it? What's wrong?'

I shook my head, but could already feel the truth rising up in my throat, like something my body needed to purge. Maggie wriggled out of the silk dress with the speed of a quick-change artist. 'These can wait for another day,' she declared, with scarcely a backward glance at the dresses she had yet to try on. 'We need tea. And we need it right now.'

Maggie spotted a vacant corner table in the department store café and parked me there while she headed for the counter. She returned a few minutes later carrying a laden tray. Without bothering to ask if I wanted it, she passed me one of the two enormous slices of chocolate cake she'd bought.

'Sod the dress,' she said, spearing a mouthful onto her fork. 'I'll just buy the next size up.' She poured our teas, disposed of the tray, and then looked across at me expectantly.

Maggie never finished her cake, and anyone who knew her even half as well as I did would agree that nothing could have illustrated her shock more than that.

'When did all this happen?'

'Yesterday. Last night.'

'And Noah knows nothing about it yet?'

I shook my head vehemently. 'I don't want him to *ever* know. Hell, *I* don't even want to know about it.'

'You can't be like that,' Maggie said, with just the right amount of best friend bossiness. 'I know this has come out of nowhere and knocked you off your feet, but you have to come back swinging now, because you can bet your life that's what the other woman is going to do.'

The last mouthful of tea changed its mind about settling in my stomach, and for a moment I panicked that I was going to disgrace myself among the Saturday afternoon well-to-do shoppers. Maggie with her razor-sharp instincts and unerring practicality had gone straight to the heart of the problem. Somewhere out there was another woman, another mother, who believed her claim on Noah was stronger than mine. I could roll myself into a ball, like a terrified hedgehog, or I could stand up and prepare myself for a fight.

Maggie's head dipped in an approving nod as she saw me sit up a little taller in my chair, my bowed shoulders subtly straightening out.

'So the first thing you need is a good lawyer. One who's ballsy, not afraid to take on a tough case, and willing to work cheap. Do you have anyone in mind?'

I shook my head, pretty certain I wasn't going to find anyone matching that description while scouring through Yellow Pages.

'No matter,' continued Maggie, smiling broadly and suddenly looking very pleased with herself. 'I happen to know just the person.'

'Here?' questioned Pete, wincing at the throb of heavy metal music pulsating from the open doorway of the record shop we'd pulled up alongside. 'Are you sure?'

I checked the number above the door and saw it matched the one written on the piece of paper in my hand.

'Her office is on the fifth floor,' I said. Our eyes travelled in tandem from the dimly lit interior of the ground-floor shop, up the facade of the small office block. It had to be said, the upper storeys didn't appear a great deal more promising. The building had the look of a place where you'd expect to find boards nailed over the windows, and 'Keep Out' signs hammered across the entrance.

'This does *not* look like the kind of place a hot-shot lawyer practises from,' Pete declared, giving the shop one last dubious look before manoeuvring effortlessly into a parking space I'd have sworn was too small for his car.

Once out of the vehicle, the area didn't look any more inviting. Pete locked his car, and fondly patted its bonnet, as though he very much doubted it was still going to be there when we emerged from the building.

Although we didn't have to go through the record shop to reach the block's upper levels, the steady throb of music still followed us as we walked around the perimeter and found a second entrance. The door swung to a close behind us, leaving us in a small airless hallway, which housed two unappealing options. The narrow lift door looked no wider than a broom cupboard so we turned towards the shadowy staircase, ignoring the fact that it didn't appear to have been swept or vacuumed in quite a while.

Somewhere between floors two and three, Pete paused in our climb to ask: 'I don't suppose Maggie happened to mention how long her niece has been a lawyer, did she?'

I stopped, grateful for the chance to catch my breath. *Must exercise more*, I mentally promised myself. 'No. She didn't.

But she did say she was very good at her job. Graduated at the top of her class, I think. She worked for one of the big companies after qualifying but has now decided to set up on her own.'

Pete's smile was weak.

'You can't judge her abilities purely by the state of this building. It's probably a statement location. You know, sort of hipster.'

'I'm not even sure I know what that means. I just want an incredible lawyer, one who knows her stuff and can make this whole damn mess go away.' *Me too*, I thought silently, too winded by the stairs to speak by the time we finally reached the fifth floor.

There were only two offices on each storey. The door to one of them was propped open, revealing a room that might recently have been visited by the bailiffs. It was stripped bare of everything except a single landline telephone, sitting in the middle of the paint-splattered floorboards.

With matching nervous expressions, we turned towards the second door. It was hard to tell whether the glass panel was opaque or just covered in a film of dust. Most of it was hidden anyway behind a piece of white A4 card with *Francesca Burrows, Lawyer* printed on it. It was stuck to the door with four blobs of Blu-Tack.

'This must be the place,' I said in a tone that strived for chirpy, but didn't quite make it.

'I'm afraid you're probably right,' murmured Pete, lifting his hand to rap on the panel.

Perhaps we shouldn't have been surprised by the slight, spiky-haired young woman who ushered us into the office, given the unconventional choice of location. My first thought on seeing the girl standing before us in her music festival T-shirt and ripped jeans was that she probably worked in the shop downstairs. But then she thrust out her hand.

'Hi. You must be Izzy and Pete.'

If I was a little slow in returning the gesture, she didn't appear to notice. Her handshake was warm and surprisingly firm, causing the multitude of silver rings on her fingers to leave tiny impressions on my skin when we were done.

She had the most unusual colour eyes, blue-violet like a Siamese cat, and as I looked into them I recognised the resemblance to the fresh-faced girl I'd often seen in Maggie's family photographs. She'd certainly changed a lot since the last snapshots had been taken.

The young lawyer turned to Pete, beamed broadly, and then repeated the handshake, as she asked: 'Not quite what you were expecting, huh?'

Pete and I replied in contradictory unison.

'Yes, it is.'

'No, it's not.'

I glared at him, but Frankie Burrows was too busy laughing to notice. A pinstripe business suit wasn't what made you good at your job, although I suspected that was what Pete would have preferred to be seeing right now.

'Come in,' Frankie invited, motioning us further into the room. There was a desk and a filing cabinet in one corner of the office, but she led us towards a small seating area furnished with two bright orange settees that I recognised from my last visit to a well-known Swedish retailer. The building and the location might be questionable, but everything in Frankie Burrows's sparse office was spotlessly clean and looked brand new.

'It's very nice to meet you, Francesca,' said Pete politely.

'Frankie,' she corrected, nodding towards the settees. They creaked under our combined weight, but Frankie was so slight, she scarcely dented the one she sat down on. She was tiny, barely bigger than Noah, I thought, and we were tasking her with something enormous. Were we making a terrible mistake here? My doubts were multiplying, running away from me like escaped ponies, and I was pretty sure Pete was already mentally halfway back down the grubby staircase.

'I apologise for the surroundings,' Frankie said, waving one skinny arm in the air. There were at least two tattoos inked into her smooth white flesh. 'You know what it's like when you're just starting out.'

Pete flashed a worried glance my way. *She's too inexperienced*, it said. *This case is too big for her.* I kept my hopeful smile pinned in place even while I reluctantly agreed with him. But Maggie had been so sure about Frankie. She wouldn't have recommended her if she didn't think she was up to the job.

'So, it's quite a shitty situation you find yourselves in.'

It was an unexpected opening remark, which broke through the ice like a pickaxe. Perhaps this *was* the right place for us, after all. I'd given Maggie permission to tell her niece everything, and it was quite a relief not to have to go through it again, because each time I did my anxiety levels climbed a little higher up the chart. Pretty soon they'd be off the scale altogether.

'So, our meeting today is kind of like a blind date,' Frankie said, drawing her legs up beneath her, like a cat getting comfortable. 'If you decide you'd like me to represent you, our next meeting will cover all the formal rubbish we have to go through, but today I just want us to get to know each other and talk through exactly what we're getting into here.'

However unconventional her office or appearance might be, I felt a sudden rush of confidence. Frankie Burrows sounded like she knew exactly what she was doing, which was certainly more than Pete and I did.

'Your case against the clinic is rock solid,' she said with a nod of her head. 'Basically, they screwed up big time and we have their nuts firmly in a vice.' Her language was certainly colourful and I liked the way she made no apology for it. There was a family resemblance to Maggie here that went way deeper than just the shape of her nose or her unusual-coloured eyes. 'But I have to warn you that financial settlements have a nasty habit of dragging on and on – sometimes for years.'

'The money is unimportant,' Pete declared, a statement I felt sure our bank manager might disagree with. 'All we care about is how this affects Noah.'

Frankie sat back in her seat, her eyes clear, direct, and brutally honest. 'I'm not going to bullshit you. This case is a challenge, and very hard to predict. We have to assume the biological parents are going to put forward some sort of claim for shared custody or access.'

I swallowed, trying to ignore the taste of bile in my throat. This was our gravest fear, and hearing it coming from the mouth of someone who – I hoped – knew what she was talking about made it all seem horribly real. Pete's hand reached out across the orange seat between us, and I gripped it hard enough to turn his fingers white.

'We'll have no legal precedents to cite,' continued Frankie, shooting down my hopes for a straightforward conclusion with two loaded barrels. 'We're going to be making legal history with this one, guys.'

The look Pete and I shared went far deeper than just concern.

'We'll need to prove to the courts that Noah's best interests are served by staying where he is, in the sole care of the only two parents he has ever known. But until we know what the set-up is with the other couple, it's impossible to guess what we're up against.'

'Can you do it? Can you handle a case this big?' asked Pete, without a flicker of embarrassment at posing the question I'd been too polite to voice.

'I can,' Frankie assured him. She smiled. 'I want this. And I can do it.' She picked absently at one aubergine-coloured thumbnail. 'You could say you had me at "embryo mistake".'

'Can we afford you?' Pete asked, clearly working his way down a list of difficult questions he had mentally compiled.

'More easily than you can afford anyone else, I imagine,' Frankie batted back in reply. 'I'll keep the costs down as much as I can, and as you can see my overheads here are pretty low.' We both smiled fleetingly, the way I felt sure she'd intended. 'I'll apply for legal aid on your behalf, but whether we'll get it, and to what level, is impossible to guess.' She leant forward and reached for a small notepad, scribbling down a figure on it. 'That's only a ballpark figure, but it gives you an idea of what it will cost taking this to the Family Courts. She watched us carefully, but we were prepared. Our eyes might have widened a little but there were no embarrassing shrieks of dismay.

'Whatever it takes. However much it costs,' said Pete quietly, and in that moment I truly don't think I had ever loved him more. Which made it doubly ironic when Frankie cited the next potential problem.

'I understand from Auntie M that you two are currently separated?'

I flushed as if she'd uncovered a guilty secret. 'We are,' I admitted cautiously, as though tiptoeing barefoot across a floor of broken glass. 'Is that a problem?'

Her small bony shoulders shrugged revealingly. 'It might be. It depends how dirty the other side want to play things. And of course it depends on Bio Mum and Dad's set-up. Maybe we'll catch a break and find out *they're* divorced too.'

'We're separated, not divorced,' enforced Pete firmly, as though clearing up the world's biggest misapprehension. 'And… and we don't have to be.'

My head snapped to the right to find Pete staring directly into my eyes. Frankie Burrows could have left the room at that moment and neither of us would have noticed.

'Isn't that something we ought to discuss first?' My voice was a croaky parody of the one I usually used. But then again, Pete's didn't sound exactly normal.

'What is there to discuss? If living apart could potentially damage our claim to keep Noah with us, then we shouldn't be doing it anymore.'

I'd dreamt of this moment a thousand times or more over the last nine months, but never once in any of my imagined scenarios had I pictured my husband saying those words in a solicitor's office, in front of a total stranger.

'This is probably something you guys need to discuss in private,' Frankie interjected, looking suitably uncomfortable. 'But I won't deny it would be good to be starting off on a level playing field. Just let me know whatever you decide to do.'

There was a sense of the meeting winding up now, and she'd certainly given us plenty to think and talk about. But Frankie had one more disclosure.

'Before you make your decision about whether you want me to represent you, I should probably tell you that I've heard on the grapevine that the other party have engaged a highly respected legal firm to handle their case. But I don't want you to think that hiring fancy fat-cat lawyers who operate out of a swanky office is going to give them even the smallest of advantage. They can hire the most expensive team of suits in the country, but that's not what you need here. You need someone who'll fight like a tiger to keep your boy with you. You need someone who's not afraid to step into the ring for you, and who won't back down – and I won't. I'm scrappy, and that's what you're going to need to win this – a scrappy lawyer.'

We said nothing as we stood in the hallway and waited for the lift to arrive. I pressed the button for what had to be the third time, but all I could hear was an alarming clanking of metal parts coming from the shaft.

'Just to clarify,' began Pete, breaking the silence of the hallway. 'She said she was *scrappy*, not *crappy*, didn't she?'

How did he always manage to find a way to do that? To make me laugh when I felt more like howling? The smile was still lingering on my face when the lift finally arrived. Its doors swept open and the most appalling smell billowed out from the carriage.

'Stairs?' questioned Pete.

'Stairs,' I confirmed.

'About what you said in there.'

I'd waited until we were back in the car and heading away from the lawyer's office before the question burning through me like a forest fire could finally be asked.

'I said a lot of things in there. Which one are you talking about?' Pete asked, but I wasn't fooled by his feigned nonchalance. I'd seen the way his fingers had tightened on the steering wheel and the small revealing twitch of a muscle beside his mouth.

'About moving back into the house.'

His sigh was long and measured. 'You think it's a bad idea?'

I was rattled to have the question batted so swiftly back to me. 'I didn't say that. I just think it's a pretty important decision that we need to discuss properly.' Perhaps I'd picked the wrong moment to bring it up. The traffic was heavy and I knew Pete had only been able to get a couple of hours off work to attend our meeting that morning. The car swerved sharply to the left, but it was a deliberate manoeuvre as Pete changed lanes and then pulled over to the side of the road. He unfastened his seat belt and turned to face me.

'So let's discuss it.'

'What, now?'

'Why not now?'

I looked out through the windscreen, suddenly unable to meet the scrutiny in his eyes. 'This wasn't how I thought it would be.' My voice was a whisper, confessing to something I don't think he even knew I'd been feeling. 'If I thought about you coming back – *when* I thought about it, it would be because we both wanted to give things another try. Because we both realised we'd made a mistake.'

'I always thought we had.' His words snapped my gaze back towards him. 'Although I know you didn't,' he added sadly.

It was *a mistake – one I wanted to take back almost as soon as I'd said it. But you* agreed *to it; you* agreed *with me.* Why couldn't I say those words to him now? Even more crucially, why hadn't I said them nine months ago?

'All I know is that things are different right now,' Pete continued, unaware of my inner turmoil. 'If being a united family is what the courts need to see, then I *have* to come back. For Noah, and also for us. You *do* see that, don't you?'

I nodded dumbly, trying my best to hide the pain of hearing him saying all the right things for all the wrong reasons.

'So, this is just temporary. Is that what you're saying?'

'I don't have an end date, Izzy. I just know that we have the toughest challenge of our life ahead of us, and I think we need to face it side by side, not living on opposite sides of town. Besides, the money I'll save on rent will at least go some way towards paying Frankie's bill. If she's the one we decide we want to go with.'

He was changing the subject, and for once I was happy to let him do so. Our living arrangements were an insignificant drop in an ocean that was far too stormy to navigate alone. Pete needed to come back home right now, and I needed him for a thousand different reasons, most of which I would probably never reveal.

'Okay,' I said, turning my head and looking out the side window, so he couldn't see the tears suddenly filling my eyes. 'Come home then.'

14

Beth

The red light on my answering machine was blinking like a one-eyed dragon in the darkness of my lounge. There was only one person who still left messages on that machine rather than using voicemail. After six weeks of almost daily phone calls, I was no longer surprised to hear my father's voice when I pressed the play button, although initially it had felt distinctly odd. He'd always been more of a 'hang on, I'll just get your mother' kind of phone conversationalist.

I kicked off my shoes and curled up in the armchair as I reached for the phone. 'Hi, Dad. Sorry it's so late, I was catching up on some paperwork at the shop and lost track of time.'

'That's okay, sweetheart. I just thought I'd give you a quick call.' He coughed then, giving us both a moment to acknowledge that he was nowhere near as good at acting as my mother was. He feigned a casual nonchalance on every single call, which frankly had about as much chance of flying as a dodo bird. 'Just thought I'd call to ask how things are jogging along.' That was father-speak for: *How is it going with the lawyers? What are the latest developments?*

I smiled in the darkness. My dad was trying so hard to give me the space I'd asked for to handle this alone, and yet the need to be involved in the legal proceedings was clearly an itch he was finding it almost impossible not to scratch. Once a lawyer, always a lawyer, I guessed.

'Can't you just let him help you?' Karen had asked when we'd spoken about it a few days earlier.

'No, for all kinds of reasons,' I'd replied. There was no mistaking Karen's sigh of frustration, which travelled with perfect clarity all the way from Sydney.

'He *is* footing the bill for your legal team,' she pointed out unnecessarily, a sister's censure in her tone. Was that the real issue here, I wondered? Did Karen begrudge the amount of financial help our parents were giving me?

'I know that. And I'm going to pay them back every last penny, if that's what you're worrying about.'

'Of course it isn't. I just think he's feeling a bit left out of things. He still *thinks* like a lawyer.'

I sighed, acknowledging she'd hit the nail squarely on the head. 'I know he does, and that's half the problem. If I open that door even a crack, he'll be in there one hundred percent. And I don't think he should be getting stressed, not at his age. I might not be able to stop him worrying about me, but I'd rather he did it with his dad hat on, not his lawyer one.'

'When is it you're meeting with Patterson – that *is* the family law expert you're seeing, isn't it, Bethie?'

My lips twisted into a wry smile, which I tried to keep out of my voice. My father knew perfectly well which lawyer William Sylvester was bringing in to assist with my application for contact with my child.

'Next week, Dad. But I'll be speaking to you before then, I imagine.'

My dad coughed again, knowing he'd been rumbled. 'Yes, love, you probably will.'

By my fourth appointment with William Sylvester I stopped dressing as though I was going for a job interview. By then I'd realised I was never going to feel completely relaxed in that unfamiliar environment, so I might as well be comfortably dressed. Today I was wearing dark skinny jeans and a fitted white shirt. Externally, I think I pulled off 'smart casual' pretty well, but inside was a different story altogether. My heart always raced as I waited in the reception area for William's PA to escort me to his office. Just being in the building sent my system into a mini meltdown, with trembling legs and palms so sweaty that shaking hands was downright embarrassing.

Surprisingly, after that first encounter I'd never bumped into Liam Thomas again. I'd heard his voice once, talking in the distance to a colleague, and I'd caught a fleeting glimpse of his back disappearing into his office, but that was as close as we'd come to crossing paths over the past six weeks. Perhaps he knew the dates and times when I was meeting with William Sylvester, and was deliberately avoiding me. It was fine if he was, I told myself as my foot drummed out a nervous tattoo against the leg of a coffee table. It was probably far less complicated if we kept our acquaintance under wraps.

As usual, the sheer number of people waiting for me in William's office unnerved me. I had to keep reminding myself that these smartly dressed, sober-faced professionals were on *my* side. It was the other party who were supposed to feel nervous of them, not me. Family X, as my lawyers referred to them. Their identity was being scrupulously protected, William had told me, his expression sombre. I'd wanted to ask *Who from?* but I already knew the answer to that one. From me. In the eyes of Family X, *I* was the enemy.

With his customary good manners, William greeted me with a handshake and came around the desk to hold out an elegant upholstered chair for me. I settled into it and then greeted the other occupants of the room with a smile and a nod. In addition to the PA, who'd positioned herself in one corner of the room, laptop at the ready, there was a legal assistant who barely looked old enough to shave, who had a habit of blushing painfully whenever he spoke. Perhaps that's why he seldom did.

Occupying the fifth chair in the room was a man who could easily get a job moonlighting as a department store Father Christmas if the family law business ever dried up. Edward Patterson got to his feet, a rotund Humpty Dumpty of a man in a Savile Row suit. His shock of white hair and matching candyfloss beard drew your first glance, and it was only on your second that you saw the tempered steel in his cerulean-blue eyes. I'm sure I wasn't the first client to have seriously misjudged the sharp legal brain beneath the Santa Claus exterior.

'Beth, how *are* you?' Edward asked in a booming voice, sandwiching the hand I held out within his two beefy ones.

'Very well, thank you,' I answered, unable to keep a smile from my lips.

'Splendid, splendid,' he enthused, still holding my hand hostage. It continued to surprise me that every one of his comments wasn't finished off with a resounding *Ho-ho-ho.*

'Don't be fooled,' my father had warned me, when I'd given him my initial impression of the man who would be championing my application for contact with the courts. 'He's nothing short of a legend within the profession. If *anyone* can make this happen for you, it's Edward Patterson.'

The 'legend' eventually released my hand and settled his considerable girth back on a chair identical to mine, which I seriously hoped was sturdier than it looked. The focus of my meetings with William Sylvester was primarily on the case for negligence he was compiling against the clinic. I nodded a lot during those consultations, which shouldn't be confused with understanding what was going on, because most of the time I had no real idea what I was agreeing with. William was the kind of lawyer who should probably come with subtitles. He spoke fast, dropping in and out of legalese and Latin as though everyone was bilingual.

It was only on the sessions where Edward Patterson was in attendance that I truly felt engaged with everything that was being said. At our very first meeting, when I was still shell-shocked by what had happened, he'd cut straight through to the heart of the matter.

'What is it that *you* hope we will achieve, Beth?' he'd asked carefully, his features – which looked like they belonged on the front of a Christmas card – suddenly as unreadable as a professional poker player. They didn't even flicker when I cleared my throat and said 'Custody. I want to know how to get our child back.'

The other professionals in the room were nowhere near as adept at hiding their reactions. William had winced sharply, as if something very heavy had just been dropped on his toe, while the trainee's eyes had widened so much he'd looked like a cartoon character. But perhaps the PA's reaction had been the worst of all, because she'd just looked so incredibly sorry for me.

Edward Patterson's fingers had steepled together, and he'd leant as close as his beach ball stomach would allow him to get across the desk towards me. 'I'm going to be frank with you, Beth.' Sentences that begin like that are never likely to end well, and this was no exception. 'Custody of a child who has been born to another woman, and been raised exclusively by her for the last eight years, is highly unlikely.'

I'd looked at every face in the room in turn, as though seeking a different response, but they'd all worn carbon copy expressions of agreement.

'But it wasn't *her* embryo.' Even I could hear the childish petulance in my voice, but the injustice of it felt suddenly overwhelming.

Edward's eyes had softened then, and there was genuine sympathy in their brilliant blue depths. 'I'm not suggesting we give up before we've even begun, but there are certain truths and legal aspects that we simply cannot ignore.' I sat up straighter in my chair, my hands clasped so tightly that each finger had turned to the colour of bone. 'In the eyes of the law, the woman who gives birth to a child is legally the mother, and her husband is legally the child's father.'

'Even though – biologically – they have no connection to that child?' I argued, dismayed to hear thick threads of emotion in my voice.

'Even then,' he confirmed. He must have seen the desolation in my eyes, which was about to dissolve into tears, for he was quick to give me hope. 'But your circumstances are completely unique and because of that I feel we are in a good position to apply for shared contact. That is the route I suggest we pursue.'

'Unfortunately, Family X's lawyer has once again rejected our request for a meeting,' Edward advised, his head shaking regretfully, as though the offending lawyer was sadly now going to have to be put on the Naughty List.

My hands fisted with frustration. If these people weren't even willing to meet with us across a table, how would we ever reach a point where they'd be prepared to allow me to become part of my child's life? As ever, I winced inwardly at the sexless phrase. It seemed so wrong that I still had no idea if our embryo had grown into a girl or a boy. The thought was like a small electrical charge, galvanising me. I bent down and plucked my handbag from the floor. Edward Patterson was outlining his next proposed course of action, but for once I wasn't listening as I rummaged among the detritus that lived in the bottom of my oversized tote for the small white envelope I'd brought with me. I'd discovered it the day before, waiting on the coconut doormat of Crazy Daisy when I'd opened up for business.

My searching fingers finally located the envelope and I held it up like a football referee sending someone off. It had the desired effect as everyone fell silent. 'This was posted anonymously through my shop's letterbox yesterday,' I said, passing it to William.

'What is it?' he asked, his long elegant fingers already reaching below the flap to draw out the greeting card. There was confusion on his face as he looked down at the blue-coloured card in his hands. He studied the cartoon drawing of a stork with a newborn infant dangling from its beak as if it was a painting in a gallery that he couldn't quite understand.

'I don't get it,' said William, looking up from the card with a frown.

'Open it,' I instructed, my voice suddenly a little huskier.

'Noah,' he said, reading the name that was neatly printed below the cheesy verse inside the card. 'Do you know anyone of that name?' I shook my head.

William shrugged his shoulders expressively. 'I don't think this means anything. It could have simply been posted through the wrong letterbox. Perhaps it's meant for one of the neighbouring shops.'

The disappointment felt like a crushing weight, as though a small elephant had suddenly sat down on my chest.

'May I?' asked a voice that for once was missing its usual jovial tone.

The card looked lost in Edward's chunky fingers. He turned it over several times, as though looking for a hidden clue, and then spent a very long time staring at the handwritten name.

'Why would someone called Noah put this card through my door?' I asked, wondering if William had been right, and that it was all just a genuine mistake.

'I don't believe they did,' said Edward Patterson, carefully laying the card down on the desk before him. I could practically hear him saying: 'With the court's permission, allow me to present Exhibit A.' I shook my head to dispel the idea, but there was something in his eyes... something that was starting to make my heart pound.

'This card isn't *from* someone called Noah, it's *about* someone with that name.'

Edward's hands gripped mine for the second time that day, but I scarcely noticed, because I was staring unblinkingly into his ruddy-cheeked face.

'Noah is the name of your son,' he said gently. And then, in a much cooler voice, he turned to William Sylvester. 'And we, my friend, now have a very serious problem, because someone, somewhere, has leaked out highly confidential information.'

15

Beth

The meeting was cut short, and forty-five minutes earlier than expected I found myself back on the street, although I couldn't quite remember how I got there. It was hardly surprising because I'd taken in very little after Edward Patterson's shattering disclosure. A little boy. A son. Together, Tim and I had created a baby boy.

'Noah.' I said the name out loud for the very first time, and earned myself a startled glance from a passing postman. I smiled at him and shook my head, before saying the name again, no doubt upgrading my status from slightly odd to decidedly crazy. I didn't care. 'Noah. Noah. Noah.'

I started to walk, with no real idea where I was going. There was a thrum of excitement coursing through me that would have made standing still impossible. The name from the greeting card looped in my head, like a song on the radio that you can't shake off. It was a silent mantra, a rhythm my feet marched to as they took me away from the main road and down narrow side streets. Noah, Noah Brandon. My footsteps faltered and brought me to a standstill on a deserted street corner. No, no, that wasn't right; not Brandon. Our child obviously had a completely different surname, and if Edward Patterson knew it – which I suspected he did – he clearly had no intention of divulging it yet.

'I'm going to need to speak with Family X's lawyer as a matter of urgency,' he had declared, his voice grave. 'This obviously changes everything.' I had nodded emphatically in agreement, but when I saw the worried expressions on my legal team's faces, I could tell we were on totally different pages from completely disparate books.

Even William's PA looked distraught as she led me back along the carpeted corridors towards the reception, making me feel like the only person in a cinema who hadn't grasped the jaw-dropping twist of a film. I might have asked her to explain why everyone was so very concerned, but she was walking so fast it was all I could do to keep up with her.

I looked around me at the unfamiliar streets. I wasn't exactly lost, more misplaced. I'd been walking for fifteen minutes and could easily have retraced my footsteps, but instead I crossed the road ahead of me and carried on. A few minutes later I found myself at the entrance to a city park. Hidden away behind the tall buildings, it was a quiet green oasis for local residents and sun-seeking office workers. The gates were pushed open as if beckoning me in, and it seemed rude to refuse the invitation.

I hesitated for a moment at the entrance and then selected one of the grey ribbons of concrete walkway that meandered through the neatly mown grass. I walked with no destination in mind, happy just to feel the warmth of the sun against my back and a light breeze lifting the hair from my neck. I shared the pathway with red-faced joggers, dog walkers carrying unmentionable plastic bags, and mothers holding wobbly-legged toddlers by the hand. I also shared the pathway with my memories. Our early visits to the clinic, when we were still reeling with the news of Tim's diagnosis, were a place and time I rarely revisited. It was a time overshadowed with fear and although neither of us admitted it, we both knew we were banking on a future we might not have.

During the last six weeks, since I'd learnt about the clinic's mistake, I'd focused only on the error and the injustice, allowing those feelings to sweep me up and carry me along on a destructive riptide. But today, for the first time, I focused on the miracle that somewhere out there, a part of Tim still lived on. He wasn't gone... He was still here. All I had to do now was find him.

I've never believed in guardian angels, but someone out there was trying to help me; why else would I have been sent that card? And perhaps they'd sent me here too, to a park I never knew existed, in an area I didn't know well? Nothing is random. There's a reason for everything.

The path bent like a dog's leg up ahead, and as I rounded the corner the peaceful sound of birdsong was drowned out by an excited swell of young voices, punctuated by shrill blasts from a whistle. I lifted one hand to my eyes, using it like a visor to cut out the midday glare as I looked towards the football pitch. Twenty-two enthusiastic children, wearing bright yellow polo shirts, were careening up and down the field, while their teachers ran along the sidelines, bellowing out cries of encouragement. I'm not a football fan. Tim once joked he'd grow old and die before I ever understood the offside rule. His words had been horribly prophetic. But this was different. This felt so much like a sign that I even glanced skywards, as though looking for celestial confirmation.

I stared at the pint-size players on the pitch. How old were they, I wondered? To my inexperienced eye, they looked about the same age as my nephew Aaron – which would make them about the same age as Noah. He could be among them, I realised, he could be right there in front of me and I wouldn't even know. I was wondering what would happen if I called out his name to see if anyone looked up, when a name rang out clearly through the park. It wasn't Noah's, it was mine.

I spun around and saw Liam Thomas standing in a pool of sunshine, his suit jacket looped on one finger, hanging casually over his shoulder. 'Beth,' he said again, 'I *thought* it was you.' I glanced back almost longingly towards the football pitch before crossing the grass to reach the man who had a peculiar habit of turning up in my life just when he was needed.

'Hello, this is a surprise,' I said.

'It is,' he confirmed, bending low and grazing my cheek with a fleeting fly-past of his lips, so light I barely felt their touch. Even so, it took me by surprise. We were still in that weird no man's land, somewhere between formal handshakes and kisses hello. Or so I'd thought.

'Weren't you supposed to be meeting with Bill this morning?' he asked.

My face must have registered surprise that Liam was

familiar with my appointment schedule with his colleague. Was that why his cheeks suddenly took on a pinker hue, or was that simply due to the heat of the day? It really *was* quite warm.

'Something came up... and William cut the meeting short.' It still didn't feel right calling him Bill, but that wasn't what brought the furrowed lines of a frown onto Liam's brow.

'Is there a problem?'

I gave a small, helpless shrug. 'I don't really know. I didn't think it was a big deal, but then everyone acted like it was a real game changer.' I sighed. 'So now I'm just confused – and unexpectedly free in the middle of the day.'

I winced inwardly the moment the words left my mouth, because they sounded embarrassingly like I was angling for company, and then winced again as I realised that wasn't so very far from the truth. Fortunately, Liam didn't appear to have noticed, although he *was* looking genuinely concerned. I had to keep reminding myself that he was a senior partner in the firm handling my case. Obviously, he had a vested interest if we'd just hit a bump in the road.

'Someone sent me an anonymous card, revealing the name of my child.' A sudden suspicion grew from a minute seed to a fully fledged conviction in the space of a heartbeat. Liam's position in the company would certainly give him access to the case files. Was *he* the one who'd taken pity on me and decided that I deserved to know the gender of my own flesh and blood? It suddenly seemed to make perfect sense, but would asking him outright put him in an impossibly awkward position?

'Hmm,' Liam said, and even though I was studying his features for a clue, I couldn't read a single one. Never ever play poker with this man, I told myself; he was totally devoid of even the tiniest tell. 'Well, that could definitely complicate things.'

You did this, didn't you? asked my eyes.

His own had deepened almost to the colour of charcoal in the sunlight. *I have no idea what you're talking about,* they replied.

'Why does it complicate things? It was going to come out anyway, wasn't it?'

Liam drew in a long breath before asking: 'What did Bill say, exactly?'

'Not much. Although Edward Patterson mentioned talking urgently with the other party's lawyers.' As much as I tried not to, my voice never failed to grow colder whenever I spoke of the mystery couple who'd received our embryo.

There was clearly some inner conflict going on within Liam. I could see it in the small grooved lines between his brows and the tightening of his lips. He reached whatever decision he'd been battling with quickly and decisively.

'Walk with me,' he said, his words falling somewhere between a request and a command. I fell into step beside him, although after a few minutes of inconsequential chatter I began to think he'd changed his mind about discussing the case after all.

'There's a mobile lunch wagon a little further on. They do great sandwiches and baguettes – it's where I was heading when I saw you.' Liam looked at me, as though seeking encouragement. 'We could grab something to eat and find a quiet bench somewhere to talk?'

My head was asking if we couldn't just cut straight to the talk, but was overruled by my stomach, which couldn't quite get past the promise of great baguettes. I'd waited this long for information; I could surely hang on for a few more minutes?

On the walk to the sandwich van Liam took a firm hold of the conversation, steering it steadily onto neutral ground. He certainly seemed to know the park well, and pointed out several landmarks as we passed them, including its oldest tree and an oversized modern sculpture in the shape of a pear.

'I come here a lot with Sally,' he explained. 'Although her habit of stopping to smell every single tree is a bit time-consuming.'

I looked at him blankly for a moment, wondering who the hell he was talking about, before suddenly remembering the cute photo on his phone of the Jack Russell terrier he'd shown me six weeks ago. It felt like another lifetime.

'Ahh, your dog. For a moment I thought you were talking about a nature-loving girlfriend.' I liked the sound of Liam's laughter; it had a depth and richness to it that made me think of soulful saxophones playing in intimate jazz clubs. Tim would have liked the musical analogy.

Liam's eyes were still smiling, which was at odds with the confession on his lips. 'No girlfriend. Not now, not ever.'

It was a conversation stopper, but fortunately we'd arrived at the mobile sandwich van, and all I had to worry about for the moment was selecting one of the freshly made baguettes, which looked every bit as good as Liam had predicted.

While Liam took charge of the cardboard tray holding our drinks, I carried the bulging brown paper bag containing the food. We spotted a vacant bench and crossed the grass to claim it. The wooden slats felt warm against my back, but as pleasant as it was sitting in the sun enjoying an impromptu picnic, there was really only one thing I wanted to talk about. I managed only half of my lunch before returning to the topic that was monopolising my thoughts.

'The card that was sent to me…' I began hesitantly.

'The one giving you your son's name?'

The plastic drink cup was halfway to my lips, and froze there. 'I didn't tell you that I had a son. I never said it was a boy's name.'

Liam's eyes held mine, but as hard as I tried, I couldn't free the secrets locked in their depths. He was far too skilled at reading mine, though.

'It wasn't me, Beth. I'm not the person who sent you that card.'

'But you knew it was a boy,' I challenged.

There was a small flush on his cheeks. He reached for his own drink, buying himself time to formulate an answer. 'I admit I may have taken more of an interest in this case than I'd normally do.' He took a long sip and then set down his takeout cup carefully, as though the manoeuvre required all of his concentration. 'It presents a fascinating legal conundrum.'

'Oh.' My reply was heavy with disappointment. Perhaps that's why Liam unexpectedly declared: 'Damn it. That's not the truth… Well, it's not the *whole* truth. I feel… invested…

in this case. Invested in its outcome and what happens to you.' He looked strangely confused, and I don't think it was an emotion he was accustomed to feeling. 'I feel like we're connected, you and me, by the things we've lived through and the losses we've experienced.' There might be only two shadows falling onto the grass beside us, but it definitely felt as though there were now *four* people sitting on the park bench. Perhaps there always had been.

'I've read the case files,' Liam admitted. 'I knew that the child was a boy, but I truly didn't know his name. I'm not the one who leaked that information, Beth. Professionally, that would be really irresponsible of me.'

I nodded, finally believing that he wasn't my mystery benefactor. 'But why is it so bad that *anyone* has told me?'

Liam spoke with slow deliberation, as though carefully selecting each word before using it, to test its suitability. 'Any leak of confidential information can damage a case. The biggest challenge with yours, beyond the uncharted legal precedents, was always going to be keeping it out of the media for as long as possible. It's naïve to expect that the story would never break, it's far too newsworthy, but Bill's hope was always that he wouldn't have to make a public statement until *after* the case had gone to court.'

'But wouldn't going to the press strengthen my case? Wouldn't getting public sympathy actually help me?'

Liam's eyes, which had looked almost charcoal in the bright sunlight, burned now with something that looked like sympathy. 'It's impossible to say, Beth, but I know Bill was very worried that Family X's case might strike a more poignant chord. His fear is that it would strengthen their claim and maybe weaken yours.'

16

Izzy

My day unravelled slowly, like a pulled thread on an old cardigan. And I unravelled right alongside it.

A wedge of sunlight had found a gap in the curtains and was falling across my pillow. I rolled over leisurely and reached for the alarm clock, wondering how much longer I had until it went off, only to discover it should have woken me an hour earlier. 'One job. That's all you have. One bloody job,' I reminded the useless piece of technology as I catapulted out of bed.

Not bothering to slip on a dressing gown, I raced across the hallway to wake Noah, and collided straight into the solid wall of Pete's bare chest as he emerged from the bathroom. Droplets of water from the shower were still speckled like dew across his torso. Some transferred to the skimpy vest top I was wearing over a pair of briefs, my standard sleepwear when the weather was too warm for pyjamas. For one ridiculous moment, I almost crossed my arms to cover my semi-nudity, as if he was a lodger instead of the man who'd seen, touched and caressed practically every last centimetre of my body – even the bits of it I didn't particularly like.

We were only two weeks into our new living arrangement and there were still some major kinks that needed ironing out. Clearly, organising some sort of rota for the bathroom was going to have to be a priority. The days of Pete shaving while I showered, or brushing his teeth while I soaked in the tub, belonged to a past we'd never again recapture. I missed them.

'Where's the fire?' Pete asked, his eyes doing an involuntarily sweep upwards from my pink-painted toenails to my cheeks, which were fast turning the same colour.

'Overslept,' I mumbled, stepping around him like a roadblock and hurrying to Noah's bedroom. I had less than thirty minutes to get a sloth-like eight-year-old ready for school and out the door, but that's still no excuse for the way I snapped at him when I saw he was already awake and surrounded by a colourful sea of Lego pieces scattered across his mattress. In his hands was the model he and Pete had been working on together the night before.

'Noah, what on earth are you doing? We're late!' My exasperation was out of character, and I hated the way it wiped my son's cheerful good-morning smile from his face.

I stepped into his room and immediately trod on a particularly evil piece of Lego, which must have fallen from the bed. Its sharp edges punctured the soft skin of my sole and I swore angrily, teaching Noah a brand-new word to impress his friends with.

'Mummy swore,' snitched my son, just in case Pete hadn't already realised I was now in training for the 'Worst

Mother of the Year' award. He must have been standing right behind me in the doorway, because I could feel his breath fanning the exposed skin on my neck right beneath my ponytail when he spoke.

'Yeah, pal. But you know the rules about clearing up your stuff.'

Noah slithered off the bed in that curious boneless way that only those under ten seem able to achieve. 'And she shouted,' he muttered under his breath, managing to sound both shocked and indignant at the same time. 'I'm very disappointed.' It was the first time he'd used my preferred expression of reproach back against me, and at any other time, on any other day, I would probably have laughed. But not today.

'Mummy's got a lot on her mind right now, big guy, so why don't we go easy on her for a bit?' Pete suggested reasonably.

My eyes prickled uncomfortably with guilt and gratitude. I was in the wrong here – all three of us knew it, and yet Pete was still defending me; still on my side. I flashed him a small, grateful smile.

'Why don't I go and fix his breakfast while you get yourself ready?' he suggested, taking charge in a way that reminded me so much of all that we'd lost, it just made me sad.

'What *kind* of things are on Mummy's mind?' I heard Noah asking as they descended the stairs. There was a familiar giggle, which I knew meant Pete had pulled one of his funny faces, the kind that always made Noah crack up.

'Just silly grown-up stuff,' Pete replied, his voice fading

as they headed towards the kitchen. 'Nothing for you to worry about.'

I had the world's fastest shower and joined them in the kitchen just as Pete was directing Noah back upstairs to get dressed for school. I stopped in the doorway and pulled our little boy in for a hug, which he tolerated for longer than he probably wanted, just to please me. 'I'm sorry, sweetie,' I whispered into his sleep-tousled hair, before gently pushing him towards the stairs.

'I'd better go with and keep him on task,' said Pete, squeezing past me. We were chest to chest in the narrow doorway and I was enveloped in a cocktail of aromas that woke up far too many sleeping memories. My nose twitched as it isolated his aftershave. It was one I'd bought, and Pete used to save it only for special occasions. It was the fragrance of anniversaries, birthdays, and date nights, and it saddened me knowing he'd now downgraded it for everyday use.

A cup of coffee was waiting for me on the marble patterned worktop, and as I reached for it I caught sight of the slim white envelope I'd left propped up against the tiles. Within it was one of those 'silly grown-up things' I'd spent half the night worrying about. Despite her promise to keep the costs as low as possible, Frankie Burrows's first bill was very probably going to empty out my bank account.

Pete had turned to leave, but paused and looked back at me with an awkward uncertainty on his face. 'Er, I won't be back until very late again tonight. I'm not sure if you want or need me to tell you that kind of thing anymore.' I turned to face him, leaning back against the kitchen units with what I hoped looked like casual interest. We were living in a curious no man's land. We were back together, sleeping under the same roof, but in different rooms. The chasm of the narrow upstairs landing was our own Grand Canyon, separating the double bed we used to share from the single one in the spare room Pete now occupied.

I ran through a list of possible responses, from an inquisitive *Where are you going, and who with?* to a breezy *Have a good time*. In the end, I settled for a neutral 'Okay'.

Absently, I plucked up the envelope from our lawyer, turning it over in my hands as though I might be able to kaleidoscope the numbers in the total box to a figure I liked a little better.

'Don't worry about that bill, Izzy. We'll find the money from somewhere.' That was easy for him to say, as he stood there with his head full of his evening plans, but for me it was a vivid moment of déjà vu. Had Pete developed selective amnesia? Had he forgotten all those rows about money and unpaid bills? I hadn't, not when they'd been the axe striking the final blows to our marriage.

I shook my head, determined to replace an unpleasant memory with a happier one, which shimmered before me like a mirage. It had been a fortnight earlier, in this exact spot, when we'd given Noah the news that Pete was moving back home.

'Temporarily', we'd both emphasised in perfect unison, as though we'd rehearsed it. We were wasting our breath. Noah was focused only on the headline news.

'Dad's coming back?' He had practically danced around the kitchen with joy. 'This is the best news. The best news EVER. Can I tell everyone at school?' he'd asked, running excitedly between us, not sure who to hug first.

I had nodded meaningfully at Pete over the top of Noah's head, which was buried deep against my chest, and he'd taken his cue. 'It's only while they do some repairs to my building, champ,' Pete explained, using the lie we'd agreed on to explain his return. 'It's not forever.'

Noah's dark brown eyes had sparkled with joy, hearing only what he wanted to hear. 'I don't care why it's happened,' he declared, his small pointed chin – which he'd inherited from neither of us – jutting out determinedly. 'You're coming home, and I hope they *never* fix your mouldy old building.'

Here, here, I echoed silently.

Apart from Maggie, no one at work knew about what had happened. Frankie had recommended that we tell as few people as possible, and that was fine by me. 'These things have a nasty habit of circulating like Chinese whispers,' she'd told us. 'It's better for everyone if we keep this on a strictly need-to-know basis.' So when the call came through just after lunch and the lawyer's name flashed up on my phone screen, I was reluctant to pick up at my desk where I could be easily overheard. I swept up my mobile and went in search of a quiet spot to take Frankie's call.

The only room I could find wasn't empty, but I was pretty sure its occupants wouldn't spill my secrets. I opened the door and slipped into the canine hospital room. Only two kennels were currently occupied: I walked past one containing an elderly Jack Russell, who'd eaten something she shouldn't have, and stopped beside a forlorn-looking spaniel, who'd lost her litter of puppies. The dog looked up at me with sorrowful, watery eyes as I answered the call.

'Oh, good, you're there,' began Frankie Burrows, sounding relieved. 'I hadn't wanted to leave this on your voicemail.'

'Is something wrong?' I asked, already knowing there had to be, to have put that worried note in the lawyer's voice.

She answered my question with two of her own. 'Can you talk? Are you somewhere private?' I didn't think it was possible for my anxiety levels to climb any higher, and yet they managed to do just that.

'I don't want you to panic,' Frankie began uselessly. A sentence that started like that was a self-fulfilling prophecy. All bets were immediately off the moment those words were spoken.

'What's happened?' My voice was low and already quivering with emotion.

Frankie was blunt. 'We've got a problem. Someone has tipped off Bio Mum; she's been given Noah's name.'

I swayed on my feet, bumping clumsily into the cage beside me. The spaniel looked up and then got unsteadily to her feet.

'By who? How? I thought you said our identities would be protected – that she couldn't track us down?'

'To be fair, I don't think *she* did. Someone appears to have sent her an anonymous note. It looks very much like we've got a mole somewhere.'

Anonymous notes and moles; they were phrases out of a spy film, and had no place in real life. Except nothing about my life felt real anymore.

'I had a phone call from their family lawyer a little while ago,' Frankie continued, sounding more rattled than I'd ever heard before. I remembered her description of the bigwig lawyer the other couple had engaged, and wondered if he was responsible for the nervous timbre in her voice. David versus Goliath is a great story, but far less so if Goliath ends up slaying David. Once again, I seriously questioned whether we were with the right lawyer. 'They've requested a meeting with all the parties present.'

'But you said we shouldn't do that. You said our case deserved to be heard in a court. You told us we wouldn't have to meet the biological parents yet.' Despite my best efforts, I could hear the accusation in my tone.

'I know. And I still stand by what I said. We're not rolling over and giving in to their demands. This doesn't mean we're going to accept their proposal for shared contact. But I do think we need to hear what they have to say, and sooner rather than later. The next anonymous tip-off might not be to Bio Mum, it could be to the press.'

I felt cold, and then hot, and then very, very sick. I was leaning heavily against the kennel, one hand splayed against the wire mesh, as though to hold me up. Through the grid the spaniel's damp nose gently touched my palm. They say animals know things, that they can sense when people are in distress. I was a stranger to this small dog, and yet despite her own loss it felt like she was reaching out to comfort me. Was that why I started to cry, or was I always going to do that anyway?

'I don't want to see them. I don't want to see *her*,' I said irrationally. 'I don't want to meet the woman who's trying to steal my child.'

I liked how Frankie didn't tell me that I was being overly dramatic, or hysterical, even though I'm sure that was exactly what she was thinking. 'I know, Izzy. I'm so sorry. I just don't see there's any way we can avoid it now.'

I closed my eyes and laid my head against the dog's cage. Everything was beginning to spiral out of control; I could feel Noah already slipping from my grip. It had been my recurring nightmare when he was a toddler whenever we'd been anywhere crowded. It was the reason that every pocket or handbag I owned had at least one EpiPen in it. Stupidly, I'd thought those hysteria-driven fears were a thing of the past, but today they felt frighteningly close again.

'Would you like me to phone Pete and give him this news, or would you rather tell him yourself?'

'I'll tell him,' I shot back, surprising myself by the assertiveness of my reply.

'Okay. I'll be in touch then, as soon as we've fixed up a date for the meeting.'

'Fine,' I said, my voice flat. 'You do that.' There was nothing left to say, at least not to Frankie.

The spaniel's eyes held a look of reproach as she lay back on her blanket and drew the toy she'd been given against her belly. She nuzzled it, as though it was one of her lost pups, and then looked up at me with almost human understanding.

'I have to disappear. You understand that, don't you?' I whispered, my eyes so full of tears the dog was now just a blurry outline. 'They can arrange as many meetings as they like, but we're not going to be here to attend them.'

17

Izzy

'What sort of surprise?' questioned Noah again, from the back seat of the car.

I concentrated on pulling out of the tight parking space, before glancing back at him over my shoulder. 'If I told you that, then it wouldn't be a surprise, would it?'

I was driving a little too fast and probably erratically, so I forced myself to slow down. I didn't want to prang the car on our way home or, worse, get stopped for speeding. Although I managed to slow down my driving, the pulse throbbing at the base of my throat refused to do likewise.

I'd been the first mum at the school gates, pacing anxiously backwards and forwards across the playground as I waited for the bell to ring and the doors to open. For once, Noah had been the first one out, a practically unheard-of occurrence, which I took as a sign. I'd been looking for them all along the familiar route from the veterinary surgery to the primary school. *If every traffic light on my journey is green, then fate is telling me I'm doing the right thing. If they're red, I should stop and rethink.* I shaved a good ten minutes off my usual journey time, for every single light had read 'Go'.

There was a voice of reason screaming in my head saying that what I was about to do was madness, but I refused to listen to it.

I left Noah in the kitchen with a tumbler of milk and free access to the biscuit tin as I pounded up the stairs two at a time. The suitcases were kept in the spare room, and as I hauled them out from beneath the bed I could almost hear Pete's voice pleading with me to stop. His belongings were all around me; the smell of his aftershave still lingered in the air.

'I'm sorry,' I told the empty room. 'I have to do this. I have to keep Noah safe.'

I shut Pete's bedroom door firmly behind me, as though his possessions were watching and judging me, and ran to my own room. There was no sign of the woman Pete had once laughingly accused of packing with military precision, as I darted between wardrobe and chest of drawers, pulling out random items of clothing and throwing them into the case. When the bag could hold no more, I dashed to Noah's room and did it all over again.

Whatever I left behind we'd have to manage without, and in truth there were only two things I needed. I reached for them now, my hands scrabbling through the detritus of my bedside drawer until I found them. Noah's brand-new passport was like an unread book; its spine unbroken, each page a mystery of where it would take him. A mystery to me too actually, for I still had no idea where we were going.

I stuffed both our passports into the back pocket of my jeans. Just weeks ago, I'd have had no means of fleeing the country with our son. The only reason Noah had a passport was because Pete had been planning to take him to Cyprus. Unwittingly, he'd given me the keys for our escape. Everything happens for a reason, he'd once told me. I hadn't believed him at the time, but I did now.

It was only in the bathroom, when I stood before the open medicine cabinet, that I forced myself to slow down the supermarket-sweep-style packing and focus on what I was dropping into the toiletry bags. My eyes ran along the cupboard's glass shelves, scooping up inhalers, steroid sprays and an assortment of antihistamine medicines and creams. Noah hadn't needed most of them in months, but I was taking no chances. Who knew how difficult it would be to find an English-speaking doctor where we were going?

'*And where exactly would that be?*' asked the slightly crazed-looking woman staring back at me from the bathroom mirror.

'I don't know,' I confessed to her in a terrified whisper. 'Somewhere far away.'

Noah was young enough to feel only excitement as I thumped down the stairs carrying two bulging suitcases and announced we were going on a mystery holiday. By the time I was done, his case weighed considerably more than mine, because I'd squeezed in as many of his toys as I could until the zipper had protested 'no more'. But separating Noah from his belongings wasn't what was worrying me.

I tore a single sheet of lined paper from a ruled pad and began to compose my note. Even if I'd had hours to write it, I doubt I'd have been able to explain my actions to Pete in a way he would ever accept. I was under no illusions here. I was about to do something truly terrible: I was going to separate a boy from the father who adored him, and I'm not sure my reasons would ever justify my actions in Pete's eyes. He'd probably hate me forever for this.

I kept imagining the moment when he'd walk back into the house that night and find it empty. It would probably be late. Whoever or whatever had been occupying his time lately had been keeping him out until almost midnight. Would he assume we were both in bed when he let himself into the darkened house? Would he look in on Noah... and find him gone? It was hard to dispel the horrible image of Pete tearing through the house, throwing wide every door and calling our names into the echoing silence. It felt so horribly vivid, my breath was starting to hitch as I drew the paper towards me and began to scribble the short note that would break my husband's heart.

I can't risk letting these people take Noah away from us. Frankie will explain what's happened. I'm going to the airport and catching the first flight we can get on. I'll message you as soon as we're settled. I'm so sorry, but I can't think of any other way I can keep him safe.

My pen hovered above the lined page. Should I tell him that I still loved him? Was this my very last chance to do that? But how could I write those words when what I was about to do was certain to make him hate me? I settled instead for signing my name with a single X beside it, and two fat tear drops that would have dried long before he read the note.

***

'Planes!' exclaimed Noah excitedly as we drew closer to the terminal. 'Is one of them going to be ours?'

'Maybe,' I said, my hands tightening on the steering wheel as I followed the confusing direction signs to the various airport car parks. *Drop Off? Short Stay? Long Stay?* Curiously, there didn't appear to be one named *Never Coming Back*. A bubble of almost hysterical laughter rose up in my throat and I quickly swallowed it back down, afraid that if I lost control now, I'd probably never regain it.

It was early evening, but the terminal was still buzzing with activity. I found a trolley for our cases and let Noah push it as I studied the overhead departure board. The whole world was up there on the screen. We could go anywhere; disappear off the grid completely if we were lucky, but then what would we do?

I scanned the board, my eyes flitting from one destination to the next as I tried to imagine each one as our new home. Sweden? Italy? Istanbul? I knew no one in any of those places, and standing in the terminal among the bustling crowds of travellers, I'd never felt more alone in my entire life.

We joined the first line we came to. In the end, my decision was *that* random. Two passengers away from the check-in desk, I pulled us out of the queue.

'Let's go and get something to eat first, and *then* we'll buy our airline tickets,' I said, with the false cheeriness of a morning TV presenter.

I ordered burgers from a well-known chain and watched Noah devour his, while my own remained untouched. I

nudged my bag of fries towards him. 'Help yourself, kiddo.'
He munched contentedly on the chips, pausing only to ask
the one question I'd been dreading all afternoon. 'What
time is Daddy getting here?'

'I'm not sure, sweetie. Later, I think.' The lie stuck in my
throat like a swallowed marble, and felt just as dangerous.

It's impossible to say when I finally realised I couldn't go
through with it. Was it when the young family in the second
airline queue innocently asked us where we were going on
our holiday? Was it seeing families say goodbye at the gates,
tears rolling down their faces as they waved off their loved
ones? How could I do this to Noah? Or to Pete?

The sun was low in the sky, painting the huge picture
window in a mural of reds and golds. Noah was nose to
glass, transfixed by the constant flow of landing and taxiing
planes. We'd been standing there for quite a while, and
eventually I knew we'd have to move – locate whichever
car park I'd dumped the car in, and go back home. But
not just yet. As long as I remained inside the terminal, the
future I had planned to protect Noah was still possible.
Even though I now knew I could no longer claim it.

Noah was spreadeagled against the window, a small boy-
sized silhouette, but he spun around instantly the moment
his name was called. My head shot up, as did my heart rate,
as the name rang across the distance of the terminal once
again, cried out with an emotion I don't think I'd ever heard
in his voice before. A second name was called out. Mine. I
got shakily to my feet, as Noah shrieked out in delight.

'Daddy! You're here!'

Pete wasn't a runner, but he covered the distance of the terminal like an Olympic sprinter. Noah took off like a rocket towards him, cannoning into his dad, who'd dropped to his knees, arms outstretched to catch him. Pete was crying. I could see that even though I was too far away to hear him. His broad shoulders were shaking, and his face was burrowed into the soft fabric of Noah's T-shirt.

Eventually he released Noah from the hug, but remained on his knees as I joined them. I had a crazy flashback to the day he'd suddenly dropped down in the middle of a busy shopping centre and proposed. Tears had been in his eyes then, just as they were right now.

'I thought I was too late. I thought you'd already have gone.' His voice sounded broken, and the guilt hit me like a bomb blast, rocking me on my feet. *I'd* done this. *I'd* caused him this pain.

Tentatively, I reached out my hand and rested it on his shoulder. 'I couldn't do it. I couldn't go. I couldn't take him away from you.' Pete turned his head and buried it against the back of my hand. I could feel the wetness of his tears against my skin and heard him whisper huskily: 'Thank God.'

'Aren't we going on a plane, then?' asked Noah, clearly disappointed. He looked lost and confused. *Join the club, my love,* I thought miserably. I definitely had no idea what I was doing anymore.

Pete got to his feet and swept the back of his hand roughly across his eyes. 'You can still go,' he said, his voice low. 'If you feel it's the only option, then you should go.'

I shook my head sorrowfully, wondering when and how the tables had bizarrely turned. 'I couldn't do it, and I still

18

Beth

'I have some bad news, sweetheart. Your dad is still running a temperature. I don't think he's going to be well enough to go with you tomorrow.'

I sank down on the edge of my bed, pushing aside the dress I'd bought specifically for the occasion. The navy silk sheath was formal without looking too business-like. 'You'll want to look smart, but not stuffy,' my father had confirmed, when I'd asked him for advice. It was the last in an exceedingly long list of questions I'd had for him, ever since I'd learnt that Family X had finally agreed to meet with us. When Edward Patterson had asked if I'd wanted someone to accompany me, there was only one person in the world I could think of.

'At least it will even up the numbers on both sides of the table,' my father had said. I'd swallowed nervously at his words, because they sounded like we were getting ready for a battle, which I was already afraid was exactly what it was going to be.

'You're going to be there as my dad, not my lawyer,' I'd reminded him.

'I've been doing this for quite a few years now, Bethie,' he'd assured me. 'I'm not going to interfere. I'll be there to support you.'

Only now it seemed he wouldn't be.

The hotel foyer was grander than I remembered. My heels clicked noisily as I crossed the marble floor, heading for a discreet velvet banquette that would give me a clear view of the main entrance. I was far too early, but after having watched every single hour come and go through the night, I'd eventually given up all hope of sleep and was showered and dressed long before the birds had finished their dawn chorus.

I looked around me as the hotel's patrons spilled from the lifts or queued at the reception desk. Porters pushing shiny brass luggage trolleys wove like downhill skiers among the meandering guests, and my eyes followed every new arrival. Was Family X here already? Had they, like me, been unable to resist the urge to gain some small advantage by being the first to arrive for today's meeting, as though extra credit might be given for extreme punctuality?

I sat in the shadows, half hidden by an oversized display of stargazer lilies, and studied the guests around me. Were the couple arguing quietly in the corner the people Noah called Mummy and Daddy? Or was the harassed woman beside the pillar, who kept glancing anxiously at her watch, the person who kissed my child goodnight? I really hoped they weren't the stony-faced couple sitting at a nearby table, sharing a morning coffee but no conversation, because they looked totally devoid of warmth or humour. Our embryo deserved a better family than that.

Despite the morning sunshine, the twinkling glass chandeliers in the foyer were all fully lit. Prisms of light bathed the room in tiny rainbows, something I would probably have found enchanting on any other occasion; but not so much today. I knew this hotel through my work; I'd supplied the flowers for several weddings here, and yet I still felt as displaced and vulnerable as a refugee as I waited for my legal team to arrive. Both sets of lawyers had agreed it was better for this meeting to be held on neutral territory. Today, this stylish Victorian hotel would be our own version of Switzerland.

I looked up as the revolving doors began to turn, disgorging an excitable Italian family from one segment, an elderly gentleman with an ivory-capped walking cane from the next, and the man who'd agreed to join me today from the final compartment.

Liam scanned the foyer and I got to my feet with a grateful sigh. It wasn't that I hadn't believed he would keep his word; it was more that the intervening hours since I'd asked him had given me too much time to question if I'd made the right decision.

The bravado I'd pinned in place on the phone to my mum had quickly disintegrated when I thought of facing Noah's parents with an empty chair beside me. I'd heeded William Sylvester's warnings and hadn't breathed a word of my situation to anyone outside of my immediate family. It was too late now to regret the decision to keep my friends at bay. But now, with my father too ill to attend, I was left with no one to ask to take his place. Except that wasn't entirely true. There was one person I could ask – someone who'd already acknowledged that serendipity seemed determined to keep drawing us together.

Liam looked different today. His choice of clothes made their own unique statement. He was not here as a lawyer. He looked relaxed and somehow younger in the black shirt with its collar unbuttoned and no tie in sight. It went well with his black denim jeans. I felt a little overdressed in the blue sleeveless sheath, even though it was perfectly simple.

'You look very nice.' It was an excellent confidence booster, and at least managed to release a few of my facial muscles to form a smile. Once again, he bent to kiss my cheek, the warm citrus of his aftershave momentarily obliterating the aroma of the lilies.

'Thank you so much for agreeing to come today. I know it was a lot to ask.'

'Not at all,' said Liam kindly, nodding towards the banquette. 'Shall we sit down for a minute? We're still quite early.'

I could feel his gaze on me, quietly assessing, as he took in my restless hands and the incessant jiggling of my crossed legs. 'I'd suggest a coffee, but I've a feeling you might already have overindulged in caffeine this morning.' My lips twisted wryly. 'Did you manage to get any sleep at all last night?' Liam asked thoughtfully. He was either very perceptive, or the concealer I'd used to mask the dark circles beneath my eyes simply wasn't cutting it.

'Not much,' I confessed. 'So much is riding on what happens today. It was impossible to switch off.'

'Everything's going to be all right, Beth.'

'Is that a professional assessment, or a personal one?'

His eyes were kind as they looked into mine. 'A bit of both.' He paused for a moment as though testing to see if this was the right moment to lighten the mood. 'Bill was certainly intrigued when I told him I was planning on accompanying you today.'

'It's not a problem, is it? Does it compromise the case having you here?' Worrying that every small thing was a potential pitfall was quite frankly exhausting, but it was a habit I couldn't seem to get out of.

'No. Not at all,' Liam was quick to assure me. His grin returned as he added: 'Although I imagine it will be a hot topic of conversation in the office once word gets out I was here.'

I heaved a sigh of relief. People could think what they liked about Liam and me; we both knew there wasn't a shred of anything inappropriate happening here. We were both still spoken for.

Liam's phone vibrated in his pocket and he drew it out, his face impassive as he read the incoming message. 'That was William. He says they're ready for us in the meeting room now.'

I gave a nervous start. I was still waiting for them to walk through the doors, but apparently everyone was already here. It was time, and I wasn't ready. I wasn't even close.

'The other people... Couple X... are they up there already?'

'No. They're waiting in one of the smaller lounges. William will call them up when you're settled and ready.' I must have looked like a scared rabbit, trapped between lanes on a motorway.

'They might be in for a long wait.' I'd meant it as a joke, but it sounded instead like a prophecy.

The booked meeting room was on the fourth floor, and without Liam's hand at my back guiding me towards the lifts, I truly don't know if I'd have persuaded my legs to take me there instead of to the exit. *This is the worst moment,* I thought, as I stepped shakily into the shiny mirror-walled carriage. This is when, more than anything, I missed my father's calming presence. He'd have known just what to say to ease my tension.

In every direction I looked, I could see multiple reflections of a tall, handsome man, dressed all in black, and a terrified-looking woman, whose eyes appeared to be three times too large for her face. Liam and I stood shoulder to shoulder, heads tilted upwards to watch the ascending numbers light up on the overhead panel. I've always been slightly claustrophobic in lifts, and more than a little relieved when the doors eventually slide open. So it was strange to find myself actually willing this one to break down. Of course, it did no such thing. As it pinged to announce our arrival on the fourth floor, my hand reached out of its own volition and clasped Liam's. His fingers immediately circled around it.

'You don't mind, do you?' I asked. My hand was holding his with such a death grip that unless he happened to have a concealed crowbar about his person, he wasn't going to get rid of me. I couldn't remember the last time I'd held a man's hand in mine. It had been a while.

'Of course not,' Liam replied, squeezing my fingers gently before guiding me down the corridor to where the others were waiting.

William's face registered a flicker of surprise and I knew he'd seen our linked hands, even though we'd separated the moment we'd crossed the threshold to enter the meeting room. Edward Patterson greeted us warmly, but for once his Yuletide-like cheer had lost its power to make me smile. The only other occupant of the room was William's PA, Keeley, who was poised at one end of the boardroom table behind a laptop. She flashed me a fleeting look that was full of sympathy. I noticed that her face appeared pale under the bright overhead spotlights, turning her normal peach-coloured cheeks to a sallow yellow. I imagined I looked even worse.

Keeley got to her feet and poured out glasses of water from a crystal jug, before sliding a typed document in front of each of us.

'This just outlines the points we've previously discussed,' assured Edward, as I frantically began thumbing through its pages, as though cramming for an exam I'd forgotten to revise for. I nodded, and drained half my glass of water in a single gulp. I caught a look I probably wasn't supposed to see between William and Liam.

'Okay then,' said William, his voice betraying just a hint of eagerness. I could tell he was psyched for this, like a racing driver revving up on the starting grid. There was a coiled-spring readiness about him as he reached for his mobile and punched out a number. 'Let's ask the others to join us, shall we?'

19

Izzy

'I should have worn the black one. The red looks too frivolous, as if I'm going to a party or something.' I plucked nervously at the sleeves of my cardigan, which I was now regretting having chosen to wear for the meeting with our son's biological parents.

'I doubt anyone today will be judging us on our clothing,' remarked Pete dryly, unconsciously running his finger around the collar of his shirt, as though it was attempting to strangle him.

'Says the man in the suit, which he normally only wears to weddings and funerals.'

Pete turned in the driver's seat and flashed me a sheepish grin. 'Touché,' he replied. His eyes dropped to my plain black pencil skirt and sleeveless silk shirt. I didn't look like me, and I didn't need to read the corroborating expression on his face to know that. He smiled slowly, not at me, but at the cherry-red cardigan. 'I've always liked that one. The colour really suits you.'

I bit my lip and turned to look out the side window to

hide the effect his words had on me. So much of my past was tied up with this man. He shared a history – not just with me, but even with the clothes hanging up in my wardrobe. How would anyone else ever know me this well? Would I even want them to? It was too big a question to think about right now, when there were so many others claiming my attention.

I switched my gaze to the majestic-looking Victorian hotel that filled our field of vision through the car's windscreen. We'd been parked outside it for forty-five minutes, as though it was a joint we were casing for an impending heist. I don't think I could have felt any more nervous if we *had* been planning to burgle the place. Sooner or later one of us was going to have to summon up the courage to suggest we actually *got out* of the car and went inside.

'Do you think they're in there already?' I asked nervously.

'I don't know. Possibly.' He knew I didn't mean the lawyers who'd set up this appointment. As intimidating as I'm sure they would be, *they* weren't the ones responsible for the dark circles beneath my eyes, or the string of untouched meals over the last few days.

Pete sighed deeply. 'Well, I for one am looking forward to finally meeting them face-to-face. I'm fed up imagining how I'll measure up against some super-dad, action-hero father. I'd rather know *exactly* who we're dealing with.'

'Would you?' My voice was as fearful as the expression in my eyes. 'I'd prefer it if I *never* had to meet this woman, her husband, or their fancy-pants lawyers.'

I pulled down the sun visor and once again checked my reflection in the small mirror fixed to its underside. It didn't seem to matter how many times I pinched my cheeks, they still looked scarily white. I looked like the ghost of a woman who *used to be* Noah's mum.

'*Fancy-pants*, Iz? Really?' Without even looking at him, I knew Pete's lips would be wearing a teasing smile. 'Do people still say that?'

'This "people" does,' I said, snapping the visor shut on my ashen reflection. I knew what he was doing – trying to lighten my despair and inject some normality back into our lives when everything around us was tumbling like skittles. He'd always been good at that, but this time I didn't think the familiar technique would work.

My phone, which I'd left on his dashboard, began to twitch and vibrate against the black vinyl surface. I opened the incoming message, while my heart tried to find a way to break free from my ribcage. 'It's from Frankie,' I announced unnecessarily to Pete, who was unashamedly reading over my shoulder. 'She's waiting for us now in the foyer.'

Pete was out of the car and holding open the passenger door before I'd even unclipped my seatbelt. He was every bit as anxious as I was to have this meeting over and done with; we just had different ways of showing it.

The hotel was far grander than any I'd visited before. In truth, I was more of a Premier Inn person, and the marble pillars, crystal chandeliers and liveried doormen made me feel like a misplaced extra from a *Downton Abbey* episode. I was grateful for Pete's large, warm hand tightly holding onto mine as we entered the opulent reception.

Frankie was easy to spot across the width of the foyer. An establishment like this probably didn't see too many patrons who favoured pink-tipped hair, a leather skirt and biker boots. She looked up from her phone, finished whatever message she was composing, and beckoned us over. The marble floor gleamed like an ice rink beneath our feet, and my kitten heels clicked noisily like tiny hooves as we crossed it. By the time we reached Frankie's side, I was practically walking on tiptoe.

'Hi, guys,' she greeted us, with a warm smile and a quick hug. 'We're still a little early, so I thought we could wait down here.' Her hand was at my back, exerting firm but gentle pressure against my spine. She was walking with purpose, and suspiciously fast.

'It's this way,' she explained, casting a quick glance over her shoulder as she guided us along a carpeted hallway leading away from the foyer. A small frown crumpled her brow when I slowed down.

'They're back there, aren't they, the other parents? They were in the foyer.'

Pete was also frowning, clearly wondering what he'd missed. In reply, Frankie gave a single sharp nod and then steered us through a pair of double doors into a reception room. 'They've booked a meeting room. That's where they've decided you should be introduced. They'll call us up as soon as they're ready.'

Frankie's bright, maximum wattage smile didn't fool me for a minute. She didn't like the way the other lawyers were taking charge of events any more than I did. This venue had obviously been *their* choice, rather than hers. Was this how it was going to be? Were they already asserting their authority and trying to intimidate not just us, but also our young lawyer?

With surprising astuteness, Frankie read each one of my

unspoken fears, as if they were tattooed on my forehead. 'Don't worry,' she said as she led us to a bay window where three wing-backed armchairs were positioned. 'Don't let them rattle you, because they sure as hell won't be doing that to me. We've *still* got the stronger case here, and they know it.'

Pete smiled and nodded, hearing only the words sitting on the surface of the conversation and not the worrying subtext ticker-taping beneath it. While we waited to be summoned, Frankie took the opportunity to run through her list of dos and don'ts one last time.

'Basically, say nothing. Do nothing. Agree to nothing. Let *me* do all the talking. And just remember, we're only here today to listen to their proposal. We're not agreeing to a single thing. Unless of course they suggest dropping their claim. We'll agree to *that*!' She laughed and then stopped abruptly as she caught sight of our hopeful expressions.

'Erm, that's probably not going to happen, guys. Sorry. Bad joke.' For the first time that day, Frankie looked less than comfortable. That expression was still on her face when her phone pinged with an incoming message a few seconds later. She read the screen and then looked up, her eyes glittering with anticipation. 'That was them. They're ready. It's showtime.'

20

Beth

She was shorter than I was expecting, and the kind of thin that makes you think she got that way through dieting rather than by nature. Her husband – I assumed they were married, although no one had ever confirmed it – was tall and solidly built, with a rugby player's physique. He looked like someone who worked outdoors; he certainly looked uncomfortable in the suit and tie he was wearing, because his fingers kept going to the collar of his shirt as though he'd mistakenly bought one two sizes too small. In contrast, Liam looked supremely relaxed and at ease, but then of course he would. The outcome of today's meeting wouldn't impact his life in the way it would ours.

A third figure entered the room with my son's parents, and in any other circumstance she would have been the one who would have drawn my attention because she looked as if she might possibly have wandered into the wrong room, or even the wrong hotel. Her jet black spiky hair, feathered with bright pink tips, gave her the look of a dangerous raven. There was a tattoo on the back of her wrist, just visible as she extended her hand to her suited counterparts. William was far too professional to register surprise at her unconventional appearance, although I imagine not many lawyers have ears so heavily pierced they appear to have run out of flesh and cartilage to decorate.

At William's invitation, everyone sat down. In the seconds before anyone spoke, the sheer incongruity of the meeting struck me like a rock thrown through a window. Apart from my own lawyer, everyone looked like they were in the wrong place. Couple X's lawyer looked like she should be at a comic book convention; Edward looked like he should be in a grotto surrounded by elves; Liam should be abseiling down a building to deliver a box of chocolates; while Couple X and I looked like we should be anywhere else on the planet... except here.

Introductions were made from our side of the table first. William had already instructed me that surnames might not be revealed initially. But being introduced as 'Beth' felt far too informal, as though we were at a pleasant social gathering and would soon be chatting about the weather we've been having lately. You only needed to look into everyone's eyes to see that was clearly not the case. No one made any move to shake hands, which seemed to be as much of a relief to the other couple as it was to me.

Liam had jumped in to perform his own introduction before William could do the honours. 'I'm Liam. I'm here as a friend of Beth's, but am not directly involved in her application.'

On the other side of the table, the woman who looked in need of several hearty dinners flinched, while her husband remained unaffected, or so I thought until I glanced down through the thick plated glass of the tabletop and saw that his hands were balled into fists on his knees. That didn't bode well.

'I'm Frankie Burrows, and I represent Couple X,' informed the young female lawyer. She glanced at her clients and I caught her giving them a small smile of encouragement. 'Who in real life go by the names of Izzy and Pete.'

The keyboard clattered quietly as Keeley's fingers flew over her laptop, minuting the meeting. I'm sure she accurately recorded the comments made by both sets of lawyers, but there was no way she could have logged the fear and mistrust that hung over the table like a toxic cloud.

'Before proceeding,' began William smoothly, 'I should inform you we've now received a preliminary report from the Westmore Clinic investigation.' Everyone immediately sat up straighter, like meerkats on alert. William reached for a file and extracted a document from within it. I recognised the clinic's logo on the front cover. 'There's a copy for each of you, but to precis the findings, the clinic now acknowledges negligence.'

On the other side of the table, the man who Noah called Daddy made a noise that sounded like an angry bear. William paused for a beat before continuing.

'We already knew *what* had happened, so the report focuses on the how and the why. Unsurprisingly, the conclusion they've reached is that human error was to blame. Your names were similar.' William looked up from the document in his hands, his eyes going to the couple on the other side of the table. 'I believe you were still using your maiden name at that time?' The thin woman with the terrified eyes gave a curt nod. 'Eliza Bland and Elizabeth

Brandon – they *are* similar, but if the clinic had followed their own protocols and ensured that the removal of the embryo had been witnessed by a second embryologist, the mistake would have been spotted.'

'That's not good enough.' The words burst from Izzy like gunfire.

'You're right, it isn't,' agreed William. 'You all deserve better answers than that, but in reality we may never get them.' His eyes dropped again to the document in front of him. 'The clinic have discovered that the embryologist responsible for the error, Melanie Cuthbert, may possibly have been suffering from post-traumatic stress. Apparently, she witnessed a fatal car accident on her way to the clinic that morning.'

'Then she shouldn't have been at work that day,' I said fiercely. Across the table, Pete and Izzy were nodding emphatically. It was, I suspected, one of the only times we might ever be in agreement about anything.

Beside me, I was aware that something had caused Liam to stiffen in his seat. From my peripheral vision, I saw him reach for the document on the desk and draw it towards him, his focus on the date of the clinic's mistake. I had no idea what had snagged his attention.

Meanwhile, William's voice was smooth and placating. 'Obviously, our claim is against the clinic, rather than any one individual. Although the board at Westmore were at pains to reassure us that Ms Cuthbert is no longer an employee of the clinic.'

'As it's highly unlikely my clients will ever use Westmore Fertility Clinic again, that's kind of irrelevant,' interjected Frankie, giving Izzy a reassuring nod and a fleeting smile.

'We've already made arrangements for their remaining embryos to be transferred to another facility.'

Her words felt like a knife stab. Izzy and Pete still had *other* embryos, other chances of a family, while my one and only opportunity had gone.

The lawyers took over the meeting from that point, both sides filling the air with words, without saying anything at all. As we skirted around the reason this meeting had been called, Edward's voice deepened with authority and gravitas. Frankie Burrows's comments were less orthodox and although I probably wasn't meant to admire her feistiness, part of me did. As long as it wasn't going to get in the way of what I hoped we'd be able to achieve.

After a particularly 'difficult to follow if you've never been to law school' comment of William's, I could sense the mood on the other side of the table begin to change. Frankie Burrows leant forward, the collection of silver bangles on her wrists jingling against the table's glass surface. 'Let's cut... to the chase,' she said. Everyone in the room knew she'd substituted the words 'the crap' from the end of that sentence at the last moment. 'What is it that your client wants?'

I hadn't known I was going to speak over the top of William until the words were tumbling out of my mouth. 'I want to get to know my child. I want to be part of his life.'

Izzy made a sound halfway between a gasp and a cry of denial. Her head was shaking fiercely from side to side, causing her hair to flay against her husband's cheek with each emphatic unspoken 'no'.

'I didn't even know if we'd had a son or a daughter until

someone leaked that information,' I said desperately.

'Yes, about that—' began Frankie, clearly looking for a diversion, but she was stopped by her own client.

'That's because *you* didn't have a son or a daughter,' said Izzy. Her voice was tight and very controlled. 'I did.'

'It was my embryo,' I said, my voice rising with emotion. Very subtly I could sense Liam leaning a little closer towards my chair.

'Which grew into *my baby*.' She turned to look at her husband, Pete, who was nodding encouragingly, his eyes overflowing with admiration. 'Our baby. Our child. Our son.'

Izzy drew in a deep, steadying breath before continuing, scything me down with every single word.

'I'm very sorry for what happened. I know it's not your fault. But we've been hurt by this every bit as much as you have.'

'Hardly,' I muttered darkly. Beside me, I could sense the lawyers were looking for the right moment to intervene and wrest back control of the meeting.

'I don't want to sound heartless, but your position is no different from anyone who donates unwanted embryos to infertile couples. Yes, the clinic made a dreadful error, and we both have a case against them for that. But you do not have any rights to our child.'

I heard Liam's indrawn breath at exactly the same moment as Edward began to speak, but they were lost beneath what Izzy must have thought was her winning argument.

'You and Liam can have other babies together. And I hope you do. I hope your next round of IVF is a success. But that still doesn't entitle you to be part of our child's life.'

There was so much that she clearly didn't understand. Not least of which was her assumption that Liam was the biological father of the embryo she'd received eight years ago. That one at least I could correct.

'Liam is not my partner. He's just a friend. The embryo that should have become my son was frozen ten years ago by my husband and me.'

Izzy's face drained of colour; I watched it ebb to a sickly shade of white. It was almost like she knew what was coming next.

'We froze our embryos before my husband began his cancer treatment. We had one last one left in storage. Or so I'd always believed.'

Izzy's eyes went to Liam and then back to me.

'My husband's treatment wasn't successful. I lost him five years ago. That final embryo was all I had left. It's the hope I've been clinging to since the day he died. Everything else is gone – our future, our dream of growing old together, the family we wanted to have.' My voice was breaking now, but I couldn't hold back the tears if I tried. 'All that was left was one last chance to have our baby. And they gave it to you instead of me.'

I'm not sure if it was my lawyers or theirs who suggested we should take a short break. The atmosphere in the room was so highly charged with emotion it felt practically combustible.

'Shall we meet back here in thirty minutes?' suggested William. Frankie Burrows, who was busy shepherding her clients out of the door, looked back over her shoulder and nodded tersely.

I counted to thirty, giving Izzy and her husband more than enough time to have cleared the corridor before getting shakily to my feet. I wasn't used to confrontation and felt physically drained by the scene we'd just been through.

'I'm about to phone down for coffee,' said William as he saw me grappling for my bag.

I shook my head. 'I need some fresh air.'

I could see Liam getting to his feet, but motioned him back with my hand. Someone was saying something, but their words were a distortion of garbled noise. I imagine they were trying to dissuade me from leaving, but I was focused only on the door and my need to get through it before I was physically sick with reaction.

Thankfully, the corridor was empty, but I didn't want to risk bumping into anyone in the hotel foyer, so I followed a sign for the emergency exit stairwell. Despite the heels and tight-fitting dress, I was still halfway down the second flight of stairs before Liam caught up with me.

'Beth!' he cried, as his hand shot out to circle the flesh of my upper arm. From the urgency in his tone, I doubt it was the first time he'd called my name. His grip unbalanced me and I stumbled forward, feeling the bite on my skin as his fingers tightened their hold, steadying me.

'Careful,' he warned, his voice jagged with concern. 'You almost fell.'

'Only because you grabbed me,' I shot back, my heart racing at twice its usual pace at the near miss.

He had enough good sense not to pursue that argument. 'Just slow down for a moment. Please,' he pleaded. His eyes appeared almost black in the unnatural fluorescent lighting and were overflowing with the kind of compassion that could very easily undo me. I was on a dangerous cliff edge, holding on by only the tips of my fingernails, but I had to pull myself back up. I couldn't let him help me.

'Let me come with you,' he implored, already knowing I was going to say 'no'. It was strange that this man who I hardly knew understood me better than perhaps even my own family did. We'd both unwillingly travelled to a place few people our age had visited, and the journey had changed us in ways that still took me by surprise. I could feel the bond between us subtly tightening.

'Just tell me this: are you coming back?'

I nodded fiercely before asking a question of my own. 'It's not going to go our way, is it?'

Liam took his time, making me wonder how many discarded replies he'd considered before admitting: 'Feelings were always going to be running high.' It was a politician's answer, and my raised eyebrows told him exactly what I thought of it.

'It could have gone better,' he admitted soberly. He looked at me for a long moment. 'I'll see you back upstairs.'

Despite my craving for fresh air, I remained on the stairwell, watching as Liam climbed back up the stairs he had just raced down to reach me. I almost called him back, not just once, but several times. His name was still on my lips waiting to be set free when he finally disappeared from sight.

Memory led me to my destination, taking me down to ground level and then along a winding passageway until I arrived at a set of steel service doors. I pushed them open and stepped into the warm sunshine-filled oasis of the hotel's courtyard garden. It was an area I'd decorated several times with garlands of flowers woven into trellised archways for outdoor weddings. Luckily, none appeared to be scheduled today, for I shared the courtyard with no one except a few milling pigeons.

Like a diver breaking the water's surface, I lifted my face to the sky and inhaled deeply, drawing in serenity – or as close to it as I could get – in huge restorative gulps. I didn't open my eyes for at least a minute, allowing the warmth of the sun, the breeze lifting my hair, and the fragrance of flowers from the rose garden to recalibrate and steady me.

These were the moments when I still felt Tim beside me – not in a creepy *'I see dead people'* way, but in a deep, almost elemental manner, connecting with nature. The breeze against my cheek was his breath as he lay beside me at night; the sun's rays warming me were his arms circled around my waist; and the whispered stirrings of the foliage were our softly spoken secrets.

I missed him suddenly with an intensity that made it hard to breathe. 'I don't know how to do this without you,' I confessed to the empty courtyard. 'I'm not even sure if I'm doing the right thing anymore. Is this what you'd want? I wish you could tell me, or give me some kind of sign.' I looked up at the thick fluffy clouds chasing each other across a bright blue sky, but there were no meaningful images hidden among their cotton wool depths; they were just clouds.

Fifteen minutes later, I reluctantly forced my sun-warmed limbs off the bench I'd claimed and prepared to return to the fourth-floor meeting room. The back of my neck was prickly with perspiration, and I was definitely in need of a ladies' room to freshen up before facing Noah's family again.

I rode the lift to the fourth floor alone, acknowledging too late how much harder it was without the comfort of Liam standing beside me. Maybe I *had* been too quick in dismissing him, I thought, as my hand slipped clammily on the handle of the door bearing a woman's silhouette.

The washroom was blissfully cool. The sound of my heels ricocheted off the marble walls and floor as I crossed to a row of gleaming white basins. Ignoring the lure of a padded velvet bench, I rummaged hurriedly in my make-up bag at the vanity area. After some quick repairs, I gathered up my scattered cosmetics and bundled them back into the bag, sighing with irritation as my mascara rolled off the shelf and onto the floor. I bent to retrieve it and noticed something crumpled on the marble behind the velvet bench: something soft, woollen, and bright red in colour. I picked it up, already knowing where I'd seen the garment before: looped over Izzy's arm when she'd left the meeting room.

My eyes flew to the row of cubicles set at a discreet distance from the basin area. At first glance they'd appeared to be vacant, but now I looked closer I could see that the door to the stall at the end of the row was shut. I reached for my runaway mascara and threw it into the bag. The very last thing I wanted was to have a face-to-face encounter with Izzy in the ladies' room, but the sound of a sliding bolt told me that was exactly what was about to happen.

Her eyes widened when she opened the cubicle door and saw me. She walked with staccato shaky steps towards the basins. Izzy said nothing, but her eyes were locked on me in the mirror, as mine were on her. There was a sheen of perspiration covering her face, giving her a cheese-like pallor, which I'm sure wasn't the look she'd been aiming for that morning. She set the cold tap to full blast and scooped up a handful of running water, using her palm as a cup to rinse her mouth.

I took a step back, knowing how much she must hate me seeing her at her most vulnerable. For just a moment a feeling of pity washed over me, as I remembered how I too had felt physically nauseous after our confrontation. I didn't want to feel sympathy for this woman who was effectively my adversary, but it was almost impossible not to. *Walk away. This is none of your business*, I told myself. *This has nothing whatsoever to do with you.* And yet it was impossible to leave the room.

'Are you all right?' I asked awkwardly.

Again, her eyes were fixed on my reflection, as though communicating through the mirror could somehow defuse the potentially explosive situation we found ourselves in.

'I'm fine,' Izzy declared, which was clearly a lie as I'd never seen anyone look less fine in my entire life.

'Would you like me to fetch your husband?'

She looked surprised, and seemed to take a very long moment before shaking her head. 'No. But... but thank you for asking.'

I fidgeted uneasily behind her, passing the soft wool cardigan from one hand to the other. The movement caught her attention and her eyes fell upon her lost item of clothing. This time she did turn around. I was taller than her, but felt immediately dwarfed in her presence in a way I couldn't begin to explain.

'Is that mine?'

I looked down, almost surprised to find the garment was still in my hands.

'Erm, yes, I think it is. I found it on the floor behind the seat.'

Her green eyes locked unblinkingly on mine. Very slowly she held out one hand.

'I *was* about to return it,' I said, still clutching the folds of fabric tightly between my fingers. The temperature in the washroom was already air-conditioned cool, yet I could have sworn it dropped then by several degrees.

'I'm sure you were. You seem honest. Trustworthy.'

The compliment sounded genuine, but to trust it would make fools of us both.

'You don't know me, or what I'm like,' I countered.

For a moment, I thought I saw a ghost of a smile pass over her lips. She nodded slowly in acknowledgement. 'That's true, I don't. But I have good instincts, and mine tell me that you're a decent person. The kind of person you can rely on to do the right thing.'

The lawyers would go crazy if they knew what was happening right now, just two doors down from the meeting room. For a start, I was pretty sure it was forbidden for Izzy and me to be alone together, much less be talking to each other like this.

Her green eyes were magnetic, and as much as I wanted to, it was impossible to break free from her gaze. Her hand was still outstretched, waiting, but when I passed her the cardigan I hesitated before releasing it. In the wall of mirrors I could see our reflection, locked in the moment with the garment stretched between us, as though we about to play tug-of-war. I don't imagine the symbolism was lost on either of us.

Izzy pulled the garment, and held it against her slender frame. 'I guess we both have to do what we have to do, Beth.'

Weirdly, there was a feeling of sisterhood in her words. In other circumstances, in another lifetime, I could imagine myself liking this woman.

I nodded slowly, turned around and left the washroom without saying another word.

21

Beth

There was a subtle shift in atmosphere in the meeting room after the break. It would be an exaggeration to say things had warmed up, but there was a discernible climate change.

'Let's be honest here,' Edward said, looking up from his papers and directing his comments to Izzy and Pete. 'It's in no one's best interests for this case to go to court.'

'I disagree,' interjected their own lawyer, her eyes glittering at the challenge. 'This case is too big and too important to be settled within these walls.'

Edward was shaking his head, pitting his years of experience and wisdom against the young female lawyer, who seemed more than ready for a courtroom battle. A little *too* ready, perhaps?

'This case will become a media feeding frenzy. Your story will be splashed across the headlines of every single tabloid newspaper,' warned Edward. 'Take a moment to think how that will affect you as adults, and then multiply it by a hundred – because that's how it will be for Noah.' Izzy flinched as though the man who looked like Santa had suddenly produced a sabre. 'Remember, the courts will be on Noah's side. They will make their decision based purely on his best interests.'

'It's in his best interests to stay with his mother,' Izzy declared, her voice impassioned.

'Which mother?' Liam asked quietly, drawing every eye in the room in his direction.

I saw the naked fear in Izzy and Pete's eyes as they faced the possibility that a shared contact ruling might end up favouring *my* claim instead of theirs.

'The law wants to ensure every child has access to their rightful heritage. They—'

'Don't you think Noah deserves to know where he comes from?' I interrupted, unable to stay silent for another moment. I was going way off-piste here, speaking when I shouldn't, and flagrantly ignoring the guidelines Edward and William had set out.

'When he's older, perhaps,' conceded Pete. He glanced at his wife, who had jolted in her seat at this hypothetical suggestion. '*Much* older,' he added hurriedly. 'Like maybe when he's eighteen or so.'

'The courts will rule otherwise,' said Edward solemnly, pulling us all back to his prepared script. As much as I imagined she wanted to, even Frankie Burrows didn't dispute that one.

'I've already missed the first eight years of his life,' I said, my hands twisting together as I spoke. 'But more than that, *Noah* has missed out too.'

Izzy instantly bristled at the implied criticism, and I knew I only had seconds to backpedal from the place my words had taken her.

'He has a whole family he deserves to know about. He has cousins – one who's almost the same age as him. Doesn't he have a right to meet them, and his grandparents?' Pete was slowly shaking his head, but Izzy looked up then, her eyes meeting mine. 'And he should know about his father.'

Izzy reached instinctively for Pete's hand and squeezed it comfortingly, but her eyes stayed on my face. I could tell that we had reached a critical tipping point and I was almost too frightened to carry on speaking for fear of saying the wrong thing, but I had to press home this small advantage before it slipped through my fingers. 'I don't even know what Noah looks like.'

For a long moment, no one spoke. The only sound was the clatter of the keyboard as Keeley captured our words and transcribed them onto her laptop screen. Izzy reached slowly for her handbag, ignoring or simply not seeing the look of disbelief on her husband's face. I was starting to feel a little light-headed from holding my breath, terrified that even the smallest sound would somehow snap her awake as if from a hypnotist's trance.

'Iz?' questioned Pete, as she drew out a plain black purse. Her fingers stilled on the clasp, hesitating for a moment, and I almost screamed in frustration. But I was panicking needlessly.

'She can see a photo,' she said, looking deep into her husband's eyes. For a moment, it was as if the rest of us had suddenly disappeared. Their eyes spoke silently for several moments, a language that outsiders could never hope to understand. Whatever she said, she must have convinced him, for Pete finally gave a small nod of agreement and Izzy unfastened her purse. It was a small photograph, the type that looked as if it had been cut from a sheet of four proofs. She pulled it out from behind its plastic window and stared at it for a long moment, holding it in her hands as if it were a playing card.

I don't know how hard it must have been to do, but I could see Izzy's fingers were trembling slightly as she laid the photograph down on the table. Very deliberately she turned it around so that the image was now facing me. My heart was pounding so loudly I'm surprised Keeley wasn't attempting to minute its thunderous beat. With one neatly trimmed fingernail, Izzy slid the photograph across the glass towards me.

I gasped, in much the way I imagined Izzy herself might have done when her newborn baby was placed in her arms. The first sight of your own child will always be one of life's most precious memories. I could feel my eyes begin to fill with tears, making it hard to see the deep brown eyes, the straight nose and the full mouth, stretched wide in a cheesy smile. His dark hair stood out against the pale blue backdrop the school photographer had used for the portrait. I already knew its springy texture, and the funny double crown that was responsible for the small irrepressible quiff on the top of his head. My fingertips held the memory of that hair in every curving whorl. I looked at the face I had never seen before, and knew it better than even my own reflection.

Wordlessly, I reached into my own handbag, mirroring the actions of the woman on the opposite side of the table. Very slowly, as though laying down a winning ace, I placed the photograph of Tim down on the glass-topped table and swivelled it towards her. Her gasp wasn't as loud as mine, but the shock that registered on her face was every bit as obvious as my own had been. The lawyers had arranged for DNA tests to be conducted, but in that moment I don't think anyone in the room thought they were anything more than a box-ticking formality. I half expected someone to call out 'Snap', for anyone could see that Noah was a miniature carbon copy of his late father.

With obvious reluctance, I pushed the photograph of Noah back towards its rightful owner. 'Do you think it might be possible for me to get a copy of this?' I turned to William and Edward, suddenly unsure. 'Is it okay to ask for that?'

Before they could answer, Izzy once again surprised me. 'You can keep that one.' Even her own husband looked shocked by the unexpectedly generous gesture.

'Thank you,' I said softly, picking up both photographs and sliding them back into my wallet before Izzy had a sudden change of heart and snatched hers back. Although something told me she wouldn't do that. I would probably never get to know this woman well enough to decide if I liked her or not, but even today, when so much between us remained unresolved, I already respected her. She had earned that.

There was a comforting completeness knowing the two photographs now resided together in the same leather compartment. Father and son. Together at last.

'Are you sure this isn't taking you out of your way? I could easily catch a cab.'

'It's no trouble,' reassured Liam easily as we crossed the busy road in front of the hotel. 'I'm parked in one of the side streets over there,' he explained, his hand resting fleetingly at the small of my back to guide me.

After Izzy had given me the photograph, the meeting had pretty much drawn to a natural close.

'You already have our proposal for shared contact,' Edward said, nodding towards the document Frankie was slipping into a bright red patent leather satchel, which was probably as close to a conventional briefcase as she was prepared to go.

'Yes. We'll be in touch when we've had time to review it.'

'I think you'll find it reasonable and extremely fair,' William assured her with a politician's smile.

'For *your* client, perhaps,' retorted Frankie, shaking her head. 'I still think mine might prefer to let the courts decide what constitutes fair.'

To his credit, William's smile didn't slip by even a millimetre. 'Let's talk soon.'

Izzy and Pete were already at the door, clearly anxious to be out of there. That was something we definitely had in common. Pete's hand was on the door handle, when Izzy leant up and whispered something in his ear. He gave a curt nod and reluctantly released her hand from his. My palms were damp and sweaty with nerves as she took a step towards me. I was wondering how obvious it would look if I wiped them on my dress as I got to my feet. But shaking hands wasn't what was on her mind. Despite the incident in the Ladies', and her generosity with Noah's photograph, we were still a million miles away from cordial handshakes.

'I'm a good mother,' she said with quiet confidence, her eyes not releasing mine long enough for me to signal a plea for help to my legal team. 'Noah has everything a little boy needs. He's got two parents who love him more than anything else in the world and a safe and secure life. He's a happy little boy with no worries. Please don't do anything to change that. Don't drag him into a confusing nightmare he's too young to understand. If you really love him – and I can tell from how you act that you do – then love him enough to walk away and leave his life intact. Please.'

It was a powerful exit line, and it stunned me so much I never even noticed when she and Pete slipped from the room, closely followed by Frankie Burrows.

'Should I make a note of that?' queried Keeley, her hands on the laptop, which she'd already shut down at the end of the meeting.

'No. The meeting was already concluded. Those comments were off the record and don't need to be minuted,' ruled Edward decisively. I agreed with him; no need to record them when they were already etched into my heart as though with a chisel.

The inside of Liam's car smelled of expensive leather upholstery and the subtle but distinctive aftershave he wore. My nose was deciphering the individual aromas, a peculiar habit of mine, but my head was still stuck in the unguarded comments my legal team had made following Izzy's impassioned speech and departure.

'From the way she spoke, you'd never know that she and her husband haven't lived together for the last nine months, would you?' remarked William. It was an indiscreet slip, an indication that he was rattled and perhaps not quite as confident about our chances of success as he claimed to be.

'A situation I'm sure their counsel will have addressed by the time we get to court,' Edward replied, rapier fast. For the first time I glimpsed the razor-sharp family lawyer my father had recommended, rather than his jovial, white-bearded alter ego.

My eyes darted between the two lawyers. 'Are Izzy and Pete divorced?' Later I would berate myself for hoping that if they *were*, it might help to level the playing field a little, should the case go before the courts.

'No. Not yet. But they *were* separated, which is something we may need to highlight should things go that way.'

'Izzy and Pete seemed very close for a couple going through marriage difficulties,' I observed as Liam pulled out into the busy stream of early afternoon traffic. I turned slightly in my seat to look at him. 'Do you think they were putting on an act? Trying to create an illusion of a united front to help strengthen their case?'

Liam overtook a badly parked van, and it was impossible to tell if the twin frown lines between his eyes were caused by that, or by my question. 'I think that's a big assumption to make, that no one can answer for sure. And I wouldn't want to sit in judgement on them, even if this *is* the thing that's brought them back together again. Adversity can do that.'

I sat back in my seat and stared out through the windscreen with unseeing eyes. Liam's words were exactly the same as those I felt sure Tim would have given. I'd never noticed even the smallest of similarities before between the two men, so it was all the more unsettling to realise that they thought along very similar lines.

'Were you and Anna happily married?' My brain was leaping around all over the place, like an agitated grasshopper, but Liam seemed to have no trouble keeping up. 'Very,' he declared emphatically, his lips curving gently at the memory. 'How about you and Tim?' he asked, batting the question back to me.

'Absolutely. I loved him from the very first day we met.'

'Then *we're* the lucky ones.'

It seemed like a bizarre assertion, seeing as we were both living our lives without the person we loved most in the world, but strangely I agreed with him.

'Yes. We definitely are.'

For a while the only sound in the car was the purr of the engine and the echoes of past memories, which we were both lost in. So it was a little startling when Liam finally shattered the silence with the most prosaic of comments.

'I don't know about you, but I'm absolutely starving. Do you feel like grabbing a bite to eat somewhere, or do you need to get back to the shop?'

'No. It's half-day closing today,' I said, realising with surprise that I was equally ravenous. I hadn't been able to eat anything since the previous night, when I'd done nothing more than half-heartedly pick at a frozen ready meal, as though excavating it with my fork.

'I *am* hungry,' I admitted, 'but I'm not sure I'm up to coping with a crowded restaurant or pub right now. I'm sorry. I guess this morning's meeting has left me a little shell-shocked.'

Liam's long fingers tapped thoughtfully against the steering wheel as though following a distant rhythm. It was something Tim used to do all the time when he drove. *Stop it!* I told myself furiously. In the years since his death, I'd been scrupulously careful about where and when I allowed my memories of Tim to run free. But recently they'd been finding cracks in the wall I'd built, and kept slipping through them when I least expected it. Like now.

'Would you feel comfortable coming back to my place? I make a pretty mean omelette, or so I've been told.'

I hesitated for only a few seconds. Perhaps I hadn't known this man long enough or well enough to blithely agree to go back to his house. But he *had* rearranged his whole day at the last minute when I'd phoned and asked him to accompany me. Surely that earned him the right to be trusted?

It's okay, Beth, spoke Tim's voice reassuringly in my head, something he was now doing with worrying frequency. *This guy's okay. You're safe with him.*

Funnily enough, I hadn't needed my dead husband to tell me that. Somehow, I'd known that all along.

22

Izzy

It was the longest and most emotionally exhausting two hours of my life. I felt like a diver going through decompression as I sat between Pete and Frankie in the busy Starbucks just around the corner from the hotel.

Frankie bought the coffees, informing us with a cheeky wink that it was okay, because *we* were actually the ones paying for them. As we'd yet to settle her account I wasn't sure how she figured that one out, but I was too tired to question it. No one had spoken more than half a dozen words since we'd left the meeting room. This debrief was crucial, because even though I'd listened intently to everything that had been said that day, I still had no idea how the meeting had actually gone.

Frankie deposited the coffees on the table and took a reviving caffeine hit from hers before speaking. 'Well, that went pretty well, all things considered, don't you think?' she asked chirpily.

Pete and I exchanged a similarly baffled look. 'It did?'

'Hell, yeah,' Frankie said, sinking her teeth into one of the three oversized muffins she'd bought along with the coffees. I suspected hers was the only one that would get eaten.

I should probably have waited until she'd finished her mouthful before asking the question that had been blistering on my tongue for over two hours. 'Did you know? About her husband, I mean. Did you know that he was dead?'

Frankie looked grateful for the delay the double chocolate chip muffin afforded her. 'Not exactly,' she said, reaching for a serviette and dabbing it with a debutante's delicacy against her plum-coloured lipstick. 'I knew she was a solitary claimant, but that could have meant anything. She could have been divorced, separated, or simply a woman who'd chosen to have a child alone.'

'It's going to make a difference though, isn't it?'

Frankie looked like she really wanted to deny it, but lying didn't seem to come easily to her. She was going to make a terrible lawyer.

'It adds a… *poignancy* that skews things a bit in their favour,' she admitted reluctantly.

Pete's head was switching from left to right, as he tried to fill in the blanks of our conversation. 'But don't we still have the advantage here?' he asked in confusion. 'We're able to give Noah the benefit of *two* loving parents. Doesn't that score more highly than just having a single one?'

I looked at him sadly. 'She's a widow, Pete, and a really young one. The child she and her husband dreamt of having is never going to happen because of Westmore's screw-up. There are no second chances for her.'

'You sound like you're almost on her side,' he said accusingly. I braced myself, because I knew this man and understood perfectly what was coming next. 'Was that why you did it? Was that why you gave her Noah's photograph, because you felt sorry for her?'

'I *do* feel sorry for her,' I defended, a little embarrassed to discover I was closer to tears than I'd realised. 'And I feel sorry for Noah, and for you, and for me. I feel sorry for every one of us.'

Pete's face was a stony mask, and there was no sign of the usual compassion in his eyes as he glared at me.

'I gave her the photo. I didn't give her Noah,' I said defensively, feeling the weight of both of them staring at me now. I dropped my gaze and studied the inside of my coffee cup. 'I realised after speaking to her that she's finding this just as devastating to deal with as we are.'

'You *spoke* to her?' I don't know if Frankie had intended to raise her voice, but the words certainly came out several decibels higher than her normal speaking tone. 'When exactly did you speak to her? And more to the point, why? You do you realise she could use whatever you said against us?'

I felt like a bug on the end of a stick being slowly dissected by the pair of them. I cleared my throat, knowing that the colour I was hoping for earlier had found its way back into my cheeks. I could feel them burning furiously. 'It wasn't like that. I bumped into her in the Ladies'.'

'What did you talk about?' fired Frankie. I took it all back. She sounded exactly like a barrister in a courtroom drama. Frankie was going to be a *terrific* lawyer.

'Nothing about the case, or Noah.'

'Phew,' said Frankie, looking visibly relieved as she pantomimed wiping her brow free of sweat. 'That should be okay then.'

'So what happens next?' asked Pete. 'Will they want to

meet with us again for further discussions?'

'They might do,' Frankie admitted. 'But if they suggest it, I recommend we politely decline.'

Pete and I both sat up a little straighter in our chairs as Frankie leant in closer towards us. 'We did our bit today. We went along and listened to what they had to say.' Pete and I were nodding in unison, like two model dogs on the parcel shelf of a car. 'They're trying to snow-blind us with legal precedents that have no bearing on your particular circumstances. They're underestimating us. And they're underestimating *me*,' said Frankie, with a wry smile. 'It happens quite a lot, actually.'

Both Pete and I remained tactfully silent.

'But it really doesn't matter, because I take it the bottom line here hasn't changed? You're both still unwilling to give Elizabeth Brandon access to Noah, or grant any kind of shared custody?'

'Absolutely not.' We said the words with perfect synchronicity, as though singing a duet.

'That's what I thought. So I'll give them a few hours to stew things over, and then I'll call William Sylvester later this afternoon.' Frankie did her best to suppress the smile, but it was a losing battle. 'I'll dress it up nicely. Thank them for the meeting blah blah blah. But basically, I have only one thing to say to them.' She paused for a beat before executing the line with perfecting timing: 'See you in court.'

The atmosphere was strangely muted after Frankie had gone.

'I don't suppose we have a choice anymore,' Pete said

dolefully. 'I guess we're going to have to talk to Noah about all of this now.'

Panic jolted through me like an electric current. 'Not yet. Let's wait until they've set a date for the hearing. Anything could happen before then.'

Pete's hands were clenched on the tabletop, the calloused oil-stained fingers jarring incongruously with his smart suit. 'Are we going to be okay with this, Izzy? Are we ready to be on the front pages of every newspaper? To be talked about – and judged – by total strangers all over the country?'

'I don't see how we have a choice,' I said.

Frankie certainly hadn't pulled any punches when she'd warned us the road ahead would be far from easy. 'There'll be support flooding your way from all over the world. But be prepared – there'll also be vilification. There'll be hate mail. You'll change your phone numbers half a dozen times, and the press will *still* manage to get hold of them. And there'll probably be trolls all over the internet.'

I'd almost laughed at the expression on Pete's face at that one. He was clearly thinking only of the kind with bright orange hair and squidgy noses, who lived under bridges.

'We're ready,' I'd said, with a whistling-in-the-dark confidence I'm not sure any of us believed in.

Something had been bothering me during the meeting – a mental itch I couldn't quite scratch, and it was only as we got up to leave that I snagged the elusive memory. 'That man today, the one with Beth Brandon – I know him.'

Pete looked understandably shocked. 'Why didn't you say something?'

'I couldn't place him until just now. He's a client at the practice. He owns a cute little Jack Russell.'

Pete's mouth was a tightly set line. 'You should probably mention it to Frankie,' he said darkly. 'It might be a conflict of interest... or something.'

Lately, we were both guilty of dropping random legal phrases into our conversation, without a clue what they meant. 'I suppose so,' I said with a sigh, not liking this new world we suddenly inhabited, where nothing was simple or straightforward anymore. 'I want to ask her about her bill anyway. I wondered if we could pay it in instalments.'

Pete rarely blushed, but there was a flush now that began at his neck and crept slowly up his cheeks. The pink was a vivid contrast to the white of his shirt.

'You don't need to. I've taken care of it.'

My head twisted so rapidly that my neck muscles twanged painfully in objection. 'How? Where did you get the money from?'

'That doesn't matter.'

'Actually, it does. You didn't...' I heard the incredulity in my voice. 'You didn't do anything... illegal, did you?'

I deserved the withering look he gave me. I knew him better than that. Pete was the kind of man who'd point out to shopkeepers if they gave him too much change. He didn't 'do' dishonest.

'A bank loan?' I queried, knowing how unlikely that was given our credit history. He shook his head and frowned, realising I wasn't about to let it drop.

'A friend helped me out,' he admitted finally. 'Can we just leave it there, please, Izzy.'

For him the subject was closed, but for me it was a

Pandora's box that I couldn't stay away from. It had to be Maya. There was no one else it could possibly be. Pete had mentioned years ago that her family were extremely wealthy. He kept insisting they were just friends, but do friends lend each other that kind of money? Was she the one he was spending his evenings with, and how much more was there to their relationship than he was willing to admit? No wonder he hadn't wanted to talk about it.

A day I'd hoped was done with delivering unpleasant surprises had actually been saving the best until last.

I'm sure it was more for Noah's sake than mine when Pete asked, almost hesitantly, if he could join us for dinner that evening.

'You don't have to ask me that,' I said, my heart in serious trouble when it saw the uncertainty in his eyes. 'This is still your home.'

I let myself pretend that our world wasn't slowly crumbling to dust as I prepared Noah's favourite pasta dinner and the three of us sat down to eat it, as if nothing bad could ever touch us. We played junior Monopoly after dinner, turning a blind eye when Noah blatantly stole from the bank when he thought we weren't looking. His dishonest streak hadn't come from his dad, I thought with a smile as I watched him embezzle a handful of banknotes. Except Pete wasn't Noah's dad, and we actually knew nothing about his biological father. What if there were important facts about him that we should know? Suddenly, a hundred unanswered doctors' questions over the years began to make more sense.

'*Are you sure there's no family history of allergies, Mrs*

Vaughan? Did either you or your husband ever suffer with asthma or eczema as a child?'

'No, *neither of us did. Nor either set of grandparents. There's no family history of anything like that whatsoever.'*

Except now, maybe there was. It was just a different family. Noah's *real* family.

23

Beth

If I'd had to guess the type of home a man like Liam Thomas owned, I would have gone for a sleek bachelor flat in a maintained block, with gated security and lots of plate glass and chrome. Or perhaps a penthouse suite with a classy roof terrace, offering the best views in town.

The sprawling development of family-style properties took me by surprise. We drove through a twisting maze of streets, passing avenues of practically identical 'executive homes'. I glimpsed porches full of colourful wellington boots, and gravelled drives with carelessly strewn bicycles, tricycles and skateboards littering a pathway to the door. This was the sort of place where summer evenings would be filled with the aroma of barbecues and the sound of children's laughter. It was a curious choice for a widower in his early forties.

Liam's spacious driveway – unlike those of his neighbours – was clutter-free, although it was immediately apparent that he didn't live alone from the sound of scrabbling claws coming from the other side of his front door. I stayed several paces behind him as he unlocked it, but was too slow to avoid being pounced on by a small wiry creature who torpedoed down the length of the hallway towards me.

'Sally. Sally. No. Get down.'

The small dog was leaping up around my knees, and it wasn't clear if those rows of tiny white teeth were bared in a threat or a cheerful welcoming grin. Liam bent down and slid his fingers beneath the terrier's leather collar, pulling her back.

'You'd never tell that we were the obedience class dropouts, would you?' he asked wryly.

'That's okay, I'm sure she's just protecting her territory… or you.'

'Hmm,' murmured Liam, as he led the feisty dog into the lounge and shut the door firmly behind her.

'I'm sorry. She's not used to visitors,' he said, still sounding apologetic. 'We don't have that many.' That told me an awful lot more than I think he had intended to reveal, and he quickly sought to get back to the reason we were there.

'The kitchen's this way,' he said, sounding more like an estate agent than a host. He really wasn't used to entertaining guests, which was strange because he certainly wasn't antisocial. It was a mystery I was still pondering as I followed him down the hallway. *And how many people – who aren't related to you – have you invited home recently?* asked a voice in my head. *Touché.* Not that many.

'What can I get you?' asked Liam solicitously. 'Tea, coffee, or a glass of something stronger? I have some wine in the fridge.'

I was trying not to stare enviously at his large,

well-equipped kitchen, and concentrate on his question. 'What I'd really like, if you happen to have them, are some paracetamols. I've got a really bad headache.'

'That's not surprising. It's been a tough morning.' He'd get no argument from me on that score. 'I've got a few different types you can choose from,' he said, turning on his heel and striding back across the hallway. It took a split second before I realised he was waiting for me to follow him.

The downstairs shower room was fairly spacious, as these things go, but even so it obviously hadn't been designed with twin adult occupancy in mind. I was suddenly very much aware of the personal space boundaries we were both breaching. I shrank back as far as I could as Liam reached up to open both sides of a mirrored wall cabinet. His reflection in the glass doors looked curiously sheepish, and when I turned my attention to the closely packed shelves of the cabinet, I knew why. The last time I'd seen that many pharmaceuticals, I'd been in my local branch of Boots.

'Whoa. I'm lucky if I can find a sticking plaster at my place.' I threw him a curious sideways glance. This was the cupboard of a serious hypochondriac, or a closet survivalist, and I couldn't exactly picture Liam as either of those.

'These aren't mine,' Liam explained in a slightly embarrassed tone. 'They're Anna's.' As his wife had died over eight years earlier, that didn't make the cache any less weird. 'She liked to be prepared.' Liam smiled fondly as his hands rifled past the medications on the shelves. 'Every time we flew we were fined for excess baggage, because she'd insist on bringing all of this with us.'

He turned to me and the humour on his face was suddenly

replaced with something far more vulnerable. 'A couple of years after the accident I threw everything out – it was all out of date anyway. But the night before the bins were emptied I crept down at two o'clock in the morning and hauled it all out again.'

The pain medication in the cupboard had suddenly got a lot less appealing, but Liam only smiled sadly and shook his head. 'I took it all to the pharmacy and replaced every single item with a new one.' His fingers settled on three slim boxes, which he plucked from the shelf. 'I've done the same thing every couple of years ever since,' he admitted, dropping the packets of painkillers into my hands. He shook his head, almost in disbelief. 'You know, I've never told anybody about that before. I thought it would sound too crazy. And now that I hear it out loud… I realise I was right. It did.'

I stayed longer in the cloakroom than I needed to, giving Liam time to regain his composure. There are times when even the most secure protective armour can slip a little; mine was certainly all over the place. When I felt enough minutes had passed, I went to rejoin him in the kitchen, only to find a small dog with a very big attitude in my way.

Sally looked up at me, a challenge in her ageing brown eyes. I considered calling for Liam, but instead took a small cautious step forward. The elderly Jack Russell gave a low rumbling growl, which I pretended didn't faze me at all.

'It's okay, little lady, everything's all right.'

The dog cocked her head on one side, hearing something in my voice, and then without warning flopped onto her back, her front legs waggling, as her tail thumped steadily against the wooden floor. I don't know much about dogs, but I recognised an invitation when I saw one. I bent down to rub the wiry fur on her exposed belly and I was still doing so when Liam emerged from the kitchen and stood in the doorway, watching us with an unreadable expression on his face.

'I've not seen her do that with anyone for a very long time,' he admitted quietly.

He'd been busy in my absence. Two places had been set at the breakfast bar and there was a bowl beside the six-ring range cooker containing an extraordinary number of eggs for just two people.

I slid onto one of the high chrome stools, my offer to help politely but firmly declined, as Liam busied himself with the omelettes. As he cooked, I looked around the well-appointed kitchen, which wouldn't have been out of place in a *Beautiful Homes* magazine feature. There was every conceivable piece of equipment you could possibly want outside of a professional kitchen, including an impressive magnetic board with every size of kitchen knife you'd need from filleting a fish to disembowelling an intruder.

'It's a great kitchen, for someone who only cooks eggs.'

'Anna was the real cook,' Liam said, telling me something I'd already guessed. He gestured towards the cockpit-like row of dials on the range. 'I still don't know what half of those actually do.' His smile was self-deprecating as he nodded towards the microwave sitting on the worktop. 'That one I can use, though.'

I laughed, feeling a thread drawing me inexorably towards him, as the confession slipped from my tongue. 'I still have Tim's baby grand piano in my lounge, despite the fact that it takes up half the floor space. I dust it every week, and get it tuned twice a year.'

'You don't play?' Liam guessed.

'Not a note. Not even "Chopsticks" – and practically everyone in the world knows how to do that one.'

Liam's smile was wry and understanding. He lived in the same world as I did, and for the longest time I'd really thought I was its only inhabitant. It felt kind of strange to discover that I wasn't.

We chatted amiably over the omelettes, which were surprisingly good. I got the impression Liam was deliberately trying to steer our conversation away from the events of that morning, but like a sore tooth, I kept going back to them, even though it hurt to do so.

'How long do you think it will be before we hear back from their lawyer?' I asked, neatly lining up my cutlery to the twelve o'clock position on my plate. I'd been even hungrier than I'd realised, and despite the size of the omelette I'd cleared my plate of every last scrap.

'It's impossible to say.'

'But if you had to guess,' I pressed.

Liam shook his head, refusing to be drawn. 'I think the longer they take to get back to Edward, the better the chances are that they'll decide not to go to court.' He took our dirty plates and loaded them into the dishwasher, shaking his head regretfully at the small dog who was staring up at him hopefully. She'd been hovering beneath my stool throughout our meal. Clearly, I looked like someone who was likely to be clumsy with her food.

'As hard as I'm sure it will be, the best advice I can give you is to put all of this to the back of your mind for now.

Let the lawyers do what you're paying them an extortionate amount of money to do.'

I spluttered slightly on my mouthful of water. 'You're not wrong there.'

Liam grinned and inside me something shifted slightly, like gears in movement. The line between acquaintance and friend had been crossed, and I don't really think either of us had seen that coming so quickly.

The breakfast bar was positioned directly beneath a huge overhead skylight, which at night would probably make you feel as though you were dining under the stars, but on a hot summer's day like today, the effect was more like eating inside a Turkish sauna. I tried, unsuccessfully, to smother a yawn.

'Why don't you go and sit down in the lounge while I make us some coffee,' Liam suggested. 'It's more comfortable in there and about twenty degrees cooler.'

'I should help you clear up,' I protested, swallowing back another yawn. My sleepless night was finally catching up on me and my eyes felt so heavy it was all I could do to keep them open as I did as Liam had suggested and moved to the lounge. It was really rather sweet to see Sally get a little arthritically to her feet, and then trot alongside me, as though just half an hour earlier she hadn't seriously been contemplating how to rip my throat out.

'You've made yourself a friend,' observed Liam, watching the tiny dog falling into step beside me. From his tone, I could tell it didn't happen very often.

'I have,' I said, my eyes going to his without any conscious thought. I felt the heat of a blush warming my cheeks, which I hoped he hadn't noticed. 'I really have.'

★★★

There was a baby in my arms, and that in itself felt strange and unfamiliar. The infant's head was resting in the curve of my arm; its weight was heavy as it lay across my stomach. Was I in a delivery room somewhere? I didn't think so, particularly as I appeared to still be fully clothed. But dreams don't always bother with the i-dotting and t-crossing details of reality. It was a good dream, and I could feel Tim beside me, even though his face was obscured by shadows.

'Is this Noah?' he asked softly, his voice awed.

I opened my mouth to reply, but another voice from somewhere unseen jumped in before I could speak.

'It's Edward.'

I shook my head. No, that wasn't the name I would choose for our child. But the mystery voice was insistent. 'Beth. It's Edward. Wake up.'

The dream played tug of war with my consciousness for several moments before finally disintegrating. The 'baby' in my arms wriggled and licked my nose, her tail beating out a tattoo on the settee cushions.

'Sally, get down,' Liam commanded, laying one hand on my shoulder and gently shaking me all the way awake. In his other hand was a slim rose-coloured device, my mobile phone, which I now remembered leaving on the breakfast bar when I'd moved into the lounge.

I blinked stupidly up at him and reached for my phone, which had now fallen silent. 'How long have I been asleep?' I asked, rubbing my eyes roughly in an attempt to get them to focus on the screen. Even my voice sounded weird, as though someone had crept in and stuffed my mouth with cotton wool balls while I slept.

'Just over an hour,' Liam said, sounding apologetic. 'You looked so exhausted I didn't have the heart to wake you.'

The embarrassment of falling asleep in someone else's home barely even registered as I wriggled myself upright. Sally shot me a disappointed look before jumping off my lap and settling instead by my feet. Finally, my eyes were capable of deciphering the words on the phone's screen.

'Three missed calls,' I read, my voice flat and fearful. 'All of them from Edward.'

'I saw,' said Liam, and although he tried to hide it, I heard the thread of concern in his voice. 'I'm sorry. I was upstairs and only heard it ringing a minute ago.'

'Why do you think he's calling? It's too soon, isn't it? You said the longer it took for their lawyer to get back to us, the better.'

'You have to remember that I frequently don't know what the hell I'm talking about,' Liam declared, a fact that I simply didn't believe for a second, even if it did make my lips spasm briefly in a semblance of a smile.

'I should call him back,' I said, looking up at Liam as though willing him to tell me to do no such thing. Instead, he just nodded solemnly. This was bad. This was very, very, bad. I could feel it with a sick kind of presentiment that in normal circumstances I simply wouldn't believe in.

My tongue still felt abnormally thick, as though it fully intended to sabotage my phone call by sticking to the roof of my mouth and silencing me. I noticed a cup on the table beside me, which hadn't been there when I'd fallen asleep, and I reached for it now, taking a huge swallow even though the coffee was unpleasantly cold.

Liam pulled a face. 'I'll make you a fresh one,' he offered, 'and give you some privacy to talk.'

He reached out for the cup, but my hand shot out to stop him, even before I knew it was going to do it. At some point he'd rolled the sleeves of the black shirt up to his elbows, so my hand rested on the warm skin of his forearm, instead of on fabric. His lower arms were more muscular than Tim's had been, although minus the covering of soft dark hair that I remembered so well on my husband's body.

'Stay. Please,' I asked, my voice not quite steady. 'I could do with the moral support. I've got a really bad feeling about this.'

I liked the way Liam didn't tell me I was letting my imagination run away with me, or that I was overreacting, or even just being stupid. He simply nodded and sat down on the settee beside me, so close that his hip bone was brushing against mine. I pressed the screen to return Edward Patterson's call, while Liam leant forward and absently scratched the top of Sally's head, right between her ears. It's safe to say she was the only one in the room who didn't look worried.

Edward was more succinct and sharp-shooting than he'd been in any of our previous conversations. There was no hint of the Santa bonhomie in his tone as he got straight to the point. 'It's not good news I'm afraid, Beth. Frankie Burrows has rejected our proposed outline for shared contact, on behalf of her clients. In addition, they've also closed the door to all further negotiations. They've decided they want to take their chances in front of a judge. It's a decision I feel sure they will end up regretting.'

'I... I see,' I said. Despite Edward's confidence, I could already feel defeat coursing through me, pushing out the earlier traces of misplaced hope that I'd stupidly allowed to creep in. After I'd explained to them about Tim, after Izzy had let me keep the photograph of Noah, I'd dared to let myself believe we could find a way to work things out. It felt doubly cruel to have those fledgling dreams stamped out.

'We always knew this was a possibility,' continued Edward calmly. 'I truly believe this won't change the eventual outcome; it just means it might take us a little longer to get there.' I don't remember hanging up the phone, or even saying goodbye. It's quite possible that I did neither. My phone was back in Liam's hands once more, and he carefully set it down on the table.

'This doesn't mean you've lost,' Liam said with a quiet confidence he probably shouldn't be owning. The truth of the matter was that no one knew how a court was going to rule in this case, because no judge had ever had to make this kind of decision before. Not ever. A battle could have been avoided today – but instead Izzy and Pete had chosen to declare war.

24

Izzy

The dream came back that night.

'Noah! Noah! Noah!' I screamed myself awake, the way I'd done countless times before. Only these days Pete wasn't there beside me to gather me in his arms and soothe the nightmare away. Although to be fair, he wasn't far away.

I was still lost in the world my subconscious had conjured up when the bedroom door burst open and Pete stood within its frame, silhouetted by the light from the hall. His eyes took it all in: the sweat-drenched bed sheets tangled around me, the hair plastered to my forehead, and the heaving of my chest, as I once again lived through the most terrifying experience of my life. He had no need to ask what was wrong. He already knew.

As if the words 'separation' and 'divorce' had never entered our vocabulary, Pete climbed onto the bed and drew me against him. I went willingly, burying my face into the familiar terrain of his bare chest.

He spoke into my hair, crooning the words like the

refrain of an old song 'Shh... shh... It's just a bad dream. Everything's all right. You're fine now.'

I struggled against the circle of steel his arms provided, tilting my face up towards his in the dim light. 'I couldn't get him into the car. Everyone had gone home. There was no one to help us. I couldn't save him.'

'But that's *not* what happened, Izzy,' Pete reasoned, a fact I knew perfectly well as Noah was currently sleeping peacefully in the adjacent room. 'There were still people in the farm shop. One of them called an ambulance. It got there in minutes.'

Gradually, nightmare and reality began to separate, parting like clouds to reveal the truth. Pete's voice was calm and measured, talking me down from the ledge the way it always did. 'We were lucky, the paramedics were carrying an EpiPen in the ambulance. They gave him the dose right there on the ground of the car park,' Pete continued, as if he'd been there himself, which of course hadn't been the case. There was only *one* parent to blame for what had happened to Noah that day – me.

'By the time you phoned me from the ambulance, Noah was already improving and breathing more easily. Remember?'

I nodded, although within me there still lived a dark parallel world where there'd been no paramedics; no life-saving dose of epinephrine; no ambulance journey to the hospital where Pete was already speeding to meet us in A &E.

He passed me the tissue box from the cabinet on what used to be his side of the bed. Our limbs were twisted together like pipe-cleaner figurines: his thigh slotted between both of mine, his right arm still firmly circled around me, holding me close enough to wake up a million old memories from hibernation. I flushed in the darkness, thankful he couldn't see. My heart was still racing far too quickly, but that was surely the residual effect of the nightmare, and had nothing to do with my almost-ex-husband's nearness.

'Why don't I make you a cup of tea? That always used to help.'

Not as much as having you hold me. For a dreadful moment, I nearly said those words out loud. 'Tea would be good,' I murmured instead. The curious feeling of abandonment as he eased himself away from me was hard to ignore.

He returned much sooner than I was expecting, catching me unawares. I'd used his absence to change out of my unpleasantly damp sleepwear and had pulled on a clean pair of briefs and was about to slip on a fresh strappy vest. My arms were raised above my head, as though I was surrendering, when Pete returned with the tea. I knew he'd seen me naked. The full-length bedroom mirror caught the moment when he jerked to a halt, even though it was too dark to read the expression in his eyes. He gave a small sound; it was impossible to tell if it was an indrawn breath or an expression of dismay.

'I've made some toast too,' he said, his voice strangely gruff as he laid the tray down on the mattress. 'You need to eat more, Iz. You've lost too much weight.' I wanted to ask if he meant in general, or whether his comment was a result of what he'd just seen.

'Will you... Will you stay with me? Just for a little while. Until it fades away.'

He needed no further explanation. He knew how the nightmare worked; he understood how it liked to bury its fingers deep into my subconscious, making it almost impossible to get back to sleep. I read the indecision on his face and saw the precise moment when he shut down the voice in his head warning him this was a line he really shouldn't be crossing. 'Sure. I'll stay until you fall asleep.'

I ate the toast, not because I wanted it, but because the approval in his eyes was worth sleeping in a bed filled with crumbs. 'That's better,' he said encouragingly. 'You need to get some of your old curves back.'

I wanted to ask why. What did it matter if my jeans hung loosely on my hips, or if every one of my bras was now just a little too big? A sudden unwanted comparison flashed through my head of Maya's voluptuous cleavage versus my own practically non-existent one. I reached for another piece of toast.

With my mug drained, I settled back against the pillows. In the old days, this would be when he'd hold me tightly against him, our legs and arms twisted and tangled together like vines. Obviously, that would be far too weird now, but he *did* settle back against the headboard, lying on top of the covers. I inched a little closer, and he looped one arm around my shoulders.

'Thank you,' I whispered into the darkness. He didn't ask if I was referring to the tea, the toast; to chasing away the nightmare; or to never once blaming me for endangering our child's life. He never would; that was *my* job – and I was very good at it.

I fell asleep to the sound of his breathing, the warm familiar smell of him filling my lungs with each inhalation.

Hours later, as the first rays of light began to filter through the bedroom curtains, I reached out for him – but he was gone. The sheets were cold, so he'd left some time ago. There was a small Pete-shaped dent in the pillow where his head had lain, and I buried my face into it and confided to the duck down and feathers how much I still loved my husband.

25

Beth

'What's it supposed to be?' Natalie asked, screwing up her eyes and taking a step backwards to get a different viewpoint. A series of small popping sounds filled the shop, like short rounds of gunfire, as she stepped on the many yards of bubble wrap that were now pooled around our feet.

'I don't think it's necessarily meant to *be* anything. It's abstract.'

Natalie frowned, and shook her head as though faced with a tough algebraic equation rather than a piece of art. 'I like my paintings to look like something, you know?'

'Well, it reminds me of a field of poppies,' I pronounced, repeating what I'd said to Liam when I'd first seen this particular oversized canvas, hanging on the wall of his lounge.

'That one is absolutely amazing. It's so vibrant and eye-catching,' I had declared.

Liam's face had transformed into an expression that was an amalgam of pride, appreciation and love. 'Yeah, I've always really liked that one.'

He glanced around the room, where every wall held at least one of his late wife's creations, and looked almost nervous, as though the paintings were listening to him. 'Well, I like them all, of course.'

He surrounded himself with them, I had quickly realised within seconds of being welcomed into his home. He surrounded himself with *her*. The paintings were in the hallway, the lounge, and followed a pathway up the staircase to the upper floor. And of course I already knew about the ones that decorated the walls of his office.

'If Anna walked in here right now, she'd be really shocked,' Liam declared.

I think we all *would be*, I had thought, but wisely hadn't gone for the easy quip.

'She had a rule about only ever putting up one of her paintings at a time. She was modest – almost shy – about showing anyone her work. Even though I told her they were amazing, I think she always believed I was irrationally biased.'

I smiled gently as his words peeled back another revealing layer of the woman he had loved. I would have liked his late wife, I realised. I knew it with the kind of certainty that made me sad, because I'd never got the chance to meet her.

'Do you still have many of her pieces?' I asked innocently, totally unprepared for the boyish grin that took up residence on Liam's face as he answered me.

'Two bedrooms full of them, and half of the attic,' he admitted. 'I'll show them to you some other time,' he said, as though it was a foregone conclusion that I would be in his home again one day. That was a surprise, because it wasn't anything I had imagined would ever happen again.

'Did she ever have an exhibition, or sell them through a gallery?'

The grin disappeared in an instant, and I could see that for some reason my question had saddened him. 'No. Never.' I'd asked the wrong question, and Liam wasn't just shutting the door on our conversation, he was positively slamming it.

And now, totally unexpectedly, a courier had arrived at Crazy Daisy with an enormous rectangular package. Long before Natalie had helped me to peel off the layers of brown paper and protective bubble wrap, I already knew that Liam had gifted me the picture I had admired in his lounge. I was so touched that my eyes were already swimming with tears, making the briefly worded card attached to the back of the painting difficult to read.

This one always makes me smile. I hope it does the same for you.

Liam

'Where will you put it?' asked Natalie, thinking far more practically than I was doing right then. It was a big thing for him to have given me one of Anna's paintings, especially as I suspected he'd allowed very few to leave his possession since she had passed away.

'Well, it's too big for my lounge,' I said, already knowing exactly where I wanted to hang the piece, 'but it will look perfect over there.' I nodded towards a large blank wall beside the counter. 'That way, everyone who comes into the shop will get a chance to see it.'

'Hmm...' said Natalie, still sounding uncertain as she squinted at the painting one last time. 'Perhaps it *does* look like flowers,' she conceded eventually. 'Maybe we should add poppies to our next order from the wholesaler.'

I smiled, feeling an unexpected lightness of spirit as I hunted in the back room for a hammer and some twine to hang the painting. If this was what Liam had hoped to achieve with his extremely generous gift, then his plan had worked perfectly.

I might have run out of family members I could comfortably talk to about my legal situation, but there was one person I could confide in, someone who'd unexpectedly become a new and welcome fixture in my life. It started when I'd phoned to thank him for the painting.

'Are you really sure you want to part with it?' I'd asked, because it felt like the right thing to say, even though I would already miss the painting, which every single customer had commented on since I'd hung it in the shop.

'I wouldn't have given it to you if I wasn't sure it was going to the right person.'

An unfamiliar emotion rippled through me at his words. Not quite pride, not quite happiness, but certainly something in the same ballpark.

'Well, I promise to take good care of it, and if you ever change your mind and want it back, then you only have to ask.'

The sound of Liam's laughter rumbled down the phone. 'I'm not in the habit of asking for my gifts back, Beth. The painting is yours, to keep.'

The next day, I'd sent him a photograph of the painting hanging in pride of place in the shop, with the caption 'My view at work today', and he'd sent one straight back of an in-tray stacked impossibly high with files, saying 'And this is mine'. And that was how it began, with silly photographs – most of his showing Sally doing something cute, and links to amusing internet memes. It was innocent banter, with absolutely no flirtatious undertones. There were no 'x's after our messages, but after a fortnight I stopped pretending that my only connection with Liam was his position in the legal firm who were working on my case. Almost without me being aware of it, he had carved out a small spot in my life, and it was a very long time since anyone had done that.

Perhaps that explains why Liam was the first person I reached out to... after it happened.

I'd slammed my front door behind me as though I was being pursued, and leant back against it as I tried to control the panicked tempo of my breathing. With tears still coursing down my cheeks, I pulled out my phone and dialled his number. The need to reach out to someone who would understand, the need to reach out to *him*, was a reflex I didn't even stop to question.

It had all started that afternoon with a name and a phone number scribbled on a canary yellow Post-it note. It was stuck in the dead centre of my desktop screen, often the only place in the back-room office where it wouldn't get lost beneath snipped stems, flower heads and offcuts of ribbon.

'Bridget?' I queried, peering at Natalie's almost illegible scrawl.

'Oh yes!' exclaimed the author of the note. 'I forgot to tell you someone had rung.'

I smiled indulgently. I'd hired Natalie for her artistic skills with flowers, not her abilities as a secretary, and this wasn't the first time I had almost missed a message.

'What did she want?' I asked, clearing up the workbench, which as usual was in a state of organised chaos.

'She's getting married and wanted to discuss hiring us to do her wedding flowers. She wondered if you'd be free to meet her after work this evening at The Crown, at half past six.'

I frowned. I didn't mind meeting clients out of work hours. Evenings were very often the only time some couples had to discuss their plans in depth, but I wasn't in the habit of conducting my business in the local pub.

'What did you tell her?'

'Well, I checked your diary and told her that it would probably be okay, but I took her mobile number so you could reschedule if you had other plans and couldn't make tonight.'

That's the thing about being single and living alone without even the benefit of having a pet like Sally waiting for you at the end of the day. You are, pretty much, permanently without a valid reason to say 'no'. Even so, I would still have preferred to choose a more appropriate and professional location than The Crown.

I glanced at the clock. It was almost five thirty, so probably too late to change the plans Natalie had agreed to. I tried to shrug off a vague feeling of disquiet, which had sprung up from absolutely nowhere. I just wished I'd spotted Natalie's note earlier in the afternoon, when there had still been time to do something about it.

'Am I meeting with her and her fiancé?' I asked Natalie.

'Did she give you her surname, or any idea how soon her wedding is?'

Natalie managed to look both guilty and embarrassed at the same time. 'Oh God. I'm really rubbish. I didn't ask any of that.'

I smiled and shook my head, letting her off the hook. 'That's okay. Just try to get a few more details next time.'

Natalie was chewing on her lip and I could see she was still worried. 'It's okay, really it is. It's all business,' I said, giving her arm a gentle squeeze. 'Everything's fine. I don't suppose she happened to let you know how I'd recognise her?'

For the first time, Natalie smiled broadly. 'She said you couldn't possibly miss her, because she has bright red hair.'

I was looking for a woman with Ed Sheeran's colouring, and had walked the length of the bar three times without finding anyone who remotely fitted the bill. Five more minutes and then I'll cut my losses and go, I promised myself, looking up and giving the sympathetic-looking barman a passing smile. I realised he probably imagined that I'd been stood up on a date, and that made my smile grow even wider, because in a way I guess you could say that I had been.

And then the doors of the pub flew open and the woman I'd come there to meet stood between them. I'd been looking for entirely the wrong kind of red, imagining it to be the kind that nature gifted you with. Bridget's was the shade they painted postboxes and buses in, and made no apology whatsoever for coming out of a bottle.

She scanned the bar and even though I don't imagine she

knew what I looked like, her face broke into a wide, tooth-filled smile. 'Elizabeth!' she called out, her voice carrying so loudly that several heads at the bar turned in my direction. My polite smile of greeting felt a little weak as I quickly closed the distance between us. There was something about Bridget that had sent my inner antennae into overdrive. Perhaps it was the use of my full name, which hardly anyone had used since the day of my christening. Surely Natalie would have told her my name?

'It's just Beth,' I corrected, holding out my hand in greeting. She hesitated for a second, but I didn't judge her for that; some people simply aren't comfortable with the formal greeting. Bridget's dark-purple nail varnish was beginning to chip, and her hand was a little unpleasant, the palm sticky with perspiration, but neither of those were good enough reasons not to like the woman I'd come there to meet. And yet I didn't like her. The feeling was instant and instinctive, and over the years I'd learnt to trust my judgement; even if it seemed irrational, it was rarely wrong.

'It's all business', I'd said to Natalie, and I reminded myself of that as I suggested we find a quiet table in the corner of the saloon. Crazy Daisy was doing fairly well, but not so much that I could afford to turn away a lucrative wedding booking just because I'd taken an illogical dislike to the bride.

'Shall I get us something to drink before we begin?' I asked pleasantly. 'At this time of the evening they'll probably still do us some tea or coffee if we ask.'

'I'd sooner have a rum and Coke, if it's all the same with you.'

I told my mouth to smile, and I suppose it must have

done as instructed, even though inside I was scowling. I used the time it took for the barman to fix our drinks to practise a little attitude adjustment. We had got off on the wrong foot here, but I was honest enough to admit that the problem was with me rather than Bridget. I pasted what I hoped looked like a genuinely friendly expression across my features and carried our drinks back to the table.

'Cheers,' Bridget said, clinking her glass against mine with such gusto that small splashes of the lemonade I was drinking speckled the back of my hand like dewdrops.

Wresting back control, while trying to make it clear that even though we were in a busy pub, this was still a business meeting, I drew a reporter's notepad and pen from my bag. Bridget watched me with slightly narrowed eyes as I flipped to a clean page and carefully wrote *'Bridget and…'*. I paused with my pen hovering a centimetre or two above the feint ruled line. Bridget looked at me blankly for a moment. Her heavily pencilled eyebrows rose a little.

'Your fiancé,' I prompted gently. 'What's his name?' It certainly wasn't intended to be a tough question, but she seemed to need a beat or two before supplying me with the answer.

'Jerry.'

The nib of my pen almost made contact with the paper. 'Is that with a G or a J?'

'Huh?' All right, this was beginning to feel a little strange. 'Oh, it's er… it's with a J,' she said, shaking her head a little as though she was now done with my Gestapo tactics.

I printed the name of her fiancé slowly and carefully, giving both of us a moment. What on earth was wrong with me? I usually had no problem getting on with people. In fact, customer contact was probably my favourite aspect of being in retail. But today it felt like pulling teeth.

'So when exactly is your wedding?'

At least she appeared to know the answer to that one. 'The seventeenth of November.'

'Oh, on a Tuesday, that's unusual,' I commented, gently double-checking that I'd heard her correctly. It might be a fairly redundant skill in any other business, but for a florist it was always useful to memorise where the Saturdays fell throughout the year.

Bridget took a long slurp of her drink, draining a sizeable amount from the glass before lowering it back onto the table. 'It's cheaper midweek.'

That was undeniably true, so I just smiled and wrote down the date on my pad. 'And I presume you already have a venue booked?'

If she answered this one with a 'no', we were probably both wasting our time here. But Bridget had her answer ready and waiting. With a smile that looked just a little smug, she revealed the location of her wedding. 'Hamley Manor. Do you know it?'

I closed my eyes for a second, and behind them an image of a cream-coloured invitation appeared, with my name and Tim's embossed in silver writing above the name of that venue. I forced my lips into a smile. 'Yes, yes I do. It's a lovely location for a wedding.'

Bridget's eyes were small and bright, like a bird's, I thought, a little ungenerously. And there was definitely something about the way they were studying me now that felt decidedly avian. It's almost as if she *knows* that I got married there, whispered a voice silently in my head. I ignored it, because how the hell would she know something like that? This woman was a total stranger to me. Her appearance was far too distinctive; if I'd ever met her before, I wouldn't have forgotten it.

'Have you given much thought to the kind of flowers you'd like? Did you bring any photos or clippings with you today?'

'No,' Bridget said, draining the remainder of her glass and replacing it on the table. I didn't offer her a refill, a deliberate oversight that made her lips tighten momentarily. 'Was I meant to?'

I shook my head, still trying to convince myself there wasn't something majorly 'off' with this appointment. 'No. Not at all.' I launched into my usual wedding flower spiel, but although Bridget's eyes never once left my face, I didn't think she was paying attention to a single word I was saying.

'What colour scheme were you and Terry thinking of?' I asked.

Bridget gave me a long, calculating look, her mouth twisting into a reluctant smile of admiration. 'Jerry,' she corrected. 'With a J, remember?'

She was toying with me, the way a cat does with a mouse, and suddenly I didn't really care how much money I was walking away from, I didn't want to work on this woman's wedding.

Bad acting apparently runs in my family, because there would be no Oscars handed out for the way I suddenly smacked my own forehead and gasped in faux dismay. 'Oh no! I've just remembered, I already have another booking on that day. I'm so sorry, but I'm afraid I'm not going to be able to help you after all.'

'I thought you said Tuesday weddings were unusual,' Bridget observed, and there was something in her voice that made my pulse beat a little faster. 'That's such a shame, because someone I know recommended you highly.'

I flipped the notebook shut and slid it back into my bag, still willing to go through the pretence that this woman really *was* getting married, which was something I now seriously doubted.

'This friend of mine was hoping to book you for her own wedding, but her plans are all on hold now. She's going through a really difficult time career-wise. Quite a few people where she works have lost their jobs recently.'

'These are difficult times, financially,' I said, waiting for the metaphorical bullet to be fired. She had come here ready armed, that much was obvious, and she wasn't about to let me leave without saying her piece.

'Indeed. She works at the Westmore Clinic. Perhaps you've heard of it?'

I felt the colour leave my cheeks; it went quickly, in one draining rush. 'I'm not sure. I don't think so.'

'Hmm… apparently there's some huge compensation case pending. But I think you probably know all about that, don't you, Mrs Brandon?'

Mirroring my own manoeuvre, Bridget delved into her shoulder bag and pulled out a notebook. 'Would you care to make a comment? I can promise you my newspaper would be willing to pay very handsomely for an exclusive interview.'

I got to my feet so rapidly I almost knocked over my chair. 'I have no idea what you're talking about.'

Bridget shook her head, as though dealing with a recalcitrant child. 'You disappoint me, Elizabeth. You must know that getting the public on your side will only help your case. I could do that for you.'

I could feel tremors begin to run through me, as if I was suddenly in the throes of a fever. I only hoped the reporter couldn't see them. 'There is nothing to discuss, because you've got the wrong person.'

She shook her head. 'I don't think so. Perhaps the child's birth mother might be more willing to talk to me.'

A small spark of relief ignited within me, because the confidence in her voice had ebbed slightly. Bridget might know exactly who *I* was, but I was almost certain that Izzy, Pete and Noah's identities were still a mystery to her. Thank God.

'I'm afraid you've made a huge mistake and have wasted not only my time but also your own in arranging this pretence of a meeting.'

It felt good to see the doubt flicker behind her eyes, even though she tried to mask it with nonchalance.

'I really *am* getting married, you know.'

I shook my head slowly in disbelief at her utter gall. 'Then good luck...' She opened her mouth to reply, but I jumped in before she could. '...to your fiancé. I imagine he's going to need it.'

My fury lasted for the rest of my journey home. But at some point during the fifteen-minute drive, the adrenaline that had powered me out of the pub like an Amazonian warrior had dissipated into trembling reaction. I was crying without realising it, or even knowing why. I'd done nothing wrong. I hadn't given the reporter any information she hadn't already known, and yet somehow I felt as though a crypt door had been forced open, and all manner of unpleasantness was now going to find its way through the opening.

They don't know who Noah is. He's still safe, I tried to reassure myself. But it didn't matter how many times I repeated those words, I still felt as though we were all playing a dangerous game of hide-and-seek, and that every lowlife reporter was now sitting in wait chanting: *Ready or not, we're coming to get you.*

'Calm down, Beth. Take a breath and tell me again exactly what happened.'

'A reporter tricked me into meeting with her this evening by pretending to be a client. I think someone at the Westmore Clinic must have tipped her off.' I took a moment to swallow down my emotions before continuing shakily. 'That's probably where the leak must have come from.'

'Actually, I don't think—' Liam broke off whatever he was about to say, and for a long moment there was silence on the other end of the line.

It made it harder to hide the fact that I was still crying.

'Are you okay?' asked Liam suddenly.

My head was frantically shaking from side to side, even while I was saying: 'Yes, I'm fine.'

There was a pause, so long that for a moment I wondered if the connection had been lost.

'No, you're not,' Liam declared in a tone I don't think I'd ever heard in his voice before. 'I'm coming over.'

'No, really. You don't need to do that. I'll be okay.'

'I'm on my way,' Liam said decisively, hanging up before I had a chance to try to talk him out of it. I stared at the silent phone in my hand for several moments. 'Thank you,' I whispered softly into the mouthpiece.

26

Beth

'I'm sorry, I don't have any beer.' I straightened up, not sure why I'd gone through the pretence of even looking. It would have been more of a surprise if I *had* found a forgotten six-pack lurking in my fridge, when it hadn't featured on my shopping list in over five years. 'There's a 24-hour shop down the road, I could—'

'Beth, it *really* doesn't matter.' Liam cut through my protests like a knife through butter. 'I'm happy with wine,' he said, his eyes dropping to the bottle of Sauvignon Blanc that I'd pulled from the fridge.

I liked the way Liam didn't do the alpha male bit by offering to take over as I struggled with the mechanics of the corkscrew. At least it proved I wasn't in the habit of solitary drinking, I thought, giving a small grunt of triumph as the cork was finally freed from the bottle. But tonight the wine was needed to dull the memory of Bridget's beady gaze, and to disinfect the really bad taste that meeting the reporter had left in my mouth.

Liam took one of the two generous glasses I'd poured

out and fell into step behind me as I led the way to the lounge. He paused for a moment after I invited him to sit down. I saw his unusual smoke-coloured eyes glance in the direction of the room's solitary armchair (*Tim's* chair, a voice in my head silently reminded me). After what seemed like a long moment of indecision, he moved to the three-seater and settled himself at one end. Leaving a vacant no-man's-land cushion between us, I went to the other end, kicked off my shoes and curled my legs up beneath me. It was taking longer than I'd expected for the sanctuary of my own home to settle my jangling nerves.

'Thank you again for coming over,' I said, aware it was probably the fourth or fifth time I'd said that in the twenty minutes since he'd arrived. Liam must have literally dropped whatever he'd been doing and got straight in his car after my call to have got here so quickly. It had been a long time since anyone other than my family had cared that much about my well-being, and each time I thought about what he'd done I had to swallow down a huge lump in my throat. After Tim had died, there'd been no end of friends who'd pledged their support, but over time their numbers had slowly dwindled. And so too had the invitations, which I declined so often that eventually they'd stopped coming altogether. I didn't blame anyone; life carries on, that's how it's supposed to be. It's only the people left behind who can get caught in a groove, cycling in a loop between the past and the present.

Perhaps that's why it was so easy to relax in Liam's company, I thought, watching him now seemingly perfectly at home in a place he'd never been before. He was the kind of man who was comfortable in his own skin, and with his own company. Had he always been like that, I wondered, even before Anna had died? It didn't seem like the kind of question I could ever reasonably ask, so I tried another.

'Can we do anything to stop this from happening again? Can William or Edward protect Noah's identity? What about a restraining order or something to stop them from tracking him down?'

Liam shook his head sadly. 'Their feisty young lawyer will already have applied to keep her clients' identity secret, but that's not how I imagine the information will get out.' My eyes searched his face for the answer. 'Any number of clinic employees could have had access to the records. All it needs is for one friend, a partner, or a relative to be told in confidence, and then they tell someone else, and then they...'

I nodded bitterly, not needing him to explain any further. It was the answer I already feared he would give me. We were playing a dangerous game of Chinese whispers, and sooner or later someone was going to murmur something into the wrong ear. It was almost inevitable.

'I know the intrusion is vile, but the press are just looking for their next big story. It's what they do. And unless they break the law or openly harass you on private property, there's very little we can do to protect you.'

'Unless I drop the case,' I said quietly.

I'm not sure which of us looked more shocked at the unexpected suggestion. Liam turned sharply to face me. 'Is that what you're thinking of doing, Beth?'

Is it? asked Tim from the numerous photo frames around the room.

'I don't know,' I said, embarrassed to hear the crack in my voice.

I'm not sure how it happened. I certainly didn't make the first move, but then I don't think Liam did either. But one of us must have done, for our wine glasses to have been set down, and for Liam's arm to be comfortingly around me, pulling me in. I leant into his shoulder, my lungs filling with the smell of him, even while my head and my heart were filled with another man. Tim looked down on us from a silver frame on top of his baby grand piano. As if he too suddenly felt the other man's presence, Liam turned towards the polished black instrument and the picture upon it. I knew every pixel of that image: my face radiant; pieces of confetti still caught in my hair as I gazed lovingly into the eyes of my new husband. That couple had been so happy, so blissfully unaware of what the future held in store for them. It made me feel strangely protective of them, living in blissful ignorance inside their silver frame. I missed him, all the time I missed him, but it was quite a shock to realise that I missed her too, almost as much.

Liam turned his head, and it felt as if a silent agreement had been reached between the two men, and a wordless deal struck. Very subtly, he withdrew his arm from around me and settled back a little further into his own corner of the settee.

'Don't make any decisions just yet, and certainly none based on what happened this evening with the reporter,' he advised. 'Give it a couple of days.'

'But there'll be more of them,' I said sorrowfully. 'They'll keep on coming. You've all warned me about that. We won't be able to keep this a secret. If one reporter has tracked me down, then another will too, and maybe the next one will be more successful at identifying Noah, Izzy and Pete.' Liam was too wise to deny my prediction. 'And let's just say we do it anyway, and to hell with the press, and *still* lose our application. Then I'll have put everyone through this nightmare for nothing.'

Liam reached for my hand, which was fidgeting anxiously on the seat between us. His palm pressed against mine, our fingers like steeple spires that slowly collapsed in on themselves. The silence stretched out, but it wasn't awkward or uncomfortable. We'd finished the bottle of wine I'd brought from the kitchen, and made sizeable inroads into a second, and yet Liam still showed no desire to rush away. He was a stabilising anchor as my mind journeyed down endless pathways that all seemed to lead me back to exactly the same place.

'Speak to William,' Liam advised, as though he'd been able to follow every random meandering *what if*. 'Discuss it with him and see what he says. Cross each bridge as you come to it.' My eyes widened as my husband's favourite expression was spoken in another man's voice. It was startling, like a glass of water thrown in my face. I tugged my hand free from Liam's and he made no move to stop me.

'Don't worry about making an appointment,' he said, getting to his feet and pulling out his phone. 'Just call by the office any time over the next couple of days and I'll make sure Bill finds time to see you.'

For a moment, I thought he might be phoning William right there and then, until I recognised Uber's familiar logo on his screen. 'You're calling for a car?' I asked, the wine making me slow in working out why.

'I've had too many to drive,' Liam stated simply.

'You could always stay here, if you like,' I said, blushing a deep red as I realised how easily my invitation could have been misconstrued. But not by Liam, who gently shook his head.

'No. Thanks for the offer, but I can't. I have to get back for Sally.'

I was suddenly very grateful that Anna had left behind one very needy and demanding terrier who commanded his return. Because I really didn't know what I would have done if Liam had taken me up on my impulsive invitation and I was more than a little relieved that now I didn't have to find out.

27

Izzy

'It's your son's school.'

It's amazing how four simple words, in precisely that order, can strike terror in the heart of any mother. In the space of time it took me to cross to the reception desk and take the receiver from the veterinary nurse's hand, I'd already run through a whole list of possible scenarios. They ranged from Noah falling from a dangerously high climbing frame to nearly drowning while pond dipping. My imagination seemed capable of conjuring up only the most catastrophic or sensational options.

'Hello, this is Izzy Vaughan.' I could hear my breathing was a little faster than usual. 'Is Noah okay? Has something happened?'

'Noah's fine,' replied the junior class teacher who'd been assigned the task of making this call. I thought I heard an almost indiscernible sigh as she dealt with what I'm sure she thought was another overly protective mother. I guessed she had no children of her own. *Wait a few years and see how it feels when you're on the* receiving *end of one of these calls.*

'We're calling because Noah's been complaining of feeling a little bit "strange" all morning. We're sure it's nothing to worry about, but we thought we should let you know.'

'*Strange?* What does that mean, exactly?' From the moment I took the call I'd been calculating how long it would take me to get to the school; now I was working out how to do it *faster.*

'He can't really explain it properly. That's why we thought we should phone you. Perhaps you'd like to pick him up?'

There was no 'perhaps' about it. 'I'm on my way,' I said, throwing a glance at the teetering stack of files on my desk, all of which were marked 'Urgent'. Not as urgent as this.

Before hanging up, there was one important detail I needed to clarify. 'Has Noah got his pen with him? There's one in his bag, and another in the school office with his name on it.' If she thinks I'm talking about a biro and not a life-saving injection of epinephrine, I might just lose it, I thought, as I gripped the phone a little more tightly. But the school was better than that, and so was she.

'Of course. It's the first thing we check on with any of our pupils with allergies. But it doesn't seem to be anything like that. He's just… not himself today.'

I exited the surgery car park as though driving a getaway car, and cursed like a marine at every red light I caught as I ducked up and down side streets to avoid the roadworks and diversions surrounding the school. It felt as if the local council were *deliberately* trying to keep me from reaching

Noah. My hands drummed the wheel in frustration as I saw the gridlocked queue of vehicles in the road leading to his school.

With a squeal that probably meant I'd left rubber on the tarmac, I braked sharply and peeled out of the queue. I executed an impressive U-turn in a road that forbids them, and swung down a side street to park the car. I was still some distance from the school, but it would be quicker to walk from here. I was driven by a burning need to keep moving, and get to Noah without delay. Like most mums, I'd been called to collect my child from school or nursery on numerous occasions over the years. But this felt different, although I couldn't put my finger on why. Was it the looming court hearing that was making me feel this way? Would I always trace every horrible thing in our lives back to that, as though it was a curse we couldn't outrun?

I hurried along the pavements past the line of idling cars, my sandals making sharp slapping sounds as they connected with the concrete, only just managing to restrain myself from breaking into a run. I recognised the middle-aged secretary who buzzed me into the school, although for the moment her name escaped me. She was small, plump and kindly, wore colourful Dame Edna Everage glasses, and had bosoms that looked like pillows. 'Noah's been waiting for you in the office with me,' she explained, leading me down a short corridor to that room.

I'm not sure what my imagination had been expecting, but a torrent of relief gushed through me when I saw my son sitting at a vacant desk, his legs swinging as he spun the swivel chair from side to side. It was only as I crossed the room that I noticed the telltale signs that all was not right.

The smattering of freckles across his nose was now the only splash of colour in a face devoid of its usual healthy glow. Noah wasn't a crier, but I could see the tracks of dried tears on his cheeks; his eyes were puffy from them. I was suddenly very, very glad I was there.

'Not feeling so great, kiddo?' I asked, bending to kiss his forehead, which doubled up nicely as a means of assessing if he had a raised temperature. He didn't.

'Tummy ache? Do you feel sick? Have you got a headache?' He shook his head in response to every symptom I fired at him. The Dame Edna lookalike gave me a comforting smile from across the room. I scrutinised Noah's face carefully, trying not to frown as I noted its overall puffiness. Noah's allergies had returned with a vengeance over the last few weeks, and despite two visits to the GP and numerous different medications, nothing had helped.

'I have all of his things here,' the secretary said, passing me a bundle of Noah's belongings. My brain was busily leafing through every page in my encyclopaedia of childhood ailments as I automatically checked in his school bag that the EpiPen was within easy reach.

'Shall we go then?' I asked, holding out my hand to Noah, and watching him closely as he got to his feet. Was he a little more sluggish than usual? 'I'm afraid I've had to park a little distance away.'

'Can't you give me something more to go on than just feeling "icky", sweetheart?'

We were walking back to the car – frustratingly slowly,

as Noah kept casting wistful glances over his shoulder at the sound of his friends in the school playground.

'Not really,' he mumbled, and looked so miserable I decided not to push it further until we got back home, which wasn't going to be for quite some time at our current snail's pace. 'My shoes are hurting,' Noah moaned, when I tried to hurry him along. 'They're too tight. I think I need new ones.'

'Well, they were fine yesterday,' I reasoned. 'Feet don't grow overnight – unless you're turning into a hobbit.' I expected him to laugh, or at least crack a smile, but he did neither. Instead, he came to a sudden halt, looking so small and vulnerable I immediately retraced my steps to stand beside him.

'Is something else worrying you, honey? You know you can tell me anything.'

Noah shook his head, but his lower lip was trembling with the weight of whatever he wanted to say. 'Roland Carter said my eyes looked weird. Like I'd been crying,' he whispered. I bit my tongue on my knee-jerk reaction to say something mean right back about Noah's bullying classmate. 'And it made me so sad that I *did* cry. And he just laughed.'

He was about to cry again, I realised, and before I could defuse his misery, the first tears were already squeezing their way past his puffy eyelids. I threw open my arms and he catapulted straight into them. His belongings fell to the pavement where I mindlessly dropped them, but neither of us even noticed, much less cared.

Even as I soothed him with *'Everything will be better soon'*, a worried voice in my head was asking me how sure I was about that. This was so un-Noah, so unlike his usual behaviour. The old paranoia was like a hopeful snake, looking for an easy chink in the wall to slither through. When I eventually lifted my head from where it had been buried in Noah's thick dark hair, the queue of cars and vans beside us were blurred by my own fear-fuelled tears.

'Why don't we go for ice creams and not bother with boring old lunch?' I suggested, which sounded much more like an idea Pete would have come up with than me. It was met with an instant smile, which only faltered slightly when I added, 'And then I'll see if we can get a doctor's appointment for this afternoon.'

I might have taken the fresh-faced young woman for a work experience student if it hadn't been for the stethoscope looped around her neck. This was our third visit to the GPs' surgery in as many weeks, and we hadn't seen the same physician twice. Today's doctor was a locum who looked barely old enough to have a *driving* licence, much less one to practise medicine.

'What seems to be the problem, young man?' she asked jauntily, directing her question to Noah. In normal circumstances I'd have let him speak for himself, but there was something about how he was acting today that prevented me from keeping silent.

'He said that he—'

The young locum cut me off with a smile that didn't quite make it to her eyes. 'Shall we let Noah tell me in his own words?'

I could already see I was a cliché in this woman's eyes.

The kind of mother who wrapped the cotton wool so closely around her child she was in danger of smothering them. But I was too worried, too old and too thick-skinned to take offence. As long as she got to the bottom of what was wrong with Noah, I didn't care what this doctor thought about me.

After Noah's mumbled explanation, the GP spent several minutes scrolling back through the medical notes on the computer screen beside her. Her eyes occasionally flashed over to me, before flicking back to Noah's medical history. I could see what she was thinking as though it was written in a giant thought bubble floating above her head. *Over-anxious mother.* I wondered if the number of visits on the screen revealed as much a picture of *my* medical history as it did of Noah's.

The doctor continued to ask Noah a slew of questions as she examined him, and when she was done the words I'd been bottling up burst from me. 'None of the allergy medications he's been prescribed seem to be working. And it's come on really suddenly—'

'I realise it might seem that way, but Noah *does* have a history of allergies going back to when he was a baby.'

'Yes...' I conceded. 'But he's been so much better for such a long time. It's been *years* since we've even come close to using the EpiPen.'

'I'm afraid that's the nature of allergies. They come, they go.' From someone who'd studied medicine for five years, was it unreasonable to hope for a better explanation? 'This is always the worst time of year for someone with Noah's sensitivity,' she continued, flashing him a quick smile. 'I bet you anything they've been mowing the grass near your school over the last few days.' Noah's eyes widened like marbles, as though he was in the presence of a genius. Me, not quite so much. The doctor smiled benignly. 'There you go then.'

'I really don't think it's—' I began, only to be shot down by the look in her eyes. You'd think I'd know better by now than to try to tell a doctor you believe they've just misdiagnosed your child. 'It's just that his face is looking so puffy, especially around the eyes,' I added, already knowing exactly how she was going to respond. She didn't disappoint.

'Those are classic signs of an allergic reaction, Mrs Vaughan,' she said, oblivious to the fact that I'd probably read more on that particular subject than she had. 'I couldn't see anything on Noah's notes, but have you or Mr Vaughan ever suffered with allergies?'

Noah had heard this question many times before, but it was the first time he'd heard me hesitate before replying. 'No. Never.'

The doctor shrugged and turned her attention to the keyboard. The room filled with the sound of her fingers clattering over the keys as she wrote out yet another prescription for a medicine I very much doubted would work any better than the ones that had come before it.

She got to her feet, our consultation clearly over as far as she was concerned. I allowed her to lead us to the door, but after she'd opened it, I rested my hand lightly on Noah's shoulder. 'Would you mind sitting in the waiting room for a minute while I have a quick word with the doctor?' I asked. 'There'll be some toys in the children's corner you can play with.'

Nothing is quite as withering as the look your eight-year-old gives you when you insult his intelligence. 'They're for the *little* kids.'

I smiled, and ruffled his hair affectionately. 'Sorry, big guy.'

The young doctor didn't direct me back to the chairs, so I knew the clock was ticking; we'd already exceeded our allotted twelve minutes of consultation time. 'Two things,' I said in a rush. 'Firstly, I was wondering if blood tests would give a clearer picture of what is going on with Noah.'

It would appear that twenty-somethings with a medical degree are pretty good at withering looks too. 'If it will set your mind at rest, Mrs Vaughan, we can arrange for that, although I'm not convinced they are warranted. Noah's symptoms are textbook classic for a child with allergies. What *would* be useful is to refer you back to the allergy clinic, for further tests.' I nodded, my hands unconsciously fiddling with the strap of my bag as I got to Point Number Two.

'You asked whether there's a family history of allergies…' I drew in a deep breath, hating the words I was going to say, because they felt like a betrayal to Pete. 'It's possible Noah's father had allergies in the past. Would it be helpful in treating Noah to know if he did?'

'Absolutely. Any information Mr Vaughan can give us can only help Noah.'

I opened my mouth to correct her, and then shut it again. I wanted no record of Noah's unique background plastered all over his medical notes. 'Okay, I'll see what I can find out.'

28

Beth

I blinked at the unfamiliar car on my drive, screwing up my eyes to check it wasn't a hangover-induced mirage. No, it was still there, as was the worst headache I could remember having in years. Tim had always claimed I was a lightweight, and it was easy to imagine his amusement as the screech of the curtain pole rings made me wince.

The previous night was starting to come back to me in small snapshot images. I could remember walking Liam to the door, the Uber he'd booked already idling at the kerbside, and promising him that I wouldn't make any rash decisions. What I couldn't remember was saying goodbye, or arranging when he'd collect his car. Those memories were lost under an avalanche of embarrassment, caused when I'd turned my head at the wrong moment, so that the kiss he'd intended for my cheek had landed instead on my surprised lips. There were two seconds, maybe three, when the wine, muscle memory, and the moment made my lips soften and part slightly under his. But then an arc of memories brought us both back to sanity. I doubt we could have pulled apart any faster if my lips had been electrified. Liam's charcoal eyes had burned briefly into mine, before we both decided to be terribly British about it, and simply pretend it hadn't happened. Except that it had, and now I couldn't un-see the horrified expression on his face as he'd hastily backed away from me.

A long shower certainly helped to clear some of the fuzziness the wine had left behind, and I was feeling much more human as I padded back to the master bedroom wearing one towel like a toga, with another twisted into a turban on my head. I was moving as fast as my hangover would allow, just in case Liam intended to collect his car before going to work. But as I shook my hair free of its towel, I heard the unmistakable sound of an engine being fired up. From the bedroom window I could just make out a shadowy figure in the car's driver's seat. Without stopping to think it through, I dashed into the hall, my feet leaving a telltale trail of damp footprints as I ran down the wooden stair treads.

Even so, I was too slow. As I unlatched the door's security chain I could already hear the vehicle driving away, and by the time I flung open the door, Liam's car had disappeared with a blink of red brake lights at a nearby junction.

Had he seen me silhouetted in the open doorway in his rear-view mirror? If he had, it hadn't changed his mind. Was it lingering embarrassment from that awkward kiss-that-nearly-was, or was it my indecision about continuing with the court case that was making him keep his distance? Perhaps he'd finally come to realise that the line between lawyer and friend was just too hard to straddle?

Feeling unsettled, I stepped back from the door and trod

on something small and hard on the coconut mat beneath my bare feet. Luckily, the sturdy blister pack appeared to have protected the contents from damage. But the outside of the box was far more interesting than what was inside it. Liam's handwritten message had been squeezed around the brand name on the front of the pack of painkillers and the dosage. I smiled as I read it.

Because you said you never have any, and I've a feeling you might be in need of them this morning.

Several cups of coffee and two of Liam's pills successfully managed to sort out the headache, but the question ricocheting around my head wasn't so easily banished. *What was I going to do?* And just as importantly: *What would Tim have wanted me to do?*

I nibbled on a slice of toast and reached for the morning newspaper. I'd never really been much of a believer in horoscopes, but working with Natalie – who was slightly obsessed with them – must have diluted my scepticism. She insisted on reading mine every day, ignoring my protests that the predictions were so vague they could be twisted to fit practically any situation. What would she say now, I wondered, if she saw me running my finger down the list of star signs, searching for whatever words of wisdom the mystic in the grainy photograph at the top of the page had to offer?

'"Don't be afraid of losing your way",' I read out loud in the sunny warmth of my cosy kitchen. '"Trust your heart and you'll find the right road to follow",' I finished with a small harrumph of scorn. 'Sounds more like something my satnav would say,' I told the grinning astrologer, folding the newspaper shut.

'I suppose it's too much to hope *you* could send me some kind of sign,' I suggested to the photo of Tim sitting on the shelf beside my recipe books.

'I mean, it doesn't have to come with a flash of lightning or a thunderbolt,' I assured his smiling face on my bedside table as I bent down to fasten my sandals.

'Just something meaningful to let me know you think I should keep going with the application,' I explained to a collage of Tims, hanging in a multi-frame by the hall mirror.

Several hours later, I found myself staring at a big black arrow in the centre of a custard-yellow diversion sign. 'Not exactly the type of sign I had in mind, hon,' I said, laughing at my own quip as my fingers drummed against the van's steering wheel. Several road workers who'd been earnestly inspecting a hole in the road looked up to see what was so amusing. I blushed, having forgotten the wound-down windows on the delivery van, and willed the temporary traffic lights to hurry up and turn green, even though the diversion sign was going to take me miles away from where I needed to go for my final delivery of the morning.

I peered through the windscreen and saw more signs further down the road, all directing me towards an area I really didn't know very well. It was yet another frustration to add to a day that had been accumulating them from the moment I'd woken up. Of course I didn't blame Val, our regular delivery driver, for phoning in sick that day. In fact, she was so reliable and off so rarely that I'd never bothered worrying about finding a back-up driver. Which meant the only option for getting Crazy Daisy's orders out that day was to deliver them myself.

I wasn't worried about leaving Natalie alone to manage the shop, because she'd been doing that more and more lately, covering my appointments with William and Edward. But I *was* disappointed that the quiet morning, allowing me time to think things through, had been unexpectedly hectic. Despite that, it had been a good day, until the local council had thrown a spanner into the works.

Back when I was a lowly trainee florist, I'd always enjoyed the delivery aspect of the job. There are very few people who aren't delighted to see you when you present them with a bouquet of flowers. But today the van felt uncomfortably hot; the air conditioning wasn't working properly; I was getting hungry, and I was now heading *away* from my final delivery address instead of towards it. At least, I assumed that's where I was going. To be honest, I wasn't exactly sure *where* I was anymore. The yellow signs had led me down several residential streets, past a park and a small parade of shops, and now, unbelievably, it looked like there was *another* set of temporary lights up ahead.

I pulled on the handbrake and joined the end of a long queue of cars at the three-way lights, keeping my fingers firmly crossed that my second-hand van, with its tendency to overheat, wouldn't decide today was the day it intended to leave me stranded miles away from home.

It seemed that only a few cars were managing to squeeze through the lights at each turn, so it looked as though I might be here for some time. Curiously, I looked around me at the unfamiliar neighbourhood. It appeared to be a nice quiet area, with 1930s'-style houses and neatly kept front gardens. A little further up ahead I could see a row of dark green railings, which looked like they might belong to a school. As my car crept further down the road I could tell that I'd been right, it *was* a school, and from the chorus of young voices floating on the summer air, I guessed it was a primary one. The growling of my stomach reminded me it was lunchtime, so the children were probably in the playground.

And just like that, the tiny sensitive hairs on the back of my neck began to prickle and stand to attention. A film of perspiration misted over my upper lip. I wiped it away with the back of my hand. What I was thinking was ridiculous. A town this size must have goodness only knows how many primary schools. There was no reason to think that fate was going to take me right past the one Noah attended. But what if it did? What if, just a few hundred metres up the road, the only thing separating me from my own child was a row of wrought iron railings?

If only I knew which school Noah went to; if only I had a way of finding out. My hands were no longer resting lightly on the steering wheel, but were gripping it so tightly that the bones of my knuckles were bleached of colour. *But there is a way, isn't there?* pointed out a voice in my head. It was persistent, and as annoying as a fly buzzing around me. *You know exactly how to find out if this is Noah's school.* I stared with unseeing eyes through my windscreen, not seeing the dirty rear doors of the van in front of me, with 'Clean Me' scrawled in the grime; not seeing anything except a hotel meeting room and something being slowly slid across the table towards me.

That's right, applauded the voice, *all you have to do is check on your phone.*

It was crazy; *I* was crazy for thinking that something – or someone – had led me down a road I'd never been on before for just this reason. My fingers were trembling slightly as I reached into my handbag for my mobile. Somewhere in the back of my head I could hear an echo of the horoscope I'd read with such scorn that morning: *Trust your heart and you'll find the right road to follow.*

I didn't need to scroll through the gallery of photographs stored on my phone, for I'd set the one of Noah on my locked screen. I stared at the image, for once not focusing on my husband's face replicated in miniature on our son, but instead on the green uniform sweatshirt with the gold embroidered logo stitched upon it. I studied it for several seconds before lifting my head and turning to look out of the window at the sign fixed to the railings beside me, which displayed the name of the school, its headteacher and, in the top right-hand corner, the school's crest. It was an exact match. While part of me was reeling from the incredible coincidence, another part of me wasn't surprised at all. Things happen for a reason. Nothing is random. I was meant to be here, in this place, at this exact time today.

I peered through the gaps in the railings, searching for my proof, searching for Noah. There were too many children. They were moving too fast to view their faces, but I could see no one with the familiar abundance of dark hair that I now knew Tim's son had inherited. The lights changed and I moved forward the length of three vehicles, to a position where I could now see the entire playground. None of the faces matched the one in my photograph.

It was her voice that I heard first. When we'd met, it hadn't struck me as particularly memorable and I hadn't realised I'd committed its tone and timbre to memory, but I recognised it instantly.

I slunk down low in my seat, the way I'd seen countless cops do in movie stake-outs. I must have looked ridiculous with my head practically on a level with the van's dashboard, but no one saw me, especially not Izzy, whose concentration was solely on the child walking beside her. I gasped out loud, but luckily they were still too far away to have heard me. He was tall, so much taller than I was expecting, almost up to Izzy's shoulder. It was as if someone had opened a door to the past, allowing me to see Tim as he must have looked at that age. My hand uncurled from the steering wheel and reached out, futilely grasping the air as if to reach him. Noah's face was tilted upwards to Izzy, and it was only as they got a little closer that I saw the tears on his cheeks. My hand was on the door handle and I was almost out of the van before sanity kicked in. I felt as if I was being torn down the middle: half of me wanted to bound from the vehicle, regardless of the line of cars queued up behind me. The other – saner – part told me to stay exactly where I was and avert my face as they approached.

But something was wrong, it had to be. Why was Noah crying and being collected from school in the middle of the day? Was he in trouble? I dismissed that idea without a second's hesitation. Tim had been the gentlest, sweetest man I'd ever met. Surely his son would have inherited those attributes as well as the more obvious physical ones.

Izzy's arms were full as she carried Noah's belongings: a Marvel-themed lunch box, and the kind of bag I immediately recognised as the type music students use. I stored those snippets of information away to devour later. Right now, it was impossible to see beyond the look of misery on the boy's face and his tears. And then, almost as though fate had orchestrated it, they came to a halt practically level with my van. If either of them had chosen to look towards the queue of cars at that moment they would have seen me, bent like a pretzel behind my steering wheel, watching them avidly with stalker-like intensity.

But Izzy's focus was only on Noah. With what looked like practised efficiency, she laid the back of her hand against the young boy's forehead, her own furrowing into a musical stave of lines at whatever she felt there. She had no idea they were being observed as she bent down low to whisper in Noah's ear. After a moment of hesitation his bottom lip trembled and he nodded miserably, before throwing his arms around Izzy's slender waist. Her bag and Noah's belongings fell from her hands, as she enfolded her child in the protective circle of her arms. I strained my ears, but all I could hear were the tone of her words rather than the specifics, and an awareness of the love that radiated from the entwined pair in palpable waves. They were lost to the rest of the world. At that moment, Noah needed nothing more than the arms that were gently rocking him, keeping him safe as they'd surely done for the last eight years. He wasn't feeling well, that much I *had* worked out, but would I have known what to do with him in that situation? Of course not; I wouldn't have had a clue. And he would want nothing from me, this child I had created. Why would he, when all he'd ever needed was standing right there in front of him?

As she held and comforted my child, I could see there were tears glistening in Izzy's eyes at his despair. By the time the lights finally changed and I drove past them, my cheeks were as wet as hers.

There were balloons, quite a lot of them, and it really wasn't the kind of place where you ever imagined seeing them. They were impossible to miss as they bobbed for freedom high above the deserted reception desk. Thin strands of ribbon kept them firmly tethered to the bouquets of flowers and pile of gift-wrapped presents. A greeting card the size of a small billboard stood beside them, with 'Sorry you are leaving' emblazoned on the front.

A quick glance at my watch confirmed there was still half an hour until the offices officially closed, but the sound of laughter and popping champagne corks floating down the corridor made it clear that everyone had already downed tools for the day. I couldn't have picked a worse time for a quiet talk with William, as I appeared to have walked straight into someone's leaving party.

I turned to go, hoping to slip out of the unmanned Reception as surreptitiously as I'd entered it, but before I reached the door a familiar voice called out to me.

'Beth.' I hesitated, but the voice was insistent. 'Beth... Mrs Brandon, wait.'

I pasted a smile on my face and turned to face Keeley Browning, William's assistant.

'Hello, Keeley. How are you?'

A tiny frown marred the smooth skin of her brow. 'Confused,' she admitted. 'I thought I'd cleared Bill's diary for the afternoon. Did you have a meeting with him that I missed?'

I shook my head.

'Phew, that's good,' she declared, pantomiming mopping her brow in relief. 'I'd hate to go out on a sloppy mistake.'

It took a couple of seconds to work out what she meant. I gestured towards the gifts, flowers and farewell card. 'Are these for you? Are you leaving?'

Keeley's eyes looked suspiciously bright, and there was something a little unnatural about the chirpiness of her reply. 'Yes, I am. It's time for something new.' Unexpectedly, she reached for my arm. 'Have you got a couple of minutes?'

I nodded, and followed her curiously as she led us down a quiet corridor, away from her partying colleagues. 'We shouldn't be disturbed in here,' she said, stopping before an unmarked door to unlock it. She slipped through the opening and I followed her, my nose twitching at the dry and dusty smell. Keeley flicked on the overhead light, flooding the room with the glare of fluorescent tubing. The supply room was lined with floor-to-ceiling metal shelves packed with stationery, and was a far cry from the crystal chandelier grandeur of the reception area. Keeley gave a small satisfied nod and pushed the door closed.

'If anyone sees us they'll just think I'm helping myself to some pens and Post-its before I leave,' she joked with a quirky sense of humour I'd never heard from her before.

'What is it you want to tell me?' I asked.

She drew in a long breath before beginning. 'Firstly, I want to say that I'm perfectly okay with how things have worked out.'

I had no idea what she was talking about, so I just nodded politely.

'To tell the truth, it's actually a relief now that everything's out in the open.'

'Oh, well… good,' I said, smiling vaguely in a mystified fashion.

'And I don't regret it, not for a single moment. You deserved to know.'

There was no way I could keep pretending I understood what was going on here. 'Know *what*, exactly?'

'Oh. I thought Liam would have told you. I thought you and he—' She broke off and her cheeks flushed a becoming pink. Mine weren't far behind her at the implication. Keeley inhaled deeply before expelling the words in a rush. '*I* was the one who leaked Noah's identity to you. *I* was the person who sent you the card.'

Whatever I'd thought she was going to tell me in the cloistered privacy of the stationery room, it certainly hadn't been that.

'I knew exactly what I was doing, and the risks, but you were in such an awful situation… and the information was right there in the files, and no one was telling you anything.' She gave a small shrug, which belied the enormity of her actions. 'So I did.'

'I… I see,' I said, processing this unexpected revelation, before remembering that Keeley – who'd broken the rules because of me – was now about to leave the firm.

'Did you lose your job over this? Is that why you're leaving?'

A smile formed slowly on the younger woman's face and she shook her head. 'Well, it didn't exactly qualify me for employee of the month, but it was more of a mutual decision kind of thing. Although in a way you *are* sort of responsible for me wanting to leave.'

'I am?'

'Well, both you and Izzy Vaughan, to be fair,' she replied. 'Working on your case has made me realise how easily something precious can be lost. My partner has been wanting us to go travelling before settling down and having a family. For a long time I wasn't sure that was what I wanted, but now I am.'

It might not have been inappropriate, but impulsively I reached out and hugged this young woman whose life I had unwittingly altered. 'I wish you all the luck in the world,' I said, feeling unexpectedly emotional. 'I'm really glad everything's worked out for you.'

'I hope it does for you, too. For *all* of you.'

No one understood, but that was all right, because I hadn't really expected them to. William hid his irritation well, but I could feel it seeping through the cracks in his restraint.

'And the case against the clinic, are you dropping that too?'

'No. Westmore Clinic was negligent and they need to answer for that. I still want you to go ahead with the claim you spoke about under the Human Rights Act.'

William nodded and looked slightly mollified, but my only interest in the financial compensation was to pay my father back the money he'd lent me.

My parents were disappointed by my decision, even though they spent an entire forty-five-minute telephone call assuring me that they weren't. Only Karen applauded the decision, quite literally as a matter of fact, clapping her hands together as though I'd just won an award.

'This is definitely for the best,' she assured me, from her sun-drenched Australian garden. 'I'm so proud of you, Beth. I know how hard this must have been for you.'

I'd been so strong up until then, so determined not to cry, but her words dissolved my resolve as if it had never been there.

'I just wanted to be a mother,' I said sadly.

Karen leant a little closer to her laptop screen as though those extra few inches would add emphasis to her words. 'You already are. You've sacrificed what you wanted for the sake of your child. And if that's not being a mother, then I don't know what is.'

29

Izzy

There are moments in life when your entire future changes. Like when your boyfriend unexpectedly drops to his knees outside WH Smith and asks you to marry him; or when – after years of believing it will never happen – you finally see two blue lines appear on the stick you've just peed on; or when your solicitor phones you up, and the first thing she says is: *'Are you sitting down?'*

The phone was already ringing as I inserted the key in the front door. I was juggling with three bags of groceries and my handbag, and although I could see that Pete was home – his car was parked on the drive – for some reason he wasn't answering the phone.

'Hang on,' I urged, using my shoulder to open the door and my foot to close it. I was running out of body parts to utilise, as I half stumbled over Pete's abandoned work boots and dived for the handset before the answering machine could kick in. Floating down from the upper floor I could hear someone singing lustily – and somewhat tunelessly

– along to the radio. That *had* to be Pete; Noah simply wasn't capable of hitting that many wrong notes in one chorus.

'Are you sitting down?'

I recognised Frankie's voice instantly, although admittedly it sounded considerably tighter than usual.

'I've just walked through the front door, so no,' I said, my heart already starting to beat just a little bit faster. It was almost as if some of my organs already knew how important the next few minutes were going to be.

'I've been trying both of your mobiles for ages. In the end I had to call the *landline*.'

I smiled. Frankie made it sound like she'd had to hop into a DeLorean and journey back to the nineties.

I set one of the shopping bags down on the floor, noticing as I did that Pete's phone was on the kitchen worktop, jacked up to the charger.

'Sorry, I must have been in a poor signal area. What's up?'

'I hope you're ready for this,' Frankie said, and it was only then that I realised her own voice was shaky. My pulse rate catapulted up another ten beats a minute.

'What's happened?'

Frankie cleared her throat, as though what she was about to say was so big it was in danger of obstructing her airway. 'She's dropping the case.'

'I... I... What?' It wasn't that I hadn't *understood* what I'd just been told; it was just that it was too enormous to immediately process it. No wonder she'd asked me to sit down.

'Beth Brandon is dropping her legal claim for contact with Noah,' Frankie said, enunciating every word slowly and carefully, as if I was a foreigner.

The remaining plastic carrier bags fell from my fingers. One part of my brain watched as half a dozen oranges rolled for freedom across the wooden floor of the hallway; the other part was quite literally stunned into inactivity.

'Izzy, are you still there? You've not passed out on me or something, have you?'

'No. I'm still here,' I whispered into the mouthpiece. My legs were like jelly and I stepped back until I could feel the treads of the staircase behind me. I sank down on them gratefully. 'How did this happen? *Why* did this happen?'

The sound of Frankie's laughter travelled cheerfully down the phone line. 'I'd like to say it's because she realised I'm a shit-hot lawyer, and that they were never going to win this one in court – but the truth is, I simply don't know. I *do* know that this is one hundred percent her decision. I got the distinct impression that neither William Sylvester nor Edward Patterson are exactly on board with it – but at the end of the day she's the client, and they have to follow her instructions.'

'And she really doesn't want to be part of Noah's life? Not in any capacity?' I was struggling to get my head around this life-changing news.

'No. For whatever reason, she has withdrawn that side of her legal action. I imagine she'll probably still pursue her claim against the clinic, but as I've mentioned before, Westmore are going to want to settle with both of you out of court, so this gets you off the hook as far as media intrusion goes too. As far as you, Pete and Noah go, this is a win-win situation.'

I'd become so used to walking in the shadows, I was finding it difficult to believe the sun had finally emerged from behind the clouds. 'But what if she changes her mind somewhere down the line? What if she decides in the future that she *does* want to get to know Noah after all?'

'Way ahead of you there, Izzy. I've already made it clear to William that we'd want a document drawn up, wherein she legally renounces this and any future claim to the embryo – to Noah,' Frankie corrected. 'We've still got the nitty-gritty details to work through, but basically this is like winning the lottery *and* finding a Willy Wonka Golden Ticket on the same day. This is a champagne-corks-popping moment, and to hell with what time of day it is.'

The smile started slowly, almost as if it didn't dare to believe the nightmare was over. It was still inching up towards my ears when Frankie spoke again. 'Now, do *you* want to give Pete the news, or should I keep trying his mobile?'

I was grinning so broadly it was actually quite difficult to speak. 'No, that's okay. I'll tell him.'

After Frankie had hung up, I stayed on the stairs for several minutes, uncaring that my frozen shopping was now beginning to defrost in the bags. Beth Brandon was about to step out of our life, as unexpectedly as she'd walked into it. I had no idea what had prompted her decision, or if anything I'd said or done had influenced her. I had no clue why she'd inexplicably changed her mind, and maybe I never would. 'Thank you, Beth,' I murmured into my empty hallway.

'Thank you for giving life to our son, but even more than that, thank you for giving him back to us.'

I ran up the stairs in the way I was always telling Noah not to do – two steps at a time, my toes hardly connecting with each tread before they were flying upwards to find purchase on the next. Fortunately, Noah wasn't home to witness the transgression. The school holidays had begun, and I remembered now that he was spending the afternoon with one of his classmates. That was probably just as well, because the jubilation coursing through me was way too big to be contained in hushed whispers. This was the kind of news that demanded to be shouted out loud.

There were certain unwritten rules that we'd put in place since Pete had moved back into his former home. One of them involved waiting for permission outside any closed door. But today I didn't even stop to *think*, let alone knock. I flung the door open so wildly I heard the handle collide damagingly against the plasterboard, marking on the wall the moment when the course of our future would once again change.

Sheer momentum propelled me across the threshold and my excitement was so intense it actually took several seconds for me to notice that Pete was completely naked. He'd spun around at the sound of the opening door; the damp towel that he'd dropped on the carpet – some things never change – was too far out of reach to provide any cover. In those first few shocked seconds, before he reached for something to conceal his nudity, the reason I was there was momentarily shunted out of my head by several disquieting thoughts. The first was that Pete too had lost weight over the intervening months, although on him it looked good. The taut muscles of his stomach – which had never quite made it to a six-pack – were much more prominent than I remembered. The second thought was surprise at my body's reaction to his, which jolted through me like an electrical charge.

My brain rapidly pressed 'reset' and the reason I was there – the phone call with all its amazing implications – spilled from me in an incomprehensible jumble of words.

'Iz, slow down. I can't understand what you're saying,' Pete declared, still incongruously masking his dignity behind what I now saw was the Paddington Bear toy he'd given me on our first wedding anniversary.

'Frankie called. It's all over. She's dropping the case.'

Pete's face crumpled into a frown. 'Do you mean she's not going to represent us anymore? Do we have to find a new lawyer?'

I shook my head, wondering why Pete had suddenly become blurry around the edges. Happy tears were pooling in my eyes and as I shook my head they were released to trickle down my cheeks.

'Not Frankie,' I said, my voice hiccupping on a tiny sob. 'Beth. *She's* the one who's dropping the case.'

Pete took a small step towards me, still holding Paddington firmly in place. Witnessing the moment when the realisation dawned in his eyes was the most beautiful thing I had ever seen. No sunrise over the Grand Canyon, no Sahara sunset or night sky of Northern Lights could ever be more wondrous.

'It's over?' he asked, his voice scarcely louder than a whisper. 'She's just giving up?'

I nodded, too choked to speak, although I did notice when Paddington fell from Pete's hand to the carpet.

It's impossible to say which one of us bridged the final distance between us first. I'd like to think that we both did. All I knew was that his arms were open and I fell into them, into him, as though I'd never been away.

The warm length of his body burned through my clothes, setting me on fire as he held me tighter than he'd ever done before.

'My God, Izzy, is it really over?' His question was murmured into the fall of my hair. 'She's not going to seek contact?'

'No. She's walking away,' I replied, my words muffled, for they were spoken into the bare skin of his shoulder. He smelled of shower gel and a mixture of pheromones that were the unforgettable cocktail of him. I inhaled him secretly, storing the memory away and ignoring the warning klaxon that was beginning to sound in my head.

Perhaps Pete heard it too, for his hold on me fell away. I took a step backwards, losing my balance as I stood squarely on the dropped bear. Pete's arms shot out to steady me. Holding me as he was, at arms' length, it was impossible to ignore his state of undress or his body's surprising reaction to my proximity.

My eyes dropped to the fallen bear, which at that moment seemed to be the safest direction to look. As I crouched to retrieve it, the humour of the situation crashed over me like a wave. Somehow, we had journeyed from Greek tragedy to French farce in the blink of an eye. 'Well, if *that* doesn't send him back to deepest darkest Peru, nothing will,' I said, my fingers curling into the plush fur, still damp from a place it was safe to say it had never been before.

Pete threw back his head and laughed so infectiously it was impossible not to join in. Our humour surfed a borderline between relief and hysteria. It was a much-needed physical reaction of release, and perhaps so too was what happened next.

Maybe it's not unusual for intense emotions to spill over and lose their way. I remember reading once that people are more likely to have sex after attending a funeral than they are a wedding. The dread that had been lurking at our door for the longest time had finally moved on and you could practically taste the euphoria in the air.

My clothes hit the bedroom floor and Pete's hands were moving over my skin as hungrily as my own were retracing their pathways over his. We fell back onto the spare room bed, our lovemaking a frenzy of celebration that took us both to a place I thought I'd never visit again.

30

Beth

'My view today – or first thing this morning, to be precise!'

It was easily the sixth or seventh time I'd clicked on the photo, and yet it still made me laugh. At first I'd struggled to recognise the room in the picture as being Liam's immaculate kitchen, for the entire floor was lost beneath an explosion of something white and foamy.

It was only when I enlarged the image that I saw it wasn't actually a sea of bubbles covering the slate-grey tiles, but the stuffing from a two-seater settee, which looked as though someone had effectively disembowelled it. Beside the ruined couch sat the culprit, wearing an innocent expression that was largely cancelled out by the lumps of stuffing still dangling from her mouth.

I smiled as I scrolled back over our exchanged messages.

'Oh no. What did she do?'

'Apparently took a dislike to the sofa in the middle of the night. We're now off to the vets for X-rays. Again!'

I set the phone down on the shop's counter, a smile still playing on my lips. However much Liam might moan about his late wife's dog, he'd be the first to admit he'd be devastated if anything ever happened to her. She was more than just a link to the past; she was a loyal and faithful keeper of his memories. And as an added bonus, she was also a source of practically guaranteed amusement.

Perhaps *I* needed a Sally in my life, I mused, as I began sorting through the morning delivery from the nursery. It would be all too easy to let myself wallow in the sadness of dreams that hadn't come true. But I wasn't going to do that, because the decision I'd made had been the right one. I'd chosen not to destroy something Tim and I had created together, so how could that ever be wrong?

My fingers stilled on the flowers I was absently lifting from the container. Calla lilies. Although most commonly known for their popularity with brides, I'd chosen these flowers not for their undeniable waxy beauty, but for their meaning in the language of flowers: new beginnings.

I hummed quietly to myself as I began work on the display, not exactly happy, but more at peace with my decision than I'd thought it was possible to be. As the arrangement took shape, words circled my head, like displaced birds finally finding a place to land. *New beginnings, new horizons, and new dreams.*

The buzzing of my phone broke the silence of the shop. Sally's face filled the screen. If dogs could grin, that's what she was doing. I read the message below the photo and sighed with relief.

'No serious damage, except to the couch and my wallet!'

I added one final item to the list I'd been mentally compiling for reasons to look forward rather than backward: *New friends.*

Was I guilty of being complacent? Had I taken for granted things that had never been spoken of? Was that why it all went so horribly wrong just a few short hours later?

It had all started with the customer in the flamboyant psychedelic shirt and designer suit. He'd ordered a very expensive floral display and at the last moment had added three dozen long-stemmed roses to his bill. It was an unexpected bonus at the end of a quiet day, and I was just processing the payment when he startled me with his desire to make one more purchase.

'That painting you have over there, I don't suppose it's for sale, is it?'

Quite a few customers had commented on the vibrant piece of artwork since Liam had given it to me, but this was the first time anyone had wanted to buy it. I think that's why I sounded so wrong-footed and hesitant as I replied.

'Er, no. I mean... no. It's not mine... Well, it is... but it's not for sale.'

'Shame,' said the man, laying his roses down on the counter and walking up to the painting to inspect it more closely, with what I was beginning to suspect was something more than just a passing interest.

After several moments, he looked back at me over his shoulder. 'And you're sure you don't want to part with it?'

And then he named the figure he'd be willing to pay, which was so much higher than I'd been expecting that I gave a very unprofessional gulp. Haggling was clearly not in my nature.

'No. I'm sorry, but my answer's still "no". It was a gift,' I added. The man nodded as though he'd fully expected to be knocked back. 'The artist's husband gave it to me,' I explained.

'Really?' questioned the man, suddenly sounding much more interested than he'd been only a few seconds before. He pulled a business card holder from his pocket, like a magician performing an illusion, and extracted one for me. I took the small rectangular card from his outstretched fingers. 'Tetra Art Gallery,' I read out loud. I'd never heard of it, but from the quality of the card and the appearance of the man, I guessed it was quite a prestigious establishment.

'Do you happen to know if his wife has any other pieces that she might be willing to sell?' Andrew Cartwright, Gallery Owner – according to the gold lettering on his business card – wanted to know.

That was the moment when I could have shot it all down. I could have taken his card and then simply thrown it away when he left the shop. It's certainly what I *should* have done. I've spent quite a bit of time rewriting my actions and examining my motives since that day, and I'm still not sure why I didn't do that.

'Actually, his wife passed away – well, she was involved in a tragic car accident – about eight years ago, so it's her husband you'd have to ask about selling pieces of her work.'

'But there *are* more pieces?' Andrew Cartwright probed, and the excited gleam flickering in his eyes should have warned me that this man wasn't the kind to take no for an answer. Instead, I just carried on, blithely digging myself into a hole that very soon I'd find impossible to climb out of.

'God, yes. There are loads. He has them all over his home and office. I think there are at least a couple of roomfuls of them in his house.'

'How interesting.'

And there was something about his voice that made me suddenly realise that perhaps this wasn't something Liam would want to be involved in. Why was this only *now* occurring to me?

'But I'm fairly certain he wouldn't want to sell any of them, given the circumstances.'

'Oh, absolutely. I totally understand. But I *would* be very interested in possibly putting on an exhibition of the pieces,' Andrew Cartwright said, glancing towards the one on my shop wall, 'especially if they're anything like this one.'

An exhibition, rather than an auction. Surely Liam would have no objection to that? Wouldn't he want Anna's amazing paintings to be seen by a wider audience; an audience who clearly appreciated and understood art?

'They *are* all as good as this!' I exclaimed, already getting carried away with excitement at being instrumental in the paintings being displayed on the walls of an esteemed gallery. 'Here,' I said, reaching for a notebook and thumbing through until I found a blank page. 'Let me give you his telephone number and then you can contact him direct.' Perhaps even then it might have been possible to have salvaged my interfering mistake, if I'd given him Liam's work number, but stupidly I didn't do that. Unthinkingly, I scribbled down his personal number on the page. And just like that, the damage was done.

Liam called me that evening, and at first I was slow to recognise the total absence of warmth in his greeting. He wasted very little time on preamble.

'Why did you tell a gallery owner that I'd like to exhibit Anna's paintings?'

'I didn't. Well, I did in a way... but not really.'

'Well, which one is it?' His question sounded as if it had come straight out of a lawyer textbook, from a chapter entitled 'How to Interrogate a Witness'. I certainly felt as if I was giving evidence on the stand as I fumbled over my reply.

'The man came into the shop and was interested in the painting. He wanted to buy it and—'

'Anna's paintings aren't for sale.' Liam cut through my explanation as if he was wielding a sabre.

'Yes. That's what I told him. But then he started talking about an exhibition and I...'

There was an unnerving silence at the end of the phone as my voice trailed away. Straining my ears, I could just about make out the sound of his breathing.

'Liam, I'm really sorry, I didn't mean to interfere.'

This was the point when he was supposed to say something like: *It's okay. Don't worry about it* or *I'm sure you meant well* or even – although this now seemed highly unlikely – *Thank you for giving the guy my number.*

He drew in a long steadying breath before speaking, and when he did his words burnt me like an icy blast from an arctic cave. 'Did the man tell you how interest in the exhibition would be so much greater because Anna was dead?'

I felt sick, actually physically sick, at his words. 'No. No, he didn't say that.'

'You didn't know Anna, so you've no idea how self-effacing she was about her work. She'd have hated to have a roomful of strangers gawping and critiquing her paintings.'

He was right. I'd stepped over the line, and trodden carelessly on something sacrosanct: Liam's relationship with his late wife. Like an intruder caught in a flashlight beam I tried to back away, but it was too late, the damage was already done.

'I'm so sorry, Liam. I should have thought it through. The guy caught me on the hop and I just got excited about the idea of an exhibition.'

'Which Anna would have hated,' he reminded me, in case I was still in any doubt about that.

'Yes, well, maybe she would. Obviously you knew her better than anyone. Although I have to say, I think it's disappointing you have so little faith in her work.'

He gasped at my words and I think I might have done too. But I'd started now, so I might as well hammer the final nail in the coffin of our friendship.

'All you talk about is how she'd have felt about the criticism. But what you don't say – what you don't even appear to have *considered* – is how she'd have felt about the admiration and the praise. Wouldn't she have deserved to hear that too?'

Liam said nothing, so it was hard to tell if my words had fallen on deaf or receptive ears. I made one final attempt to put things right.

'Why don't I phone Andrew Cartwright and explain that I acted impulsively and ask him not to bother you again.'

'That really won't be necessary, thank you. Mr Cartwright *won't* be calling me again.'

I shivered at his words, not realising then that the gallery owner wasn't the only person Liam had no intention of speaking to in the near future.

31

Izzy

'Are you sure no one is going to mind if I go with you?' It was probably the fifth time he'd asked me that question over the past two days. I set my morning cup of coffee down on the kitchen table and smiled in Pete's direction. It was something I'd been doing quite a lot over the last forty-eight hours, testing my facial muscles to see if they still remembered how to do it. It would appear they did.

'Maggie will be absolutely fine about it. It's going to be a very relaxed wedding, and the original save-the-date card *had* included you,' I reminded him, conveniently forgetting that by the time the actual invitations had been sent out for her son's wedding, we'd no longer been living together.

Pete's eyes crinkled at the edges. How could I have forgotten how much I loved the way they did that? 'Hmm, but a lot has changed since then,' he observed, neatly skirting a topic we still hadn't properly addressed. It had been two days since Frankie's phone call; two days since we'd stepped blinking and dazed out of the shadow we'd been living under; and two days since we'd made love for the first time in more than a year...

We'd never intended to fall asleep afterwards. But the bedroom, bathed in afternoon sunlight, had been warm and cosy. My head had naturally found its way to the familiar hollow of Pete's shoulder, and his arms had locked tightly around me, holding me close as our breathing slowly synchronised and our eyelids grew heavy. It was the sound of persistent knocking that had forced me awake. The first thing I noticed was that the sun had travelled to the furthest corner of the bedroom and my naked limbs felt chilled without its warm caress. For a heartbeat, I couldn't remember where I was or what had happened. Then the memories returned, bringing with them a hot flush of colour to my cheeks.

'What the hell is that noise?' Pete mumbled sleepily, slower than me to realise that someone appeared to be hammering extremely loudly on the front door.

'Shit! It must be Belinda, bringing Noah back,' I exclaimed, my eyes widening as I glanced at my watch. We'd slept for *hours*. I sat bolt upright, forcibly breaking apart Pete's hold on me. Something soft stirred inside as I realised he'd never released me while we slept, but it was pushed aside by the need to answer the door before Belinda remembered the place I'd told her the spare key was hidden.

I twisted off the bed, my arms instinctively covering my naked breasts as I scrabbled on the floor for my discarded clothes. I thought I saw the vaguest twitch of Pete's lips when he noticed my sudden attack of modesty, but I was struggling into my shirt before he could comment. I thrust my legs into my jeans and was still pulling up zips and securing buttons as I ran barefoot down the stairs to answer the door.

'I was just about to indulge in a spot of breaking and entering,' said Belinda, sounding almost disappointed that I'd thwarted her plans as I flung open the door. A curious expression slid over her face as she took in my tousled hair and the revealing flush that was fast travelling south from my face to my chest. Her lips moved, as though she was savouring a delicious toffee, and then formed a small O of surprise as Pete, also barefoot and dishevelled, ran lightly down the stairs behind me.

'Hi, B,' he said easily, looking past her dancing eyes and smiling warmly at the two boys flanking her like miniature guards. 'Hey, guys, have you had a good time?'

'I bring with me two very tired young men: one yours, one mine,' Belinda replied, as Noah broke rank to give his dad a massive hug. I smiled at both boys, but couldn't help noticing that Noah looked appreciably more exhausted than his best friend, Archie.

'We've been swimming, and cycling, and then we built an enormous den in the garden,' Belinda listed breezily as the boys moved to follow Pete down the hallway. 'We've had quite an afternoon.' Her eyes danced mischievously as the trio moved out of earshot. 'As, I suspect, have you.' She leant a little closer and dropped her eyes briefly to my top. 'You missed a button,' she whispered, only just managing to suppress a Cheshire-cat grin. Like a chameleon, my cheeks morphed to the exact shade of pink as my shirt, but fortunately Archie's return to his mother's side ensured the subject was dropped.

Back in the kitchen, Pete was listening to Noah's account of his afternoon activities, while I tried my best to stop thoughts of our own from surfacing. It felt beyond inappropriate to be slicing vegetables and preparing our evening meal when my head was full of snapshot images of Pete poised above me, and the way he had trembled before joining his body with mine, as if it was our very first time.

It was only when Noah ran off to watch his favourite TV show that we were finally alone. Almost shyly, I looked at him across the distance of the kitchen. For a moment, everything else faded away: I could no longer hear the whir of the washing machine; the theme tune from the television; or any of the hundred and one other mundane noises that formed the soundtrack of our home. All I could hear was my heartbeat, banging like a drum in my ears. Some of the sauce I was stirring slopped over the top of the pan, and I scarcely even noticed.

'We should probably talk,' Pete said softly, stealing what I had intended to be my opening line. I nodded, the heat from the stove added to the warmth already flooding through me as his eyes held me captive in a look I knew was going to keep me awake that night.

'I just want you to know,' he said, his eyes glancing towards the doorway to make sure Noah wasn't about to put in an appearance, 'that it wasn't just a heat-of-the-moment thing – at least, it wasn't for *me*.'

How was it possible to suddenly feel so shy in front of a man who'd been by your side through the very best and worst moments of your life? But that was exactly how I felt. Very gently, Pete lifted my chin with one finger, forcing my eyes to meet his. 'I do *not* regret what happened today,

Izzy. And I really hope you don't either, but...' It had all been going so well until the introduction of that worrying conjunction. '...but I don't think we should rush into things or make assumptions about where this might lead.'

I tried to hold his gaze while hiding the fact that I'd been doing nothing *but* making assumptions ever since Belinda's hammering on the door had woken us.

'We need to take it slow. Not just for Noah's sake, but for ours too. I'm scared of getting it wrong again.' It was crushing to think that even before this thing was fully formed, he was already thinking of it failing.

'No. No, of course not,' I lied, suddenly pretending that the sauce I'd been busily splattering all over the hob now deserved my full attention.

By the time Pete had disappeared upstairs to put Noah to bed – a ritual that hadn't grown old for either of them since his return – I'd managed to rein in the disappointment coursing through me. I listened through the ceiling to the creaking floorboards as the pair moved from bathroom to bedroom. I muted the television, preferring to hear the deep timbre of Pete's voice as he read the next chapter of Noah's bedtime story.

While I waited, I extracted a bottle of wine from the fridge and poured out two generous glasses. This was *still* a day of celebration, I reminded myself as I took a long sip of the crisp Pinot Grigio. Okay, so it wasn't ending in the way a Hollywood romcom script would have written it, but this was real life, and I was old enough and sensible enough to know that not every story ends with a *happily ever after*.

★★★

Pete drained the remainder of his morning coffee as though downing a shot, and placed the cup back on the table. The clearing of his throat was the only warning I had that he was about to say something important.

'I had a long talk with Maya yesterday and told her I thought it was best if we called a halt to everything from now on.'

I could feel a variety of expressions spinning like a wheel of fortune as they kaleidoscoped across my face. What *was* the appropriate one when your husband informs you that he's broken up with his girlfriend?

'How did she take it?'

'She was relieved, I think,' Pete replied, resting his splayed fingers on the tabletop. They were broad, and blunt, and never entirely free of lingering ingrained oil stains. They were the hands that still wore his wedding ring, and had held our newborn son within their strong grip. They held a thousand memories.

'Why do you think she was relieved?'

'She was worried about her job. It might not be a sackable offence, but it certainly would have earned her a reprimand.'

'Huh?' Had Maya's job really been in jeopardy by dating a co-worker?

'Siphoning off the jobs the garage didn't get and passing them to me to do privately after hours isn't exactly something I imagine Barry would approve of.'

Barry was the garage owner; a scary man, who resembled a slightly less menacing cousin of the Kray twins.

There was a sudden knowing look on Pete's face as he continued. 'You *do* realise that's how I've been earning the money to pay Frankie's bills?' he questioned, seeing the look of astonishment on my face. 'Obviously, now we won't be going to court I can pull the plug, before it gets both of us into trouble.'

'I thought that Maya... I thought she was lending... I thought you and she were—'

Pete was staring at me with a look of growing incredulity on his face. My cheeks were getting warmer, and there was absolutely nothing I could do about it. One of the hands I was so fond of travelled across the kitchen table and took hold of mine.

'Never. Not even once. It simply never crossed my mind.'

It wasn't the time or place to say that I was still pretty sure it had crossed Maya's. Despite that, I was grateful for the help she'd given us, whatever her motives had been, and when I next saw her I would thank her.

'So that's *one* thing cleared up. That just leaves... us,' Pete began, leaving his sentence dangling, unfinished, for me to pick up.

'Maybe we could talk properly later today, at the wedding reception?' I suggested tentatively. Weddings always put people in a romantic mood, and perhaps after a glass or two of champagne the conversation we'd been keeping on ice for the last two days could finally be aired.

'I don't understand how these shoes can possibly be tight,' I exclaimed, dropping to my knees on Noah's bedroom carpet. 'We only bought them a couple of weeks ago because your old ones didn't fit.'

'And now these don't fit either,' Noah added, quite unnecessarily. Even with the laces loosened as far as they could go, the flesh of Noah's foot bulged uncomfortably against the leather. I reached for the shoe box, certain the sales assistant must have given us the incorrect size, but there was no disputing the large numeral printed on the side of the carton. Noah had had another inexplicable growth spurt since our shopping expedition – or at least, his feet had.

'What are we going to do?' I said despairingly to Pete, who'd paused on his way from the bathroom to the spare bedroom to see what the trouble was.

'Get him a job in a circus?' he joked.

'Very helpful,' I muttered, turning my attention back to the problem before me. We were due to leave for the wedding in less than an hour, and there was no time to replace the shoes. Even the suit I'd bought him only a month ago looked a little tight, I now noticed. How on earth do children manage to grow that fast?

'You're just going to have to wear your trainers. At least they're black,' I said, getting to my feet.

If only all of our problems were that easy to resolve.

The wedding was joyful, if perhaps a little bizarre. After a conventional registry office ceremony attended only by immediate family, the day became an extravaganza of celebration, including a second exchange of vows 'officiated' by the couple's friends and family.

It was gloriously warm, a real gift of a day, which was fortunate, for the reception was held in the middle of a field owned by the bride's uncle. Guests were seated on 'pews' of hay bales, which scratched sharply against the back of my bare legs and made me very glad it had been too warm for tights beneath my floaty sleeveless dress.

Noah thought it was all tremendous fun, leaping from bale to bale with shrieks of laughter with a clutch of other young wedding guests, who'd gravitated towards each other like magnets in instant friendship. Watching him play happily in the afternoon sunlight, the blood tests and allergy clinic appointments we'd attended that week felt almost pointless. He looked fine; he *was* fine, I assured myself, as I sat on the hay bale, Pete's leg almost but not quite brushing up against mine.

I cried during the ceremony, although from the sound of rustling tissues and blowing noses, I don't think I was the only one to do so. When Maggie read out a poem about watching your child grow up, and then went on to say how proud she was of the man her son had become, Pete reached for my hand, his fingers curling around mine and squeezing them gently. 'That'll be us one day, you and me at Noah's wedding,' he whispered, sounding a little choked himself as an image of a much older Noah, a young man we'd yet to meet, filled our heads.

'You may have guessed, they're off to Mexico for their honeymoon,' informed Maggie, who found me among the assembled cluster of guests a little later. Her cheeks were flushed a becoming pink, which may or may not have something to do with the champagne that had been flowing freely all afternoon.

'Ah, well, that explains the Mariachi band and the piñatas,' I said, my eyes travelling to the edge of the field where Noah and his new friends were currently beating a paper donkey to smithereens in order to release its hidden cache of sweets.

Maggie turned to leave and then paused and spun back to face me, unexpectedly swooping in to kiss my cheek. 'It's really good seeing the three of you together again. You look so happy today.'

I hugged her briefly, looking over her shoulder to watch as Pete weaved through the crowd towards me, two paper plates stacked high with buffet food balanced in his hands. His eyes were on me the entire time, and the look within them made my heart skip and trip in a way it hadn't done for quite a while.

'I *am* happy,' I whispered in my friend's ear, before stepping out of the hug. 'It feels like all the missing pieces in my life are finally falling back into place.'

As dusk began to fall, a snaking row of tea-light candles in glass jars set around the edge of the field were lit. They twinkled like fireflies in the fading light. The hay bales had been moved to form a square around an area designated as a dance floor, and I wondered how long Pete would be able to resist the lure of the music, although to be fair he showed no signs of wanting to leave my side.

'So,' he said at last, passing me a glass of champagne, although he'd switched to soft drinks several hours earlier. 'We said we'd talk…'

My heart rate increased, revving upwards like a car going through a gearbox. Nought to sixty in seconds. I smiled at the analogy. Once a mechanic's wife, always a mechanic's wife. At least, I hoped that was what I still was. I shifted on the treacherous hay, not even noticing how it stung my legs.

'I've been thinking really seriously since what happened the other day…' That sentence had the potential to end in one of two ways, so I kept my features neutral as I waited for him to finish. 'And what I really want to say is—'

'I need a wee.'

Both of us had been so intent on what was possibly one of the most important conversations of our marriage, neither of us had heard Noah approach. Our heads spun towards him with the synchronicity of tango dancers. I loved that child more than life, but at that moment I really wished he'd taken a few more minutes before joining us.

Pete's smile was rueful as he got to his feet. 'Do you want me to come with you?' he asked, already knowing the answer.

Noah nodded and looked relieved when Pete's hand came to rest on his shoulder. 'Come on then, big man. The portaloos are over in the far corner of the field.'

I could hear Noah giggling with schoolboy delight at the word 'portaloo' as the two of them disappeared into the lengthening shadows. I was still watching them as my clutch bag vibrated silently against my thigh. I slid my hand beneath its flap to retrieve my phone, frowning slightly as I recognised the number displayed on the screen. Why was the doctor's surgery calling me long after they should have closed for the day? *Don't answer it*, urged a voice in my head. *Leave it. Whatever it is, it can wait until tomorrow. Don't let anything ruin this perfect day.*

Ignoring the warning, my finger pressed down firmly on the green icon.

★★★

The bride and groom were circling the makeshift dance floor, executing moves that had probably taken weeks to master at the local dance school. But I scarcely even saw them. They were blurry shapes swirling past my field of vision, which was focused on... well, nothing, really. I felt rather than saw Pete return. The hay crackled as he sat back down beside me. There was a tension in him that initially I thought was coming off me, arcing out like an electrical current.

He twisted slightly, following Noah's gangling run as he jogged back to join his new friends. Even though he was too far away to hear us, Pete's voice was low and a little hurried.

'I don't want you to panic...' What a perfectly ridiculous way to begin a sentence. It was a self-fulfilling prophecy. *Of course* you were going to panic after hearing those words. The only thing you didn't yet know was *why*. Except that I did.

'I think Noah may have a problem.'

Perhaps if it hadn't been for the phone call I'd just received, my head would have shot up at those words. As it was I lifted it slowly, as if it was suddenly too heavy for my neck to support.

'There's something up with his pee. I noticed it just now. It's the wrong colour and kind of... I don't know... frothy.'

My stomach flipped as the vague hope that the doctor's tests had been wrong and that Noah's results had mistakenly been muddled with someone else's slipped through my fingers like wisps of smoke.

'Do you think we should take him to A&E? Get him checked out tonight? We could leave right now.'

It felt strange seeing my usually capable and calm

husband playing the role that had been mine for so long. I'd spent practically Noah's entire life panicking about his health, and yet now, when there was clearly something that warranted that concern, I was strangely calm.

'We have an appointment at the GP's first thing in the morning.'

'You phoned them already? How did you know?'

My smile was sad, not surprising really, as that was how I felt. Sad and terribly, terribly scared. 'I didn't. They phoned me. Something has shown up on the tests we had done this week. They want to see us both first thing in the morning to discuss it.'

It was 3 a.m. and even the house had ceased its creaking and settled down for the night. Across the hallway Noah slept soundly, oblivious to all the ways his life was about to change. Pete, I imagined, was also asleep; there'd been no light coming from beneath his bedroom door on my last two coffee trips.

The last cup was cold on my bedside table, an unappealing skin forming on its surface. Not that I needed the caffeine to stay awake. I shifted my legs and the laptop slithered a little to one side. The duvet was hot where the computer had sat as I scrolled through page after page on the internet, cross-matching symptoms with conditions and case histories; searching for answers. And there were plenty out there to be had, but none of them were to my liking, so I just kept on looking.

We'd left the wedding as soon as it was acceptable to do so. Noah had already fallen asleep by the time we'd pulled into the driveway and Pete had carefully unfastened his seat belt and carried him in from the car, in a way he hadn't done since Noah was a toddler. Pete had stood in the bedroom doorway, watching as I eased the trainers from Noah's feet, saying nothing as I winced when I saw the deep indentations they had left in his flesh. How had I not noticed this? How had I been so busy worrying, first about the court case and then about what would happen between Pete and me, that I'd neglected my duties as a mother? I'd spent almost all of Noah's life practically paralysed by the fear that some dreadful illness would befall him. I'd been so vigilant in guarding against it I had practically driven my husband away with my obsession. And now, the ultimate irony: the universe's slap in the face – because there really *had* been something genuine to worry about. My greatest fears had come true, and what had I been doing? Looking the wrong bloody way.

'We don't know anything for sure yet,' Pete had soothed as I eased shut Noah's bedroom door. 'We may be worrying about nothing.'

The look I gave him spoke volumes. Doctors don't just phone you up late on a Friday evening about test results that aren't causing serious concern. 'We should cross that bridge when we come to it,' Pete said, reaching his hand out to rest it on my shoulder. I took an unconscious step backwards and his hand fell into the abyss between us; a chasm that was growing so wide I could hardly see him on the other side of it anymore.

'I should have known,' I whispered into the darkness of the hall. 'I'm his mother. It's my job to look out for him. It's my job to never look away.'

'It's *both* our jobs,' Pete corrected, the crack in his voice betraying his emotion.

I turned towards my bedroom, trying not to see the unasked question in Pete's eyes and my own unshakeable reply. I wanted to be alone.

'Well, I'll see you in the morning then,' he said, his weight shifting, making the floorboards creak noisily. It was like the end of an awkward date, where no one is sure if they should kiss, shake hands, or simply turn around and walk away.

We both walked away.

32

Beth

'So, what did you think of Bondi?'

I wrinkled my nose and my sunglasses bobbed upwards before falling back into place. 'It's okay, but very crowded and commercial. I'm glad we went – I'd always wanted to go there, but I think I'm possibly ten years too old to appreciate it properly.'

'That's *exactly* how I felt, ten years ago!' Karen laughed as she leant forward to retrieve her wine glass from the table I'd insisted on, which was as close to the water's edge as we could find. It was such a touristy thing to do, but Karen was so pleased to finally have me here, she was happy to indulge every one of my whims.

The late afternoon sun was still warm enough to bathe our table in a hazy glow, and with the iconic Sydney Opera House behind her I couldn't resist taking one more photograph of my sister to add to the several hundred I must have snapped over the last three weeks. It was technically still winter – but not as we Brits know it, I thought with a smile. Karen and I were both wearing T-shirts, and our sunglasses weren't just a fashion statement but a necessity to protect us from the glare of the water that sparkled like quicksilver in the harbour.

I looked towards the famous Harbour Bridge, watching the tiny black figures – no larger than ants from where we were sitting – inch their way upwards in their climb to the top. I lifted my phone and took yet another photograph. Out of a habit I still couldn't seem to break, I sent it off in a WhatsApp message, which I doubted Liam would answer, with the caption: *'My view today.'*

Smiling at my sister, I settled back in my chair. 'It's so nice here,' I said, which was probably the understatement of the century.

Somehow Karen managed to resist saying *See!*, even though it was written all over her face. 'I knew you'd like it,' she said, trying not to look smug and failing a little. 'And if you feel that way now, when you've every reason to feel sad, just imagine how much more you're going to love it when you feel happier again.'

I turned my gaze to the harbour, with the ferries chugging in and out, and the impressive cruise liner docked majestically behind them. 'I don't think deciding to give up your claim to your own child is something you ever really get over,' I said sadly.

Karen's sun-bronzed hand reached over and clasped mine, the way it had done when we were children walking through the school gates; and after she'd fixed my veil in place on my wedding day; and when she'd walked beside me from Tim's freshly dug grave. Her hand and mine had been linked through joy and tragedy; this was just one more life experience to add to the list.

'It *will* get easier,' she promised, which was easy for her to say when her own children were no more than a couple of hundred metres away, craning over the edge of the harbour wall with their dad, looking for the Opera House's resident seal. I didn't want to ruin my final evening with yet another conversation about my decision. It had been made, and it was time to move on with the rest of my life.

My phone pinged with an incoming message and a flicker of hope fluttered in my chest, even though I told it not to. Had Liam actually decided to reply this time? My eyes scanned the message from my phone's service provider, and as much as I tried to disguise the disappointment on my face, Karen still managed to spot it.

'Not from him, I take it?'

I shook my head, thankful my sunglasses were dark enough to provide protection from more than just UV rays.

'Well, I'm sorry, but your new friend isn't impressing me one little bit with his radio silence. I still think this has a lot to do with you dropping such a high-profile case that would have given their firm incredible exposure.'

I remained silent, because nothing I said would convince Karen otherwise. But I was the one who'd been there, not her. I remembered how anxious I'd been when I'd left William's office and hesitantly knocked on Liam's door, to tell him about my decision. He'd sat me down on the green leather chesterfield, his eyes probing mine as I repeated what I'd just told his partner.

'I'm not going to insult you by asking if you've really thought this through,' Liam had said when I'd finally got to the end of my explanation. His eyes were kind and his voice was gentle as he added, 'I imagine you've thought of nothing else for days.'

I had smiled the way I always did when either a passing comment or an expression on his face revealed how well he'd come to understand me in such a short period of time.

'Was Bill gutted?' he asked, his eyes holding no blame at all.

'I think so.'

Liam shook his head, but the smile never left his lips. 'He'll get over it.' The smile sobered a little as he looked at me. 'But will you?'

I sighed, and gave a small, helpless shrug. 'I think I have to. It's the best thing for Noah, and I think when all's said and done, that's what I have to keep reminding myself.' Liam nodded wisely, and nothing about his demeanour changed when I'd added softly: 'Besides, I truly believe it's what Tim would have wanted me to do.'

A sudden blast from the cruise ship's horn brought me back with a jolt to Sydney Harbour. A crowd had gathered at the harbour wall to watch the gigantic white ship slowly leave the port, but I wasn't seeing that; I was still stuck on thoughts of Liam and how I'd carelessly ruined our burgeoning friendship by sticking my nose in where it hadn't been wanted. Because it wasn't dropping the case that had ruined things between Liam and me, it was speaking to the gallery owner about Anna.

Two days after that last phone call with Liam, and after a decade of excuses and putting it off, I finally took the plunge and purchased a return flight to Australia. I needed to get away, to lick my wounds and make peace with my decision about Noah. I yearned for the comfort that only my sister and her loving, chaotic family could give me. My decision was out of character and impulsive, but I told myself it had absolutely nothing to do with what had happened with Liam. Nothing at all.

'Under twenty-three kilos for a three-week holiday,' Karen exclaimed, lifting my suitcase off her bathroom scales. 'How did you do that?'

I gave a rueful shrug and took the case from her, preparing to carry it down to the waiting car. 'It's probably because I don't pack any medicines.' Karen looked confused. 'It's… It's just something silly Liam told me, that's all.'

A vaguely disapproving look passed over my older sister's face. 'You talk a lot about someone who's ignored every single communication you've sent him over the last three weeks.'

I'm sure she wasn't deliberately trying to rub salt into an open wound, but her words still had the power to sting. 'It's because we're friends. *Were* friends,' I amended regretfully. If truth be told, I had no idea if Liam would ever want to pick up where we'd left off because, as Karen had so accurately pointed out, he'd apparently forgotten how to reply to his phone messages.

I'd sent him countless *'My view today…'* picture messages, and hadn't received a single one in return. And mine had been pretty amazing: the spectacle of the Blue Mountains; Sydney's Botanical Gardens – a florist's paradise; and endless miles of deserted Australian beaches. Liam had lost either his phone or any desire to hear from me again. I guessed I was going to have to wait until I got back to the UK to find out which one it was. And yet I still shouldered all of the blame.

'I should have realised that if Liam had wanted an exhibition of his wife's paintings, he'd have organised one himself by now. I mean, it's not like he's stupid, or anything. He *is* a lawyer, after all.'

'Those two aren't mutually exclusive, you know,' Karen had observed, which at least had made me laugh.

I thought I'd done well to avoid it, but Karen caught me unawares, somewhere between the check-in desk and the security gate.

'It's really hard saying goodbye to you guys,' I said, sniffing slightly. My eyes feasted one last time on my two adorable nephews, and of course their mum, who had all insisted on coming to the airport to see me off.

The holiday had given me a poignant taster of what life was like with young children, particularly one who was almost the same age as Noah. *They'll exhaust you,*' Karen had warned. And she was right, they had. But I'd fallen asleep each night with memories of laughter, sand-castle building and sticky ice-cream flavoured kisses filling my head, and of arms thrown around my waist as the boys launched in for one more cuddle.

'You'll fall in love with Australia', everyone had predicted, and in a way they were right, I had. But I'd fallen in love with being Aaron and Josh's Auntie Beth even more.

'Goodbye doesn't have to be for so long this time. Please promise me that you'll think about it seriously when you get back to the UK.' My sister's voice was starting to wobble the closer we got to the security gate.

I nodded and pulled her to me for one last hug, the kind I thought would have to last me for years, but if I said 'yes' to Karen's suggestion, then perhaps it only had to keep me going for a matter of months.

As I buckled myself into my economy airline seat, and prepared for the gruelling twenty-four-hour flight home, I thought again about what Karen had said.

'It's going to be so hard, you know, now you know where Noah is. I worry that you're going to find yourself looking for him in every crowd, or street corner, or driving past his school hoping to catch a fleeting glimpse of him.' She'd shrugged her shoulders, her eyes soft with sympathy. 'It's what I would do.'

'If I have to, I could move anywhere,' I'd reasoned. 'I've always said that one day I'd like to move back to the coast. But the UK has beaches too, you know. I don't necessarily have to relocate to the other side of the world. Besides, if I moved, what would I do about Crazy Daisy?'

'Keep it, or sell it,' Karen had fired back, finally getting the chance to use every tool of persuasion in her arsenal. 'It doesn't make it any the less something you and Tim dreamt up and created together, even if you decide to move on. And with the money you get from the clinic settlement you could open up a *second* Crazy Daisy, right here in Sydney.' The idea dangled enticingly before me, like a twirling jewel. 'You could go global,' she said. I was still laughing at the thought when she went in for the kill with all the skill of a matador. 'And if *you* move out here, then I bet Mum and Dad would come too.'

As the plane took to the skies, it was impossible to tell if I was flying back to my old home, or away from my new one.

33.

Izzy

'I couldn't remember if you said you wanted the blue jumper or the black one, so I just brought everything from your drawer.'

I took the canvas bag, inside which a large section of my wardrobe appeared to be stuffed.

'That's fine,' I said, sliding the bag out of the way beneath the hospital bed. 'Was everything okay at home?' It was surprising how quickly the hospital had started to feel like the only place we had ever lived. It was the cosy three-bedroom house, where we'd spent the past ten years, that felt alien, as though it belonged to an alternate version of the Vaughan family; people whose lives were untouched by the devastating diagnosis of kidney disease.

Pete lowered himself onto the uncomfortable straight-backed chair on the other side of Noah's bed. It was where he'd slept for the first two nights, before the nursing staff had taken pity on him and had found us a second camp bed. Apparently, there was some dumb rule about only allowing *one* parent to stay with their child in the hospital. So far, everyone was pretending it didn't exist.

'He's looking a little better, don't you think?' asked Pete, staring down with hopeful but tired eyes at our sleeping son. I didn't need to glance towards the bed to know that he was wrong. Noah's face was still puffy, his eyes practically disappearing in the soft folds of swollen flesh. He looked like a very tiny boxer who'd been bounced around the ring by a particularly vicious opponent. It wasn't fair. None of it was fair.

'Yes, a little better,' I lied, giving Pete the closest thing to a smile I could manage to summon up. I was exhausted, both mentally and physically, but despite Pete's daily urging, I refused to leave Noah's bedside for anything more than just a few minutes. I took thirty-second showers in the doctors' on-call room they were letting us use, and bolted down meals I couldn't even taste in the hospital cafeteria. There was a constant dull aching pain lurking in the middle of my chest, which was probably indigestion, but felt more like my heart was breaking. It certainly felt like shattering every time I looked at Noah, and the battle he was fighting.

It seemed far longer than just ten days ago since we'd sat anxiously in the GP's office on the morning after the wedding. The rest of the building had been in darkness and the junior doctor, the one I'd had no confidence in, had let us into the building and through the deserted surgery to the consultation room. Her eyes had darkened in a concern she wasn't experienced enough to hide as she briefly examined Noah. Her chirpy demeanour as she carried out her checks jarred worryingly with the expression on her face when she asked Noah if he'd mind waiting in the reception for a moment while she spoke to us.

Eight is young, but it's not stupid. Noah knew straightaway that something was very wrong. The look he gave me as he walked out of the doctor's office tore my heart wide open, and it was still there, burnt behind my lids, every time I closed my eyes.

The young medic had turned her troubled gaze in our direction as she slid a single sheet of paper across the leather-topped desk. I glanced down at the paragraphs, the medical words I had been reading through the night jumping off the page at me.

'This is a copy of a letter I've emailed to the hospital, requesting Noah undergoes further investigation. His recent tests have revealed that he may be experiencing some issues with his kidneys.'

It was a sugar-coated version of what I now suspected was way more serious than just an 'issue'. Pete took the letter and read it slowly and determinedly, as though the scary Latin words could be defused if he faced them head-on.

'You found protein in his urine?' I asked, earning me a look of respect from the doctor. I'd been wrong about her. I had underestimated her and her abilities, but perhaps she'd been equally guilty of under-estimating me.

'We did. And that coupled with the oedema – swelling,' she translated for Pete, who was looking increasingly sick with every passing second, 'and the weight gain makes me feel that we should really get this investigated further without delay.'

'So you're arranging for an appointment for him to see a consultant?' frowned Pete, still not fully understanding just how serious this had all suddenly become.

'No, you need to take him today. Right now. They're already expecting him on the children's ward.' What little colour there still was on Pete's face had rapidly drained away.

'We have the results of Noah's kidney biopsy.'

The flinch that ran through me was involuntary. Every time that word was mentioned, all I could think of was standing beside Noah, humming a lullaby I hadn't sung to him for years as the general anaesthetic flooded his system and fluttered his eyes to a close. I'd tearfully collapsed into Pete's waiting arms even before they'd wheeled Noah into the operating theatre for the procedure.

'As you know, the biopsy was essential to give us an accurate picture of what is going on with Noah's kidneys,' the doctor continued. Pete and I both nodded, bracing ourselves for the words that I suspected would hit us like a blow. 'I'm afraid the test revealed that Noah has a condition called FSGS.'

Beside me I could hear Pete's sudden indrawn breath, like the hiss of a tyre. The paediatric nephrologist was silent for a moment, allowing his words to filter down slowly. They seeped into our lives like an indelible stain.

'I imagine you're wondering what those letters stand for—'

'Focal Segmental Glomerulosclerosis,' I murmured, my tongue working its way around the unfamiliar words. It was the first time I'd said them out loud, but I already knew it wouldn't be the last.

'You've heard of it?' Mr Clinton asked in surprise, his thick black eyebrows inching upwards towards his hairline. 'Are you a nurse?'

'No. A mother.' I wasn't being facetious, just truthful.

'And are you aware of what this condition means?' Noah's consultant asked, angling his question slightly in Pete's direction. The bridge my husband hadn't wanted to cross until he had to was suddenly right there in front of him.

'Perhaps you can give it to us in layman's terms,' he asked.

Throughout the paediatrician's explanation Pete wore a stony expression, but he listened hard, as though Noah's recovery was dependent on his ability to grasp the situation. It broke my heart the way he pulled his chair closer to the desk as though afraid of missing a single word, and how his eyes scrutinised each of the doctor's hastily drawn explanatory diagrams.

'It's a chronic condition that we will manage with a variety of medication and diet. And of course he will have to be closely and regularly monitored to ensure his kidneys are functioning correctly.'

Noah's uncomplicated childhood was evaporating away before our eyes, and there wasn't a damn thing we could do to help him.

'How did he get this? And why wasn't it spotted sooner?' Pete's voice was a low growl. He was angry and wanted someone to blame. The doctors who had missed the initial symptoms were an easy target.

'It's a tricky condition to recognise in its early stages and very easily overlooked when the child in question has a long history of allergies, as Noah does. Even if it were my own son, I can't guarantee I'd have spotted it,' confessed the doctor, his eyes unconsciously travelling across the desk and coming to rest on a silver-framed photograph of a flaxen-haired boy around Noah's age. When he spoke again, he sounded much more like a parent than a physician.

'You mustn't blame yourselves. You couldn't have known it was serious and in cases such as Noah's, where there's no family history of kidney disease, we simply don't know what causes this condition.'

Did the doctor notice the way we suddenly both sat up a little straighter, or the quick worried glance that telegraphed between us?

'Would it have helped to know if there *had* been a family history? Would it have been easier to diagnose? Would it have been found earlier?'

The doctor looked confused. 'Has anyone else in Noah's family ever suffered from renal failure?'

Pete's head dropped, leaving me to answer the question. 'We don't know.'

34

Izzy

The face was truly monstrous. The eyes were deep sunken hollows and lingering traces of blood could be seen on the row of jagged fangs. I studied the Halloween pumpkin on the kitchen table carefully, as if it was a piece of art.

'It's incredibly authentic,' I said. 'I particularly like how you got the blood-stained teeth effect.'

'Very funny,' replied Pete dryly, holding up one hand and wiggling his fingers comically for Noah's benefit. Three of them wore plasters.

'And you were worried *I* was going to cut myself,' laughed Noah weakly. It was how he did everything lately. Weakly.

'Next year, *you* can be in charge of the carving,' promised Pete, deliberately turning his gaze from mine so that he wouldn't see the question in my eyes. The future, which had once seemed so very clear and straightforward, had become much murkier over the last few months.

'Can I go trick or treating tonight?' Noah asked hopefully. 'You said I could if I felt better.'

'Let's wait and see, shall we?' I said, feeling every ounce of his disappointment as he despondently pushed his uneaten slice of toast away.

'That means no,' Noah said, his lower lip jutting and beginning to tremble. My own wasn't that far behind his. I bent down and planted a kiss on the thatch of thick dark hair. 'That means wait and see.'

'We'll have a quiet morning and see how you're feeling later when Mum gets back,' Pete compromised, managing to reignite the hope in Noah's eyes. He was good at that; far better at it than I was, I acknowledged.

'Have you taken all your pills this morning?' I was looking at Noah, although it was really Pete I was asking.

Noah opened his mouth impossibly wide, as though he'd just completed an eating challenge on *I'm A Celebrity*, closing it only to ask a question I already knew I was going to have to answer with a lie.

'Where are you going, Mum? You're all dressed up. You look fancy.'

'Not really,' I countered, looking down at the blue jumper dress, the one that always managed to make me feel good. I had pulled it from the wardrobe that morning as if it was a suit of armour. 'I just have some errands to run.'

Pete waited until Noah had left the room before allowing his smiling mask to slip a little.

'Do you want something to eat before you go?'

'I think I'd probably throw up.'

He nodded in understanding and began to silently replace Noah's collection of medication in the kitchen cupboard. So many pills and drugs, and none of them seemed to be working anymore.

'*It's trial and error,*' the doctors said each time they wrote out yet another new prescription. '*We just have to keep trying to find the right balance.*'

'*These are old people's pills,*' Pete had declared on the day we'd brought Noah back home, weighed down with a bulging bag from the hospital pharmacy. '*He's got pills for high blood pressure, raised cholesterol and God knows what else. They're what my dad had when he was in his seventies.*'

To be fair, initially the cocktail of medications had helped. They got rid of the massive amount of fluid that had built up in Noah's body, until he finally looked like our little boy once again. They helped his failing kidneys to function. But the last three months had been hard on him. He'd missed more days of school than he had attended and had to give up so many of the things he loved – at least for now. We'd overcompensated, but I defy any parent in the world not to do that when you see your child lost and bewildered in a place he'd never asked to visit.

When Noah wasn't well enough to take part in the new school show, we'd bought him a piano and arranged for lessons. When he'd had to step down from the five-a-side team, we'd bought him a dog.

'You do know we're spoiling him?' Pete had asked, as we broke all our own rules and allowed Marvel, the three-legged greyhound and the newest addition to the Vaughan household, to sleep in a basket beside Noah's bed each night.

'I know, and I don't care,' I'd replied, my throat constricting when I remembered how Noah had walked past the cages with the perfectly healthy cute dogs and stopped determinedly in front of the one with the sad-looking creature who was so used to being passed by, he hadn't even bothered looking up. 'I want that one,' he'd said, his eyes huge and pleading in his too-pale face.

'Noah *will have good days, and bad days,*' the doctors had warned us, so often you'd have thought we'd have been much better prepared to deal with the inevitable decline when it came. I'm not sure what we'd been expecting, but it hadn't been this avalanche of new symptoms that made me almost scared to ask Noah how he was feeling.

Pete's eyes were fixed on Marvel now as he wolfed down a bowl of food, almost as though he couldn't bear to look at me as he asked his question.

'So you're going to do it, then?'

The blue dress had probably told him that I was, but he still deserved an answer.

'I have to. I thought we were both agreed on this.'

He nodded, and it was only then that I realised how close he was to crying. We alternated, like scales trying to find a balance. Sometimes he was the strong one; other times it was me. On this issue, he was all over the place, but I was titanium strong. I had to be, for Noah.

'I should go,' I said.

Another nod, but as I turned to leave, Pete spun around and pulled me into his arms, crushing me almost painfully against him.

'Good luck,' he said, his voice gruff with all the things he couldn't say. It didn't matter. I already knew them.

35

Beth

The columns of figures on my laptop screen blurred and then came back into focus as I wearily rubbed my eyes. The shop was quiet, and with the rain bouncing like bullets onto the pavement outside, it was likely to stay that way for the rest of the afternoon. It should have been the perfect opportunity to catch up on some paperwork, but somehow I couldn't seem to concentrate.

I refused to admit Natalie's parting comment several hours earlier was the reason for my distracted state. 'Has that tall guy you're friendly with moved into this area?' The question had been dropped casually, like a carelessly thrown grenade, as she pulled on her jacket.

'Not that I know of,' I replied carefully, without choosing to correct her. There was no need for her to know that I'd not heard from Liam in months.

'Weird,' Natalie said, unaware of the unsettling chain reaction her question had triggered. 'I keep thinking I see him. He must have a double.' She shrugged, and by the time she'd crossed to the door and left for her afternoon off, she'd probably forgotten all about it.

I wished I could do the same. My attention kept straying from the laptop screen and travelling to Anna's painting, which still hung on the wall beside the counter. I should probably have taken it down or at least offered to return it to him, because it was certainly a distraction, and not just today. I found it almost impossible to look at it and *not* think of Liam or the unfortunate way our friendship had petered out.

Even so, I was sure Natalie must be mistaken. Whoever it was she'd seen, it was unlikely to have been Liam. But good sense and logic weren't enough to stop me from glancing up every time a tall figure walked past the shop window. It was almost as if I was preparing myself; so when a shadowy shape cloaked in a dark raincoat and hidden beneath an enormous golf umbrella stopped in the porch, I think I already knew they weren't just taking refuge from the downpour, or admiring the window display of pumpkins and orange roses on a crunchy bed of red and gold leaves.

I sat up straighter on the stool I was perched on, my hands unconsciously gripping the edge of the counter as the figure stood on the threshold, shaking droplets from their hooded raincoat and umbrella, before turning around to enter the shop.

My usual smile for greeting customers faltered and then dissolved completely as Izzy Vaughan walked further into Crazy Daisy. She slipped off the dripping raincoat, turning it inside out to protect the floor. The action implied she wasn't about to rush back into the street and confirmed her appearance here was no random coincidence. She'd known *exactly* whose shop this was, and I very much doubted she'd come here to buy flowers.

Beneath the coat Izzy was wearing a hyacinth-blue knitted dress, which really suited her colouring. Her hair was smartly styled and she was wearing make-up, which didn't quite manage to disguise the lines around her eyes she was too young to have, or the twin panda circles beneath them.

One of us had to speak, and as the seconds stretched on, I eventually realised it was going to have to be me.

'Hello, Izzy.'

'Beth,' she responded, as she chewed nervously on her lower lip. She seemed fidgety and kept readjusting her grip on the strap of her bag, which she was holding so tightly I could see the bones of her knuckles outlined through the skin.

I could feel myself paling beneath the tan I'd brought back from Australia as I slid off the stool and stood as tall as I could to face the woman I'd never imagined I would see again.

Izzy's eyes darted around the shop, but I doubted she was taking in the exotic blooms or the autumnal floral displays. I breathed in deeply, inhaling their fragrance, which usually calmed me, but for once their magic failed to work.

'Why are you here, Izzy?' My voice was calm, belying the maelstrom of emotions swirling inside me. 'Is it about Noah?' What a stupid question; *of course* it was about Noah. There was nothing else we had in common.

In answer, Izzy glanced once again around the shop. 'Is there somewhere private we could go to talk?'

My pulse rate went up a good ten beats a minute, but I hoped my face remained composed. 'My assistant is out for the afternoon, so I can't leave the shop.' Izzy didn't challenge me, or ask me to close up, which I could easily have done. In truth, I wanted to stay right where we were. The shop was my haven and my sanctuary. Whatever she'd come here to say, I wanted to hear it somewhere familiar, where I felt safe. 'We can talk here without being disturbed. It's been a quiet afternoon.'

I emerged from behind the counter and crossed to a small shabby chic bench beneath Anna's painting. I sat first, and after a moment of hesitation Izzy lowered herself onto the blue-painted slats beside me. Ignoring good manners, I didn't ask if she wanted anything to drink. Even the two minutes it would take for the kettle to boil were too long to wait. I needed to know why, after all these months, she was here.

Izzy cleared her throat and then closed her eyes for a long moment, as though the words she had come here to say were written on some internal autocue inside her lids.

'Before I say anything else, I want to thank you for what you did in the summer... for walking away and not putting Noah through a media circus of a court case. I know how hard that must have been for you.'

My gaze was level and steady; unfortunately, the same couldn't be said for my voice. 'Actually, you have no idea.'

She bowed her head in acknowledgement. There was a composed stillness about her now, but it was her hands that gave her away. They were writhing in her lap, the fingers twisting and contorting as though playing their own game of Twister. They made me uncomfortable, but I couldn't look away.

'If we could find a way…' Izzy began hesitantly, 'a way that didn't involve lawyers, judges or courtrooms, for you to be involved in Noah's future, would you be interested?'

My gasp sounded ridiculously loud, but it was impossible to suppress. 'Do you even need to ask me that?'

Izzy nodded slowly, as though she had expected no other answer.

I had about a hundred questions that were screaming to be asked, but Izzy silenced them all with her next words.

'Noah needs you.'

'Needs me? How?' I hardly recognised my own voice.

I could tell how hard this was for her, because her words sounded raw, as if they were being hacked from her. 'Noah needs you to be his mother.' She took a long steadying breath. Clearly, however much she had rehearsed this speech, it was still much harder to deliver than she'd been expecting.

Wordlessly, I strode to the door, flipped over the 'Closed' sign and slid the latch, giving us both a very necessary moment. I leant back against the locked door, as though I could no longer trust that my legs were capable of carrying me across the room.

'You made it very clear at our previous meeting that Noah needs only one mother. You. So why the sudden change of heart?'

Each word Izzy spoke seemed like a blade being slowly drawn across her skin. 'Noah needs something I can't give him. No one else can help him. Only you.'

My heart was pounding so hard, I could feel it beating against my chest as though trying to escape. 'What is it that you need from me? Is it money?'

She looked almost pityingly at me, as though I'd said something unbelievably stupid.

'Noah is sick.'

The world seemed to tilt and for a moment it felt as though I was actually falling... falling back into the past, into a consultation room where an oncologist with sad eyes was saying: *'I'm afraid it's not good news...'*

With jerky steps I walked back to the bench, sitting down at an angle to Izzy, so close that our knees were touching, but there was still a chasm between us.

'What sort of sick do you mean? What's wrong with him?' In my head I could hear nothing except the word 'cancer' tolling like a bell.

It was almost a relief when Izzy said, 'Noah has a kidney condition – quite a rare one. It's called FSGS.'

I could feel relief washing through me, but Izzy's eyes were filled with a fearfulness that made the dread come flooding back.

'Is it... Is it serious?'

She gave one brief, hard nod. And with that everything fell into place. I knew in that moment *exactly* why she was there. Izzy was busy pulling sheets of paper from her bag; pages and pages downloaded from the internet, filled with diagrams and closely printed text. She was talking about how Noah's condition had initially been missed, and of the cocktail of drugs he'd been on over the last few months, and the numerous hospital stays. It was all just white noise.

'He had so many allergies, you see, at first they thought the symptoms were—'

'Yes.' My voice was clear and decisive. The word rang out through the shop.

Izzy faltered to a stop, as her carefully structured speech was derailed. Our eyes met and for a moment I heard nothing. Not the cars driving past through the deep puddles, the rumbling of buses, or the pounding of the rain on the roof. There was a new silence in a world full of noise.

'Yes, Izzy,' I repeated slowly and carefully, as though talking to a person unfamiliar with English. 'It's what you came here to ask, isn't it?'

She coloured in embarrassment, but what was the point in making her go through whatever it was she had planned to say? The decision was already made. 'You came to ask me to donate one of my kidneys, didn't you?'

She'd not planned for us to reach this point in the conversation for quite some time, and it was almost funny to see her mentally fast-forwarding to the right part of her speech, or it would have been if it wasn't all so deadly serious.

'Last week the doctors talked about dialysis for the first time. I don't want him to have to go through that. Not if... not if there's another way.'

I nodded slowly.

'I got them to test me almost as soon as he was diagnosed. Pete too. They thought I was being a catastrophist, but I just wanted to know that I could help him when he needed me. Only it turns out I can't.' Her voice cracked on the admission. 'It's my job to look after him. When he's ill, I'm supposed to be the one who makes him better. But I'm failing him now.' Her eyes were twin pools of unfathomable misery. 'The only person who can make Noah well again is the person who gave him life in the first place. You, Beth.'

If she'd been stabbed I doubt she could have looked in greater pain. Almost of its own volition, my hand reached out for hers. I'm not sure which of us was the most surprised.

'I can only imagine how hard it must have been for you to come here today and ask me to do this.'

Izzy shook her head fiercely and wiped the back of her free hand roughly across her cheek, banishing any errant tears. 'Noah is everything. Nothing else is important. I would walk through fire for that boy.' She took a long shaky sigh. 'And I'm banking everything I have on the hope that you feel exactly the same way.'

'I do,' I said solemnly.

She nodded, and then seemed to pull herself up a little straighter, as though drawing on an inner well of strength. 'Doing this incredible thing for Noah will obviously change everything. Pete and I both understand that, and we're prepared to work out a way of bringing you into Noah's life. He deserves to know what you're doing for him, and why.'

'No. Absolutely not.' Izzy looked momentarily panicked. 'I'm not doing this to buy his love for me.'

Izzy frowned. 'It wouldn't be like that. I just meant that your place in Noah's life from now on will never be challenged by either Pete or me.'

It felt like we were playing hopscotch on the edge of an emotional minefield, each of us fearful of taking a wrong step and watching everything blow up in our faces.

'I will do this. I will *willingly* do this. But I don't want Noah to be told who I am before the operation.' I could sense Izzy was poised to disagree, but I talked over her objections before she could voice them. 'This is non-negotiable. When Noah is better, *that's* when we can discuss how much time he will be able to spend with me.'

As much as she believed she was ready for this, Izzy was powerless to disguise an involuntary flinch at the thought of having to share Noah with anyone else but Pete. But there was a core of steel in her that I was only just beginning to understand. It was apparent in her next words.

'Obviously, you're going to have to go through a great many tests over the coming months: physical and psychological. They need to make sure you're a good match, and that you're healthy enough to be a donor. But I want you to know that if things don't work out, that if for any reason you *can't* give Noah your kidney, this arrangement will still stand. We're still... *willing...* for you to be a part of Noah's life.' 'Happy' would have been a better word for her to have used, but perhaps that was hoping for too much. Besides, Izzy had made the offer with clear sincerity. I didn't doubt her for a single moment. From this point on there was no need for lawyers. We were just two mothers quietly working out what was best for our child.

'We don't need to worry about not being a match,' I said with the kind of confidence that would have had the doctors shaking their heads at our folly. 'I will be. I will give

Noah a new kidney, and the rest of it will all fall into place after that.'

Izzy left a short while later, leaving me with the name and contact details of the doctor heading up the transplant team who would begin organising the tests I'd have to undergo. We stood awkwardly by the door. Not friends, but no longer enemies. It was Izzy, not me, who finally closed the space between us, and impulsively threw her arms around me. I could feel she was trembling, or perhaps that was me? It was hard to tell.

'Thank you,' she whispered into my hair. 'Thank you for being his mother.'

'It was all I ever wanted to be,' I said softly to myself as I watched her walk back out into the driving rain.

36

Beth

Everyone in the airport seemed to be crying. It reminded me of the scene in *Love Actually* where loved ones fly like magnets into the arms of their waiting relatives. Except we weren't in the Arrivals hall, but the Departures one, so I suppose the tears all around us were ones of farewell as people said goodbye to their loved ones for the holidays.

As if that wasn't poignant enough, a choir of school children were positioned in the middle of the terminal, serenading the bustling passengers with sweetly sung Christmas carols. They were gathering quite a crowd, as everyone suddenly forgot the deep queues waiting at the check-in desks, or last calls for their flights, and stopped to listen. The male teacher conducting the choir was beaming enthusiastically from beneath a pair of reindeer antlers and just for a moment, as my vision blurred, his face disappeared and I saw Tim in his place. With that uncanny empathy that always took me by surprise, my mother's hand reached over and covered mine where it rested on the bar of their luggage trolley. When I turned to look at her, the memory of her lost son-in-law sparkled in her eyes. It was how he lived on in all of us. And today, of all days, he seemed closer than ever.

Who knows how long we might have stood there, lost in memories of the past as the strains of 'Silent Night' filled the terminal, if my father hadn't come up and laid a hand on our shoulders. 'You're so busy looking at other people's grandchildren, you're going to make us late for the flight to see our own,' he warned. There was actually very little danger of that happening, as we were at the airport at least two hours earlier than we needed to be, but that suited my plans for the day just as much as it did theirs.

Both of them were worried about me, which perhaps was to be expected as this would be the first Christmas I'd be spending apart from them since Tim died.

'Come with us,' my mother had urged impulsively after dinner last night. They were staying overnight with me, and I was going to drop them at the airport before going to work in the morning. Except that I actually had no intention of going to work; something they obviously knew nothing about.

'It's not too late to change your mind,' my mother had said persuasively, and for just a moment I wondered if she was referring to what I was intending to do while she and my father took to the skies for the long journey to Australia.

'I've only just come back from a three-week holiday visiting Karen,' I reminded her, as I bent to load our plates into the dishwasher. 'And I have a business to run, remember?'

'Couldn't your assistant look after it again? You said she did a fine job last time. And isn't it all just poinsettias and holly wreaths at this time of year?'

I smiled wryly at my mother's oversimplification of my business model.

'She did do a fine job.' *And she will do so again,* I added silently, finding it surprisingly tricky to straddle the precarious line between the truth and the lies. 'But I need to be here myself – there are some things that only I can do,' I said, echoing the words Izzy had used at the end of October when she'd come to tell me about Noah's condition.

'You could close the shop and join us,' said Mum, unable to resist one last try.

My dad had looked up from a guidebook of Australia, which he was studying with the intensity of a student cramming for an exam. 'If it's just a question of the money, Bethie, then your mum and I are happy to buy you a plane ticket.'

Unexpected tears had pricked at my eyes and blurred my vision, but I had somehow managed to hold myself together and smile back at the two people who meant the world to me.

'It's not only that, Dad. I really *do* have lots planned for the next few weeks, and I can't just disappear off to the other side of the world and let people down.' I softened my refusal with a smile that held them both in its warmth. 'But I love you both for offering.'

'It's such a shame that we won't be together for the holidays,' my mother had commented that morning, while I surreptitiously tried to pour my cup of untouched tea down the sink without anyone noticing.

'Christmas is all about family,' she said, as though I might still be persuaded to change my mind and join them.

'You sound like a Hallmark card, Mum,' I teased, stepping

away from the sink to envelop her in a huge hug. 'You don't have to worry about me, you know,' I said, giving her an extra tight squeeze. 'I'm a big girl now.'

She wiped her eyes carefully, mindful not to smudge the make-up she had still applied, despite the early start. 'It's just that you've had such a difficult year, Beth. What with the clinic, and the lawyers...' She was getting dangerously close to an area I really didn't want her venturing into.

'Well, if we don't get a move on, we won't have to worry about me being alone for Christmas, because you're going to miss your flight.' That was never even a remote possibility, but it got me off the hook and them into the car. We actually reached the airport in record time, which allowed me to come into the terminal to see them off. Despite my professed independence, I was suddenly reluctant to see them leave. I had a strong feeling that my mum wouldn't be the only one in tears when they disappeared through the gate at Security.

After a brief tussle with my dad at the check-in desk, which happily I won, I swung the heavy cases, packed to the brim with Christmas presents, onto the conveyor belt. It would be the last time in months I'd be able to lift anything that heavy, and it felt good to feel the pull and strain on my muscles.

'Carry on like that and you'll end up in hospital,' chided my father, totally oblivious that his warning was actually an uncannily accurate prediction. That was *exactly* where I was going to be in three hours' time.

'I'm used to carrying heavy things for the shop,' I assured him as I dropped a kiss on his softly wrinkled cheek. 'And besides, I'm as strong as an ox.'

Fortunately, that was pretty much what the doctors who'd

been running tests on me for the last couple of months had also said. I'd passed every single one of them with flying colours, even the psychological ones, which had worried me far more than the physical examinations. Everything was set. Everything was in place. Noah had been admitted to hospital the day before, and I was going straight there as soon as I left the airport.

37

Izzy

It was the day I hoped would never come. It was the day that couldn't come soon enough. I was so conflicted that I couldn't even begin to untangle my mixed emotions. The date in December had been ringed in red on the kitchen calendar for weeks. Beside it hung Noah's advent calendar, and with every window he excitedly opened each morning, the day of the operation crept closer. And now it was finally here.

I stood at Noah's bedroom doorway, watching him carefully choose which of his toys to add to the case I'd packed for the hospital. 'If I'm not back home by Christmas, how will Santa know where to find me?' he asked worriedly. Of all the concerns racing wildly through my head, that particular one hadn't been high up on my list.

'He'll know, champ. He's clever like that,' assured Pete, coming up behind me, laying a hand on my shoulder and squeezing it gently.

Last week we'd visited Father Christmas in a local department store grotto and Noah had been surprisingly secretive about sharing what he wanted for Christmas. I only hoped that whatever he'd asked for was in one of the brightly wrapped parcels hidden away at the back of my wardrobe.

'Goodbye bedroom,' Noah said sadly as I shut the door of his room behind us.

'You'll be back home before you know it,' I said with a false cheeriness that even an eight-year-old was able to see through.

'Are you *absolutely sure* we're not allowed to bring Marvel to the hospital with us?' Noah was kneeling on the floor beside the dog, his thin arms wound around the bony canine in an enormous hug, which surprisingly the dog seemed quite happy to tolerate.

'It's against the rules, sweetheart. Dogs have a lot of germs,' I explained.

'Not *my* dog,' declared Noah. He drew his face so close to his pet that they were practically eyeball to eyeball as he whispered, 'Be a good boy. Do what Mummy and Daddy tell you, so they won't send you back to the dogs' home.'

'He's going to be right here waiting for you when you get back, son,' promised Pete, who'd joined us in the kitchen, car keys in hand. He cleared his throat noisily, yet his voice still sounded oddly thick as he added, 'Come on, big man. It's time to go.'

They'd let us stay with Noah until the anaesthetic had been given. 'Your mum can hold your hand until you get sleepy,' the anaesthetist had said kindly. Noah reached out to me, his dark eyes starting to grow fearful, and I wound my fingers through his as I'd done a thousand times before, from his very first steps to the last road we'd crossed together. But this was a journey he'd have to take without me, and eight suddenly seemed far too young to go anywhere alone.

Without Pete beside me, I'd have been a mess. But he was amazing – cracking jokes and making Noah laugh in the way that only he could. I watched as the only man I'd ever loved clowned around, being strong for Noah and for me in the only way he knew how, and felt something subtly shift within me.

The anaesthetist stepped closer to the bed and I forced a smile on my face, because it was important to make that the last thing Noah saw as he fell asleep.

'Do you want to know a secret, Mummy?' Noah whispered.

'Always.'

His voice dropped conspiratorially. 'I asked Santa if I could have a new kidney for Christmas.'

Above their surgical masks, I saw the eyes of the medical team soften at Noah's confession.

'Well, maybe Santa helped,' I said gently as I stroked back a thick lock of dark hair from Noah's forehead. 'But do you remember Daddy and me telling you about a kind stranger who has decided to help you get better by giving you one of their kidneys?'

'I remember,' Noah said, his eyelids already drooping sleepily as the drug the anaesthetist had administered began to take effect. 'Do you think Santa asked an angel to give me a kidney?'

I thought of the woman who Noah had yet to meet, who at that very moment was in another operating theatre not far away. A woman who'd already lost so much, and yet when asked to give more hadn't hesitated for a second.

'Do you know what, I think he did,' I replied, bending down and leaving one last kiss on my child's cheek.

38

Beth

'I'm an idiot.' The voice was distant, as if it was coming from the end of a very long tunnel. 'Probably the world's biggest idiot.'

I struggled to open my eyes, which felt as if someone might possibly have sealed with superglue. With an enormous effort, I forced them apart and then immediately snapped them shut against the glaring brilliance of a room that seemed full of white.

The voice was still talking, pulling me awake because I recognised those deep tones, even though it had been quite a while since I'd last heard them.

'Liam?' My voice was hoarse; its frog-like croak felt like a graze running the length of my throat. Once again I forced my eyes to open and this time there was a figure, blurry but recognisable, which swam into focus.

'I'm sorry,' he apologised. 'You're still really drowsy from the anaesthetic.'

Anaesthetic? The word danced in my head, dissolving

out of reach every time I tried to grab hold of it. *Had he had one, or had I?*

'Ah, she's starting to wake up properly now, is she?' asked a female voice from somewhere unseen. 'I'll get her some fresh water.'

I twisted towards the sound of the retreating footsteps and immediately wished I hadn't as a sharp stab of discomfort ran across my lower stomach. It brought me back to reality quicker than a douse of icy water.

'Noah?' I asked urgently, all drowsiness gone from my voice. 'Has he had his operation? Did it work?'

'He's still in surgery. I've been checking for updates every twenty minutes or so,' Liam continued with a wry smile. 'The nursing staff might possibly hate me.'

That seemed highly unlikely, I thought, as I eased myself back against the stiff hospital pillows, moving slowly so I wouldn't aggravate the small incisions the surgeon had made.

'Liam, why are you here?'

His expression was hard to read. 'Because you've had an operation to donate a kidney.'

I shook my head slowly but carefully. 'No. That's why *I'm* here. What I want to know is why *you* are.'

There was a set to his jaw that I don't think I had ever noticed before. He may, or may not, have been incredibly angry. 'I think a far more interesting question is: why am I the *only* person here? Where are your family? Your friends?' I flinched under his steely grey stare. 'You're very close to your parents, and your sister. Why aren't they here at your bedside instead of someone who—'

'—who has studiously ignored me for the last four

months?' I interrupted. The effort to summon up a cutting retort sapped me of strength, but it was so worth it.

'You're right. I deserved that,' Liam said, his head bowing, but not before I saw the regret in his eyes. 'Like I said, I've been an idiot. I acted like a total dick.'

The vulgarism almost made me smile, but the hurt still ran as deep as cuts from a scalpel.

'Why didn't you tell anyone what you were doing?' Liam asked, holding up his hand to silence whatever lie I was about to offer. 'And don't pretend that you have, because I'm just not buying it.'

'There was no need to tell anyone before the operation.'

'Because you didn't want them talking you out of donating?'

I shook my head with unexpected emphasis. 'That would *never* have happened.' A flash fire of admiration burned brightly in his eyes. 'Right now, my parents are about to land in Sydney. It's their first trip in years to visit my sister and their grandchildren. The visit was planned months ago, long before I knew this was going to happen, and I didn't want them to cancel it.'

I could see Liam weighing up my words, getting ready with a counter argument. It's hard to sound authoritative when you're lying in a hospital bed, looking up at a six-foot-plus man towering above you, but I gave it my best shot. 'This has nothing to do with anyone except Izzy, Pete and me.'

The sound of the door opening startled us both and gave me a welcome reprieve as a nurse entered the room and began rearranging the items on the bedside locker before placing a fresh jug of water on it.

'Don't let your wife have more than just a few small sips,' she advised solemnly.

I waited for Liam to correct her, my eyebrows rising incredulously with every passing second that he remained silent. As soon as she left the room, I challenged him. 'Why does that nurse think you're my husband?'

Liam's tone was deceptively neutral. 'They may have made that assumption when I got here several hours ago, and I might have chosen not to correct them. I don't suppose they'd have let me in if I had.' His eyes darkened, and I guessed what was coming next. 'I imagine their mistake might have something to do with the fact that *Tim* is listed as your next of kin on the hospital paperwork.' It was almost impossible to meet his steady gaze without flushing. 'It would have been tricky for them to reach him if anything had gone wrong, don't you think?' There it was again, that brief flash of anger. I was too tired and too sore to deal with it right now.

'Well, thankfully nothing *did* go wrong. And I don't understand why you're so bothered about it, anyway.'

Liam moved so swiftly I never even saw him; one minute he was on the other side of the room, and the next he was right beside me, his hand gripping mine. 'What if something had happened to you? How do you think the people who love and care about you would have felt if that was the first they'd known about what you were doing?'

'All the people who love and care about me are currently in a different hemisphere, so it's not as if they could have got here in a hurry anyway.'

'Not *all* of them are on the other side of the world.'

The statement was so big, so all-encompassing, it filled the entire room, making it suddenly much harder to breathe normally. I had no response. None. Fortunately, Liam didn't seem to expect one.

'I assume you put Tim's name down because you were afraid they wouldn't let you go through with the operation without someone at home to look after you?'

'Something like that,' I mumbled, feeling suddenly as though I was being cross-examined by someone who knew exactly what he was doing. Liam should definitely have specialised as a barrister, he clearly had a natural talent for it.

'Was it Natalie who told you I was here?' It wasn't a Sherlock Holmes worthy deduction, because aside from Izzy and Pete Vaughan, she was the only person who knew. So much for her sworn promise not to tell anyone.

Liam must have read my thoughts. 'Don't blame her for telling me. She held out for a long time. And solicitors are pretty good at getting at the truth.' He looked away for a moment, not allowing me to see the expression in his eyes. 'We're just not that great at accepting *home truths*.' I wondered if somewhere in that statement was a veiled apology for the way he'd reacted when I'd unthinkingly come between him and his late wife's memory.

Liam reached for the newly replenished water jug and poured out a measure in a plastic cup. He held it out for me, considerately sliding one hand beneath my neck for support as he lifted the beaker to my lips. Swallowing was difficult, but that might have had nothing at all to do with my recent surgery.

'Enough?'

I nodded and he gently lowered my head back down onto the starchy pillowcase. I could see he was really trying to make amends, and wondered how long it would take before I forgave him for ghosting me the way he had. He set the drink down on the locker, and then looked through the plastic jug at the framed photograph I'd positioned on the bedside unit. Very carefully, Liam picked up the picture of Tim and brought it to the front, turning it so that I could see my late husband's smiling face whenever I wanted. Perhaps that was the moment when I realised Liam was already forgiven.

On his third foray for information, Liam returned to the room with a smile. He'd been gone much longer this time, and I was beginning to worry that there *had* been news... and that it was bad.

'Noah's out of surgery, and already awake. They're going to be transferring him to the paediatric ICU very soon. I managed to catch Pete Vaughan for a few moments in the corridor.' Liam's face softened at the memory. 'He was pretty emotional, actually.'

'Because something went wrong?' My voice was small and fearful.

Liam shook his head and the smile was back, if anything even broader than before. 'Because everything went right. Apparently, that's one hell of a kidney you gave away. It's already doing a great job.'

I fluffed up with pride at the organ everyone had hoped would change Noah's life for the better. 'Did you see Izzy?'

'No. She was already in with Noah,' Liam replied

unthinkingly. Of course she was. That was a mother's place, at her child's bedside. There was an ache inside me, an emptiness and a feeling that something was missing; something far more vital and important than just a functioning kidney.

I prodded at the food on my plate, and then pushed the dinner aside.

'I'll bring in something tastier tomorrow.'

I looked over at Liam, who'd settled himself comfortably in the visitor's chair and showed no signs of intending to leave. He'd been there all afternoon while I dozed the rest of the anaesthetic out of my system.

'You really don't have to come back again, you know.'

The room was quiet except for the sound of our breathing and the muted strains of a Christmas carol playing on a radio in the ward.

'It's not a question of *having* to, but of *wanting* to.' I swallowed the lump in my throat as his eyes held mine and wouldn't let go. 'I realise I've still got some explaining and apologising to do, and I know that now's not the right time to do it. But leaving you here alone without your family, without visitors...'

He paused and suddenly the confidence I was so used to hearing in his voice was strangely absent. 'Don't fight me on this, Beth. Please. Give me one more chance, even though I don't deserve it.'

'I don't think I've got the strength to fight *anyone* right now,' I said quietly. It was a sitting-on-the-fence reply, which effectively dodged anything personal. Liam took a moment and then nodded, apparently satisfied that I was willing to keep the door ajar, rather than slamming it shut.

A little later, when a young ginger-haired nurse stuck her head around the doorframe and politely reminded us that visiting hours were technically over, Liam somehow managed to wangle a thirty-minute extension. 'Oh, go on then,' the nurse said, looking slightly dazzled by the charm of his smile. 'You're such a lovely couple, and after all, it *is* Christmas.'

Her words lingered in the room after she'd gone, begging one of us to correct them. 'It's not Christmas yet,' I said eventually. 'And we're not—'

'—telling anyone that you plan to go back to an empty house in a couple of days' time,' Liam completed, not at all fazed that my lie was tangling us up in knots that were becoming too complicated to undo.

I shrugged, all at once too exhausted to work out how I felt about the silly charade I had created. I could feel my eyelids growing heavier, and although I fought against sleep like a determined toddler, it came and claimed me before I could work out a suitable riposte.

Someone had turned off the main overhead light while I slept. I blinked sleepily in the low-level amber glow that filtered down from a panel above the bed, casting the room in shadows. The sheets scratched in the silence as I stirred and turned my face towards the figure still sitting on the visitor's chair.

'Liam?' My voice was a whisper, but the figure in the chair jerked as though shot.

The shape got to its feet, too slight and short to possibly belong to the man who had occupied that seat for most of the day.

'No,' a female voice replied. My heart gave a lurch, which if I'd still been hooked up to a monitor would probably have brought the medics running to my room.

'It's Izzy,' my unexpected visitor announced.

My mouth went inexplicably dry. 'Is everything all right? Is Noah okay?' This new level of worry felt completely alien to me. Was this how parenthood was for everyone? How could anyone possibly function in this perpetual state of anxiety? The woman stepped forward and into the pool of light, and I saw exactly the cost of that love. It was there in the deep lines radiating from her eyes and the black circles beneath them. I knew Izzy was a year or so younger than me, but at that moment she easily looked a decade older.

'Noah's doing well. Exceptionally well,' she said, a smile of pure relief making her look instantly better. 'The doctors are actually amazed at how quickly the new kidney began to work.'

'That's wonderful news. I hope he's not in any pain.'

Izzy shook her head. 'A little, but he's being really brave.'

Something unexpected clutched at my heart and I turned involuntarily to look at the photograph of Tim. 'His father was the same. I never once heard him complain, however bad things got.'

Izzy's eyes flashed to the photograph on the locker, which showed her son's features on a much older face.

'I mean Tim,' I immediately corrected. 'My late husband, and not Pete. Obviously.'

There was a serenity on Izzy's face as she continued to stare at the image of the man I had loved. 'No,' she acknowledged quietly. 'You were right the first time. Noah takes after his father, Tim... and also his dad, Pete.' It was far more than just an olive branch she was holding out to me, it was the whole tree. 'He's a hybrid of all four of us: the best parts of each one, I'd like to think,' she added softly.

I was too choked to speak, which was perhaps just as well, for there was nothing I could add to such a generous comment. With what looked like considerable effort, Izzy pulled her gaze away from Tim's smiling face. 'That's why I'm here now, in the middle of the night,' she admitted. 'I've come to take you to Noah. If you want to see him, that is.'

Seeing him was *all* I had ever wanted, from the moment all those months ago when I had first learnt of his existence.

'But we agreed,' I began hesitantly, wondering why I was protesting when my heart literally yearned to be beside the child Tim and I had made. 'I thought we said we would wait until he was fully recovered from the operation before I met him.'

'We did. We shall,' agreed Izzy solemnly. 'They've given him something strong to help him sleep, so he won't wake up.' Her smile looked a little sad, and I was shocked to see the sympathy in her eyes was for me. 'He won't know you're there, but *you* will. After what you did today, you deserve to see...' A small pause that must have cost her a thousand heartbreaks. '...you deserve to see your son.'

It was too dark for her to see that I was crying, but somehow she must have known, for she waited a long moment before stepping to one side, and drawing something out of the shadows. The chrome on the wheelchair caught a shaft of moonlight slicing in through the curtainless window. 'Your chariot is waiting,' Izzy said, hinting at a sense of humour I hadn't even suspected existed.

'You stole a wheelchair from somewhere?'

I heard her soft snigger in the darkness. 'More borrowed than stolen,' she admitted.

'Am I allowed on the ICU ward? Or out of bed, come to that?' I asked, even though I was already throwing back the covers.

'I never imagined Beth Brandon was the type of person who was scared of breaking a few rules,' Izzy challenged, with just the right amount of goading for me to slide my legs to the floor and ignore the tug of protest from my stitches.

'Slow down,' Izzy warned, as I went to stand up. 'You're going to have to let me help you.'

How many thousands of miles had we travelled since we had first learnt of each other's existence? The distance was practically immeasurable. She held out an arm and I took it; I had to, when the alternative was to crumple to the floor at her feet. Even though she'd pulled the chair as close to the bed as possible, the effort to manoeuvre me into it took its toll on both of us. My hospital gown was plastered unpleasantly to my back by the time I was securely seated, and there was a fine sheen of perspiration on Izzy's forehead when she finally straightened up.

The corridor was dimly lit, although in the distance I could hear the muted sound of nurses talking, leaving me to wonder how we were ever going to get off the ward without anyone noticing us. Izzy pushed the chair, keeping to the shadows on the far left of the corridor whenever possible. The exit was almost in sight when the doors swung inward and a nurse I'd not seen before came through them. I closed my eyes and braced myself for a confrontation, or maybe barrelling straight through the opening, but instead the nurse just looked at Izzy and gave her a small nod of approval. 'You managed okay by yourself?' she questioned.

I looked up at the woman who was currently holding on tightly to the handles of my chair. 'Yes. No problem. Thanks for all your help.'

The nurse smiled and then reached down and squeezed my shoulder gently. 'Happy to assist,' she said, holding open the double doors she'd just walked through so Izzy could negotiate the chair through the opening.

'I thought this was an illegal outing?' I asked, as Izzy summoned the lift for the ground floor, the level that was home to the paediatric intensive care unit.

'It still is… in a way, but I needed to make sure it was okay for you to be moved so soon after surgery.'

As she pushed me into the lift, I was no longer sure what my feelings were about this woman who I had once been so certain was my enemy. I wasn't sure if I liked her; perhaps such a leap would always be too far for either of us to take. But I knew one thing for sure, she fought for the things and the people she believed in, and I admired the hell out of her for that. As role models for my child went, I doubt I could ever have picked a better one.

We met one nurse who almost thwarted our plans. Within metres of the ward where Noah slept, oblivious to the activities of his mothers, we were pulled up by a uniformed figure who appeared better suited to a career in border control than nursing.

'Halt right there,' she cried, even holding up a hand like a policewoman directing traffic. 'Where exactly are you both going at this hour?' We'd travelled down three floors in the lift and walked the entire length of the Children's Unit without passing a single soul, but it looked as though our luck had just run out.

'My son, Noah Vaughan, is in there,' Izzy said, her head pointing in the direction of the doors bearing the acronym PICU upon them. 'He had transplant surgery today.'

'Fine,' said the nurse, with no appreciable softening to her tone. 'Then of course you're allowed in, but we permit only one visitor per bedside after visiting hours. And that's usually the mother.'

I could feel my heart sinking lower in my chest. This was probably the only chance I was likely to get in months to actually get close to Noah, but short of running down this nurse with the wheelchair, it now looked as if that wasn't going to happen.

'She *is* the mother,' said Izzy. I could feel she was trembling, so strongly that it shook the frame of the chair, but there was no trace of it in her voice. 'I'm going to push her to Noah's bed and then I'll wait out here.'

She never gave the older woman the chance to either protest or enquire exactly how many mothers this child had. But I did catch a very satisfying glimpse of her mouth dropping open slightly as Izzy wheeled me through the door.

Noah was in a bed beside the window. There were six bays in the unit, but only three of them were currently occupied. A mother sitting beside a toddler's cot looked up from her vigil and flashed a brief sympathetic smile at Izzy. Each bay appeared to have a dedicated nurse, whose only task was to monitor their designated patient. Noah was in good hands; I could tell that by the kindly smile from the nurse who had just finished adjusting a drip attached to the figure in the bed. His whispered hello included both Izzy and me, and from the fleeting twinkle in his eye as he looked down at my mode of transport, I suspected he was the one who'd helped Izzy get hold of the wheelchair. 'I'm going to be just over there,' he said, indicating a small table a few metres away from Noah's bed.

Izzy carefully manoeuvred the wheelchair as close as she could to the bed, mindful of the Spaghetti Junction of wires and tubes surrounding it.

'I'll come back in a little while,' she whispered into my ear, and before I could thank her she turned with a sound that might have been a smothered sob and strode quickly to the door.

It was then and only then that I allowed my gaze to travel up the length of the figure lying in the bed. I started at his feet, moving slowly upwards, as though afraid of what might happen when I finally saw his face. For the rest of my life I knew I would always remember this moment. I had seen Noah from a distance; I had a copy of his photograph on my desk at the shop, beside my bed, and even in my handbag, but nothing, nothing, could ever have prepared me for the explosion of emotions that engulfed me when I saw the child Tim and I had longed for that very first time.

My gasp was low, but sounded as loud as a scream in the hush of the ward. The nurse in charge of Noah looked up, and then nodded encouragingly as I gestured towards his hand lying on the hospital blanket. Noah's skin was warm; his fingers were long, just like Tim's had been. It was a pianist's hand, I thought, wondering if Noah was even interested in music. I knew practically nothing about this small boy lying before me, hooked up to monitors and softly bleeping machines. I had no idea what he liked to do, or the things that made him happy. In fact, the only thing I knew for certain, knew it with every fibre of my being, was that I loved this child with all my heart. And that there was nothing I wouldn't do for him. The unconditional swell of love that hits new mothers when their infant is first placed in their arms might be eight years late, but it still rocked me to my core.

It's impossible to gauge how long I sat at Noah's bedside, silently planning the future we would have together. I imagined a time when we would slowly get to know each other, hoping that he would one day realise that having *four* parents who'd loved him unreservedly made him the richest little boy in the world, even if one of them was sadly no longer around to tell him in person.

'I'm going to tell you all about your daddy,' I promised into his small, shell-like ear. 'He would have loved you so very much, Noah,' I whispered, my tears falling and making a small damp spot on the pillow beside his face.

Noah never stirred, not even when I reached up to touch the springy shock of dark hair. My heart contracted at the memory, for it had been many years since I'd felt that familiar texture beneath my fingertips.

A shaft of light split the darkness of the ward and I glanced towards the doorway to see Izzy silhouetted within its frame. It was time for me to go. I craned closer to the sleeping child, scarcely noticing the stab of protest from my incisions. 'I love you, my darling boy, and even though when we meet you won't know who I am, I hope someday you'll understand it wasn't just science that brought you into the world, it was also love.'

Izzy was now halfway across the room, and I glanced towards her, before stretching across to leave a single feather-light kiss on Noah's velvety cheek. 'And another love – just as strong as ours – helped you grow into the amazing little boy you are today.'

39

Beth

Even though I told myself not to expect him, that he was probably far too busy in the run-up to Christmas to take another day off work, I couldn't quite manage to stop myself from glancing towards the door as the afternoon visitors began to arrive. For someone who'd been so determined to handle this thing alone, I was suddenly craving the support of a friend.

With a helping arm from one of the nurses I'd managed the short walk to the bathroom at the end of the ward, which filled me with ridiculous pride, even though an eighty-year-old could easily have beaten me to the finishing line. The effort of taking a shower, even with the nurse's assistance, absolutely exhausted me, but it was *so* worth it.

It had felt especially good to finally ditch the unflattering hospital gown in favour of the new blue satin pyjamas I'd brought with me. *That's quite a lot of effort you're making, for someone who isn't expecting visitors*, my reflection observed mildly, as I combed my hair dry in front of my handbag mirror. I snapped the compact shut, before it said anything else I didn't want to hear.

'Just remember you're going to have to take things very carefully over the next couple of weeks,' advised the kindly red-headed nurse, who I was beginning to suspect had developed a small crush on Liam. 'Let that lovely hubby of yours look after you. I'm sure he can handle the Christmas preparations for one year,' she said, as she settled me into the upright chair beside the bed. Her fascination with Liam didn't concern me. I imagined lots of women must find him attractive. He *was* attractive, I acknowledged objectively. Just not to me.

What *was* beginning to worry me was how everyone kept emphasising how much help I would need when I left the hospital, which could happen as soon as the very next day. I'd been so focused on the surgery to give Noah my kidney and on *his* recovery, I realised a little late that I hadn't given much thought to my own recuperation.

The sound of footsteps coming to a halt outside my room brought me back to the present, and this time when I looked up it was to see Liam standing in the doorway. He paused for a moment, watching my expression change from greeting, to astonishment, and then finally to amusement. By the time he'd entered the room, I was already laughing hard enough to aggravate my stitches.

'Don't say a word. You don't have to. I've already heard it all from every passing cab driver in town. They're an incredibly witty bunch, you know.'

I tried to smother my laughter, but it was practically impossible as I watched him disentangle himself from the myriad of strings attached to the most enormous bundle of helium balloons I'd ever seen. He knotted them loosely to the end of the hospital bed frame and then turned to face me with a rueful expression on his face. He was waiting.

'Did you mug a clown on your way in?' I asked innocently, and then ruined my own quip by dissolving into giggles.

Liam gave a self-deprecating grin. 'I may possibly have ordered too many. But in my defence, what exactly *are* you supposed to give a florist when they're in hospital?'

'Grapes might have been easier to transport,' I murmured, still struggling to visualise the immaculately suited lawyer carrying the enormous bundle of multicoloured balloons through the town.

Liam pulled up a spare chair and set it close to mine. 'It was worth the abuse, just to see you laugh like that,' he said, which oddly made my smile wobble a little.

'It's a really lovely gesture, Liam. Thank you.'

'How are you feeling today? You look so much better,' he observed, his gaze journeying from the top of my head to my bare feet. The ward was too warm for a dressing gown, and although the satin pyjamas were far from revealing, it still felt odd to be sitting next to him in just my nightwear.

'I feel fine. Even better now I know how fantastically Noah is doing.' Liam's eyes flickered briefly. 'I actually got to see him late last night.'

The charcoal of his pupils seemed to grow darker as I told him of Izzy's surprising appearance in my room, and our journey through the sleeping hospital to Noah's bedside. Liam had worn a very similar look when I'd explained about the arrangement Izzy and I had reached about my future role in Noah's life. Perhaps it was the lawyer in him that prevented him from trusting anything unless it was signed and witnessed in triplicate.

'We didn't need to consult a lawyer,' I'd told him. 'We just agreed we'd do what was best for Noah.'

'I'm concerned you're going to get hurt,' Liam said now, leaning forward and resting his elbows on his knees. The manoeuvre brought his face close enough for me to see the tiny spot just below his jaw that he'd missed when shaving. I clasped my hands together in my lap, as I fought an unexpected urge to graze my fingertips over the skin there.

'I was fine. Izzy pushed the wheelchair.'

'Not *physically* hurt.'

I looked down, my eyes going to the thin band of gold on my left hand. I raised my head slowly. 'We both know there's not much you can do to guard against that. Getting hurt is the flip side of the coin toss when you love someone.'

However deeply you bury the pain, it's always there somewhere; it's a stain that you never quite manage to wash away. I recognised it from the first in Liam's eyes, just as I knew he had in mine.

'And as far as getting solicitors involved – well, no offence, but that didn't work out so well for us last time.' Liam's eyebrows clearly disagreed with me. 'Izzy isn't going to go back on her word – surely what she did last night proves that? And I'm certainly not about to ask for my kidney back.' It was meant to make him smile, and it did. Briefly. Then his face sobered, and his eyes darkened once more to the colour of storm clouds.

'I just hope you both know what you're doing.'

★★★

'Mr and Mrs Brandon.'

My head shot up. It had been a very long time since I had heard those words. Liam missed several beats before turning towards the group of doctors who had entered my room. I hoped no one had noticed that the man who was supposed to be my husband hadn't appeared to recognise his own name. Two of the doctors were strangers, but I'd met the senior consultant before. His was the last face I'd seen as the anaesthetist had put me under.

'I apologise for intruding on your visiting time, but we're running a little late with our rounds today.'

Liam got to his feet as the medics came further into the room, looking vaguely alarmed when the nurse accompanying them firmly shut the door.

'If you don't mind, we'd just like to have a quick look at our handiwork, and see if we can think about letting you go back home.'

'I... I should probably wait outside,' Liam said, sounding more awkward than I'd ever heard before.

'That's all right. We'll only be a moment or two,' assured the surgeon, stepping back as the nurse helped me onto the bed. Liam shrank into the furthest corner of the room and had already turned to look out of the window before the dressings on my wounds had been removed.

'Is your husband a little squeamish?'

'A bit,' I replied, wondering if this was actually the most excruciatingly embarrassing moment of my life. If it wasn't, it certainly ranked high up in the top ten.

Thankfully, the physical examination was brief. 'Everything is looking very good,' the consultant declared. 'I see no reason why, with the right aftercare, we can't let you complete your recovery at home. Is everything okay when you pee?' he asked, almost as a conversational afterthought.

I glanced over at Liam and thought very possibly his shoulders had begun to shake. 'Just perfect,' I answered.

'Well then,' declared the surgeon, turning now to include Liam in the conversation. 'I think you'll be able to take your wife back home tomorrow.'

The moment to correct the mistake had long since passed and my eyes sent a pleading message to Liam, asking him to play along. Sportingly he did, nodding seriously as the doctor outlined a comprehensive list of dos and don'ts for my recuperation. 'Remember, no heavy lifting for several weeks,' reminded the doctor, shaking first my hand, and then Liam's. 'And no strenuous sex for a month or so.'

'Absolutely not,' agreed Liam solemnly, who I strongly suspected was now having the best afternoon of his life.

I waited until the group of doctors had left before I turned to him, my cheeks still glowing hotly. 'If you could just please erase the last fifteen minutes from your memory, I'd be really grateful.'

Liam's smile was wide. 'As amusing as that was, it must have made you realise that you're going to need some help for a few weeks. You don't have anyone to look after you, do you?' I suppose I could have lied, but he was a lawyer, skilled at spotting a falsehood from a mile off.

'No.' I already knew what he was going to say next.

'Then the only sensible solution is for you to stay with me.'

'That's very kind of you,' I began, 'but—'

'But nothing,' Liam interrupted. 'You've just undergone major surgery and can't manage alone.' He was pacing as he spoke, as though delivering a closing argument in a courtroom. 'You want to get out of here tomorrow, don't you?' I nodded reluctantly. 'Well, that isn't going to happen unless you have someone to help you.'

I was marshalling my arguments, which involved hiring a private nurse or a carer, although in reality I had no idea how to arrange either of those at short notice, when Liam suddenly stopped pacing and dropped to a crouch before my chair. 'Let me do this for you, Beth. Let me at least try to make up for the way I behaved over the last few months.'

'But it's Christmas,' I protested. 'Surely you've already made plans for the holidays?'

'Actually, no, I haven't. I still find Christmas and New Year somewhat... difficult.'

I could feel the bonds that linked us growing a little stronger. Very slowly I nodded in acceptance.

'Okay then.'

40

Izzy

Christmas music was playing at the nurses' station from an oversized radio cassette, the kind teenagers had once carted around on their shoulders in a time before music downloads. There was a definite festive feeling on the ward, which had begun with a visit from an uncommonly slender Father Christmas earlier that afternoon. He'd gone from room to room distributing small gifts and hearty ho-ho-hos with equal enthusiasm. It was a nice touch, especially as several of the young patients he'd visited weren't going to be well enough to go home for Christmas. As to whether Noah was one of them was still undecided.

The bright orange helium balloon tied to Noah's bed frame bobbed up and down like a lifebuoy as he wriggled restlessly, trying to get comfortable. It was three days since the transplant and thankfully many of the tubes and wires he'd been hooked up to had been removed that morning. But he was still confined to bed, and growing more bored and restless by the hour. Which were good signs, the consultant had declared on his rounds that morning. The physician looked almost as delighted as we'd been when he pronounced that Noah's recovery was virtually textbook perfect. Beth's kidney was performing splendidly in its new home, just as she'd said it would.

'Where did Daddy go?'

'He just needed to get something from the car, sweetheart. He'll be back in a moment.'

I hadn't set foot outside the hospital since the day of Noah's operation, but Pete had been eating up the miles on the motorway, journeying back and forth between Noah's bedside and home to feed and exercise Marvel. It would have been easier to have put him into kennels, but we'd promised Noah that he could stay at home. A small shudder of anticipation ran through me and I glanced at my watch and smiled. Not long now.

This had been Pete's plan, and initially I thought we'd be met with resistance or an outright refusal, but surprisingly that hadn't been the case. Apparently, this was something that was actively encouraged on children's wards. Medical benefits aside, I couldn't wait to see the look on Noah's face, and as my ear tuned into the sound of Pete's footsteps in the hospital corridor, I knew I didn't have long to wait.

There are moments in your child's life that as a parent you treasure. Mental snapshots that you know you will cherish for years to come. And the expression on Noah's face when Pete walked into his hospital room carrying Marvel in his arms was definitely one of them.

A chorus of joyous squeals and excited whines filled the room as dog and boy expressed their mutual delight at seeing each other. Pete set the dog down on the bed, one arm casually looping around my shoulders as we stood side by side watching the reunion.

'He'll pee on the bed,' warned Pete darkly.

'I will not,' declared Noah hotly, and then wondered why his parents had dissolved into peals of laughter. It kept happening to us. We were still in a state where all our emotions were heightened. Like wires stripped of their protective outer sheath, everything got too close to us. I imagined things would eventually calm down and we'd find a new level of normal, but it was still very early days.

The future remained a huge unknown. Noah might have decades with his new kidney or just weeks, nobody knew. That kind of uncertainty was admittedly harder for me to deal with than it was for Pete. *'You can't spend your life worrying about things that haven't happened yet, Iz,'* Pete had said, after we'd been told the operation had been a success. That was easy for him to say; he'd always been more of a 'cross that bridge when we come to it' kind of person.

But I knew he was right. I'd spent my life worrying about Noah getting sick, and it *still* hadn't stopped that from happening. All it *had* done was almost tear Pete and me apart and if I didn't want that to happen again, if we were ever going to move forward, I was going to have to find a way to get past those feelings.

Pete's arm was still in place and he used it to pull me a little closer to his side. I breathed in the smell of him, like a drug I never wanted to quit. The threat of Noah's court case and then his illness had brought us to the same page in our story, but those couldn't be the only reasons for us to stay together.

I slipped an arm around him, enjoying the way his laughter thrummed through me. Once we'd always been like this; two halves of the same person. And now, finally, I was ready to admit how much I wanted that back.

41

Beth

'Got everything?' Liam asked, watching as I folded the last of my belongings into the overnight bag and snapped the clasps in place. 'We'll stop off at your place and pick up anything else that you need.'

I smiled weakly, still far from comfortable with how things had panned out. I had lain awake for most of the night trying to find another more workable solution, but with Christmas only a week away, I didn't feel I could ask any of my friends if they wanted an invalid house guest for the holidays.

'I realise there's nothing I can do to stop you from whistling for a cab to take you home the moment we get down to the street,' Liam said, which uncannily *had* been one of my middle-of-the-night solutions. 'But I really hope you won't do that.'

I pressed the button to summon the lift, keeping my eyes fixed on the overhead panel as I shook my head. 'I won't. Although I still think I could manage on my own.'

Liam gave a soft grunt of disapproval, but fortunately the arrival of the lift cut short an argument I no longer thought I could win.

The impulse struck me somewhere between floors four and three as the lift descended to the ground.

'I'd like to see Noah again before I leave.'

We were the only occupants in the lift, making the carriage as private as a confessional booth.

'I thought you'd agreed with Izzy that you were going to wait.'

'I know. And I will. I don't want to talk to him. I just need to see him – even if it's only from a distance, to reassure myself that he's still doing as well as everyone says.'

Liam thought it was a bad idea, I could see that. And yet after a moment of consideration he gave a small nod. 'Shall I come with you, or would you rather do it alone?'

A strange sensation swept over me. Since Tim's death I was used to doing things alone: spiders in the bathtub; complicated tax returns; the weekly supermarket shop for one. I'd learnt to cope by myself. But sometimes, when you think life has no more surprises to throw your way, along comes an unexpected friendship, and the ground shifts subtly beneath your feet.

'I'd really like you to come with me.'

It all looked different in daylight. I was walking the right way, but everything felt wrong. No one challenged us; no one questioned our right to be there; but that didn't stop the overwhelming feeling of being somewhere I didn't quite belong. Liam walked at my side, carrying my case and saying nothing. We passed recessed bays with quartets of beds; most of them were occupied and surrounded by parents and relatives. Every single bed had a helium balloon tied to its frame.

'You don't mind, do you?' I asked when I saw Liam's look of surprise.

He smiled. 'Not at all. I was wondering where the rest of them had gone.'

I'd kept a single red balloon from the cluster, but had asked for the rest to be distributed to the patients on the children's ward. Coupled with foil-cut decorations, tinsel wreaths and fairy lights, they helped to give the ward a festive cheer, which almost made you forget that there were some very poorly children here. And one of them was mine.

I was heading towards the intensive care unit when I heard the sound of Izzy's voice coming from a recessed bay immediately ahead of us. It was followed by a low rumble of laughter, which spilled out into the corridor from a voice I was pretty sure was Pete's. Like a striking python, my hand shot out and grabbed Liam's arm, bringing him to a stop.

'What—?'

I shook my head and nodded in the direction of the voices. We stood frozen in the corridor, like misplaced contestants in a game of musical statues. A new sound joined the voices from the bay, higher in pitch and curiously alien. I inched a little further forward, until two of the beds came into view. One of them was Noah's. I immediately shrank back, although I was sure none of them had been looking our way. The family bubble that encased them looked pretty much impenetrable.

'What's that weird noise?' asked Liam, whispering the question into the fall of my hair. I was blocking his view, but I didn't move. *Couldn't* move. I was rooted to the spot as if I'd been glued there. If either Izzy or Pete had turned to look over their shoulder they would certainly have seen us, but they were completely absorbed with Noah and the antics of the very excitable greyhound, which was whimpering and squealing with joy as it attempted to wriggle into bed with its favourite human.

I hadn't realised my fingers were still curled like claws into Liam's lower arm. The fabric of his jumper was puckered into folds beneath my grip, yet he made no move to shrug me off. Noah's face disappeared in and out of view, hidden by his parents and the cavorting dog, which was clearly ecstatic to be reunited with its owner.

I drank in the sight of him. I tuned in to the sound of his laughter, trying to capture it and commit it to memory. He looked and sounded so happy. And so loved.

Something happened at that moment. I could feel it shifting inside me, like gears realigning. Curiously, I think my eyes were drier than Liam's when eventually I tore my gaze away from the bay. 'Okay. I've seen enough. We can go now.'

Soft flurries of snow began to fall on our drive from the hospital. According to the weathermen, the odds of having a white Christmas were no longer worth placing a bet on. The pathway up to my front door was already slippery underfoot with a sprinkling of snow, and Liam automatically took my arm, as though I was a frail old lady with a dodgy hip. It was only when I caught sight of my reflection in the bedroom mirror while I hastily packed a suitcase that I realised I *did* look fragile and weak. My cheeks were pale and ghost-like and I quickly rummaged in my make-up bag for something to remedy that. The haunted look in my eyes wasn't quite so easy to fix.

While Liam carried my case back down the stairs I emptied my fridge of perishables, unable to shake the feeling that I was leaving something important behind. I crossed to the lounge and took my silver-framed wedding photograph from the top of the piano and slipped it into my handbag. I expected the feeling to settle, but strangely it didn't.

When I turned around, Liam was watching me from the doorway, an unreadable expression on his face. Almost as though he'd been caught out, he quickly switched the direction of his gaze to the opposite side of the room.

'That's an impressive tree you have there,' he remarked randomly.

'You don't have one?' I asked as I reached beneath the dense Nordic pine branches to pull the fairy-light plug from the wall.

Liam shrugged. 'I never really bothered after Anna.' There was so much more behind that sentence than just a decision not to decorate his house with tinsel and holly, but it wasn't the right moment to delve deeper. I'd already fallen through thin ice once before when mentioning his late wife; I wasn't about to make the same mistake twice.

'Tim was always like a little kid at Christmas. We'd have decorations up as soon as the advent calendar was opened.' Liam smiled, but I could see he thought we'd been a little strange. 'He'd be rehearsing carol concerts from around October and would be humming them in his sleep for months.' I laughed softly at the memory. 'I've always felt he'd be disappointed if I didn't celebrate Christmas the way we always did together.'

Liam made a small sound that defied interpretation.

The windscreen wipers were soporific, and combined with the mesmerising snow shower we were driving through, I was more than half asleep by the time we arrived at Liam's home. He hadn't been exaggerating about not 'doing' Christmas. His was the only house in the street not festooned with twinkling lights or inflatable Santas and reindeers on the front lawn. 'The neighbourhood kids probably call me Scrooge behind my back,' he joked, watching as I marvelled at the row of houses competing to get the largest electricity bill in January.

A Christmas junkie was probably the very last person he'd ever choose as a houseguest, I realised, as we entered the warmth of his hallway. But someone who *did* seem pleased to see me was Sally, his dog – or rather *Anna's* dog. The terrier stuck close to my heels, as though superglued there, even trotting up the stairs behind us when Liam showed me to the bedroom that was to be mine for the next week or so.

'Bed. Wardrobe. Chest of drawers,' Liam pointed out like an awkward estate agent. 'And the bathroom's just opposite.' It was odd to see him stripped of his usual confident air.

I suspected there hadn't been many guests who'd stayed under this roof since Anna had passed away.

Liam turned to leave me to unpack, calling the dog to follow him, but the terrier had other ideas. Settling herself on the rug beside the bed, she was putting on a good show of being totally deaf. Liam sighed theatrically, and it was almost impossible not to laugh. I bent down and fondled the dog's ears. 'Can she stay for a bit? I've always loved dogs.'

Liam turned towards the door, shaking his head at his pet. 'She clearly prefers your company to mine,' he said without rancour. He paused at the doorway as a question occurred to him. 'If you love dogs so much, why don't you have one? Have *mine*,' he offered with a laugh.

Sally's chocolate-button eyes were practically rolling in her head as I scratched a spot between her ears. 'I couldn't when Tim was alive. He suffered terribly with all kinds of allergies.'

'But afterwards?' Liam prompted.

I shrugged. 'I don't know, really. The shop. The responsibility.' They weren't good enough excuses, but how could I explain the irrational fear of living a life different to the one I had before, a life that held no trace of Tim in it, when I didn't even understand that myself? 'I grew up on the coast and when I was younger I used to dream of one day living in a cottage beside the sea, with maybe two or three dogs, and taking long walks along windswept beaches.' Even to my ears, my voice sounded sad and wistful.

'You should do it. Life's too short not to follow your dreams.'

Our eyes met and an unspoken acknowledgement was read and received, without a single word being said.

I slept a great deal during the first three days of my stay, which made me either the very best or the very worst kind of houseguest. Liam was still going into the office for a few hours each day. He said they were winding down for Christmas, but I suspected his reduced working hours were because of me. Despite reassuring him I was perfectly capable of sitting on a settee for most of the day without a responsible adult in the house, I could tell he was taking his duties as a carer very seriously.

On the fourth day I was alone in the kitchen, rummaging for the makings of a fresh cup of coffee, when the sound of someone unlocking the back door startled me. I jumped violently, spilling a sizeable puddle of coffee onto the worktop.

'Gosh, I'm sorry. I didn't mean to startle you,' said a woman I'd never seen before. She walked into the kitchen and shut the door firmly behind her. For a burglar, she was awfully polite. Sally raced across the floor to greet her, her claws skittering over the tiles in her haste, so I guessed the woman was a frequent visitor.

'I'm Gina, from next door,' she explained, as she bent down to rub the terrier's head. The dog clearly loved all women, or missed its first owner dreadfully, I realised with a pang of sadness. 'I usually pop in a couple of times a day when Liam is at work to let Sally have a run in the garden or take her for a walk.'

'Oh,' I said, reaching for a cloth to swab the mess I'd made before it dripped onto the floor.

'Here, let me do that for you!' exclaimed Gina, practically racing over, presumably to take the cloth from my hand. There was something odd about the way she was looking at me, as though I was in danger of collapsing at the smallest exertion. I realised then that Sally wasn't the *only* reason she was there.

'Has Liam asked you to check up on me?'

His neighbour turned a delightful shade of pink. Lying was something Gina clearly didn't do often – or well – because she was really bad at it.

'No. Not at all. Goodness me, no. Well, perhaps he might have mentioned... Oh, okay, yes. He *did* ask me to pop in every couple of hours, just to make sure...' She had cracked like a nut, and I hadn't even been trying that hard. 'But I was happy to do it. *Really* happy,' she said with curious emphasis. 'We're all just so delighted that Liam has finally found someone.'

So many questions jumped into my head, I hardly knew which one to ask first. 'We? Who exactly are the "we"?'

Gina swept her hand meaningfully in the direction of the road outside. 'All of us. We all moved in around the same time. What happened to Anna was such a tragedy, and we've been waiting a very long time for Liam to move on with his life. We can't tell you how happy everyone is that he finally has.'

'I'm not... Liam and I aren't... We're just friends.'

Poor Gina went even redder at her gaffe, which almost made me feel like pretending we *were* a couple before the poor woman combusted with embarrassment. Her eyes dropped to my hands, still busily working on the coffee puddle, and spotted the thin gold wedding band.

'Oh, gosh. I'm so sorry. What a complete idiot I am. You're *married*.'

Often I still said 'yes' to that statement, because it felt so much closer to the truth than a denial. But not today. 'I'm widowed,' I corrected. 'My husband passed away five years ago.'

Even while Gina was offering me her condolences, I could see a kernel of hope had reappeared in her eyes. Instead of quashing those rumours, I suspected all I'd actually done was put extra fuel on the fire.

I didn't mention the visit until much later that evening, even though it had been on my mind throughout the day. It was one more vaguely unsettling thought to add to the troublesome ones already niggling quietly away at the back of my head, like mice gnawing through cables. Everything still felt vaguely off-kilter and slightly wrong. As though the compass I'd been following was suddenly spinning wildly. I put these weird sensations down to the lingering after-effects of the anaesthetic, although, despite extensive googling, I couldn't find similar instances on the internet. I just hoped this odd feeling of unease – which kept waking me up in a state of panic in the middle of the night – would soon wear off.

'So, I met your neighbour Gina today.'

A tiny muscle twitched fleetingly beside Liam's right eye, but he managed to sound believably casual. 'She lets Sally out during the day for me.' I could see he hoped that would be the end of this particular conversation.

'And babysits your visitors too, when required.' I wasn't really cross; it was quite sweet how he worried about me, so I don't know why I was making him feel guilty. We were sitting in front of his fire, on a scattered bed of floor cushions, which I found more comfortable than a chair as my wounds began to heal. 'Thank you for worrying about me, Liam, but it's really not necessary. I actually feel so much better, I could probably go back home and leave you and Sally to have Christmas in peace.'

'No!'

I think he was as startled as I was that his reply had come out so sharply it sounded almost like a command. The room was lit by two low-wattage table lamps, but even by their dim light I could see the small flush on his face.

'Don't go,' he said. 'Even if you do feel better, don't go.'

My lips suddenly felt really dry and I licked them nervously, until I saw him looking at them in a way that started to make the room feel really warm.

'You can't go, anyway,' he said, thankfully finding just the right bantering tone to lighten what had suddenly become quite a strange moment. 'I ordered a huge turkey from the butcher yesterday, and I have absolutely no idea how to cook it, or use my own oven come to that.'

'Oh, well. When you put it like that, how could I possibly leave?'

42

Izzy

It was almost midnight when I crept back down the stairs, Noah's undelivered stocking still in my hand, instead of at the foot of his bed where it ought to be. He *should* have been exhausted, because *I* certainly was. But there's something about Christmas Eve that chases sleep away from bone-tired children, even those who've only been discharged from hospital that afternoon.

'Not sleepy, kiddo?' I asked, snuggling the duvet a little tighter beneath his chin. Noah turned his head away from the window with its undrawn curtains; it was how he always liked them on this night.

'I'm waiting,' he said solemnly.

My heart melted, knowing this could very well be the last year he'd be a true believer. 'For Santa?' I asked, looking through the window at the crisp, clear December sky. It was filled with a storybook moon, full and impossibly white, a perfect backdrop for a sleigh.

'For the Christmas magic to start,' Noah corrected in a whisper.

It's already here, I thought, as I bent down to kiss his forehead gently. It started when the doctors said you were well enough to come home. That's all the magic Pete and I could possibly have wished for.

'Well, magic only happens once little boys fall asleep,' I declared, wondering how many parents all over the world were saying something very similar at that exact moment.

Noah's small harrumph was full of doubt that I had my facts right, but he dutifully snuggled a little further down beneath the covers. 'Night night, Mummy. I love you.'

'I love you too, sweetheart. Sleep tight.'

'Still awake,' I declared as I entered the lounge. But there was no one there to hear me. I glanced towards the settee where Pete had wearily collapsed after his last trip to check on Noah. The cushions on his favourite seat had permanently moulded into a Pete-sized dent a long time ago. That imprint had haunted me during the months we'd been apart, and more than once I'd pummelled the resistant foam with angry fists, tears rolling down my face, as I tried to reshape not just the seat, but also my life without him. I'd never managed to do either very successfully.

I turned to leave the room, noticing as I did that Pete had been busy during my absence. The previously clean fireplace flagstones were now covered with a light film of soot, into which several large boot prints had been left. I was still smiling as I entered the kitchen and saw that phase two of Pete's plan was underway. He was nibbling up and down the length of an enormous carrot, sinking his teeth into the vegetable in a manner I guess he imagined a reindeer might do. He stopped when he saw me, running his tongue over his lips to capture any stray carrot debris. How wrong was it that I should find that so unexpectedly sexy?

'Asleep?' he asked hopefully, placing the carrot back on the plate alongside a drained glass of milk and scattered mince pie crumbs.

'Not even close,' I sighed, pulling out a kitchen chair and lowering myself onto it like someone twice my age. As I did, I noticed the trail of sooty footprints on the kitchen tiles leading to the table.

Pete grinned, looking closer to Noah's age than a man in his thirties had a right to. 'I'll clean it all up in the morning. I just wanted to go to town this year.' He paused for a moment and I caught a fleeting sadness in his eyes, which I don't think I was supposed to have seen. 'I missed doing all of this last year.'

'Noah did too,' I admitted sadly. As much as I'd tried to fill Pete's shoes during our separation, there was a bond between father and son that no one could ever match. For a brief moment, I wondered what kind of dad Beth's husband, Tim, would have been. I guessed we'd learn more about him once Noah was well enough to meet Beth. I parcelled up that thought and shoved it into a corner of my mind so it couldn't ruin our first night back home.

'I imagine I won't be doing any of this next year,' Pete said regretfully as he repositioned the Christmas props on the table.

'Because you're moving out again?' I had no idea where that question had come from. But perhaps when you're tired and distracted, buried fears have a way of erupting like escaping lava.

Pete turned two shades paler at my words and his eyes looked troubled. 'Well, actually, what I meant was that Noah would probably be too old to buy into any of this. But… I guess you're right. I suppose it's something we should be thinking about.'

No I'm not. I'm not right at all. I have no idea why I said that, because it's not what I want to happen. I don't even want to think about it. The words were all there, screaming deafeningly in my head, but somehow I couldn't unlock my voice to release them.

'We never said this was a long-term solution,' Pete continued, carelessly crushing my fragile dreams with his pragmatism. 'And now with the court case a thing of the past, and Noah's transplant a success, he—'

'—still needs you,' I completed on a rush. 'Sick or well, he still needs you here.'

Pete was so still, it was almost as though he was frozen. His hand moved just a fraction, as though it wanted to reach out to me, but he wouldn't let it.

'You and I can't live together just for the sake of Noah, Eliza. We both deserve something more than that.' His use of my full name wasn't lost on me. If I needed further proof of just how important this conversation had suddenly become, there it was. 'Sometimes you can't turn back the clock to how things were before.'

I wondered which 'before' he was talking about. Before Noah got sick? Before we learnt he wasn't our son? Or before we called time on a marriage we should have fought a damn sight harder to save? The fault for that lay with both of us; it was the unspoken spectre that slipped in and out of the shadows, but never entirely went away.

I got jerkily to my feet, turning away from him so he wouldn't see the tears that were starting to roll down my cheeks.

'At least you'll get your spare room back,' he said, trying to make a joke out of something that wasn't even remotely funny. I spun around so fast that the room actually swam out of focus for a moment. Perhaps I needed that centrifugal force to finally release the words lodged in my throat.

'It's not the spare room I want back again,' I said, lifting up my head even as I threw my pride down at his feet.

Where we were now was partly down to me. Pete had reached out several times over the past months, trying to mend the broken bits of us, but each time I'd held him back, unable or unwilling to focus on anything except Noah's health. Three times he'd pulled me into his arms and three times I'd backed away. The pain in his eyes had been real, and it had haunted me for days, but I hadn't been ready then. And now when I finally was, I might have left it too late.

Suddenly, I could feel the shackles I'd locked myself up in springing open. I didn't have to wait for Pete to tell me he wanted me again. *I* could tell *him*, because it was the truth and it always had been.

Our eyes met and held.

'Don't,' I said, my voice shaky and almost unrecognisable.
'Don't what?'

'Don't go. Don't move out. Don't give up on us. And please don't stop loving me... because I never stopped loving you.'

His smile was slow but worth every moment of agony that it took as I waited for it to change his face. He was suddenly the boy I'd met and fallen for all those years ago, as well as the man I wanted to end my days with.

'I got it so wrong last year,' I continued. 'I was an idiot for pushing you away and telling you to move out. It was never what I wanted.' Why had it taken me so long to finally find the courage to tell him that?

Pete shook his head, taking his share of the blame as he slowly closed the gap between us. 'I should never have gone. I was so busy trying to fix everything that I didn't see the most precious thing in the world was breaking right in front of me.' His eyes were bright as they held mine. 'I've spent every day since then trying to find my way back to you.'

He stood before me then, his heart open and vulnerable, as was mine. We'd kissed a thousand times before, but never like that. Never with such desperation, such longing, such feeling.

'Oh God, I'm never letting you go again,' Pete said huskily into my hair when eventually we broke apart. 'Nothing has made sense in my life since I stopped being your husband.'

I reached up on tiptoe to recapture his lips, confessing as I did: 'You never stopped being my husband, not in here.' I held my hand against my heart, which was racing as if I'd run a marathon. In a way, it felt as though we both had; a gruelling long aching journey to get back to the place we should never have left.

Neither of us noticed when we slipped into Christmas Day but as the clock in the hall chimed the half hour, Pete raised his head from mine.

'Do you think it's safe to assume Noah is now asleep, because I think my days of making love on a cold kitchen floor might be over.'

Unbelievably, I blushed, which he found absolutely delightful.

Hand in hand we climbed the stairs, Noah's Christmas stocking swinging over Pete's shoulder. We crossed the hallway and peered in through our son's open door. Noah had fallen asleep with his face turned towards the window, still waiting for his Christmas magic.

'He's out like a light,' whispered Pete, tiptoeing in exaggerated steps to the foot of Noah's bed and leaving the stocking. I stared at the gentle rise and fall of the shape beneath the duvet. There was something about it that made me look twice before allowing Pete to tug me gently out of the room.

His arms were already around me and his mouth on mine as he fumbled behind his back for the door handle to the room that would no longer be just mine from this moment on. We tumbled into the bedroom, but as I pushed the door to a close I realised I'd been right.

Across the space of the hallway, in a glimmering shaft of moonlight, I saw one slender arm emerge from beneath the duvet and punch the air in victory.

43

Beth

'Happy Christmas!'

'You're a bit early – it's still only Christmas Eve here. And isn't it the middle of the night in Sydney?'

I'd still been half asleep from an afternoon nap when the familiar Skype ring tone had me hurrying down Liam's staircase to reach my laptop.

'It's nearly five and the boys will be awake soon, so I wanted to say hello before it starts getting crazy at this end.'

Liam's kitchen, like the rest of the house, had been in darkness when I'd answered the call and settled myself on one of the chrome bar stools. I was halfway through asking Karen how our parents were enjoying their stay when unthinkingly I reached over and switched on the light, illuminating the room behind me. I instantly realised my mistake, but it was too late, for Karen was already craning towards her own screen.

'Whose kitchen is that? Where are you?'

A hundred lies ran through my head, and none of them

were believable. 'I'm at a friend's house. I'm staying here for Christmas.'

'What friend? Who?'

'No one you know. Now, did the presents I sent arrive safely?' I should have known better than to think I could distract her that easily.

'Are you with who I think you're with?' she asked perceptively.

Liam was out, but could return at any minute, and the last thing I wanted was to be caught discussing him with my sister in his own home.

'Yes, I am. And I know what you're going to say. I promise I'll explain everything, but not right now.'

I could see how hard this was for her. It didn't matter how old we were, or that we lived on opposite sides of the world. She was my champion, fighting my corner and on my side, even when she believed I was in the wrong. Like now.

There was an incredibly long silence, which finally she broke. 'Just tell me this: are you all right?'

I nodded, and something on my face drew her once again closer to her tablet screen. 'You look different somehow.' Were her sisterly powers of observation so great she could actually spot I was down one internal organ since we last spoke? But then she smiled, almost in wonder. 'You look... more at peace, somehow.'

Her words surprised me, because even ten thousand miles away she'd managed to spot something I hadn't even acknowledged myself. I *was* feeling more settled than I had in a very long time. And I think I knew why.

Somewhere in Sydney, out of camera range, came a loud

shriek, which sounded like the cry of a native bird. It wasn't. Karen's smile widened. 'I do believe that was the sound of two young boys ripping open their presents. I'm going to have to go, hon.'

I blew a kiss at the screen. 'Wish everyone happy Christmas from me and tell them I love them.' My voice sounded thick with emotion and a sudden longing to be on the other side of the world. I kept waving at the screen as Karen disappeared into a mosaic of dissolving pixels.

Next year, I promised myself as I drew in a deep calming breath, *I'll be with them all for Christmas next year.* I inhaled again, and my nose twitched as it picked up a subtle aroma. Pine... and not the disinfectant type. Like a bloodhound following a scent, I slid off the stool and let my nose lead me out of the kitchen, into the hallway, and finally to the closed door of the lounge. I was pretty sure what I'd find on the other side of it.

The tree was huge. Easily double the size of the one in my own home. It was also right in the middle of the floor, as though Liam had run out of strength to move it even one centimetre further. I walked up and stood before it, so close that the tips of its branches tickled against my face. It was a giant redwood of a Christmas tree, but what it represented was even more enormous. This was the first tree Liam had brought into the house in eight years. And he'd done it for me. And right now I wasn't entirely sure how I felt about that.

The sudden trilling of a phone startled me. It appeared to be coming from a corner of the room that, thanks to the tree, was currently inaccessible. After the fifth ring, Liam's answering machine kicked in.

'Hello there,' said a cheery voice. Just two words, but they already told me that I would have liked her. There was a genuine warmth and friendliness to Anna's tone that lived on in the recording.

'I'm really sorry, but neither of us can get to the phone right now, so you know what you're going to have to do.' She sounded as if she'd been on the verge of laughter when she'd recorded the message, and I would have bet anything that Liam had been right there in the room with her, smiling at his wife.

My eyes felt scratchy and I blinked furiously, knowing that if I allowed even one tear to escape, I'd never be able to stem the tide. I'm not sure what upset me most: that in all these years Liam had never recorded over his wife's voice, or how easy it was to picture him in this empty house, listening to that message play again and again and again.

A long beep from the answering machine made me jump, and then a new voice filled the room as Liam's caller began to speak.

'Hi, Liam, it's David. I just wanted to wish you a happy Christmas, mate. Charlotte and I are really going to miss seeing you this year, but we totally understand why you couldn't make it. So have a good one, and we'll catch up in the new year for a drink or something.'

Through the branches of the tree I could see the machine blinking like a winking dragon, long after David-Whoever-He-Was had hung up and gone back to his own life. Liam had clearly intended to spend Christmas with those friends, until he'd found out about me. Why had he lied and told me he had no plans? Just when I thought I was beginning to understand this man a little more, I uncovered yet another layer that left me confused.

Liam's headlights scythed through the window and into the darkened room a short while later. By the time his key was in the lock, I'd replaced the vaguely troubled expression on my face with something far more innocuous. He smiled as he saw me sitting in one of the chairs angled beside the fireplace.

'You found the tree,' he said artlessly.

'It's a little hard to miss.'

Our heads turned towards the pine and despite myself I began to laugh. 'Would you like a hand moving it into the corner, or shall we just dance around it like a maypole?'

Liam's grin was wide, but his voice was stern as he reminded me of my limitations. 'Absolutely no lifting, remember?'

He pulled off his jumper before attempting to drag the tree across the room, and the sight of his broad shoulders and defined arms beneath his thin T-shirt took me by surprise. He was far more muscular than I'd imagined... more than Tim had been. It was a vaguely disquieting thought that felt a little disloyal, so I pushed it away into a dark corner of my mind where it couldn't bother me.

My suggestion of making popcorn garlands for the tree, in the absence of decorations, was quickly shot down. 'Not unless we want to spend Christmas at the vet's surgery,' Liam said dryly, giving Sally, who was snoozing by the fire, a meaningful look. 'She'll eat the lot as soon as our backs are turned. Anyway, I *have* decorations.'

He was gone no more than ten minutes, returning with a large cardboard box still covered with a film of grime from the garage. He set it down beside the tree and I bent to brush off most of the dust, revealing when I did a large handwritten label stuck onto the lid. Behind me, I heard Liam's indrawn breath as my hand swept the label clean. I understood. I was exactly the same whenever I unexpectedly came upon Tim's writing on something. Anna had written 'Fragile' and 'Tree Decorations' in neat cursive script, the kind teachers use when writing on a blackboard. Yet again the peculiar similarities in our lives threw me for a moment. Both of them had been teachers. Both of them were gone, and yet both of them were still very much here.

Liam was remarkably tolerant when I insisted that decorating a tree without Christmas music in the background was practically a criminal offence. With carols playing quietly from my phone, we set to work on the tree in companionable silence. I was confined to decorating only the lower branches, directing operations from ground level as Liam climbed a stepladder to reach the top of the tree. He was busy winding a string of lights through the branches when I delved once more into the box of decorations and extracted an oblong package cocooned in bubblewrap.

The sellotape was brittle with age as I pulled the wrapping apart to reveal an egg box. I opened the lid and realised at once what I was looking at. The vibrant patterns painstakingly painted on each silver bauble were instantly recognisable from her paintings. Tiny crystals stuck on each glass ball winked up at me from the light of the fire.

Liam had descended the ladder without making a sound, and was beside me before I had time to close the box.

411

'She made a new one every Christmas that we were married. She said by the time we were done there ought to be around sixty of them.' I looked down sadly at the seven baubles in the egg tray and then at the five empty spaces. Very carefully I went to close the box, but Liam's large, warm hand settled over mine, stopping me.

'What are you doing?' He sounded genuinely confused.

'Putting them back in the box. Keeping them safe. They're too precious to risk breaking, aren't they?'

He shook his head, his hand still covering mine. 'No. Use them. That's why she made them, not for them to sit in some dusty box at the back of the garage. In fact,' he declared, getting suddenly to his feet and walking towards a rustic chest of drawers on the other side of the room, 'I have something here for you.'

I felt confused and wrong-footed. My heart was beating faster and I didn't know if that was because Liam's hand had been on mine, or how curiously abandoned I felt now that it was gone. He was back in an instant, carrying a plain white envelope, which he passed to me. Printed on the front was my name in his familiar bold pen strokes.

'Oh. I didn't know we were doing cards,' I said awkwardly. I'd ordered him a small gift for the following day, but buying a card simply hadn't occurred to me.

'It's not a Christmas card, Beth.'

I dipped my head, allowing my hair to provide a privacy curtain so he couldn't see the expression on my face as I slid my finger beneath the seal and ripped open the envelope. The style I had so easily recognised on the Christmas tree decorations was replicated on the front of the card. In fact, that particular piece looked incredibly familiar.

'You have this painting of Anna's on your office wall,' I told him.

He smiled, looking pleased that I'd recognised it. 'Open the card,' he instructed.

I had to read it three times – not because I didn't understand the words, but because it took that long for me to get control of my voice.

'You're having an exhibition of Anna's paintings,' I said, holding the invitation out to him, as though he might have forgotten what it said.

'I am,' he agreed. 'In February. And I'd very much like it if you'd come with me as my guest.' I could feel my mouth dropping open to form a small O of surprise. 'Because without you, it never would have happened.'

I glanced back down at the unfamiliar gallery name. 'You've found a different gallery,' I observed, not surprised in the least that he hadn't chosen to go with Andrew Cartwright's establishment.

'This is a much smaller place,' he said. 'Less flashy, and far more Anna.'

'What made you change your mind?'

He looked surprised that I needed to ask. 'You. Of course, you.'

It was suddenly much warmer in the room, or so it seemed to me.

'You were right. I was holding on to the past so tightly I was in danger of suffocating it.' I didn't remember saying those exact words, but it didn't seem the right moment to correct him. 'What you said about Anna and how she would have wanted people to see the work she loved made me think that perhaps *you* understood her better than I did. Because you were right. It *was* what Anna would have wanted.'

I nodded encouragingly, hopefully without any trace of 'I told you so' on my face.

'I spent months trying to find a way of telling you that I was sorry, that I finally understood what you were saying. But…'

'But?' I prompted.

'I didn't know how to. No, it's more than that. I was scared of getting it wrong again. So I waited, and waited. And when I finally told myself not to be such a damn idiot and just go to the shop and see you – you weren't there. You were on an operating table, with no family around to support you, doing something amazing for your little boy.'

My eyes were glistening in the light of the fire. We had unexpectedly arrived at a place I hadn't planned on venturing yet. But strangely the moment felt right to say the words out loud.

'Not my little boy. *Izzy's* little boy.'

What had I been expecting? A gasp of shock? A recoil in surprise? A denial? I got none of those. Instead, Liam just nodded slowly, his eyes never once leaving mine.

'You knew this was going to happen?' My voice was incredulous, because for me the decision was still a surprise.

'Yes. I did.'

'When? How long?'

There was such a look of tenderness on his face that it could have easily broken my heart, if it wasn't already in pieces.

'When we went down to the ward on the day you left the hospital. I saw it then in the way you looked at Noah.' He reached over and slotted his fingers through mine. 'I saw the goodbye in your eyes.'

'It's the right thing to do,' I said, as though Liam was the one in need of convincing, which I really didn't think was the case.

'Something has felt wrong ever since I had the operation. Not physically—' I said quickly when I saw his eyes darken in alarm. 'Something in here,' I said, pointing at the region where I thought my heart resided. 'And also in here,' I added, my finger lifting to my temple. 'I think I always knew deep down that this was the right thing to do. I just got a little... dazzled... by Izzy's offer. It took a while for me to see clearly again.'

'When will you tell her?'

'After Christmas,' I said, surprised by the feeling of rightness that seemed to settle over me, as I spoke the words out loud for the first time.

'I'll tell them that this time I'm walking away for good. No contact, no nothing. I'll be out of their lives forever.'

It was a subdued Christmas, but it was just what I needed. It had been a long time since I'd cooked in a kitchen alongside anyone, and I enjoyed it far more than I had expected.

After eating more food than a human should possibly consume, we moved once again to the lounge. The tree was twinkling prettily in the corner of the room, and ignoring the armchairs I settled myself on the floor in front of the crackling fire, to see it better. We'd exchanged gifts that morning, and Liam had seemed genuinely pleased with the cashmere scarf I'd chosen for him. I'd had to bite my lip to stop myself admitting I'd picked it because it was the exact same shade of grey as his eyes, which was an odd thing for one friend to say to another.

He'd bought me a designer handbag and almost in the same breath as giving it had told me he'd kept the receipt in case I wanted to change it, which I found oddly endearing. Not that I would change it, I thought now, as my fingers grazed over the bright red leather.

'I could have gone for black or brown,' Liam confided, coming towards me carrying two glasses of champagne. 'But somehow red seemed more "you". Bold and vibrant, and brave.'

'Is that how you see me?' I asked, wondering where that odd little wobble in my voice had come from.

He passed me one of the delicate crystal flutes, putting it in my outstretched hand while his eyes never once left mine.

'I don't think you have any idea of exactly how I see you, Beth.'

My heart was thumping all the way up to the back of my throat.

'I think… I think maybe I might do… but…'

I was almost too scared to look at him, but when I did there was a soft smile on his lips, and no blame in his eyes.

'But you're not there yet?'

I didn't want to lie to him. Nor hurt him, but I had to be honest.

'No, I'm not.'

'That's okay. I knew that anyway.' He looked perfectly at

peace with what I was saying. 'There's no rush or pressure here. We have all the time in the world.'

As much as I wanted to leave this topic, I had to be honest with him.

'What if I'm *never* ready? What if I always feel this way?'

'Don't worry about it,' Liam said gently, and for a moment everything he felt was right there, shining brightly in his eyes. Then with a single blink it was gone again. 'These things have a way of working out exactly how they're meant to.'

He lifted his flute of champagne towards mine. Our glasses chinked, backlit by the dancing flames of the fire, and within the sparkling golden liquid I caught a fleeting glimpse of our future.

44

Later

Beth

The December sunlight was slanting in through the window and falling squarely onto the Christmas tree. Even though it was far too early for its lights to be switched on, the Norway spruce seemed to glow as the sunbeams were captured and held by the glass decorations hanging from its branches.

The tree drew me across the room, until I was close enough for its sharp, sweet aroma to fill my senses. I inhaled deeply, taking a hit of what for me would always be the quintessential smell of Christmas. Very carefully, I straightened up one of the precious glass baubles, which was hanging a little crookedly. The thought of breaking one of Anna's cherished decorations filled me with dread, although Liam was strangely far more philosophical about them. 'They're not her, any more than that piano is Tim,' he'd said, sliding an arm gently around my waist as he turned me towards the instrument that occupied a corner of the room. Neither of us played, but it would always be with us. *'Where else would you put all those photographs if we got rid of it?'* Liam had teased. He made a good point, for the lid of the baby grand was crowded with an ever-growing collection of them. There were other photographs in the room, too; ones that were just as precious. Three of them sat in silver frames on the rustic beam above the inglenook fireplace. In two of them, Liam was a groom, and in two I was a bride. I loved how we looked equally happy in all three portraits, which was exactly as it should be. Falling in love for a second time shouldn't devalue the relationship that came before it. If anything, loving Anna and Tim as much as we had made us better together than we might otherwise have been. And in a way, they were the ones who'd brought us together, for we'd first met at the cemetery. Maybe it *was* unusual to have filled our house with memories of Tim and Anna, but they were with us anyway, they always would be, so why shut them away in a drawer or at the back of some dusty cupboard as though they weren't important? And our spacious home on the rugged Cornish coast certainly had more than enough room to accommodate not just our present life, but also our past ones.

The house had been a real find. Built by an architect with a passion for gardening, I was instantly entranced by the practically industrial-size greenhouse in the garden. By the time the estate agent threw open the lounge doors to reveal the wall of glass and the view of the ocean beyond, I was ready to sign on the dotted line.

I'd worried that Liam was giving up too much just to make me happy. This coastal retreat had been *my* dream, after all, not his. When he'd chosen to step down as partner and taken ridiculously early retirement, I was concerned about how he'd fill his time. But it turned out I wasn't the only one with an unfulfilled dream. These days, Liam was far busier with the charitable art foundation he'd set up in Anna's name than he'd ever been as a partner in the legal firm. I was so impressed that he'd found a way of paying forward Anna's passion for art. Now, thanks to the foundation, students with limited funds had the opportunity to study art at college or university. I liked to think that somehow Anna knew what Liam was doing, and that she was incredibly proud of her husband. Because I certainly was.

Beyond the wall of glass, the tide was now all the way out, and as the beach was empty it was easy to see the path Liam had taken by the trailing line of footprints in the wet sand. His were deep and straight, while those of his two four-legged companions criss-crossed crazily backwards and forwards.

As if sensing the direction my thoughts were taking, a low whine from the elderly Jack Russell at my feet made me look down. She was a very old lady now and no longer capable of keeping up with our much younger Labradors on their long walks across the beach. These days I let Liam have a head start and met him on his way back. The dog's tail thumped insistently on the floor, and I smiled down at her. Like Sally, who'd passed away many years ago, Bella was feisty and full of personality.

Almost as if proving a point, she now trotted over to the Christmas tree and began to snuffle determinedly among the enormous pile of brightly wrapped presents.

'You definitely should have waited until they got here before putting them out,' Liam had said that morning, holding in his hands yet another half-opened package, the ribbon and rosettes now in shreds. Bella's latest handiwork. He was probably right, I thought, as I set the cashmere jumper – one of Josh's gifts – down on the kitchen counter. This would be the third present I'd had to rewrap for my visiting family, but I was so looking forward to the reunion that nothing could dim my excitement. It was the first time in years that everyone, including Mum and Dad, were making the journey from Sydney back to the UK for Christmas, and my preparations were now in hyperdrive.

'Just out of interest,' Liam had asked, his voice dancing with amusement, 'did you buy *every* single item the supermarket was selling this Christmas?' In his hands was a carton of milk he'd been trying to find space for in our enormous American-style fridge. I took the milk from him and with a bit of creative tessellation managed to find it a home.

'You know how much the boys like to eat. They could easily clear a fridge like this in twenty minutes.'

Liam smiled at the memory. 'Yes, but that was back in their student days. They're refined young men now.'

I gave a snort of amusement. 'That's not how Karen tells it.'

We shared a look that I knew took us back to the time when first Aaron and later Josh had decided to attend university in the UK, and how our home had become their base for holidays, or whenever their pile of laundry had grown too daunting to handle.

They'd both called us their UK Mum and Dad, a title that had delighted and also saddened me a little. The whole family obviously knew about Noah, the child I'd had who knew nothing of our existence. He was the absent ghost at every family celebration. The son, grandson, nephew and cousin we'd love to meet, and never would.

Liam and I had never made a conscious decision not to have children of our own. We'd just let fate and biology make that choice for us. I suppose we could have gone for tests or investigations when nothing had come of our efforts. But he'd never pushed it, and neither had I. *'You have to admit the practising bit is fun, though, isn't it?'* Liam had declared with a twinkle in his eye. Given my unique history, I'd been understandably reluctant to venture down the road of medical intervention. *'You know I'm happy to follow you down any path you want to take,'* Liam had said, and just knowing that made it easier to let fate decide.

I was beyond lucky, I was blessed. I'd found the kind of love they write songs and novels about, and I'd done that not once, but *twice*. I had a wonderful family who we were able to visit whenever we wanted, and a man who still made me smile every morning when I woke up beside him. To have asked for more would have been greedy. And yet sometimes the hunger was still there, gnawing silently away at the empty Noah-shaped hole in my life.

Bella huffed with canine impatience when I paused to pull off a couple of wilting leaves from one of the many poinsettias I'd positioned in the lounge. I didn't care if they were a cliché, I couldn't imagine a room decorated for Christmas without their vibrant red leaves, or a vase crammed with Christmas roses and holly. This time of year always made me a little nostalgic for the hustle and bustle of Crazy Daisy. Even after all this time, I'd never been able to bring myself to sell the shop, because so much of it still felt tied up with my memories of Tim. But when Liam and I had moved to Cornwall ten years ago I'd happily passed the management of it over to Natalie, who in fairness turned out to be a far better businesswoman than I ever was.

The distant click of the garden gate made Bella and I both look up, although only one of us raced like a lunatic into the hallway when it was followed by the clatter of the letterbox. Bella jumped up at the door, all skittering claws and ferocious yapping at the postman, who'd wisely retreated back to the safety of his van.

I bent to pick up the collection of mail, most of which appeared to be Christmas cards. I began flicking through them, identifying each one by the handwriting as I made my way back to the lounge. I was standing beside Tim's piano, which felt oddly appropriate, when I reached the bottom card in the stack. It was the only one addressed just to me, rather than to us as a couple. I held it in my hands for several minutes, long enough for Bella to grow bored and return to her position in front of the fire.

It was strange how something I'd insisted I never wanted had become something I now looked forward to so eagerly. '*No contact. Absolutely none,*' I'd adamantly told Izzy all those years ago. '*Let Noah continue to think his new kidney came from a stranger. There's no need for him to ever know anything about Tim or me.*'

I'm not sure if it was for my protection or Noah's that I'd also insisted there should be no further communication between us.

'Fortunately, it would seem Izzy is just as obstinate and pig-headed as you are,' Liam had observed, softening his words with a kiss, when the first envelope had arrived, just six months after the transplant. And so they had continued. One each year. I never wrote back, nor did Izzy seem to expect me to. I never gave her a forwarding address when we moved to the coast, but somehow she found us anyway. The contents of the letters were always the same: a single photograph, with a briefly worded update written on the back. They were all there now, lined up like dominoes on top of the piano and spilling over onto the nearby bookcase shelves. My eyes travelled along the row, following Noah's history as though it was an unfolding story in a pop-up picture book. I knew the message written on the back of each one by heart. The words hidden beneath the frame had been etched into my memory. *First day at senior school*; *Captain of the football team*; *Grade 8 piano, with honours* – how Tim would have loved that one, as well as the one where Noah stood in a cap and gown, holding his music degree proudly in his hands. The photographs followed Noah's progress through the years, from school to university, from boyhood to adolescence, and then on to his adult years. In a house fire, they were the things I would save first. Without question.

Just as they did every year, my fingers were trembling slightly as I tore open the seal on the envelope. Impatiently, I tipped it up and the photograph slipped through my eager fingers and fluttered down to the floor, where it landed face-up. Noah looked up at me from the print as I bent to retrieve it, only he wasn't the only person doing so. He wasn't alone in the photograph and as I tilted it towards the light to study it better, I saw why. A pretty blonde girl was standing in front of Noah, his arms encircling her and pulling her back against him. The girl was holding her left hand at an unnatural angle, turned around to face the camera. The only thing brighter than the diamond on her finger was the brilliance of their smiles.

Mine was wide too, although a little wobbly as I studied the photograph, pixel by pixel, committing it not to memory, but to heart. Eventually I turned it over to read Izzy's message. *Noah and Carly got engaged! She's a lovely girl. You'd like her.*

'I'm sure I would,' I said a little sadly, turning the photograph over once more and looking into the face of the daughter-in-law I would never meet. Noah looked more like Tim with every passing year, and my fingers traced the outline of the face I'd loved and lost, not just once, but twice. 'Be happy, both of you. That's all I want. Be happy together.'

I took a step towards the piano to prop the photograph up against the others, and felt something small and hard beneath the sole of my shoe. I bent down and saw a small, neatly folded square of paper. It hadn't been there before, so it must have fallen out of the envelope with the photograph.

I bent to pick it up, my heart already beating faster than normal. The paper was folded over and over, so tightly that I almost tore it trying to get it open. Izzy's handwriting, with its forward tilt, was familiar, but getting a letter from her certainly wasn't. I crossed to the window, with its calming backdrop of the ocean, and began to read.

Beth,

If I've timed it correctly, this letter will reach you on a very important milestone date. Today is exactly twenty years since Noah's transplant. Twenty years since you sacrificed so much for a child you'd never even met. Your own child.

For twenty years he has lived an almost 'normal' life, because of you. What a spectacular gift you gave him. Your donated kidney has far exceeded how long the doctors expected it to last – and it's still going strong!

Thanks to you, Noah has had a life full of joy and happiness, and as you can see from the enclosed photograph, that looks set to continue with his lovely fiancée, Carly.

Pete and I are so proud of the man that Noah has become, as we're sure you are too. But there's something wrong, and it's been wrong for a very long time.

I gasped then, suddenly afraid of what I would learn as I read on, but knowing there was no way of stopping now.

Noah is twenty-eight. He's a man about to embark on a whole new life with a partner he adores. Someday – perhaps not too far in the future – he'll become a dad himself and make us both grandmas – can you believe that?

Twenty years is a long time, not just for a kidney, but also for a secret I never wanted to keep. But I've kept it all these years, because you asked me to. And now I'm breaking it, because it feels like it's the right time to do so. Or rather, I've already broken it.

Noah deserved to know everything, and so I've told him. He knows about the clinic, about the mistake, and how you selflessly stepped out of his life, to make it better. And obviously he now knows that his anonymous donor wasn't actually so anonymous after all. He was pretty mad to begin with – it was a big secret to keep from him. But do you know what? The sun still rose the next morning and the world didn't stop spinning, and Noah didn't collapse or fall apart in shock.

He asked for your name, and you can hate me as much as you want, but I gave it to him. He knows how to find you, if he wants to. To be honest, I don't know if he will or not. But it's only fair that I tell you what I've done. And it felt good, Beth, to finally tell him the truth.

So forgive, or don't forgive me, it's up to you.

Izzy

The sunlight was no longer on the tree. It had moved across the polished oak floor like a sundial, telling me I'd stood there too long with Izzy's letter in my hands. Bella was saying much the same thing as she ran meaningfully back and forwards towards the door.

'Okay, I get the message,' I told her, my voice sounding a little shaky. I reached for my waterproof jacket and her lead, driven suddenly with a burning need to find Liam. This news was too big for me to process alone. I needed his wisdom and calming influence. I needed *him*, and always would.

I'd clipped the lead to Bella's collar and was two steps away from the back door when a sound stopped me. I paused, for a moment torn by indecision and the need to find my husband. But then the noise came again, and it decided me.

So many times our life had felt like a kaleidoscope made from broken fragments of dreams, thrown randomly together. And yet each time they twisted and turned, something new had been created. Another possibility. It had happened twenty-eight years ago, when a tragic car accident had affected a young embryologist so much she'd made a careless mistake and the lives of four people – people who'd never otherwise have met – were changed forever. And somehow it felt as though it was happening again today.

I walked back into the hallway. The lead slipped from my fingers as I saw there was someone at the door. I could make out the vague shape of them through the frosted glass panels. I could see they were tall and broad-shouldered, but beyond that I had no clue. A third knock rang through the quiet of the hallway, and my legs, which felt frozen to the floor, finally remembered how to move.

I went to the door and opened it.

About the author

DANI ATKINS is an award-winning novelist. Her 2013 debut *Fractured* has been translated into sixteen languages and has sold more than half a million copies since first publication in the UK. Dani is the author of four other bestselling novels, one of which, *This Love*, won the Romantic Novel of the Year Award in 2018. Dani lives in a small village in Hertfordshire with her husband, one Siamese cat and a very soppy Border Collie.

Acknowledgements

Thank you for reading this book, and for allowing me to take you on a journey that I hope you enjoyed.

If you've read any of my books before *A Million Dreams,* you probably know fate and the part it plays in our lives is a theme I keep coming back to. I've always been a big believer that things happen for a reason – it's a phrase the characters in this book mention more than once. I'm very grateful that fate – or the stars – were on hand to help this book find its way to the amazing team of talented professionals at Head of Zeus, and that I've once again had the opportunity to work with my incredible editor there, Laura Palmer. Thank you all for loving this book as much as I do.

Thanks as ever go to my amazing agent Kate Burke from Blake Friedmann, who has been with me from Day One and continues to guide me both figuratively and literally through the world of publishing as well as from Point A to B (the curse of having absolutely no sense of direction!)

When I was a child, I remember being told in story writing lessons to 'only write about what you know'. What kind of terrible advice is that? Fortunately authors are a pretty obstinate bunch and happily choose to ignore those kinds of restrictions. But sooner or later you do need to check out certain facts with people who are wiser than you, people who can steer you straight on things you clearly haven't got a clue about.

Two of those people are the author Gillian McAllister and her partner David Evison, who I turned to with a barrage of questions about the law, when this book was still at the *'I wonder what would happen if...'* stage. Gilly is someone whose writing I admire enormously and I am so grateful for her encouragement, generosity and expertise as both a lawyer and an author and also for choosing a boyfriend who just happens to be a medical negligence expert! What a bonus. Thank you, Gilly and Dave, for answering my dumbed-down questions without making me feel in the least bit stupid. If any legal facts are incorrect, the mistakes are mine, not theirs.

I knew next to nothing about the work of a florist, but thankfully Karen Huseyin, the owner of my local florist shop, generously gave up her time to explain a little about the workings of her business and even allowed me to borrow the name of her shop (yes, there really is a Crazy Daisy).

Another professional I am deeply indebted to is Lucy Richardson, an embryologist and Laboratory Director at Herts & Essex Fertility Centre. During one extremely long and informative phone call, Lucy explained to me about the workings of a lab in a fertility clinic and also about the duties of an embryologist. I think it's safe to say she sounded fairly horrified when I told her the plot of the book. 'It's my job to make sure that kind of thing never happens,' she told me, to which I replied 'And it's mine to pretend that it did!' What I *did* learn was that the dreadful situation Beth and

Izzy find themselves in would be virtually unheard of these days with clinics utilising technology such as electronic doubling witnessing to ensure that mistakes like the one in A Million Dreams stay firmly within the pages of a book.

No acknowledgement would be complete without giving a heartfelt thank you to the book bloggers who do such an amazing job in supporting authors and our books. Like most unsung heroes, most of your incredible work is behind the scenes and never receives the praise it deserves, but please don't ever think it goes unnoticed or is not appreciated.

I've met so many lovely people in the world of publishing who I now feel lucky enough to call good friends. From our 'office Christmas lunch' to 'summer works outing' I'm grateful for the friendship, laughter, and support from a group of amazing women. Thank you, Kate Thompson, Sasha Wagstaff, Faith Bleasdale and Fiona Ford. None of this would be as much fun without you.

To all the other authors and publishing folk who've made writing down thoughts from my head the most enjoyable and sociable career – I am lucky to have met you all. Thanks to my lunch buddy Paige Toon, and to Kate Riordan, Isabelle Broom, Holly Hepburn, Catherine Isaac, Penny Parkes, Juliet Ashton, Heidi Swain, Kate Furnival, Alice Peterson, Milly Johnson, Julie Cohen, Jenny Colgan, Gill Paul, Louise Candlish and last (but never least) Sara-Jade Virtue.

Thanks also to my first readers Hazel and Debbie (who never asked for the job, but were given it anyway). And thanks too to the friends who've been in my life for decades, or have only just arrived: Annette, Christine, Sheila, Kim, Mary, Barb and Heidi.

And lastly to my loving and (let's be honest here) long-suffering family. You make this possible and I probably don't thank you enough for that...so I'm doing it now.